Twin Beeches Books

Los Olivos

PS 232

marialeonhauser.com

MARIA LEONHAUSER

maria leonhauser

TWIN BEECHES BOOKS

Murder at Twin Beeches is a work of fiction. Any references to current or historical events; to real people, living or dead; or to real places are used fictitiously. Other names, characters, places, and events are products of the author's imagination, and any resemblances to actual events or places or persons is entirely coincidental.

Cover illustration: Cathy Gendron
Logo and back cover photo: Doug Brown

Printed in the United States of America

ISBN: 979-8-9872881-0-8 (paperback)
ISBN: 987-8-9872881-1-5 (eBook)

Twin Beeches Books
2232 S. Main Street
#354
Ann Arbor, MI 48103

marialeonhauser.com

In memory of my daughter
Ariel L. Gold
You showed me how to live vibrantly

MURDER AT TWIN BEECHES

I

Monday, May 7, Three days after the party

"No blood on the champagne bucket," said Ruth Richards.

"It's because the floor is uneven," Louise Jenkins explained. "The blood would naturally pool to the right of his head and flow away from the bucket."

"What luck. Silver can be so hard to clean."

Louise and Ruth sat in Windsor chairs just outside the dining-room entrance to the walk-through kitchen pantry at Louise's estate, Twin Beeches. Between them a butler tray held two glasses, a pitcher of martinis, and a small plate of olives. Beyond them, partially tucked under the bottom shelf in the pantry, lay a body.

"Care for an olive?" asked Louise as she poured their martinis.

"No thanks." Ruth watched as Louise added three olives to her own drink. "Actually, can I taste yours? My doctor says I have to watch my sodium, but what could a couple of olives hurt?" She sipped. "Mmm, I'll keep this one."

Louise smiled. She and Ruth had been friends for seventy years. In second grade, Ruth had already cultivated her propensity for changing her mind in favor of someone else's selection. Back then it was sandwiches. Ruth loved ham and cheese, until she saw Louise had a peanut butter and jelly.

Louise took Ruth's untouched glass and popped three olives into it for herself.

"I imagine the head injury is what killed him," said Louise.

"No doubt." Ruth's hand trembled.

"Oh, Ruth, are you all right? Is this too much?"

"I'm fine. My drink was just a touch too chilled. Made me shiver." Ruth rose from her chair and paced back and forth across the doorway to the pantry. "I must study this scene. I have excellent powers of observation. After all, I did find the body."

"Yes, you did, Ruthie." Louise looked away from the body, scanning the rows of china, crystal, silver, pottery, and baskets lining the shelves, hesitating periodically while taking a sip of her drink and then moving on. "I certainly have a lot of everything. I thought I had eliminated the excess when I sold the house."

"You did a good job, Louise. I couldn't have parted with half of what you did, though I think a quarter of it is now at my house." She laughed. "Remember that footstool embroidered with the map of New Jersey? It's in my study."

"Trigger?"

Ruth let out a loud snort. "Oh, that's right. It's stuffed with horsehair. Do you want your pet back?" They giggled like twelve-year-olds, the martinis erasing the decades.

"You know," Ruth said as she studied the set of dishes on the middle shelf, "that pattern is growing on me."

"Oh no you don't, Ruth. I agreed to swap my pottery from

our trip with yours. If you want this pattern you'll just have to go back to Cabo and buy another set."

"Well, I hope Robert doesn't find out. He helped me pick it out. I think he had an eye for me."

"Robert owns the Travel Club. His job is to make us old people feel special."

"Well, it was fun." Ruth finished her drink and turned to Louise. "Let's drink to another trip!" Ruth held up her glass for a toast, realized it was empty, and set it down. "We've had some great adventures together over the years, haven't we?"

"I'm going to cut you off if you start getting morose," said Louise, eyeing Ruth's empty martini glass.

"No, no, I'm fine. Pour me a small one. I'm just reminiscing. Remember our weekend trip to the shore when we were twenty-one? My secret rendezvous with Paul?"

"Your mom never understood how you could go to the shore for an entire weekend and return home lily white."

"Oh, to be young again." Ruth studied her bright-red nails. "Like my polish? It's called 'Sex on the Beach.'"

"That would have gotten you a tan!"

"Hello! There's a kid here." The body rolled out from under the shelf and stood up.

"Goodness, Winnie, I'm sorry. Ruth and I got a little carried away."

A familiar *thwop-thwop-thwop* came from the field on the west side of the property. Louise looked at her watch. "Must be Elliott."

She turned her attention back to Winnie Miller. "You've been such a big help. The ketchup in your hair was quite a dramatic touch."

"What in God's name is going on here?" Elliott stood in the doorway of the kitchen.

"Hello, dear." Louise set her martini on the table. "Care for a drink?"

"Mother!"

"It's a reenactment," said Winnie Miller proudly. "I was the body."

"And a very good one," said Louise as she dabbed ketchup off Winnie's eyebrow. "But perhaps you should wash your hair before your parents return. It would give them a fright."

Winnie's parents, Wills and Claudia Miller, had moved to Twin Beeches a year ago to manage the house and gardens for Louise. The Millers were grateful that Louise considered their eleven-year-old daughter an added benefit.

"Dear," Louise said, turning to Elliott, "why can't you drive or take the train from New York like everyone else?"

"It takes too long," said Elliott's girlfriend, Kirby Dunbar, as she stumbled through the doorway with two oversize suitcases.

"But it scares the bunnies and pheasants, it's bad for the environment, and—"

"I'm staying at Kirby's this week," Elliott interrupted. "I want to keep the pressure on the police to solve the murder. Of course, we can stay here if you'd feel safer."

Kirby nudged him. Louise noticed.

"Thank you, dear, but I'm fine." Louise poured herself another martini. "Quite a to-do, wasn't it? Imagine, someone murdered here. That's a first."

"And during your lovely party," added Ruth. "I wish I hadn't opened the pantry door. The party was such fun. Who knows how long it would have gone on if I hadn't discovered the body? What bad luck!"

"For you or the victim?" asked Kirby.

"For everyone, don't you think? Of course, it's worse for that young man. He's dead. But finding him gave me such a fright I could have had a heart attack. Fortunately, I didn't, and I can now apply my astute eye for detail to assisting the police. You know, a reenactment can trigger a memory. It's quite possible I saw something in the pantry that could be a clue. That's what we're trying to determine." She arched an eyebrow. "We're investigating." Ruth looked around. "Now, where did I put my martini?"

2

The event committee for the Bucks County Historical Society had been deliriously happy when Louise offered her estate for the preview party of the annual house and garden tour. It would be a sellout, given the history of Twin Beeches. The more than two hundred years that the Jenkins family lived there was certainly interesting, but it was the brief time Frankie Vincent had owned the house that gave it its notoriety—wild parties fed by alcohol and cocaine, and spectacularly gaudy taste. And then Frankie disappeared. That was a year ago. He was still missing. The town was still gossiping. And Louise Jenkins was back at Twin Beeches.

Her ancestors were grateful, especially Samuel Jenkins Sr., a wealthy merchant who built the estate in 1790 for his wife and children. He named the property after two conjoined beech trees that stood sentry at the entrance.

Samuel Jr. followed in his father's footsteps, though he significantly increased their imprint with timber and textiles. He, too, raised his family at Twin Beeches, including the next Samuel.

Each generation followed the other up the driveway and into the house. And each lived up to his father's expectation of success.

Louise Jenkins, the only child of the fifth Samuel, was grateful that she had not been named Samantha and relegated to an identity as a derivative. She didn't like the repetitiveness. *The poor Samuels*, she thought, *always following the same path.*

Not Louise. After college, she packed a suitcase and set off to follow her creative spirit. At times she caught up with it. Briefly. She danced with it around a campfire at a commune in California, but when the smoke cleared they both realized they were just living in an old house with too many people. Her spirit left first; Louise followed.

She dabbled in art, history, and even religion, though ultimately she considered herself only spiritually hopeful and historically bored. Until she visited the gardens of Hidcote Manor in the Cotswolds.

It was there that Louise caught up with her creative spirit. It was sleeping on a petal fallen from an exquisite flowering yellow peony. Its heady perfume induced a sweet slumber for her spirit, which was exhausted from Louise's constant pursuit. She gently scooped the petal into her hand, smoothing its colorful shadows. As she carried it out of the garden, her spirit awoke.

And Louise took it back to Bucks County. Soon Karl Fritz Keller and Louise Jenkins walked down the aisle and up the driveway to Twin Beeches. Their family and Louise's gardens flourished. With the birth of each child—Elliott, Amelia, and Andrew—Louise propagated a new genus of peony—Paeonia elliotii, Paeonia amelea, and Paeonia andrewii.

For decades it was a good life. Until the house overpowered Louise. Her beloved Karl Fritz was now in Friends Cemetery. Her children had homes of their own, and Louise was left to live in the big house with her ancestors and their memories. They followed her around like stalkers, insisting she take care of them.

One evening as she sat in her study, a dish of gumdrops on the side table next to her unopened book, Louise looked up at the portraits of her ancestors, the Samuels, preserved in paint and held in place by their heavy gold frames and stoic expressions.

Perhaps she should sell the house, she thought. At this stage in their lives, none of her children were prepared to take it on, and she didn't want to be the caretaker of curios and the Jenkins' family ghosts until one of the children could, if they even would, settle into a future at Twin Beeches.

Louise snuggled deeper into her down-filled chair and thought of her children. They had grown up in this house, celebrated birthdays here, suffered broken teenage hearts here, and buried their pets in the garden. She picked a red gumdrop from the bowl and thought of Amelia's middle school science project. Toothpicks, licorice, and gumdrops. A DNA model, the spiral ladder that carried their family from one generation to the next; ancestors piled on each rung, waiting to meet their relatives.

"I think it's time to sell Twin Beeches," she said to the portraits. The Samuels, shocked by such a thought, lost their genetic footing and began their descent down the double helix ladder, knocking against each other along the way.

Suddenly, Samuel the First held up a hand. He had seniority by almost two hundred years and needed to catch his breath. The others, arms and legs flailing, frantically reached for a rung. Samuel the Third executed a smooth double somersault and then grabbed Samuel the Fifth, who was slipping away. Samuel the Third was always more athletic than the others. Probably got that from his mother's side.

And they sat, their legs dangling from the rungs, just like

when they were children perched on the stone fence at Twin Beeches at dusk waiting for deer to appear silently in the field. Tonight their wait was different. They were five generations wondering about the future.

In the wait, in the quiet, Louise heard a plea—or perhaps it was just a gasp—from Samuel the First. It felt like a longing, a wistfulness that someday a Jenkins would return to the house. Louise understood. It was the way they were.

After the sale, the Samuels watched as their portraits were loaded into a truck along with books and furniture for the trip down the driveway and into a storage facility.

* * *

Frankie Vincent paid cash for Twin Beeches. He had made his fortune from a chain of drive-in burger joints called Steer Here. Hamburgers were good for the property. They nourished the gardens and maintained the house. But Frankie couldn't resist the desire to showcase his wealth in the only style he knew —excess.

The two-hundred-year-old twin beech trees now shared the entrance with a pair of massive stone lions, each sitting atop a column on which was etched "Twin Beeches." The trees repeatedly dropped leaves on the lions' heads to annoy them. Velvet, mirrors, and foil wallpaper smothered the understated, natural beauty of the house. Frankie brought exotic animals indoors—dead ones, skinned and sprawled on the floor or heads mounted over a fireplace.

During the day, the house appeared quiet. The curtains were drawn, possibly to protect themselves from fire should a ray of sun refract off one of the crystal objets d'art, a term Frankie's decorator, Phyllis, insisted on using. More likely the house just needed to rest before one of Frankie's frequent all-night parties. He only invited the right people, until they were the wrong people.

On the morning Frankie disappeared, his nephew, who was rewiring the dining-room chandelier, showed his uncle a bug nestled among the gilt leaves that clung to ornate crystal flowers. Frankie was under surveillance. He and Phyllis disappeared.

The police reclaimed the electronic bug.

Louise reclaimed her house.

And Frankie remained missing.

* * *

"Amelia!" Louise waved as her daughter steered her car around a large truck parked in the driveway of Twin Beeches.

"I've come to witness the rehabilitation of your garden," Amelia said as she walked past a statue of Zeus. Amelia Halliday was happy for the diversion. She had recently moved back from California, disgraced, unemployed, and fixated on how she had killed her career as an investigative reporter. "There's enough statuary out here to fill a cemetery," she added as she watched the gardeners load onto the truck Frankie's Greek gods and signs of the zodiac.

Twin Beeches enjoyed its rebirth. The exposed oak beams in the kitchen, stripped of their bright-yellow paint, discreetly reveled in their oiled nakedness. Windows were flung open, exorcizing the cloying sweetness of the gelatinous mounds called "Spring Rain" and "Morning Dew." *Air fresheners, what a ridiculous notion,* thought Louise. *More like chemical warfare.* After a few days of fresh air, a bee flew through an open window, circumnavigated the living room, and executed a few loop the loops before returning to the garden outside. A victory lap.

The wide-plank floors exhaled loudly as workmen dragged heavy black-and-gold carpeting out the front door. The portraits of the Samuels, back on the walls of the study, swung ever so slightly to and fro. A happy dance.

Samuel the Second, always the most accommodating, convinced the others that they should take care of their own pasts—manage their own memories, not push them on Louise. They selected their favorites; the others they simply tossed up the chimney and away forever. They enjoyed reexamining Louise's mementos that were scattered throughout the house. Her life was filled with such a variety of experiences, though they had to admit some were, at the very least, unique. But every family has one of *those* relatives. The Samuels just had to reach forward six generations to find theirs.

They did hope that with time, Louise would forget her commune-living experience. It made the Samuels uncomfortable. It was indecorous.

So was the body in their pantry.

3

Friday, May 4, The party

"The house looks lovely," cooed Ruth, always the first to arrive anywhere.

"Ruthie, I'm so glad you're here." Louise greeted her at the door.

Charles Thornton, president of the Bucks County Historical Society, walked over to them. "Welcome, Mrs. Richards. On behalf of the historical society, thank you for coming. This year's house tour will be that much more exceptional because of Louise's gracious hosting of our preview party. Enjoy the tour of Twin Beeches."

"Oh, Charles, I'm here almost every day." Ruth patted his hand. "I know everything in this house."

"Ruthie, let's find a glass of champagne," said Louise. "Holler if you need me, Charles."

"How do you like my dress?" asked Ruth. Small birds, butterflies, and masses of cabbage roses and hydrangea filled the chintz landscape that folded across Ruth's sturdy frame. One of the birds, a chickadee, was perched atop her ample left breast; its slightly tilted head appeared to be eyeing the large purple bauble that hung from Ruth's neck.

"You look like a garden, Ruthie, and smell a bit like one, too."

Ruth sniffed her left wrist. "I hope it's not too much. It's new, called 'Tudor Rose,' though what the Tudors knew about roses, I don't know."

"I think your perfume is tuberose, and it's a lovely scent. It complements the floral pattern of your dress. Ask the photographer to take a photo of you by the arrangement in the dining room. You match it!"

Ruth beamed. "Oh, there's Amelia. Amelia! Yoo-hoo, over here," she called out.

Amelia entered through the side door. Her delicate blue silk dress floated as she walked toward Ruth and Louise.

"You positively shimmer," gushed Ruth, "like a morning sky." Ruth's chickadee wanted to fly to her. "Oh, there's my friend Kitty. Excuse me."

"Everything looks beautiful, Mom, including you."

A butter-yellow sheath draped Louise's slender frame. Her skin was flawless save for a few laugh crinkles around warm, gray eyes; only her silver hair testified to her age. Her friends wondered aloud whether she had had "work" done to erase the rest of the wrinkles. Louise would remind them that she wasn't interested in doing anything surgically to hide her age, though she was more than happy to do whatever she could not to act it.

Physically, Amelia was a decades-younger version of her mother, tall and slender. Temperamentally she was a mix of both parents—strong-willed, gentle, fierce, determined, kind—though at times she didn't know which trait came from whom because they each revealed them so differently. They wore their traits like a coat, sometimes covering one with another, ready to strip it off if necessary to defend or to comfort.

"I'm so glad you're here." As she hugged Amelia, Louise's gold charm bracelet tinkled like a tiny wind chime—soothing, gentle, and welcoming. Each charm, commemorating a trip or a milestone, gently tapped its neighbor hello. A double-decker bus, the Eiffel Tower, a Tyrolean hat, a heart, a peony.

"It took me fifteen minutes to get up the driveway. Cars are backed up to the road."

"I'm sure there's a curiosity about Twin Beeches, particularly after Frankie Vincent's brief ownership," said Louise. "I planted a few surprises for the nosy parkers who just can't resist peeking into a cupboard or closet. I thought I'd add a little excitement."

"Mother?"

Louise gleefully squeezed Amelia's arm. The rustle of the charm bracelet sounded like a giggle. "I put an owl in one of the linen closets. You can't miss it when you open the door. Oh, and a turtle in the drinks cabinet in the billiards room. Andrew found them for me at a taxidermy shop."

"Ladies and gentlemen." Charles Thornton stood with a champagne glass in his hand. "Welcome to our seventy-fifth annual house and garden tour. Thank you, Louise Jenkins, for opening your home to us for tonight's preview. And a special thanks to tonight's cochairs, Kirby Dunbar, a board member of the historical society, and Louise's son, Elliott Jenkins-Keller, who grew up here at Twin Beeches. So he knows it *very well.*" He laughed. "Elliott's company, Revere Investment Group, is the lead sponsor for tonight's soiree. Docents are available throughout the house to answer questions about the art and furnishings. A few of the smaller rooms have rope-and-post stanchions across the entrance. You are welcome to view the interiors, but please do not enter." He held his glass aloft. "Enjoy the evening. Cheers."

Kirby and Elliott moved through the crowd, greeting guests. She was dressed in Givenchy. He wore a bespoke suit, Italian shoes, and a perfect smile. His only ornament was a wafer-thin Patek watch. He kissed Kirby's friends on both cheeks, lingering for a moment after the second kiss to leave behind his scent, a barely perceptible imprint of soft leather, delicate spice, and lime. A cocktail on a private jet.

"More champagne?" A server in a crisp white shirt refilled Louise's glass.

"Do you think Kirby's after his money?" Ruth whispered as she followed Louise into the study after finding no fresh gossip from her friend Kitty.

"No, Ruth, she appears to have plenty of her own. She is intense, though—rather high strung."

"How old is she? Thirty-five?"

"Probably in that range."

"Do you think they're serious?"

"About marriage? I don't know. They haven't been together all that long."

"He does seem married to his work."

Louise laughed. "True. I should have known better than to give him *Samuel* as a middle name." She looked up at the portraits. If their hands hadn't been painted in place, the Samuels would have high-fived each other.

Ruth looked down at her empty glass. "Young man, where might I find a martini?" She batted her eyes at a server.

"Allow me, madam." He escorted her to the living room.

"Hello, Winnie," Louise said with a smile as Winnie Miller walked up, holding a plateful of shrimp.

"Hello, Mrs. Jenkins. This is a very nice party," she said as she dipped a shrimp into cocktail sauce and then, holding it up, said, "Would you like one?"

"How nice of you, dear, but I'm fine for now. You enjoy."

"Thank you. Mom said I could mingle with the guests for a little while and then I get to watch the chef make pastry swans filled with chocolate mousse." She paused. "If it's OK with you."

"Of course it is. Enjoy your evening."

Winnie set off into the sea of people, ducking under the occasional sweeping hand gesture of an adult.

"Who's this ravishing lady?" Andrew kissed his mother on both cheeks. "Quite a to-do."

"Yes, it is. Is Dean here?" she asked, looking for Andrew's partner of five years.

"He wouldn't miss it. He's getting us some champagne. We're celebrating. I sold a few major pieces, including that massive mahogany sideboard. Now, there's plenty of room in the shop, so we're off on an antique-buying junket next week." Andrew searched the room for Dean. "Holy Christ!" He laughed when he spotted Ruth. "I think I have an upholstered side chair in that fabric. Maybe I can sell it to her."

"Andrew! Be nice. She's just being Ruth," scolded Louise.

* * *

"Excuse me." Winnie tugged on Amelia's arm. "I think there's a problem in the kitchen. Miss Dunbar is yelling at the chef."

Amelia peered through the beveled glass window of the kitchen door. Kirby was holding a silver tray as if poised to send it sailing across the oak floor like a giant skipping stone across a lake. The catering staff was scurrying through the back door to the herb garden, their white aprons flapping like flags of surrender.

"Don't even think about it!" commanded Oliver Quinn, his toque at his feet, possibly knocked off his head by Kirby. "I will ask you one more time to stop interfering with the waitstaff so they may serve the guests."

As Amelia pushed the door open, Kirby casually set the tray on the kitchen island and smiled at her. Only the lock of hair fallen from her elegant updo and dangling across one eye belied her attempt at composure. The staff peered in from the garden.

"I believe the cochair is expected at the party," Amelia said calmly as she turned around, leaving the kitchen door swinging back and forth, perhaps cooling tempers with its rhythmic movement. She waited in the breakfast room for Kirby.

"An unfortunate outburst on my part." Kirby attempted to walk past Amelia.

Amelia blocked her path. "What was that all about?"

Kirby paused.

A server walked past. "Those." She pointed to his tray of Swedish meatballs. "I hate Swedish meatballs! They are utterly déclassé. What's next, pigs in a blanket?"

Amelia laughed. At her. "Mom loves them, and, I expect, ordered them."

"I'm just trying to maintain the *élégance* of your mother's home."

Wills rounded the corner.

"Did you remove the boxes?" Kirby snapped at him.

"Done. It was a simple misunderstanding." He turned to Amelia. "The rental company stashed boxes in the pantry. A couple of waiters removed them."

"The pantry is part of the tour, not some storage closet," said Kirby.

Amelia was about to argue that it was, in fact, just that. It wasn't worth it. "You might want to check a mirror, Kirby. Your hair is a touch *sans élégance.*"

* * *

The party had settled into a pleasant rhythm. Amelia even noticed Kirby nibbling a meatball. Music floated through the air; strings stretched their notes over the laughter and tinkling of crystal. Guests moved in and out of rooms and clusters of conversations. Harmony.

Until the social symphony reached a crescendo with Ruth's piercing scream.

"He's dead!" Ruth shrilled as she rushed into the living room. "A man. In the pantry!"

The room froze, a momentary still life, wineglasses held midsip, guests riveted as if the vines of the Aubusson rug had ensnared their feet. Only the faint sound of the violins' bows sending their last notes floating across the room gave a hint that the air was breathable. Then the landscape of guests began to stir. Heads turned away from Ruth and toward their fellow guests, perhaps searching for who was missing, who was dead. Glasses clinked as they were set down. And then the tableau of an elegant cocktail party erupted into frenetic exclamations, but still little movement.

"Elliott, stay with Ruth and Mom. I'll check the pantry," called Amelia as she rushed toward the dining room.

The body lay on the brick floor, partially under a shelf of serving trays. His lanky frame was folded and tucked as if he had curled himself up for a short nap. Except there was blood. It snaked through the blond curls and surrounded his head like a halo.

Amelia reached down to pull him out from under the shelf.

"Don't touch him," a voice behind her snapped.

Amelia lurched back.

Chief Detective Anthony Mardi reached under the shelf and put his fingers to the side of the man's neck. Sirens in the distance announced the long night that lay ahead for the guests.

4

A makeshift interview room across the main hall saw a steady stream of guests give their statements and contact information one by one. Louise, her family, and Ruth returned to the study after their interviews. Detective Rita Cole joined them. And there they waited.

Amelia chose the window seat. Car headlights periodically flashed across the window, winking at her as another guest, statement given and car keys received, retreated down the long, winding driveway. Her mother was seated in her yellow chair, Ruth in the one opposite. They were such good friends, yet so different. Ruth chattered away about how devastated she was over finding the body. Amelia knew that soon the devastation would turn to delight as Ruth positioned herself under the I-found-him spotlight. Louise sat patiently, letting Ruth ramble on. At times, Louise reminded Amelia of Yoda, the Star Wars Jedi Master. Not physically, of course, but it was in her eyes—gentleness, kindness, and power.

Louise suddenly looked over at Amelia. A Yoda moment.

Detective Cole sat in a chair near a wall of bookcases. They were filled with clusters of family photographs and books—art, history, and literature. Oversize architecture books lay horizontally and were topped with more photos. Cole's position in the room allowed her to remain on the periphery, giving the family a bit more privacy while allowing her to observe their behavior.

Andrew and Dean made room on the sofa for Kirby, who finally tired of sitting alone on the settee. Elliott had initially joined her, but only briefly. He preferred standing, pacing, and looking at his watch.

"Have you had anything to eat, Kirby?" asked Louise, noticing Kirby's trembling hands and ashen complexion.

"Thank you, I'll be OK. This is just very upsetting."

"We need information," Elliott barked at Cole. "Who's in charge?"

"Chief Detective Mardi," said Cole. "He'll be here as soon as the medical examiner is finished."

Elliott turned his back to her for another lap around the study.

"Elliott, since you're up, please bring me some water," said Louise. "Kirby, what would you like?"

"Perhaps a Perrier."

"Elliott, please stop pacing!" snapped Amelia. "It's not helping."

He glared at her as he walked over to the bar. Wine and sodas bobbed in the gleaming buckets of melting ice. A tray of hors d'oeuvres sat untouched. He dipped his hand in the cold water and pulled out a Perrier, wiping it with a linen napkin. "Sparkling for you too, Mom?"

Louise nodded, and the room relaxed. Water. Such a simple request, and they were revived.

"Think the shrimp are safe to eat?" Andrew asked, pushing off the sofa.

"Are there any crackers?" asked Kirby. "That would settle my stomach."

Elliott looked again at his watch. His impatience was not quenched. "Must we remain in this room?"

Dean brought Kirby a plate of cheese and crackers.

The study door opened.

"Finally," muttered Elliott when he saw Mardi.

"Sorry to keep you, but these things take time," said Mardi. He looked at his notes. "The victim's name is Michael Porter. Twenty-six, from Lambertville, New Jersey. Do any of you know him?"

"No." The word repeated like a weak echo until it reached Ruth.

"Yes," she said. "I recognize him from somewhere."

"Did you move the body?" Mardi snapped.

"No, of course not. I ran out as soon as I saw him."

"Mrs. Richards, his back was to you. How could you recognize him?"

"It's not his face, it's his name. That's what I recognize. Let me think, I know I've heard it before. He introduced himself to someone and then said, 'But call me MP.' I remember that because I thought of the army. You know my husband was a war hero," she added. "I also remember smelling Old Spice. My husband used to wear it, so I think that's why MP stayed in my memory."

"He's young for Old Spice," mused Louise.

"I don't know if he was wearing it. I just remember the smell."

"That's a lot of detail from a name," quipped Kirby, apparently revived by the cheese and crackers.

Mardi ignored her. "Very good, Mrs. Richards. Do you remember where or when this happened?"

"I just don't know. I'll try to think harder."

Suddenly Louise chimed in. "I remember now!"

Everyone turned to her. "You're Anthony Mardi. You were Amelia's boyfriend."

"A long time ago." After an uncomfortable pause Mardi turned to Amelia. "I heard you were back in town."

5

"OK, people, let's talk." Chief Detective Mardi sat down at the conference table in his office. He looked at his bleary-eyed team: Detective Rita Cole, Officer Harry Barnett, and Officer Tom Crayson. It was 3:00 a.m. by the time they had completed the interviews at Twin Beeches. The rest of the weekend had been fueled by caffeine and adrenaline.

Mardi convened his team as soon as possible after a serious crime. Their written reports would come later. It was during these talks that the evidence would begin to assemble itself for inspection and ultimately reveal a motive, identify a suspect, and solve the case.

"We know Michael Porter delivered pizzas for Tony's Pizzeria in Lambertville," began Mardi. "No criminal record. Lived with his fiancée, Carol Anne Jackson. Preliminary time of death is between seven thirty and nine p.m. last night. Medical examiner's preliminary report: death by blunt force trauma to the head. The likely weapon was a brass candlestick."

Cole almost spewed her coffee across the table. "A brass candlestick? What next, killed by Professor Plum?"

"No, that would have to be in the library," added Crayson.

All but Mardi laughed.

"Murder is not a laughing matter," snapped Mardi.

"I'm sorry," Cole said. "Of course it's not. It's just that when I was with the Trenton Police, the only blunt force deaths I investigated were by tire iron, hammer, or baseball bat. Never a candlestick."

"We're all tired," said Barnett. "Give her a break."

"No, he's right," said Cole. "I *am* sorry."

Mardi nodded. "Let's move on. What else do we know?"

Cole quickly composed herself. "According to Carol Anne, she last spoke to him around four p.m. the day of his death. He called her at work to say he would be home late because he had an extra job that evening. Personal calls are frowned upon, so she didn't ask any questions. Apparently, Porter often took on odd jobs for extra money, so this wasn't out of the ordinary. I contacted the pizzeria where he works. Thursday was his day off, and they didn't call him in."

"Still checking with the vendors hired for the party," Crayson said. "But so far nobody hired him."

"The caterer, too?" Mardi asked. "Porter was wearing a white shirt and black slacks, like the servers."

"Of course we interviewed the caterer," Barnett snapped. "Got nothing other than a pissed-off chef who's worried people will think his company is tied to the murder."

"Any leads on Porter's van?" Mardi asked Cole, ignoring Barnett's attitude.

"Not yet."

"Let's get back to your interviews. Who was at the party around the estimated time of death?"

"Who wasn't?" grumbled Barnett.

"Enough, Barnett!" Mardi knew Barnett was still angry. He had been passed over for a promotion to detective. He wasn't ready, too quick to jump to conclusions. His evidence gathering was good; he just didn't let it talk to him. He told it what it was supposed to mean.

"Details, people, details," said Mardi. "You've got the list, talk to me. What do you know about them?"

"We know that everyone had access, so anyone could have slipped into the pantry," said Crayson. "Guests were primarily members of the historical society, community benefactors, the social clique. There's no obvious connection to Porter, at least not yet. It's going to take time."

"I interviewed the Jenkins family," said Cole. "None of them knew Porter or noticed anything unusual. Louise Jenkins's son Elliott and his girlfriend, Kirby Dunbar, arrived early, around five thirty p.m. He apparently went to an upstairs bedroom for a six o'clock conference call with his office in New York. He came down to the living room around six thirty. He and Miss Dunbar were introduced to the crowd about seven p.m."

"Your impression of them?" asked Mardi.

"Both are strong willed, used to being in charge," Cole said. "And snappy dressers. Seriously expensive clothes."

Mardi thought of Elliott's shoes. The medical examiner was still with the body when Mardi checked in with the family. Elliott's impatience was palpable. He wanted answers. When Mardi returned to the dining room where the evidence team was working, Elliott followed him.

"I want this body out of my mother's house," he demanded. "This has nothing to do with our family. Our home is nothing more than a location."

"The location of a murder." They stood face-to-face in the

dining room, Mardi blocking Elliott's view of the pantry. "The medical examiner will determine when the body can be removed. And while this may feel like an inconvenience to you, keep in mind that one of your guests may have murdered Mr. Porter. Now, if you will excuse me, I have work to do."

Elliott glared at Mardi, refusing to cede his space. Mardi stepped aside, giving Elliott a clear view of the body of Michael Porter. Elliott turned ashen and tried to walk away. He vomited on his handmade Italian shoes.

Mardi brought his attention back to Cole's report. "Kirby Dunbar said she used her early arrival to fix things. According to her, everything was wrong, from the location of some of the flower arrangements to the food. Later she had an argument with the chef, Oliver Quinn. Knocked the toque off his head."

"Toque?" asked Crayson.

"Chef's hat," said Cole.

"Ah. Like the Pillsbury Doughboy." Crayson grinned.

"Don't ever let a real chef hear that," she said.

"That would require me going to a real restaurant. I like my food fast and cheap."

"Like his women," Barnett mumbled.

"The argument was over meatballs," Cole continued, ignoring Barnett. "She thinks they're low class."

"Probably has no use for them. She's got her own set of balls," Barnett said.

"You're an ass, Barnett," Cole replied.

"Wills Miller, who works at the estate, may have seen something," interjected Crayson. "He said he was in the kitchen around seven thirty, when he asked two servers to remove boxes that were stacked in the pantry. They apparently were from the rental company. The pantry was part of the house tour, so the boxes needed to be cleared out. One of the servers could have been Porter."

"And the other his murderer," said Barnett.

Cole shook her head. "They were standing in the kitchen one minute and the next minute one of them kills the other? Doesn't make sense."

Barnett glared at her.

Mardi quickly circled back to the vendors. "Are all the companies local?"

"Yeah," said Crayson. "They do most of the big parties in the area. They have a lot of staff turnover, college kids mostly. Nobody noticed anything unusual."

"Not even the argument between Dunbar and the chef?" asked Mardi.

"No one considered it important," Crayson said. "It's part of what goes on behind the scenes at these shindigs. Tempers flare. Both Dunbar and Quinn are considered difficult to work with. Quinn is a high-strung chef; Dunbar is a high-strung socialite."

"Get eyes on these." Mardi passed out copies of a recent photo of Porter. "Barnett and Crayson, show this to everyone who was working there that night. Cole and I will follow up with the guest list. And, people, try not to piss each other off. We're a team."

"Rah, rah, rah," muttered Barnett as he aimed his Starbucks cup at the trash can as he walked out. The cup hit the rim and the coffee dregs streaked down Mardi's office wall.

6

As Amelia sat at her dining room table reading the *Bucks County Courier Times*, she felt like she was on the wrong side of the story. She should have been reporting the news, not reading about a murder in her family home. Of course the reporting aspect could only happen if she was still employed by a newspaper. She wasn't.

"Oh my God, did you read Ruth's quote?" Amelia exclaimed to her brother Andrew. She read from the paper: "He was covered in blood. I tried to find a pulse but he was already gone. If only I could have saved him."

"Leave it to Ruth to find a dead body," said Andrew as he positioned an antique fire screen in front of Amelia's fireplace. "I know this isn't a great time to be making deliveries, but I needed to get this out of my van before Dean and I leave on our buying trip. I love these trips, but for Chrissake, it's only been three days since the murder. Should I still go? I'm worried about Mom, about the publicity."

"I talked to her this morning." Amelia held up the newspaper and laughed. "This is her doing. She called the *Courier Times* and invited them to the house yesterday."

"That's Mom!" He walked around Amelia's dining room. "How does it feel to live in the town library?"

"It's perfect!" When it was built in 1888, the red brick, Gothic-style Victorian building looked more like a house than a library. The books probably appreciated the homeyness; it was familiar to them. They had been living with Quaker families in the area who created their own book-lending system until a bequest by Anna Mary Williamson provided the funds to build the library, giving the books their own home.

Over the decades their numbers outgrew the oak shelves, so they were moved into a concrete-and-glass building with ample room and stricter organization. No more jostling for space on the stacks or being misfiled. *Huckleberry Finn* once spent a month in the food section, alongside *The Fannie Farmer Cookbook*. None of the books ever came back to the old library, which dearly missed the words of philosophers and poets, physicists and biographers, historians and humorists. It had tried its best to protect them, to keep them from deteriorating, but it couldn't compete with the climate-controlled environment where they now resided.

And so the old library sat empty, until six months ago when Amelia walked through the door and made it her home.

Andrew poured himself a cup of coffee. "You've done a nice job with the renovations, but how can you stand that obnoxiously loud ticking? It's like having Big Ben in the room."

"I like it." She looked up at the tall case clock. "It's always lived in this library. It fits. Anyway, it reminds me time is passing. Soon no one will ask me how I like being back. That's code for 'We know what happened at the *Los Angeles Times*.'"

"It's not code; it's a simple question. It's called small talk."

"Well, not to me. Andrew, Ben Adams died because of my story."

"No, he didn't. He killed himself because he was an embezzler who got caught. You exposed him."

Amelia sat silently, letting the clock tick off the time.

Andrew paused in front of the bookcase holding Amelia's collection of Nancy Drew mysteries. "You always loved these books. I remember when you asked for a magnifying glass for your birthday."

"No I didn't. I asked for a blue roadster. And Ned."

"Well, we all wanted him."

Amelia laughed. "I've got to run. I have a meeting with Tony Mardi."

"Getting reacquainted?"

7

Tony hadn't changed much. He still had the same all-American good looks that he had in high school—tall, muscular, with a chiseled face that was saved from perfection by a scar across his left jaw. His looks were born from his Italian and Irish ancestry, the best features of each. They had dated in high school and the first two years at the University of Pennsylvania. But each wanted more. Amelia wanted to study abroad; Tony wanted the blonde in his psychology class.

"So you're back home," he said as Amelia sat down in his office.

"Yes, been back about six months. You never left?"

"I like it here. I like continuity."

"You like being a detective?"

"Yes, I do."

"I remember when you wanted to be a lawyer."

He chuckled. "Not enough action. I like the investigative process and evidence gathering more than preparing legal arguments. This is the right fit for me. Why'd you move back?"

"It's a long story." When she was fired from the *LA Times* she grabbed her family ties and pulled herself home. Now she was trying to slip back onto the pages of the family album without anyone noticing the ten-year gap.

"Must be tough for you. Four Lanes End is hardly LA."

Amelia had left her small town because she didn't want her glory days to end there. She wasn't going to succumb to Bruce Springsteen's small-town anthem. She would be different. Her glory days would continue. She'd have glory days galore. Until the inglorious happened.

"LA is hardly Four Lanes End," she said. She needed her small town now. It was like a pair of old slippers, their alpaca lining holding the imprint of her feet, each toe owning its own little valley into which it settled, warm and protected. "It's good here."

She could have stayed in California, but without her husband and her job at the *Times*, why would she? Miles Halliday had left her because being a reporter was more important to her than being married to him. Or so he said.

He was wrong; she loved him. She just wanted Miles to accept her drive. She was good, relentless actually, at getting a story. But it had to be *her* story. *Her* byline. And it cost her *her* job. Maybe Miles was right.

"You married?" Amelia asked.

"Divorced. How's your mom coping?"

She laughed. "With me being back or with the murder?"

Mardi paused. "Do you mind if we go over your statement? You said you were in the kitchen around eight p.m. Porter was probably killed between seven thirty and nine."

"Does that make me a suspect?" She smiled.

He didn't smile back. "What did you see?"

"It could have been a little earlier. I was there only a minute. Walked in, Kirby and the chef were arguing. The kitchen looked like a regular kitchen during a big party. A lot of people, a lot of movement, a lot of noise."

"Was the pantry door to the kitchen closed?"

Amelia thought for a moment. "I don't know. I walked into the kitchen from the breakfast room. The pantry is located in the back, near the door to the herb garden. I wouldn't have been able to see it from where I stood. Anyway, my full attention was focused on Kirby. She's pretty tightly wound."

"She and your brother appear to be quite the power couple."

Amelia laughed. "Yeah, sometimes it feels more like a power surge. You want to get out of their way."

"I understand the argument was over Swedish meatballs."

"Ridiculous, isn't it?"

The door to Mardi's office suddenly opened.

"Chief Sullivan." Mardi stood up from his chair. "This is Amelia Halliday, Louise Jenkins's daughter."

"Good!" he barked. "Then you're just the person to tell your mother to cease and desist." He threw the *Courier Times* on Mardi's desk. "This is an ongoing police investigation. We don't need her gossiping to the press and getting in the way."

"Gossiping? A man was murdered in her house. What would you like her to do, send reporters to you so you can say '*No comment*'?" Amelia added air quotes for impact.

Sullivan glared at Amelia and then Mardi. "Just tell her to knock it off." The door slammed.

"What an ass!" Amelia said.

"He lacks people skills."

"That's no excuse. He's still an ass."

After an uncomfortable minute, Amelia handed Tony a list.

"This is why I wanted to see you. These are people Mom invited to the party. They were her personal guests, so they're not on the historical society guest list."

Mardi looked at the single page of names, across from each a description:

1. *Devin Dykas. My hairdresser. She owns the salon. Hard worker, very trustworthy.*
2. *Danny Dykas. Master gardener.*
3. *Sharon something or other. US postal worker, a.k.a. my mailperson.*
4. *Rebecca Serenity, last name may be Severson but Serenity is more fitting. My yoga instructor.*
5. *Ned Pritchard and his wife, Agnes. Farmers, at least he is. They sell produce and pies at the farmers' market on Thursdays. Lovely couple, possibly Amish or maybe just like plain clothing. I think it's the latter because they were there at the party. You must try their strawberry rhubarb pie; it's out of this world.*

At the bottom of the list Louise wrote: "They are all innocent." *Innocent* was underlined.

Mardi looked up at Amelia.

"According to my mother, none of them could ever murder anyone. They have a special aura about them."

"Amelia, I can't go by your mother's feelings."

"I know. I'm just the messenger. Mom thought this would help you eliminate a few suspects."

"Tell your mother thank you." He held up the sheet of paper. "You know this is irrelevant."

"Not to my mother," she replied. "You'd be surprised how

often she's right about things without any apparent cogent fact to support it."

"I'll keep that in mind."

"Well, I better go."

"Thanks for coming in."

Amelia left and closed his office door. She paused in the hallway when she heard Tony's phone ring.

"I'm on my way" was all she heard him say before he flung open the door.

"Does that call have to do with the murder?" Amelia asked as she ran with him down the hall.

"Gotta go, Amelia. I'll be in touch."

It was remarkably easy to follow him. His siren at intersections gave her audible bread crumbs to follow. However, once he entered Core Creek Park she pulled her car off to the side of Tollhouse Road. Mardi would have spotted her immediately had she followed him onto the road that wound through the park. The twenty-five mph speed limit was intended for a leisurely drive through the 1,200-acre park, not the surreptitious tailing of a police vehicle.

A young couple with bikes mounted on the roof of their Volvo appeared over the crest of the hill. *Turn into the park. Turn into the park,* Amelia willed the oncoming car. She high-fived the sun visor and followed the Volvo. They wound past picnic groves and a basketball court until the Volvo turned into a parking lot at a mountain bike path.

Amelia continued until she saw police cars parked on a grassy berm. Below was Lake Luxembourg. She drove past and found a parking area near another wooded trail. She grabbed her cell phone and set out on foot. The woods would shield her until she was within fifty yards of the lake.

The police cars sat empty, abandoned by their drivers who were gathered around a tow truck as it backed down a concrete boat ramp.

The huge winch on the truck groaned as a thick cable slithered into the water. Amelia looked past the water's edge. Shiny black forms, like seals, bobbed in the lake. The cable seemed to grab them and pull them under.

The lake's surface began to move. Ripples at first, then large mounds of water spilled onto its bank. The truck's groaning became a howl as a white hulk, snared by the tow truck's cable, slowly rose out of the water. It was dragged across the boat ramp and pulled firmly onto land.

The seals surfaced and came ashore, their flippers slapping the wet sand. Police divers. Having released its victim, the lake grew still again. Amelia remained riveted to her spot.

* * *

A park ranger approached Mardi. "They flagged me down," he said, pointing to a young couple sitting on the grass. "They were out fishing for bass and he snagged something. Assuming his line was caught on a log, he rowed over to it and saw the top of the van. They got out of the lake pretty quick."

He paused and then added, "It's possible the vehicle went into the lake Sunday night. This morning I found the chain on the Bridgetown Road entrance cut. It's not the first time. Usually just kids drinking beer and joyriding after the park closes."

Mardi studied the van. Its windows were open. No driver, only lake water and debris.

"See anything interesting?" he asked the police photographer who was shooting the inside of the van.

"A pair of glasses is wedged between the passenger seat and

the center console," he said. The metal-framed glasses were held together by orange duct tape.

Mardi walked to the rear of the van where Barnett stood and peered in the window. More lake water, though only about six inches remained. Empty Red Bull cans bobbed on the surface. An orange lump of material floated like a small island, a Philadelphia Flyers sweatshirt. Mardi saw something move. He peered past a pair of sneakers. A fish flopped about as the water slowly drained from the vehicle.

He wanted to rescue it. He couldn't. Not yet. He had to wait for the photographer to finish chronicling the drowned van. It was clear there was no body inside. He looked back at the fish. "Hang in there, buddy."

"It's Porter's van," said Detective Cole as Mardi walked over to the folding table she had set up to collect evidence. "I just got the call confirming it was registered in his name."

"Someone drove it off the dock," said Mardi. "If it were pushed the rear would be damaged."

The photographer moved to the rear doors. He turned to Barnett. "OK, you can open them."

Barnett yanked open the doors and reached inside. "Hey, we got lunch," he yelled as he scooped out the bass.

"What the hell are you doing? I'm just getting started."

Barnett held up his hands, the fish slipping to the ground. "Sorry, I thought you said all clear. I got gloves."

"Barnett," Mardi yelled as he stormed over to him.

Mardi looked down at the fish and saw a faint flick of its tail. He picked it up and carried it to the lake's edge. Cradling the fish in his hands, he lowered it into the water. The water washed over its silvery skin. And then the fish swam away. Mardi wondered if the van driver had been as lucky.

* * *

A black SUV drove slowly along the paved road past the turnoff to the boat ramp and headed for the exit. Its passenger stared through binoculars at the police activity and then at the woman behind the trees.

8

Amelia awoke early. Her body ached from crouching behind a tree for two hours while the police pulled the van from the lake. She downloaded the iPhone photos and video to her hard drive. The first thirty-two looked like a photo burst of the same shot, but on closer inspection incremental changes occurred as the tow truck dragged the van onto dry land. If she printed them, they would make a perfect flipbook of the action on Lake Luxembourg.

She assumed the van belonged to Porter. When she finally left the park, it appeared the police were dragging the lake for a body. The murderer? She could wait for that answer. First, she wanted to know more about Michael Porter.

* * *

Amelia pulled into the parking lot of Riverview Apartments. Across the street behind a thick grove of trees and down a steep embankment was the Delaware River. Only the distant sound of rushing water announced its presence. The two-story apartment building, vinyl-sided with gray plastic shutters riveted on each side of the windows, had no view of the river—not from a doorway, not from a window. Maybe from the roof. Maybe its tenants were hopeful, aspirational. Someday they'd catch a glimpse, a river view. Maybe in the dead of winter when the trees were bare and the river icy and barely flowing.

She knocked on the door to apartment 4, the apartment Michael Porter had shared with Carol Anne.

The door opened only as far as the security chain lock allowed.

"Carol Anne? I'm Amelia Halliday."

The door closed. Amelia heard the chain scrape across its track.

"Hi, come in," Carol Anne said. She quickly closed the door behind Amelia and motioned to a dinette set across the room. "I made coffee. Would you like some?"

"If it's not too much trouble. Thank you for agreeing to see me."

Amelia walked across the tiny living room engulfed by a massive sectional. A crocheted afghan was tossed over its side, as if hiding part of the sofa to bring it into better proportion with the room.

The noonday sun tried to shine through the large picture window. Its radiance would have helped lift the dark sadness that resided inside. Instead, the unwashed glass filtered it. A brown valance hung across the top like a giant furrowed eyebrow wondering what had happened to the brighter days.

Amelia peered into the backyard. A vegetable garden stood wilting in the hot sun. Plants bent over the hard, cracked ground searching for just a trickle of water to sip. They weren't brittle yet. That would come soon after this limp stage. Leaves from tomato, cucumber, and zucchini plants were draped over each other. They could no longer produce a seed or flower. Barren. They just held on to each other, forming a tender blanket, a shroud.

Carol Anne slowly walked from the kitchen, head bowed, shoulders drooped, jeans barely hanging on to her slender hips. Amelia turned from the garden.

On the Formica table, Carol Anne set a plastic tray holding two mugs of coffee, sugar in a jelly jar, and a pint-size cardboard container of milk. Amelia thought of school lunches. The cafeteria filled with the chatter and laughter of students released from their classrooms to talk about anything and everything while they gobbled cheeseburgers and fries off their beige plastic trays. They had so much to learn during their brief lunch period: the answers to test questions, who was cheating on whom, and which of the rumors being passed from table to table were true.

Amelia hoped at this table she could learn something, too.

"I'm so sorry about Michael," she said as Carol Anne put teaspoon after teaspoon of sugar into her coffee.

"It's really hard," Carol Anne said, clutching the coffee mug with both hands for warmth, or maybe comfort.

"I appreciate your willingness to talk to me," Amelia began. "I'll try not to ask too many questions about—"

"Mikey and me were supposed to get married next year." Carol Anne jumped in before Amelia could finish her sentence. She had been waiting for someone to come sit at her table and talk to her. The lonely kid in the cafeteria.

"He was everything to me. We went to the same high school, but we didn't go out. Just friends. But I always liked him more than that. Then we met up again a couple of years later when I was working at the Dairy Queen. He walked up and ordered two cones and said, 'Is that you, Carol Anne?'"

Carol Anne relaxed. She was back at the DQ. "I couldn't

believe it." The grief-stricken young woman who answered the door ten minutes earlier had transformed into a giddy twenty-three-year-old. Her light-blue eyes were translucent, as if you could look through them into her mind or her heart.

"There he was. He looked so good, and he remembered me. But he was, like, with some other girl. So I gave him his cones and said, 'Nice seein' ya.' He came back the next day by himself."

She put her coffee mug down, sat up, and leaned toward Amelia. "It was the most exciting moment of my life. He came back to see me! He said he often wondered whatever happened to me. Figured I had got married and had kids or something. I told him I'd been here all along, just waiting for him." She blushed. "I saw that in a movie once and couldn't believe I had the guts to say it to him. He winked and said, 'How about we go on a date.'"

Carol Anne took a deep, quavering breath. Her eyes welled with tears, occluding any further access into her heart.

Amelia reached across the table and gently placed her hand over Carol Anne's, which trembled like a small, frightened bird.

Another deep breath. "Why would someone kill my Mikey? We were going to have such a good life together. I left the DQ and got a job working at a restaurant. He was working extra jobs. We were saving for our wedding and to buy a house. We moved in together two months ago." Carol Anne stared into the dark pool swirling in her cup. Her shoulders slumped. "Why would someone kill him? He was so good."

Carol Anne was shrinking before Amelia's eyes. Alice in Wonderland. Amelia wanted to catch her before she fell down the rabbit hole. Or maybe that would be a safe place for her to go, away from her grim reality.

If she fell, how far?

Down, down, down.

If she shrunk, how small?

"She waited for a few minutes to see if she was going to shrink any further: she felt a little nervous about this; 'for it might end, you know,' said Alice to herself, 'in my going out altogether, like a candle.'"

Carol Anne was not Alice. She was not a child napping on a warm riverbank on a summer's day, dreaming. She was sitting in a gloomy apartment beside a dying garden. This was not a dream. And unlike Alice, she would not awaken and wander home to tea.

Amelia sipped her coffee. "Do you know why he was at my mother's house?"

"No. He called me and said he got a delivery job. It must have been for your party, but why didn't he tell me that? I would have been so excited."

Amelia looked at her quizzically.

"I got tickets for the house tour. It's kinda fun to see how people with money live. The party was way too expensive. But if he was going to be working there that night, why wouldn't he have said so?"

"Do you know who hired him?"

"No, but he's a good worker. Gets calls about extra jobs like deliveries, some carpentry work, landscaping. He does a lot of packing and moving, too. Houses mostly, some offices. He makes good money. He also has a regular job delivering pizzas, but carpentry is what he wants to do. Wanted to do."

"Does he have any close friends? Someone who might know who he was working for that night?"

"He's got lotsa guy friends. His main guy is Jerry. Jerry Baker. He's real successful. Mikey's been working for him for a few months now. It's part-time; they're renovating a house. Sometimes the crew goes out for beers afterward. He and Jerry hit it off. Jerry knew we were saving to get married and gave Mikey extra work sometimes. Jerry's a good guy. One time he gave Mikey tickets to a Phillies game. He's got season tickets and couldn't go, so we went. It was awesome."

"Would you mind if I called Jerry?"

"I got his number on my phone. I think he lives in Newtown or somewheres close. Most of the jobs are in that area. They got money there." She pulled her phone out of her pocket and held it gently, looking at the screen.

She turned her phone so Amelia could see its wallpaper. Michael Porter holding a Dairy Queen chocolate waffle cone. With his curly hair and impish grin, he looked sixteen.

"Mikey said I was sweeter than any DQ they could make. We went there every month on the eighth. That's the day he came to the DQ alone."

To be with Carol Anne.

9

Back home, Amelia debated calling Tony. *I'll be in touch,* he had said yesterday. She hoped that he would. Hoped that he would confirm what she suspected—that the van pulled from the lake belonged to Michael. Surely he would know that she would be interested.

As she headed for the stairs to her loft, she noticed an envelope on the floor beneath the brass mail slot in her front door. Inside was a single sheet of paper with words cut from a newspaper. *Temperance House. 1 pm. Don't forget.*

She had forgotten, but if she hurried, she could get there in time. Amelia grabbed her car keys. The call to Mardi would have to wait.

* * *

A lone figure sat on the bench in front of the stone facade of the Temperance House, an inn with a restaurant and a bar—ironic, given that its founders were teetotalers. A plaid deerstalker cap hid all but a wisp of brown hair on the bent head; eyes stared at the brick sidewalk watching an ant carry a leaf.

"Do you know an ant can lift up to five thousand times its body weight?" Winnie said as she looked up at Amelia. "I learned that from a biomechanics article."

Amelia held up the note. "Your communications have taken on a ransom-note style."

"You said I text too much."

"You could call me," Amelia said. "Did you ride your bike?"

"No, Kirby and Elliott were at the house. Kirby gave me a ride, even though I know she thinks I'm weird. She was nicer than usual, though. She agreed to stop by your house so I could leave the note and then I went with her to Bangles and Butterfield Boutique. I walked from there. Can you give me a ride home? Kirby bought a dress—cobalt blue with a touch of burnt sienna."

Winnie peppered her sentences with Crayola Crayon colors the way most adolescents sprinkled theirs with "like," "um," and "whatever." But unlike most adolescents, her crayons sat alongside chemistry and calculus books. At eleven, she had skipped numerous grades and still was firmly positioned on the GPA apex in her freshman class. Maybe the crayons let her hang on to childhood while she read Bertrand Russell. She pulled her backpack from under the bench and opened it.

"Is that a new box of crayons?" Amelia asked as she peered inside.

"Yep. I already removed the black and white ones. They're not colors," she told her. "A color has to have a wavelength. It's light. This is physics," she added, in case Amelia didn't know. "Black and white don't have their own wavelengths, so they're not colors.

"And this gets really interesting," Winnie said excitedly.

"White is all, and I mean *all*, colors added together. Black is none, because you only see black when there's no light. Of course I understand why Crayola still puts in a black and a white crayon; it's a visual thing. In the visual arts, black and white are called *distinct colors*, but not by physicists. They stick with spectral color, or as I call it, *spectacular color*. I just love science. It's so, it's so black and white." Winnie laughed. "That's hilarious, isn't it? Science gives you unambiguous answers. That means they're black and white even when it's about color."

Winnie pulled a package wrapped in pink paper from her backpack. "This is for you. It's about a murder, but not the one you think."

Amelia studied the wrapping. "Carnation Pink?"

"You're close, it's Tickle Me Pink! But you're better than most."

"Oh, sweetie. Wherever did you find this?" Amelia held in her hands a Nancy Drew book, *The Hidden Staircase.*

"At an estate sale I went to with my mom. It's a first edition. A thank-you gift. I got an A." Winnie's art history class required a final paper on an artist. Most kids gravitated to the impressionists, but not Winnie. Amelia had suggested William Hicks, the American folk artist.

"Of course." Winnie had smacked her forehead. "There are two at the house, a landscape and George Washington at the Delaware River. It should have been obvious."

"Your choice of the Temperance House is perfect," Amelia said as they walked into the dining room and sat next to Hicks's *A Peaceable Kingdom*.

Amelia thought back to her own life as an eleven-year-old and to her beloved library, now home. She would ride her bike there on Saturday mornings, hopeful she would find a Nancy Drew she hadn't yet read.

She'd lock her bike onto the iron fence that surrounded the building and amble up the steps, pushing on its brass knob the size of a grapefruit. Once inside, she'd slip into the youth section. Her room.

It was a narrow room. An enameled brick fireplace anchored one wall. Opposite it stood bookcases snuggled in between a set of tall windows that sent rays of sunlight across the room, streaking the oak floor. Amelia would turn to the fourth bookcase from the door, seventh shelf. There Nancy Drew was waiting for her. Each book covered in clear plastic with the Dewey Decimal number typed onto a sticker at the base of its spine.

Amelia would sit on the floor cross-legged and read the first chapter, the afternoon sunlight resting on her shoulders. Tranquility. The tall case clock counted off the seconds. Occasionally a chair leg would scrape across the oak floor. The air smelled of polished wood and books, mostly of books. Their pulpy scent perfumed the air. Their pages, like delicate petals, fluttered as fingers gently turned them, so eyes could pick at the words they held, pollinating the imagination.

Sometimes Mrs. Eichel, the librarian, would push the wooden cart of returned books along the rows to restack them. She would stop and, using her library voice, quietly wish her good day. Years later, when Mrs. Eichel was honored for her years of service to the community, Amelia discovered that she, too, had been a newspaper reporter. But she left journalism and New York for the beauty and tranquility of Bucks County. Not to retire, and, unlike Amelia, not to escape.

"Have things quieted down at the house?" Amelia asked as she and Winnie ate lunch.

"A smidge. I'm conducting my own investigation." Winnie touched her hat. "Your mom gave me this. Sherlock Holmes wore one just like it. I also have a private-eye kit, including fingerprint powder, though it would make a mess and the police have already done that part. I'm looking for things they might have missed. Can you tell me what I should be looking for?"

"Me?"

"Mrs. Jenkins said you once were an investigative reporter and covered crime."

"I was."

"So let's team up!"

"Let's get you home."

IO

"You can drop me off at the mailbox and I'll walk up," Winnie said as they approached Twin Beeches.

"That's OK. I want to pop in to say hi."

Amelia joined her mother in the study. "The fireplace screen Andrew found is perfect in my living room," Amelia said. "I need a side table and a few more pieces for the bedrooms and I should be pretty settled. Is there anything in the attic you might part with?"

"I'm worried about you," Louise said. "Someone was murdered in our home and you want to talk about decorating."

Amelia was silent for a moment. "I'm trying to reset my life. I want to feel settled. It's not easy after Kevin Morgan blew my career to bits."

"Amelia!" Louise snapped. "Kevin may have used you, but he didn't destroy your job. You did."

"Is that supposed to make me feel better?"

"Oh, stop pouting."

"I'm not pouting." In her mind she was also stamping her feet. "I'm pissed off, Mom. I loved my job."

"Well, it's gone. Time to move on, or at least be in the present."

How many more times must she relive it? The outcome wasn't going to change.

* * *

There he was, sitting in the office of Ed Lagonda, the *Los Angeles Times*'s editor.

"Amelia, come to my office. Now!" Ed had barked through the phone moments earlier. She was used to Ed's gruffness. She had worked for him for a decade.

She grabbed her notebook. Ed was stressed. Must be major bad news. It would be another story for her. The *Times* was submitting her recent series on Tripoint to the Pulitzer committee. She broke the story that CEO Ben Adams had embezzled $60 million from his company. A Pulitzer. Maybe this would be the year. She knew she had made an ethical misstep journalistically, but it didn't change the facts. It did wreck her personal life. At least she had her career.

She walked through the newsroom toward Ed's glass-walled office. Working in a fishbowl. The debate was always over who were the fish: the newsroom staff or Ed and Peter Daniels, the executive editor in the office next door. It all depended on which side of the glass you were looking through.

It was the slouch that stopped her. It was always so appealing, a man so powerful, a posture so casual. Not today. He was sitting in the chair across from Ed's desk. Today Ed's office was clearly the fishbowl, but it had a shark in it.

"Amelia, come in," said Ed. The door closed behind her with a thud. Ed's office, with its panoramic view of the Hollywood

Hills, suddenly felt claustrophobic. Amelia took the chair next to Kevin Morgan, her heart racing.

Her heart always raced at the sight of Kevin. But at this moment, it wasn't the quiver of heartstrings; it was a fight-or-flight response. She knew he was going to ruin her career.

"Dead?" stammered Amelia after Ed briefed her. "Ben Adams?"

"Overdose," said Kevin. "Unknown if it was accidental or a suicide."

Amelia stared at Ed, whose complexion was changing from California suntan to a slow, steady red burn. And then he erupted.

He slammed his fist on his desk, sending the crystal globe rolling off its Lucite stand straight toward the framed photo of Ed's hunting dog, Lucy. Ed grabbed for Lucy's photo; he loved that dog.

"Amelia," he bellowed, "you have violated your ethical responsibility to this newspaper."

Amelia jumped from her chair as if a gun had gone off, and she was going to beat Lucy to the kill. Kevin was all hers. "How could you?"

It had taken Amelia nearly a year to even go on a date after her husband, Miles, left her for Simone, a personal shopper at Neiman's. Amelia met Kevin through an online dating service. That alone was almost too much for her; so pathetic, she thought. Cupid on the internet trading his arrow for an algorithm.

It took only a few dates for Kevin to hint at trouble at his company, Tripoint, where he was CFO. Soon he brought copies of files, financials, and memos. They would dissect the juicy details over wine and sushi at her apartment.

She knew that their relationship was a conflict. It was her responsibility to tell her editor, who would decide if the story needed to be reassigned. She knew the answer to that. But the story was too big, too explosive for her to let someone else take over.

The series ran and Amelia's world crumbled. First, personally. After Kevin was named interim CEO pending the outcome of the investigation, he dumped her. He said it was best if they backed off for a while. She bumped into him a week later. Ben's secretary was on his arm. Amelia's humiliation was complete.

Until now.

Ed asked her to wait in his office as he escorted Kevin to the door.

When he returned to his desk, his anger carried a slight patina of sorrow. Very slight. And then he fired her.

* * *

"Amelia." Her mom's voice brought her back. "I know I'm being harsh, but you have to move on. You made a mistake. We all make them."

"It was catastrophic."

"Well, yes, but nothing's going to change that. It's time to push forward. Live your life. I sold this house because I wasn't living mine. I was too busy taking care of our relatives, the dead ones. I needed to get away from them. No offense, my dears." She smiled up at the Samuels. "Now that I'm back, the house feels different. Our ancestors are still present, but they seem to be more self-sufficient now. They survived, in a manner of speaking, and so did I.

"If Mr. Vincent hadn't gone on the lam—I do wonder what

he was up to—I wouldn't have come back, but I'm glad I did." The Samuels performed their tiny happy dance. "I'm supposed to be here," Louise added. "And you are, too, Amelia. A man has been murdered in this house. Use it to get your mind off the mess you made in California."

II

Use the murder to get your mind off the mess you made in California!

This is what a mother says to her daughter? Amelia was still angry over yesterday's conversation. Angry that her mother was capable of making such a direct hit to her self-pity. Most moms would just say *Don't worry, things happen for a reason.*

Growing up, Amelia had wanted her mom to be like the others. Normal. Living an unnoticed life. Planning vacations to Disneyland, not to a farm in France to make goat cheese or to England, where they spent a week in a cottage in Gloucestershire learning to create topiaries and make proper scones.

When she returned from LA, Amelia had hoped that she could live an unnoticed life. She wanted the party to allow her to hit reset, to smoothly blend in, like entering a conversation in the middle without anyone noticing. She had studied the faces at the party that night, so many familiar ones from her past, though she couldn't quite bring their names forward. That was OK. She wanted to be unnoticed for a while longer, just until she recovered. But to recover, you actually have to do something. She picked up her cell phone.

"Jerry Baker?" she asked.

"Yeah?"

"My name's Amelia Halliday. Michael Porter's girlfriend gave me your number."

"I don't know no Michael Porter."

"Carol Anne said he worked for you. House renovations."

There was a long pause. Amelia looked at her phone to make sure she still had a connection.

"Oh yeah, wait a minute. You mean MP. You need renovations? I'm booked pretty solid, but tell me what you're looking to get done."

"I'm not calling about a job. I'm looking for information on Michael. MP."

"Uh, you know he was murdered, right?"

"He was killed at my mother's house."

"Oh shit, that's a bad deal."

Amelia strained to hear him above the sound of hammers and power tools.

"Listen, I gotta check on my guys here," Jerry yelled above the din, "and I don't know anything about the murder. Talk to the cops."

"I'd still like to talk to you. I'm trying to help his fiancée."

Only the sounds of construction came through the connection.

"Jerry?"

"Yeah, uh, I usually end the day at the Pineville Tavern, if you want to stop by. It's a free country."

* * *

The bar area was already crowded when Amelia arrived. Built in 1742, the Pineville Tavern had served many purposes: a feed mill, a hotel, a general store, and a tavern that seated nine and served cold sandwiches. Over the decades it was expanded, renovated, and as a result, ensured its future while protecting its historically significant past during the Revolutionary War. It had been a dozen years since Amelia last dined there. She hoped steamed clams were still on the menu. Maybe she would stay for dinner after talking to Jerry Baker. She found a spot at the bar and ordered a chardonnay.

"Is Jerry Baker here?" she asked the bartender.

The bartender looked down the bar. "Hey, Jerry." Her head tilted in Amelia's direction. "Somebody wants you."

"Finally," someone said with a laugh. Jerry picked up his beer and walked toward Amelia. Tall and muscular, he was dressed in jeans. A blue T-shirt stretched across his broad shoulders, and the laces of his work boots were undone.

"Hey, you the girl that called me today?" He pulled out the stool next to her and sat down.

Amelia cringed at the "girl" reference. "If the call was about Michael Porter, then yes, I am."

"I really got nothin' to tell you. MP worked for me for a few months. I had extra work. They're my regular crew." He motioned to the other end of the bar. Five guys waved back, swigging their beers. Jerry laughed. "Bunch of clowns."

"Was he working for you the night he was killed?"

Jerry put his beer down. "Hell no, and if he was, he wouldn't have been killed. He would have been renovating a farmhouse. What are you getting at?"

"Nothing," Amelia said, trying to keep the edge out of her voice. "I'm just trying to find out who he was working for that night. No one seems to have a clue."

"Well, just call me clueless then," he said. "Talk to the cops. Hey, Harry, com'ere. This lady doesn't think you guys are doin' your job."

At least I moved from a girl to a lady, Amelia thought. She was sure "ma'am" would be next.

"What's the problem?" Harry Barnett strode over to Amelia, planting himself just behind her barstool. He waved his empty beer bottle over her head. "Hey, Barb, get me another one."

"This is Officer Barnett," Jerry said as he stood up from his barstool. "Maybe he can answer your questions."

Amelia felt claustrophobic as both men hovered over her.

"She's askin' about MP," Jerry said. "The guy that was killed. Says you guys don't know what you're doing."

"I did not," snapped Amelia. "I *said* no one seems to know who he was working for that night."

"She said you were clueless." Jerry smirked, enjoying himself so much he sat back down.

"Oh for God's sake. I'm just trying to find out why he was at my mother's house." She took a sip of her wine, hoping she could swallow her defensiveness with it. "I expect if you knew you'd tell us."

"Not necessarily, ma'am," Barnett said.

Amelia rolled her eyes. There it was. She was ma'amed.

"This is an ongoing murder investigation. Information is on a need-to-know basis."

"Oh, spare me." She slammed down her glass of chardonnay. It was hardly the effect she hoped for. A mere clink echoed off the oak bar. A shot glass of whiskey would have been much more impactful.

"Lady, why don't you let us do our job and you just sit tight. This is a murder investigation. We don't need amateurs getting in the way." He looked down at her half-empty glass of wine. "Hey, Barb, this lady hasn't been overserved, has she?"

He and Jerry laughed.

Amelia threw money on the bar and walked out the door. Just before it closed she turned and flipped them off. She got into her car and took a deep breath. Then she started to shake. With laughter.

Her old self had moved back into her body, evicting the self-pitying squatter who took advantage of Amelia's shame. She wasn't proud of flipping them off, but it was certainly better than the white flag she had been waving. It felt good to feel angry. She liked the adrenaline rush.

Driving home, Amelia felt like she was finally overtaking her past.

* * *

She turned on the lights in her kitchen and poured herself a glass of wine—this one she would finish—and climbed the stairs to her loft. Amelia looked at the mess of papers strewn across her desk—media coverage of the murder, the guest list from the party, her interview with Carol Anne. What was it about that night that led to Porter's death? Did his past catch up with him?

Amelia had allowed her past to travel with her every day, running alongside her, tripping her, knocking her down, and still she held on to the vestiges of her ruin. She opened her top desk drawer and removed a file folder. It contained her termination letter from the *LA Times* and a copy of the letter sent to the Pulitzer committee withdrawing her Tripoint series from consideration. She had been cc'd on it just in case her own private shame wasn't enough. Why was she keeping them? She didn't need them to remember. She would never forget her actions.

Amelia fed the documents into the gnashing teeth of her paper shredder.

It was time to go to bed. Time to get her mind off the mess she made. The party may not have allowed her to hit reset, but tomorrow's dinner at Twin Beeches with the family offered her a second chance.

12

"Good evening, Louise." Kirby walked into Louise's study at Twin Beeches. She was surprised when Elliott told her the Thursday family dinner was still scheduled. The murder was less than a week ago. "Elliott is just finishing a business call. He'll be in shortly."

"Hello, Kirby," Louise called over her shoulder. Louise sat on the window seat below a pair of casement windows whose copper muntins created a grid of ten small panes of glass. Louise was pulling on a lower right pane.

"Is the window broken?"

"Not at all. Look, isn't it darling?" Louise pinched her fingers around a bit of copper attached to a muntin. The small pane swung inward like a tiny door. "The casement window is too difficult to open every time Florence wants to come in," said Louise, looking up at the towering window, "so Wills made this little door in one of the panes."

"Who's Florence?"

"Our squirrel," said Winnie as she rounded the corner carrying an antique English biscuit jar.

Louise opened and closed the little door several times. "Not a squeak."

Kirby saw that the tiny door had a copper acorn doorknob.

"I didn't put a doorknob on the outside," added Louise. "Florence's little paws can't turn a knob. She rings when she wants to come in."

Outside on the stone windowsill, an antique brass service bell inscribed "Waldorf Astoria" sat ready to summon assistance. "But it's a squirrel," said Kirby.

"She, dear, not it. She's a squirrel. She jumps up on the sill, taps the little bobber on the top of the bell, and waits until I open her door. Winnie and I taught her. Very Pavlovian, don't you think?"

As if on cue, a tiny ding sounded and a gray squirrel, perched on its hindquarters, peered in.

"Do you have the peanuts, Winnie?"

Winnie held up the biscuit jar. "I just refilled it." She walked over to the window seat and placed a peanut on it.

"Well then, come in, Florence." Louise opened the tiny door and took a seat in her wingback chair near the fireplace.

Kirby looked around the room, expecting to find a groundhog curled in a chair or a raccoon sleeping on a bookshelf. Her eyes stopped at a small table. "Is that a Georg Jensen bowl?"

"It is," answered Louise. A gleaming silver bowl held colorful strands of knitting wool and bits of cotton swirled into a nest. The mottled mass resembled melted crayons, blobs of color morphed into a gray clump at the bottom of the bowl. "It's a perfect little nest for Florence. She likes it."

"It's a squirrel's nest? Do you know what that bowl is worth?"

"Oh, quite a bit. To Florence," said Louise.

"Elliott could certainly use it in New York. He entertains a lot."

"Well, I'll be sure to put that in my will."

Kirby had once again put her foot in her mouth. She just didn't get Louise. Louise valued things for their utility or their whimsy. It seemed to matter little if a bowl was sterling silver or Tupperware. Maybe that's what privilege is—ignoring the money it takes to have it.

Kirby wasn't born with a silver spoon in her mouth; she had to buy it, along with the knife and fork. Fortunately she knew what she was looking for in things and in people. Her interior design firm, Dunbar & Co., gave her access to both.

"Oh, I didn't mean it that way," Kirby stammered. "I'm sorry. But this squirrel, it's a wild creature. You can't have it living in the house."

"She doesn't live here. She visits. Winnie and I enjoy her company, don't we, Winnie?" Louise's soft gray eyes twinkled.

Winnie sat down in the chair opposite Louise, eating peanuts and occasionally tossing one to Florence, who caught it in midair. "We need to teach Florence to shell the nuts in one place. She makes such a mess."

"So have you heard anything more from the police?" Kirby asked Louise as she moved closer to the doorway, distancing herself from the squirrel and the discussion of its eating habits.

"No, I haven't. I believe they talked to Ruth again. She'll be here shortly. I'm sure she'll give us all the details. You're staying for dinner, aren't you?"

"Yes, thank you." Kirby looked down the hallway, hoping Elliott would appear soon. Elliott. He must take after his father. He's so normal, although he did name his helicopter Skip. But that was endearing, like a little boy with his toys. Expensive toys.

Elliott was the one. It was early in their relationship, but he was what she had always wanted. Being in the right place at the right time—that's how life worked. Though Kirby knew that it wasn't just kismet that got you to that place. You had to travel in the right circles first. And for some, like Kirby, it was a bumpy road, but she had made it. She had found Elliott.

"Are you full?" Kirby heard Louise ask.

"What?" Kirby said, before realizing Louise was talking to the squirrel.

"Winnie, see if your exit strategy works."

Winnie opened the squirrel door, placed a peanut on the window seat and another on the sill outside. She carried the biscuit jar over to the fireplace mantel.

Florence jumped onto the window seat, grabbed the nut, and scampered out her door. On the sill she maneuvered the second peanut until both were in her mouth, then she jumped down to the patio below and ran across the garden toward an oak tree. Winnie giggled at Florence's puffed cheeks.

"I'll go check on Elliott. His call must be over by now," said Kirby.

"And I need to wash up and get the hors d'oeuvres ready," said Winnie.

* * *

Cocktails in her study. Louise liked to include the Samuels, so the evening began with cocktails below their portraits, which adorned the wall opposite a sofa and two yellow upholstered chairs. Beyond them an antique desk was centered in front of French doors that opened out to a softly sloping lawn, a pond, and gardens beyond. Louise was certain the Samuels appreciated the exceptional view.

"Here they are," Winnie announced as she entered the study carrying a tray. She carefully set it on a side table and placed a white card next to it. "I've named this hors d'oeuvre 'The Princes of Melonland Ride through a Verdant Forest.'" Slices of melon draped in prosciutto capes sat atop a bed of asparagus. Winnie enjoyed helping her mother, Claudia, prepare meals, and her hors d'oeuvres were now a tradition at the weekly family dinner, a dinner that included Winnie, Claudia, and Wills.

"Very good," said Amelia as she sampled an asparagus. "I feel like I'm eating a scene from *A Midsummer Night's Dream*."

Elliott mixed himself a martini and looked around the room. "Last time we were all here we had a police chaperone."

"Speaking of which . . . ," Amelia said as she nibbled another hors d'oeuvre. "They pulled a van out of Lake Luxembourg, a white van. I lay odds it belonged to Michael Porter. Carol Anne told me he drove a van."

"Who's Carol Anne?" asked Elliott.

"Porter's girlfriend. I met her for coffee."

"Oh, are we investigating?" asked Elliott, arching his eyebrow.

"Asking questions," said Amelia.

Before anyone could ask another one, Ruth rushed in. "I'm sorry I'm late. I've had the most distressing day."

"Were the police there?" Louise asked.

"Yes. Let me just sit for a moment and get my wits about me."

"Have a martini, Ruthie," said Louise. "Elliott, fix one for Ruth."

Everyone watched and waited while Ruth sipped her drink.

"I feel much more under control now." She looked around the room. "Well, where do I begin? I'm so disillusioned. The way they treated me. It's almost criminal."

"Did they harass you?" asked Louise.

"Worse. They just didn't care. I told them everything. Even my tips."

"Your tips?" asked Elliott.

"You know, emergency information, currency, safety."

"Ruth, what are you talking about?" asked Louise.

"My article in the Travel Club's magazine, Louise, don't you remember? Robert D'Angelo, the owner of the Travel Club, wanted me to chronicle my travel experiences. I believe I'm considered a bit of an expert, and they thought this would be informative to their readers. It was a wonderful interview, and the photographer must have taken fifty photos of me with my various souvenirs. Robert scoured my photo albums for other unusual shots." Ruth blushed. "He paid quite a bit of attention to me."

She took another sip, more of a gulp, of her drink. "Well, today the magazine arrived. I expected to be on the cover. Instead there's a tiny article and only one picture of me. That's it!" She looked around the room, expecting everyone to feel her pain.

They were speechless. Ruth was comforted.

"But, Ruth," stammered Louise, "what about the police?"

"Oh, Louise, it's not a crime, though the reporter certainly stole hours of my time. No. I'm afraid I have no recourse."

"No, Ruth, I mean the police investigating the murder, your interview with them today."

"Oh, that. It was the woman detective, Rita something or other. She's very nice. We talked about the party, and if I remembered anything unusual. As if the body wasn't unusual enough." Ruth was exasperated. "I did tell her my investigative insight. I also remembered where I first heard Michael Porter's name.

Newtown Hardware. I'm sure of it. I must have been there to buy light bulbs."

"Oh yes," said Kirby as she rolled her eyes. "The scent of Old Spice."

"Aromas are powerful," snapped Louise. "They can embed a memory and trigger an emotional response. Every time I smell cotton candy I think of poor Andrew stuck on top of the Ferris wheel at the Lancaster Fair. The firefighters had to rescue everyone. Of course, I don't really need the cotton candy as a reminder. Who could forget such a thing? But there it is, that association." Louise walked over and patted Ruth's shoulder. "Good memory, Ruth. Now, let's have dinner. I prefer that we abstain from discussion of the murder. It's bad for digestion."

The meal was excellent, the conversation less so. Each topic raised fell almost immediately. It was time for dinner to be over.

"Ruth and I are going to the study for a nightcap and to organize my photos from our trip to Mexico," Louise said. "Or would you rather we finish my scrapbook another time, Ruth?"

"Heavens, no. I love scrapbooking. It brings back such wonderful memories."

"Ruth has quite the creative spark when it comes to chronicling our adventures. Anyone want to join us?"

"I'm heading home in a minute," said Amelia. "I'll come by on Saturday."

"Wills and I will clean up," said Claudia. "And Winnie needs to finish her homework, so we'll all say good night."

"Let's go, Ruthie."

Ruth followed Louise out of the dining room.

* * *

"It seems odd the help join you for your family dinner," said Kirby.

Elliott looked stricken. "Kirby!"

A voice came from the hallway. "My dear." Louise stepped back into the room. "I do not consider them the help, and this dinner is not exclusively reserved for family now, is it?"

"Mother," Elliott intoned. "Kirby is just looking out for your well-being. The Millers do work here."

"And they create beautiful art. We have a lovely arrangement. They help me, and I provide studio space for them in the barn. Have you actually seen their work? Claudia's pottery and Wills's paintings are highly sought after."

"Yes, but I worry they're taking advantage of you," said Elliott.

"Oh, tsk! I'm enjoying my life, Elliott. I'm not sure you can say the same. You're always in a rush. Breathe a little. Take a yoga class. I'm perfectly fine and the Millers are my friends." As she turned to leave, she paused and added, "And never refer to them as 'the help' again." She walked out of the dining room.

"Elliott, what's your problem?" Amelia slapped Elliott's arm.

"What? I'm just worried about Mother. And Wills shouldn't cater to her whims. He should check with us. He put in a door for a squirrel. What next?"

"You can be such a jerk," Amelia fumed. "The Millers are great for Mom. Do you have any friends who work for you or are they all just *the help*?"

"At least I don't confuse news sources with sex partners."

Amelia and Elliott's eyes locked, daring the other to blink first. A stare-down. It had always been this way. Always competitors. In school, in sports, in careers, and even in arguments. Each one determined to win. It was never a tie.

"Oh for God's sake, will you two stop," demanded Kirby. "What are you, ten?"

They ignored her and continued to stare, teeth clenched, hands pressed flat on the table, preventing it from levitating and fleeing the dining room. Finally, Amelia blinked.

"Ha! Gotcha," said Elliott with a triumphal grin.

Kirby rolled her eyes and poured herself more wine.

13

"It was a nice trip," said Ruth as she and Louise sorted through Louise's Cabo San Lucas photos. "My article would have been so much better if they had included a couple of my pictures. I have a great one in front of that lovely pottery shop."

* * *

Cabo San Lucas

"May I help you?"

"Goodness, there are so many choices," said Ruth. "I like the animals. The birds are nice, too." Ruth maneuvered down narrow aisles lined with massive wooden tables holding brightly painted vases, pitchers, dinnerware, and souvenirs. It was the last day of the Travel Club's trip. The saleswoman followed closely behind.

"I enjoy entertaining with the luxuries I've purchased on my many travels," Ruth said, her back to the saleswoman. She paused and turned to her. "Do you remember me? I was here last year. When I booked this trip I just knew I had to get back to this nice little shop. I see you've increased your selections, and your prices." She tittered. "But you only go around once, and I'm not getting any younger. Ooh, look at those lovely dishes over there. I must have a look. I'll let you know if I need your assistance." She dismissed the saleswoman with a flutter of her hand.

"Ladies, we're leaving in fifteen minutes," said Robert D'Angelo, dazzling his group with his smile and biceps. His starched white shirt and black trousers perfectly fit his muscular body. His silver-streaked hair added a distinguished quality, while his red Converse sneakers gave him just enough boyish charm. The combination made hearts flutter.

"Yes, Robert. I'm almost ready," cooed Ruth, her cheeks flushing at the sound of his voice. "I'm a bit overwhelmed with all the choices."

Robert sidled up to her. "That's understandable." He led her over to a wall of dinner plates, each a different pattern. "What strikes your fancy?"

"I was considering birds, but I just don't know."

He reached up and selected a plate. "This is one of my favorites. It's elegant with a hint of boldness, just like you."

"Oh my goodness." Ruth clutched her bosom. "Do they have service for twelve?"

"Angela," Robert called. The saleswoman instantly appeared next to him.

"Mrs. Richards would like service for twelve in this pattern, and as a favor to me, please include a matching vase, one of the large ones."

"Oh my," Ruth gushed.

"I'll personally see that your purchase is taken to the bus, Mrs. Richards." Robert patted her arm.

"Oh please, Robert, call me Ruth."

He added a little squeeze. "I'll see you on the bus."

Louise joined Ruth at the cashier counter. "I really don't need any more dinnerware, but these colors are so vibrant. They remind me of Majorca."

"Make sure they give you a vase," said Ruth, watching the clerks pack Louise's purchases. "It's free when you buy service for twelve."

The cashier motioned to Robert, who walked up beside Ruth. He guided her a few steps away from Louise and whispered, "It's not the shop's policy. I asked them to include the gift with your purchase because you're such a special client." He squeezed her arm and winked.

"Oh, you dear man," she replied, almost swooning. "But Louise is my good friend and this is her first experience with our travel club. You can treat her, too, can't you?"

"Well, for you, Ruth, I'll make an exception." He nodded to another salesclerk.

"My, my, aren't I getting the VIP treatment? Ooh, that's a nice pattern, Louise. I don't think I noticed that one."

* * *

Members of the Travel Club gathered in the lobby of Los Cabos International Airport. Their orange-and-navy-blue Travel Club totes looked like life jackets bobbing in a sea of luggage and souvenirs.

"Smile, Louise," said Ruth as she snapped a photo. "I've gone through six rolls of film this trip."

"Why don't you use the camera on your phone?" Louise

asked, eyeing the Canon slung around Ruth's neck like an oversize pendant.

"Because I can't control myself. I would have so many photos on my phone that I'd never be able to decide which ones I should print for my albums. Until I can't get any more film, I'm sticking with my trusty camera."

Ruth watched fellow travelers lug pottery, sombreros, and other souvenirs on board. "It's a good thing this is the club's private plane. Imagine trying to bring that pig piñata on a United flight."

Louise laughed. "Maybe she could claim it as a service animal."

Ruth and Louise settled into their seats. "You know what my dear, departed Paul always said," mused Ruth. "If you can't go first class, stay home." The Travel Club's reconfigured fleet of A320s had only first-class seats and plenty of cargo space.

Ruth sipped her champagne. Her gray neck pillow nestled on her shoulders like a short, fat python. "I hope I picked the right pattern for my dishes. Oh my, doesn't that look good," she exclaimed as the flight attendant served Louise a seafood salad.

"Excuse me," Ruth said. "I'd like to change my order to the seafood, and I'll have another one of these." She waved her glass at the flight attendant.

14

The silk sash dripping tiny brass bells announced Amelia's arrival as she pushed open the heavy oak door of Bryson's Bistro. She wasn't sure it was a good idea to meet with a reporter, especially the reporter who had texted her during the family dinner last night. It was too late to cancel, so she arrived early. It would give her a bit of an advantage, and the opportunity to have a drink.

"Amelia!" Mitchell Butterfield, owner of Bangles and Butterfield Boutique, waved her over. He was anchored at the corner of the bar.

She slid in beside him. "What are you drinking?" she asked, eyeing a concoction of cucumber, orange slices, and mint."

"It's Pimm's."

"Quite the change from your usual scotch and soda."

"I'm varying my beverage. This week it's Pimm's, though it's a little early to celebrate Royal Ascot."

Amelia raised her eyebrow.

"You know, Royal Ascot? In England?"

Amelia added an eye roll to her facial expressions.

"In honor of it, I drink traditionally English cocktails, though this is a bit fruity for me. I think I'll switch to champagne. Bollinger, of course. Nothing says Royal Ascot like a bit of bubbly."

"And nothing says royal ass like Mitchell Butterfield, said Charlotte Cartwright, a Bryson's regular, sipping a pinot noir.

"Well, at least I add a dash of imagination to my libations."

Bryson's Bistro was a popular gathering place for Newtown's locals and the faculty at Arbor College, a small, private university founded by the Quakers in 1827. Its ivy-covered walls might have aspired to join the likes of Harvard and Brown, but its student body was less competitive. No Nobel Prize winners or Fulbright scholars, at least not yet. Instead Arbor taught, graduated, and welcomed into the alumni association smart, congenial people who often reached pinnacles in their careers, though the heights did not require Sherpa-like guidance to reach the summit.

Stephen Bryson opened his eponymous brewery after an uneventful four years at Arbor College and an eventful five years at a restaurant in Negril Beach in Jamaica. His inheritance beckoned him back to Bucks County by providing the resources to open the bistro. He was still adjusting to the weather and need for punctuality.

At times the area's mix of Manhattan weekenders, college students, and fourth- and fifth- generation Bucks County residents presented an amusing balance. The weekenders, with their second or third homes and often as many marriages, mixed with the more discreet Quakers.

"Drink, Amelia?" asked Gus, one of Bryson's bartenders.

"Just a soda. I'm meeting Leslie Clark."

"Spilling the goods on the Twin Beeches murder?" asked Mitchell.

"It's my mom's house. Have a little tact."

"Yeah, but you didn't know the guy, did you? Don't you feel more intrigue than grief?"

Amelia wasn't sure why she had agreed to the interview. Maybe it was to irritate Chief Sullivan, or more likely curiosity about Leslie. Perhaps they had both matured.

They had attended the Pine Street School together, where they competed for the job as student reporter for the school newsletter. Amelia won. The rivalry continued into high school, though it sank to new levels of pettiness. Leslie was the more popular of the two and always took the last seat on the bus. She would decide who sat with her. She never picked Amelia.

Amelia was surprised when years later Leslie congratulated her on her hire at the *LA Times*. Unfortunately, in an out-of-character moment, Amelia replied that perhaps now she was worthy to sit on the bus with her. It was a total mean-girl moment that reduced her to a fifteen-year-old. And now Leslie was covering the murder at Twin Beeches for the *Courier Times*. Amelia feared this could be Leslie's touché.

"Hellooooo!" Leslie's greeting drowned out the bells. "Well, the big-city girl returns." She laughed as she swiftly walked over to Amelia. Mitchell squeezed Amelia's hand, either in friendship or to keep her from doing something violent. Amelia squeezed him back and then walked with Leslie to the dining area.

"It's been years," Leslie said as they settled into a booth. "How long have you been back?" She forced a smile to cover up the smirk that was fighting its way to the corners of her mouth.

"Six months," Amelia said, smiling gamely, ready to shut down any questions about her firing.

"Where are you working?" Leslie tilted her head ever so slightly.

"I'm freelancing at the moment. It's a surprise how busy I am. I'm pretty much committed through this year. It's actually a nice change, a lot of variety. I'm editing articles for a couple of magazines and a collection of essays by Kathy Hacker. Do you remember her? She was a columnist for *The Bulletin*? It's all interesting."

Stop talking! Amelia knew she was rambling. She should have stopped after "freelancing." It was a simple question that she was still defensive in answering. She was trying to convince anyone who asked her about work that she was in a good place. She knew she was still trying to convince herself.

"Your poor mom," Leslie said, satisfied or indifferent to Amelia's current occupation. "How is she coping? What an awful ending to a wonderful evening."

"You were there? Were you covering it for the *Courier Times*?"

"No, I was there as a guest," Leslie said, a tinkling of ice in her voice. "Richard and I were there. Richard Powell is my husband."

"As in the Powell estate?" Amelia remembered that her brother Andrew had sold Richard Powell a number of antiques, though he was disappointed when they were relegated to a two-room potting shed. The rest of the house was gilded, columned, and frescoed into an Italianate villa. Very un-Bucks-County-like.

"The same," she said coyly, resting her chin on the palm of her left hand, her ring finger flashing a dazzling diamond in Amelia's direction.

"Wow. That's quite a property," said Amelia, staring at the ring.

"Yes, it is. We were at the party as guests of Charles Thornton. We wanted to get a feel for the event. We're thinking of offering up our little house for the historic tour next year."

"But isn't your house new?"

"Well, newly constructed. But we imported material from significant estates in Europe. Paneling from a castle in England that dates back to the fourteenth century. We snatched that up just before the wrecking ball." Leslie's face flushed with excitement. "But the best are the frescoes, seventeenth-century frescoes. They were in the grand ballroom of an estate outside Paris. Giant, thick slabs of painted plaster. We just cut out the frescoes and shipped them home. It reminded me of slicing a giant wedding cake, each delicious slice more satisfying than the next."

Amelia thought of Marie Antoinette.

"If we do decide to go on the tour next year, Ricky and I will, of course, make a very generous gift to the historical society. I don't think they'll turn us away."

"You're still working at the *Courier Times*?"

"Yes, but only part time. Ricky and I travel a lot, and I don't want to miss out on any grand adventure! I'm fortunate that I have a very agreeable arrangement with my editor; I pitch story ideas to him and he says yes. I can't imagine walking away from the newspaper business. Was it hard for you to leave?" This time, cruelty won out over the smirk.

Amelia leaned in toward Leslie, closing down her personal space.

"I'm sorry, that was unkind of me," Leslie stammered.

"Why don't we get down to business?" said Amelia.

* * *

Leslie closed her notebook. "As you said, you don't have any real news, but I appreciate you meeting with me." She paused and then added, "I can share something with you. A source told me they found Porter's car. A van. It was at the bottom of Lake Luxembourg."

"Really?" Amelia wanted to add: *I was there. I watched them drag it out of the lake.* Instead she took a deep breath and said, "Any details?"

"Not yet. I'll let you know when I hear something." She dropped her notebook into her purse. "Or you can read it in the paper."

Amelia watched as Leslie made her way toward the door. The bar was now crowded with the after-work crowd. As she scanned the bar looking for someone she might actually want to talk to, she saw that the person now sitting on the barstool previously held by Mitchell was staring at her. Amelia turned around to see if he was trying to catch the eye of someone else. She turned back. Her eyes met his again. The rest of him was tall, sandy-haired, with the casual slouch of a thirtysomething. He looked vaguely familiar.

She glanced around to make sure Leslie had left and walked over to him.

"Miss Halliday? I'm Tim Watson," he said, setting his beer on the bar. "Can I buy you a drink?"

"No, I'm good. Do I know you?"

"I work for Jerry Baker. You talked to him at the Pineville Tavern. I was one of the guys at the other end of the bar waving at you. We thought you were a date or something, so we were just being goofy."

"Gus." Amelia signaled to the bartender. "I'll have a beer." Time to drink like one of the guys. She turned her attention back to Tim.

"We saw you flip him off when you left, and, well, I wanted to talk to you."

"Because I flipped him off?" she asked incredulously. Will high school never end?

He laughed. "No, though we were all impressed. Jerry can be kind of a jerk sometimes." Tim looked up at the TV above the bar. The Phillies were playing. "After you left, Jerry said you asked him about MP. He said we should ignore you if you called us."

"So you're here to tell me this in the event I called?" Amelia was reconsidering whether she should stay for the beer Gus just brought her.

"No," he said. Amelia was grateful there was no "miss" or "ma'am" after it. "I just think that Jerry knows something. Maybe he even offered MP the job that night."

Amelia scanned the bar. Everyone was chatting amicably or watching the ball game. No one seemed interested in her or, more importantly, in Tim, who sipped his beer while watching the front door. Amelia wasn't sure if he was expecting someone or considering bolting.

"Why do you think that?" Amelia pulled her barstool closer to him.

"Me and MP were working together, putting up wainscoting. It was late afternoon when we finished, and MP mentioned to me that Jerry had offered him an extra job."

Amelia looked at him skeptically. "Why are you so sure it was the night Michael was killed?"

Tim averted his eyes. "Because Jerry usually lets me in on the extra work first. I had plans that night, so I couldn't have done it anyway, but I was just surprised Jerry didn't ask me first.

"And then Jerry gets all bent out of shape because you were asking him questions about MP. It just doesn't feel right. Jerry loves knowin' stuff. He likes being a shooter. Ya know? Setting people up, knowing what's going on in town."

"Maybe he doesn't know anything."

"Well, yeah, that's possible. But normally he would have been bragging that somebody came to him for information, and even if he didn't have any, he'd try to come up with something to tell you." Tim downed the rest of his beer and set the bottle on the bar. "I dunno, it just doesn't feel right." He pulled a few wadded bills from his pocket. "I gotta go."

"I'll treat. I appreciate you finding me. How *did* you find me?"

"Easy." He motioned toward Gus, who was laughing with a customer. "He's just as nosy as Jerry."

Amelia grabbed his arm as he stood. "Wait, why didn't you go to the police with this?"

"Because I don't know if it means anything, and if it doesn't then I'll have pissed off Jerry. Not a good idea. This is still a small town, even when it's crowded with out-of-towners. Thanks for the beer."

Amelia remained at the bar, sipping her beer. She scanned the room and saw Elliott and Kirby in a booth in the corner. She considered joining them but their body language told her it was a bad idea.

15

"Let's take a trip, get away for a week," Kirby said as she picked at a salad.

"We can't. I want to make sure the cops stay on the murder investigation and that Mom is safe."

"But you don't need to get involved in this. The police will figure it out."

"I expect they will, but I don't want to worry about anyone being in danger. We were all there that night."

"Oh, Elliott, we're not in danger. That guy has no connection to us. How could he?"

Elliott swirled the wine in his glass. "You worried you might be a suspect?" He arched one eyebrow and grinned.

"Very funny," she snapped. She thrust the newspaper in front of him. "Look at this photo." Kirby and Elliott were caught in a perfect moment. Elegant, sophisticated, arrived.

"I love this photo. It belongs in the *New York Times* Style section, not the local paper beside a story about a murder. He ruined our party!"

"That's a bit insensitive."

"I'm not insensitive, I'm practical. His death and our party are not related."

"Kirby, lighten up!"

"Lighten up? I don't like the attention, this kind of attention. I don't like being scrutinized."

He looked into Kirby's eyes. They were not the eyes he first stared into when he was sitting in Bryson's, sipping a beer and reading the *Wall Street Journal* while periodically glancing up at the Phillies game on the TV above the bar.

"Here you are, Kirby," he'd heard Gus say as he set a drink on the bar to Elliott's right. Before Elliott turned to see who this Kirby was, he'd made a bet with himself that Kirby was a frat boy with an MBA with three or more names, none of which sounded like a first name, ending in III.

The "three I's," he called them. He'd interviewed a lot of them for his company. They wanted to work for him, yet they rarely asked any questions about him or his business, but were eager to talk about themselves. *I* did this. *I* know people. *I* know your company. Elliott wanted the three I's to ask questions, to demonstrate their IQ. Not their *intelligence quotient* score, their *I question* score. They needed to be inquisitive, not assumptive.

He accepted that he saw his own partial reflection in their faces, the part of him that he was born to—the privilege, the right school, and the right parents. But their images weren't as distinct. It was like he was looking at an old mirror whose silver backing had faded, the image now hazy, the reflectivity diminished. The three I's he interviewed had lost their ability to be reflective. Their lives were mapped out at birth, and they followed it without question. Questions. Elliott asked a lot of them. Of himself, of his friends, of his choices.

Elliott set his glass down on the bar. So who was this Kirby? He'd made a small drumroll in his head and turned.

And stared into Kirby Dunbar's eyes. Mesmerized. They were violet or blue, depending how the light caught them. He wanted to dive in, to swim with the silvery flecks that sparkled when she spoke, danced when she smiled. It was a beautiful beginning.

But now her eyes were hard, like granite.

"Scrutinized? Kirby, what are you talking about? It's a murder investigation."

"I don't like people digging into my private life."

"Well, maybe you should rethink your social posturing."

"What's that supposed to mean?"

"*The New York Times*, *Town & Country*? You have their photographers on your radar at every event we attend."

"That's not my private life. That's my philanthropic life."

"I see. So you give to get noticed? Why not take out a full-page ad in the *Times* and save yourself the expense of donating to charities, since it appears you're the more needy?"

"Go to hell!" She stormed out of the restaurant.

16

Jimi Hendrix stared at Chief Detective Mardi as Mardi surveyed the living room. An orange sofa was strewn with purple and green tie-dyed pillows. Behind it a wall of shelves held record albums, books, and a few photos. On the coffee table sat a candle, a couple of music magazines, and a small mirror edged in fluorescent orange duct tape. On the mirror was a razor blade and a rolled- up twenty-dollar bill.

"This place is right out of the sixties," Mardi said as he looked up at the Hendrix poster.

"Except for the electronics," said Officer Barnett. "This is seriously state of the art and very expensive."

Mardi examined framed photos on the shelves. They were underwater shots of a scuba diver. One was a close-up with a school of brilliant orange and blue fish encircling his head. It looked like a psychedelic lion's mane.

The medical examiner appeared at the bedroom door. "We have to stop meeting like this. Two Fridays in a row. I hope it doesn't become a trend." She smiled.

He smiled back. They had worked together for seven years, but months could pass without a suspicious death.

She stepped aside as her assistant rolled a gurney carrying a black body bag into the living room toward the front door. Inside was James Carter.

“What do you think?” asked Mardi.

“Looks like a drug overdose. I’ll get my report to you as soon as I can.” She looked at the mirror on the coffee table. “You guys and your duct tape. His suitcase in the bedroom is taped up.” She followed the gurney out the door.

Barnett and Mardi searched the bedroom. Mardi examined the roller bag. A strip of orange duct tape covered a rip. The American Airlines baggage tag was still attached to the handle.

“Nassau.” he said inspecting the tag. “He returned yesterday.”

Barnett opened a duffel bag next to it. Inside was scuba gear—a dive computer, regulator, and mask.

The call had come in three hours earlier from Mrs. Claire Green, who lived in the apartment next door. A noise complaint, too much bass. She said it was a recurring problem, but she had never resorted to calling the police. She always simply knocked on his door and asked him to turn it down. He would. He would also apologize to her. She said the last time she complained he said he would move his speakers to keep the reverberation away from the wall they shared.

This time it was different. He never played his music this loud or this long. It was on when she returned home about 11 p.m. last night. She knocked on his door five times. He never answered, and the music never stopped. By morning she had had enough and called the police.

Other than his music, she liked that he lived next door. There had been robberies in the area and she felt safe knowing he was there, just in case. She hoped he was OK.

He wasn't, and had Claire Green known about his criminal record she would not have felt so secure. James Carter's record included theft and drug possession. The last five years he appeared to have given up his criminal life, or gotten better at not getting caught. The glass vial of white powder on the nightstand indicated the latter.

17

Amelia moved slowly along the perimeter of the front lawn of Twin Beeches, ducking behind trees and shrubs until she reached the low fieldstone wall that separated the property from the road. The car was still there.

Winnie had noticed it when she returned from a bike ride. It wasn't there minutes earlier when Amelia arrived. *Am I being followed?* Amelia wondered. She was still unsettled by yesterday's conversation with Tim Watson.

While it was now fairly common for cars to drive slowly past the house—gawkers wanting to see where the murder happened—this one was stopped. Engine off. There was no good reason to stop, other than car trouble or an urgent need to pee. There was nothing else around except acres of woods and meadows.

Twin Beeches was set back, almost completely hidden by trees and shrubs. The view from the road offered only a glimpse of parts of the house—a piece of the roof, a chimney, a window, a chunk of a fieldstone. The image would make a great, though challenging, jigsaw puzzle—bits of a house surrounded by a thousand pieces of green.

It would take tedious dedication to complete. Like the one Amelia had worked on last winter—the surface of the moon. One thousand gray, black, and white puzzle pieces. What was she thinking when she bought it? She was still on the dark side then. Still in LA. Still trying to cope with being fired. Might as well focus on the moon and its barren landscape. No one would bother her there.

Twin Beeches wasn't tucked behind its landscape to be left alone. It was there to fit in. To be a part of nature like the trees for which it was named. It belonged and welcomed guests. It made the ribboning driveway feel like the unfurling of a beautifully wrapped gift as a car crunched along the gravel toward the front entrance. The gift, of course, was its inhabitants; the house was just the packaging.

The old Ford Escort sat motionless on the side of the road, dented and dirty, a victim of abuse or neglect. The lone occupant sat hunched over the steering wheel.

As Amelia leaned over the wall for a better view of the license plate, the car engine started. The Escort pulled onto the road and traveled no more than a hundred feet before its red brake lights winked at Amelia. The car lurched into reverse and sped back, screeched to a halt, and then gunned it up the driveway.

Amelia sprinted across the lawn as the car roared alongside her toward the house. "What the—" She grabbed her cell phone. "Wills. There's. A. Car." Each word was punctuated by a gasp for air. "Get everybody in a room and lock the door. I don't know what's going on. Keep everybody together."

The car slammed on its brakes, but not in time to stop the front bumper from shoving its way into a boxwood border.

Amelia leaped over the koi pond. *Great, if it's the murderer, I just made it really easy. Like shooting fish in a barrel.*

The driver stepped from the car.

"Carol Anne?"

Carol Anne jerked her head toward Amelia. "Oh, hi, I, um. . ." She covered her face with her hands. "I'm sorry, I'm sorry," she wailed through tears. "I needed to see where Mikey died. I just had to." With each sob she seemed to collapse into herself. Her shoulders folded in, and her head dropped lower.

Amelia raced to grab her.

"Amelia! What on earth? Oh, my dear." Louise ran toward them, arms outstretched. Carol Anne fell into them like a frightened child waking from a nightmare, a nightmare that couldn't be exorcised by the light of day.

* * *

Carol Anne was curled up in an upholstered chair beside the fireplace. The scent of lemon and ginger swirled in the steam from the cup in her hand. She hadn't slept since—well, she wasn't sure. What day was it? She couldn't stay in the apartment, so she drove. Around. No destination, just away. Away from the apartment that smelled like pizza and spearmint gum—that smelled like Mikey.

"Lunch is almost ready," said Claudia as she stood at the kitchen counter making sandwiches.

Carol Anne didn't belong here. She set her teacup on the small table next to the chair. "Thank you for the tea, but I should go. I'm sorry I scared you. I didn't mean any harm."

"Of course you didn't," said Louise. "Please stay for lunch."

Winnie walked in from the garden carrying a small vase filled with daisies and rosemary. "These will make you feel better." Winnie smiled shyly at Carol Anne as she placed the flowers on the oak kitchen table.

“All set,” said Claudia, setting down a platter of sandwiches.

“Come, dear, you need to eat something,” said Louise as she motioned Carol Anne to sit next to her.

Amelia sat down across from Carol Anne. “We’re glad you’re here.”

Carol Anne felt cared for for the first time since Mikey died.

“Thank you.” She barely got the words out as she gobbled a ham and cheese sandwich.

“When did you last eat?” asked Louise.

Carol Anne quickly put the remains of the sandwich back on her plate. “I’m sorry. Am I eating too much?” She blushed.

“No, no, eat!” exclaimed Claudia. “You need your strength. You’re like a little bird. You need nourishment.”

Carol Anne looked across the table and noticed a closed door. The food and company made her stronger. “Is that the closet? I mean pantry?” she asked, quickly looking away from it. “Can I look inside? I feel like I hafta see where, see, you know, where . . . Can I? I think I need to see him, I mean, to see where he died. I sat in the car across from your house for an hour asking him to tell me what to do. I don’t think he answered, except when I tried to drive away, I couldn’t keep my foot on the gas. I had to stop and come back.” Her eyes welled, her irises drowning until the tears breached the edge and fell. Two tiny waterfalls filled with enormous grief.

“I’ll go with you,” Louise said. She took Carol Anne’s hand and led her there.

Claudia whispered to Winnie, “I’d like you to go up to your room. Carol Anne may need some privacy.”

Carol Anne stared into the pantry. Her eyes scanned every shelf. Searching. She saw only china, crystal, and silver. It sparkled.

* * *

Louise remembered when it didn't. After the body was removed and the evidence team packed their bags and boxes, the pantry was given back to Louise. She simply closed its door. "This can wait."

Three days later, Claudia and Louise were ready. They stood before the closed door. They knew it had to be done. The pantry needed to be cleansed, exorcised, and then left to resume its simple purpose—a storage room to hold things.

"We'll do this together," Louise had said to Claudia as she handed her latex gloves.

They emptied the pantry, piling everything onto the kitchen counters and, when they were filled, onto the dining room table, breakfront, and floor. Candlesticks were clumped together like groves of trees; serving platters became small islands on the wide-plank floor.

They washed the walls, the shelves, and the brick. In silence they scrubbed with a disinfectant, twice. Then they filled buckets with fresh lemony soap and scrubbed again. They turned to the contents of the pantry; Louise knew they were begging for a bath. They had been there, in neat rows, immaculate before the chaos happened. Some of them bore witness. A spattered wine decanter, several candlesticks with drips that could have been from deep-red candle wax but were not, and a crystal bowl speckled with what looked like candy cinnamon hearts that had melted in the sun, sticky at first but now dried and hard. Blood and oxygen had separated, leaving black marks. Death.

One of the candlesticks had lost its mate. It was sealed in an evidence bag and carried out, along with Michael Porter's body.

Everything needed to be washed, even those things that escaped Michael's blood. They still held the scent of death.

Louise and Claudia methodically filled trays with crystal and china, carrying them to the kitchen, washing, drying, and refilling the pantry. They repeated the process over and over until it was time for the final step. Louise placed a bowl of dried lavender on the shelf where the missing candlestick had stood.

"It will provide calm," she said. Then she closed the door. Until now.

* * *

"It's so pretty in here," Carol Anne whispered. She turned back into the kitchen. "You have such nice things." She walked to the sink, rolling up her sleeves to wash. To cleanse.

"No, no," said Claudia. "I'll clean up."

"Please let me. I'd like to help after all the commotion I've caused."

Louise nodded to Claudia. "Well, thank you, Carol Anne," Claudia said. "I'll be outside in the herb garden if you need me."

Carol Anne turned to Louise. "I'll be very careful. I promise."

"I'm sure you will. It's very considerate of you to offer. Amelia and I will be in the study down the hall. Please join us when you're done."

Carol Anne ran the hot water. *They trust me,* she thought as she breathed in the lavender that sat in a pot on the kitchen sill. A black-capped chickadee flew past the window and lit on a bird feeder. She watched it peck at the seeds.

Kirby walked into the kitchen from the side door. She paused when she saw Carol Anne. "Oh, hello."

Carol Anne grabbed a kitchen towel from the hook and dried her hands. "Hi. I'm Carol Anne. Carol Anne Jackson." She extended her hand. "Mrs. Jenkins invited me. My boyfriend, uh, my fiancé was Michael Porter."

"The guy who was murdered?" Kirby asked in disbelief as she answered her ringing cell. "Yes, I'm here. Where are you?" she snapped as she walked across the kitchen, her heels clicking on the oak floor. "You won't believe who's at the house. The dead guy's girlfriend. It's ridiculous. You need to talk to your mother." She pushed open the door that led to the breakfast room, paused, and turned back to Carol Anne, who stood paralyzed.

Her ears were ringing. *The dead guy. The dead guy.* No. He was Mikey.

"Oh, sorry," said Kirby to Carol Anne.

At least she was apologizing.

"Sorry for your loss, but imagine how terrible it's been for *us*. We were here. We're victims."

"So was he," Carol Anne whispered under her breath, her eyes riveted to the floor, hoping it would open up and swallow her. The kitchen door swung closed with a whoosh. The air helped Carol Anne lift her eyes from the floor.

"I see you met Kirby," Claudia said simply as she walked back into the kitchen.

Moments later a man rushed through the kitchen without even a glance at them.

"That's Mrs. Jenkins's son, Elliott," Claudia said gently to Carol Anne. "Kirby is his girlfriend. Don't worry, all will be well."

"Why is she here?" Elliott yelled as he stormed down the hall.

Carol Anne walked to the doorway and stared after him, twisting the kitchen towel in her hands.

"You don't know anything about her!" she heard Elliott continue. "What will the police think? They'll start asking more questions, invading our privacy again."

"Oh, Elliott, shut up," snapped Louise.

Carol Anne's eyes grew wide.

"No, Mother, I won't. This is absurd. She could be involved in whatever he was up to. She shouldn't be here."

Silence. Then Louise spoke. "I'll decide who should and should not be here."

Carol Anne trembled as she moved away from the doorway and stood next to Claudia.

Claudia took Carol Anne's hand and held it. "Mrs. Jenkins invited you to lunch."

Moments later Elliott and Kirby marched back through the kitchen and out the door, letting it slam behind them. Carol Anne and Claudia were still invisible to them.

"I'll be right back," Carol Anne whispered. She slowly walked down the hallway and knocked on the study door, even though it stood open.

"I don't mean to cause any trouble," said Carol Anne to Louise, who was sitting on the sofa. Amelia stood at the window watching Elliott's Mercedes and Kirby's BMW race down the driveway, spewing angry clouds of dust behind them.

"Elliott's a bit overly protective and a little short-tempered," said Louise. "He means well, but sometimes he's just a horse's ass. He works in finance. That would make anyone cranky." Her eyes twinkled.

"You're such a nice person, Mrs. Jenkins." Carol Anne stepped across the threshold and looked around the room. She walked over to Louise. "I just want you to know that I'm in gratitude, uh, I'm grateful to you. As Mikey always said when he liked someone, you're good people."

Carol Anne stood very still for a moment, feeling slightly confused. She reached up and smoothed her hair as if the wind had mussed it. She felt comforted. She looked behind her and saw the portraits of the Samuels. She smiled up at them.

"Thank you," she said quietly.

18

Elliott sat in Amelia's living room, staring at his clasped hands. He had called her at 7:00 a.m. to say he was coming over. He hadn't slept; he needed to talk. She assumed it was related to his tirade at finding Carol Anne at Twin Beeches. It wasn't.

"It's about Kirby and me," he said.

"You're not getting married, are you?"

Elliott grimaced. "I believe the correct question is, 'Are you getting married?' At least feign potential delight if I said, 'Yes, we are.'"

"Sorry, Elliott. I just don't connect with her."

"Well, Amelia, this isn't about you; it's about me and Kirby."

"I know, but she creates an edge to your personality."

"What is that supposed to mean?"

"It makes you harder, less warm and fuzzy. OK, you were never really warm and fuzzy." She tried to laugh to stop the tension from building. "Somehow when you're together everything is so serious. You're both uncompromising and not always in a good way. Maybe you just need to lighten up."

"Oh, that's helpful. That's what I said to Kirby. It didn't work for her, either."

"Elliott, I *want* to be helpful. Let me make some coffee. I don't normally start my Sundays this early."

Amelia returned from the kitchen with a tray that held a silver coffee service. "I have some scones, too," she said as she placed the tray on the ottoman.

"You always liked Mom's silver coffee service," he said as he spooned sugar from a sugar bowl. "I'm glad she gave it to you."

"She still has another one." Amelia laughed. "You, too, could serve coffee in style."

"Keurig suits me just fine. One pod, one cup, done."

Amelia sipped her coffee.

"She was married," Elliott said finally.

"And? That's no different than most of the other women you've dated. How many times?"

"Once."

Amelia gently returned her cup to its saucer. This wasn't about a divorce. Elliott looked up and their eyes locked, but this was no stare-down. His eyes showed uncertainty or confusion. Amelia didn't know which. He rarely displayed either.

She waited, just as she had during hundreds of interviews for news stories. When the scandalous, tragic, or embarrassing revelations began to mumble quietly, Amelia would give them space. Keep the air silent so there was plenty of room for the words to tumble into it, to be swept into the current of relief and release. She would wait. He would talk. Just like all the others.

Elliott stood and began to pace from one edge of the rug to the other, toward the window, back past the coffee table to the opposite edge. The rug was his boundary. Back and forth.

It reminded Amelia of watching Elliott's tennis matches. He was unbeatable. Always prepared, focused, powerful. The ball flew with such force it was almost invisible until the *twonk* announced its return and immediate departure to the other side, back and forth until he wore his opponent down. Until he won.

This morning's competition was between his silence and his words. But what would winning mean? Amelia sat as an observer or perhaps a referee. Finally he spoke, and silence retreated to the sidelines. Just in case.

"It was illegal, a green-card marriage. A guy she met in college. He was from South America and wanted to stay in the States. They were good friends. His family offered her fifty grand if she married him. After two years she took her money, moved here, and started her interior design business."

"Wow, that's quite a deal. Talk about friends with benefits!"

"It's outrageous. I thought she was self-made. I admired her for that."

"She is self-made in a way. She just took a unique approach to getting ahead."

"Are you defending her?"

"I'm too fascinated to know just yet."

"Well, enjoy your fascination at my expense. I feel like I've been played."

"Played for what? It didn't involve you."

"Give me a break. It does involve me. What if we did marry?"

"This is a conversation we've never had. Marry? Really? You?" And then she stopped; she knew she had gone too far. Elliott had never confided in her about his relationships and now she was dancing gleefully on his vulnerability. "I'm sorry, Elliott. I'm not being helpful."

"That's an understatement."

"Well, Kirby must have it bad for you. She didn't need to tell you."

He stood by the window, his back to Amelia.

"If you do marry her, you can forget about ever running for president." Amelia released the sentence into the air like a balloon, floating toward Elliott, its string dangling. He would either puncture it in anger or grab hold of it and experience a moment of levity.

He turned and laughed. "No risk there. I'm not willing to take such a drastic pay cut." The balloon carried him back to the sofa.

19

Maybe Mardi should have recommended Barnett for a promotion to detective after all. He had come in over the weekend and discovered a link between James Carter and Michael Porter. Barnett had listened to the evidence regarding Carter's death better than anyone, including himself.

Duct tape and a trip to Nassau. That's what led Barnett to link Carter to Porter's murder, so ridiculous or ridiculously obvious. It led the team back to Porter's van.

The prescription for the orange duct-taped eyeglasses that were wedged between the front passenger seat and console of Porter's van matched the glasses Carter was wearing when his body was found. He was nearsighted, very nearsighted. Glasses were a necessity for him, but Core Creek Park was less than a mile from his apartment, an easy walk even in wet clothes and blurry vision.

Carter must have driven the van into the lake on purpose. It explained the open windows. He had to neutralize the pressure of the water and get out fast. His glasses were probably pushed off his face as the water rushed in.

But why dump the van in the lake? Perhaps he thought it less risky than ditching it on land and trying to remove fingerprints; he knew his were in the police database. They also were on the metal frames of the glasses in the van and on the ignition key. Latent prints protected by the water.

It was a start. It wasn't conclusive that Carter killed Porter, but it made him a very good suspect.

"At first I thought, what crazy ass would drive a vehicle into the lake?" said Barnett. "Unless he wanted to commit suicide. It was more likely he would drown than escape. But Carter was a diver. He probably knew what to do."

Mardi recalled the scuba photos in Carter's apartment. "When did he travel to Nassau?"

"Last Sunday, two days *after* Porter was killed. He returned Thursday. Found dead on Friday. And get this, he didn't buy the airline tickets until the day before he left. It got me wondering, if he did kill Porter and wanted to get out of town, why not go to Nassau on Saturday. Why wait a day?"

"Maybe Saturday flights were sold out."

"I checked. Plenty of seats available. So why wait?" Barnett grinned and held up a receipt for prescription glasses. "I found it in Carter's wallet. It's from Specs, a store at the Neshaminy Mall. They confirmed he bought new glasses on Saturday. He paid extra for a rush job.

"And this also was in his wallet." Barnett held up a C-card, a scuba diving certification. "He would have known how to get out of the van. He had rescue diver status."

James Carter rescued himself, walked home, and died.

"You and Cole go talk to Porter's girlfriend," said Mardi. "Maybe she knew him."

20

"Do you need a smaller roller, Winnie?" Louise asked as she poured vivid yellow paint into a paint tray.

"No thank you." Winnie stared into the color. "It's Dandelion. Perfect." She stepped onto a tarp, on which stood an ornately carved oak dresser primed the color of chalk. "Get ready, dresser." Then she and Louise dipped their rollers into the paint.

If the dresser had eyes, it would have closed them. For the moment. To focus on the sensation of the paint rollers as they glided down its sides, onto its legs, and then across the top surface. Massaged. Pampered. And then it would have blinked its eyes open and looked across Winnie's room at the mirror propped on the opposite wall. The dresser was being dressed. The yellow paint warmed the wood beneath it.

Winnie and Louise switched to brushes and painted around the ornate carvings. They remained white. Primed for something more dramatic.

"We'll have tea in the garden while this coat of paint dries," said Louise, "and then the real fun will begin. Do you have homework tonight?"

"No, I had study hall today and did it then. Thank you for not making me wait until next weekend to paint the dresser. I just couldn't bear it."

They sat at the patio table listening to the birdsong. "Mrs. Jenkins, is Carol Anne going to be all right?" Winnie asked.

Louise reached out and stroked Winnie's hand. "We're going to make sure she is. I called her this morning to check on her. Her visit here was rather traumatic, but she said she slept most of yesterday. I told her that was appropriate. Sunday is a day of rest, after all."

"She seems nice," Winnie said simply.

"How is your masterpiece coming along?" Winnie's mom asked as she walked up the garden path to the patio.

Winnie pulled a handful of crayons out of the breast pocket of an old dress shirt that had belonged to her dad. Her painting smock. Its long sleeves were rolled numerous times until they stopped at her wrists, where they were held in place with purple ribbons.

"We're done with Dandelion," she said, putting the yellow crayon back into her pocket and fanning out the remaining six crayons in her hand. "These are the colors of the vase."

Her mom studied them. "It's a beautiful mix of contrasting colors."

"I agree," said Louise. "The vase may be from Mexico, but the color combination sends me straight back to Morocco. I lived in Tangier for a year, a city of nonstop energy fed by light and color. So extraordinary. One of my neighbors had a pet rooster named Gregory Peck. It was as exotic as the city. He had blue, orange, and yellow feathers with a blood red cockscomb. You would have loved him, Winnie. He was so colorful."

Winnie beamed at Louise just as she had when Louise gave her the vase, a gift from Cabo San Lucas. It was a grown-up gift. Not a piñata or an embroidered blouse that most eleven-year-olds might receive. And it told Winnie that Louise understood the allure of color and its emotional language.

"Winnie, you are a lucky girl. Mrs. Jenkins certainly understands you."

"Just like you, Mama." Winnie was having a wonderful day.

"The farm just called," Claudia said to Louise. "The goats will be here in about an hour."

"Wonderful. Is the small barn ready for them?"

"It is. And Wills is on his way back with the hay and feed."

"Goats are such lovable creatures. They'll be so entertaining. And no more helicopter landings in the field. I hope Elliott isn't too put out."

"Can we get back to painting?" Winnie asked, with a sudden turn toward impatience, barely keeping her jittery legs from pushing her off her seat.

"Let's go!" said Louise.

Winnie dropped the crayons back into her pocket and raced up the stairs to her bedroom. She carefully lifted the vase off her desk and placed it on the tarp next to her box of Crayola Crayons and seven cans of paint.

"Time to accessorize," said Louise. "But be careful. The yellow paint hasn't fully dried."

"I will." Winnie walked around the dresser studying its ornamentation while clutching the crayons that had been nestled in her pocket. "I think the flowers should be these two." She looked at their names. "Periwinkle and Plum. The leafy things . . ."

"Acanthus leaf. It's a Mediterranean plant. The Greeks and Romans used its design in architecture. You'll see it on Corinthian capitals," explained Louise.

"The acanthus should be Granny Smith Apple. The upside-down seashells will be Salmon, and the ovals on the edge will be Robin's-egg Blue. They look like eggs, don't they?"

"Yes, and they are. That pattern is called egg-and-dart molding."

"And last but not least, the scrollwork will be this." Winnie held up her final crayon. "Macaroni and Cheese! Oh, Mrs. Jenkins, it's going to be beautiful."

Two hours had passed when Winnie and Louise heard the crunch of tires on the gravel driveway.

"It must be the goats! Let's go meet them." Louise took Winnie's hand.

* * *

"Oh, Anthony," Louise exclaimed as Mardi stepped out of his car. "I was expecting my goats."

Mardi smiled. He didn't know what else to do. "Sorry to disappoint you."

"It's not a disappointment. You're just unexpected, but welcome, of course. I hope you're here to tell me you've solved the murder."

"Not yet, Mrs. Jenkins, but we're making progress." He handed her a photograph of James Carter. "Do you recognize this man?"

Louise studied the photo intently. "A nice-looking young man, but no, I don't. Is he a suspect?"

"He's part of our investigation."

"Was he here that night?" Louise asked.

"Possibly. We're circulating the photo. Perhaps someone will recognize him."

"Is he a friend of Michael Porter's?"

"We don't know. My team is checking with Miss Jackson now."

"Why not just ask him if he knows Michael?"

"It's not possible at this time." He quickly turned to Winnie, ignoring Louise's perplexed expression. "Would you mind having a look?"

Winnie beamed. "Absolutely!" She held the photo carefully and then frowned. "No, I don't recognize him. Darn!"

In the distance, the bleating of goats could be heard.

"Here they come." Winnie shoved the photo back into Mardi's hand. Mardi watched as a truck slowed to a stop. Other than the driver, it was filled with goats.

21

"Hello, Miss Jackson. We're sorry to bother you. May we come in?" Detective Cole asked as she and Officer Barnett stood outside Carol Anne's apartment.

Carol Anne, wearing a limp cotton pullover and distressed jeans caused by wear and washing, not by fashion's dictates, stepped aside to let them pass. She realized she wasn't prepared for news about Mikey, assuming that's why the police were at her door. Wasn't prepared to hear who killed him. Wasn't prepared to learn why. How do you prepare for such a thing? She knew she wanted answers, but what would the information include? Did Mikey do something bad? No, he wouldn't have. He couldn't have. Carol Anne's heart pounded in her chest.

"May we sit down?" Cole asked.

"Oh yes, of course, I'm sorry," she stammered. Cole sat down on the sofa. Carol Anne joined her, but at the far end. Barnett remained standing.

"Did you find out who killed Mikey?" Carol Anne asked hopefully, fearfully.

"Not yet," said Barnett. "But we may be close."

Cole handed her a photo. "Do you recognize him?" she asked.

Carol Anne stared blankly at the photo.

"Maybe he's an old friend of Michael's or someone he worked with?" asked Cole.

"No, I've never seen him before. Who is he?"

"His name is James Carter," said Barnett.

"I don't know him; Mikey never mentioned his name."

"His fingerprints were found in your fiancé's van," added Cole. "It appears he drove it into the lake at Core Creek Park."

"Into the lake?" Carol Anne stammered. "Why did he do that?"

Cole hesitated. "We don't know."

"Well, did you ask him?"

"We can't, Carol Anne. He's dead."

Carol Anne covered her mouth with her hands, trying to catch the gasp that rushed out.

"He died of a drug overdose," said Barnett. "Did Michael ever use drugs?"

Carol Anne snapped her head up and glared at Barnett. "How could you say such a thing? Never. He never used drugs. He wouldn't. Why are you asking about drugs?" She wrapped her arms across her chest, hugging herself or perhaps holding herself together.

Cole reached for her. "Carol Anne, are you OK?"

She took a deep breath. "Mikey didn't know him and he doesn't—didn't—do drugs! Ever!"

"I'm sorry, Miss Jackson," said Barnett, "but sometimes we have to ask difficult questions."

"Nothing makes sense," said Carol Anne. "First Mikey's killed, now this other guy's dead." She flashed back to the day she was at Twin Beeches and Kirby referred to her Mikey as simply *the dead guy*. She now felt ashamed for referring to James Carter in such an anonymous way. He probably had people who loved him, too. Just because he used drugs didn't make him bad.

In her mind she was laying a bouquet of flowers on Carter's grave, until she realized the absurdity of it and snatched back the flowers. Why was she feeling sorry for him? He was a murderer. He must be.

She let out a whimper. "I just don't understand what's going on." She looked around the apartment that once held her future as Mrs. Porter. Now it just looked old and worn and sad. "Why did he drive the van into the lake? It was pretty new. Mikey took good care of it. Now it's ruined." Carol Anne looked from Cole to Barnett. "Oh, that's a stupid thing for me to say." She turned to Cole. "I'm scared."

"I can check your apartment to make sure it's secure," offered Barnett.

"Am I in danger?"

"No, we don't have any reason to think so. But I can have a look around, check your windows and the door locks for you."

"Uh, OK. Thanks." Carol Anne sat rigidly, the only movement the trembling of her lower lip. After a few moments she sucked in a breath and turned to Cole. "Are you telling me he took the van, drove it into the lake, and then died from a drug overdose? Did he kill Mikey and then steal his van?"

"We don't have the answers yet," said Cole. "But we will. Someone must have seen him at the party or driving the van. We're circulating his photograph. We're doing everything we can to find Michael's killer, I promise you."

"Miss Jackson," Barnett called from the hallway, "would you mind taking a look at something outside the bedroom window?"

Carol Anne walked slowly down the hall to her bedroom. She

peered out the window. The faded gray plastic shutter alongside the left window frame was riveted at the top to the white siding; the bottom was secured with duct tape the same color as the shutter. A lump protruded from it.

"What is that?"

"I don't know," said Barnett. "I saw it when I checked your window."

Carol Anne leaned out the window. "I can't reach it."

"Do you want me to get it?" asked Barnett.

"Sure. I don't know why it's there. I've never noticed it before."

Barnett tugged at the duct tape; the tape tugged back. After working the edge of it, Barnett slowly separated the cocoon of tape from the shutter. "Almost there," he grunted.

Carol Anne looked around her bedroom at the unmade bed and clothes piled on the floor. A mess. She picked a pillow off the floor, hugged it, and placed it on the bed against the headboard.

Barnett held up a waterproof bag. "May I have your permission to open it?" Barnett asked.

"It's not mine, but sure, open it. I want to know what's in it."

Tucked inside was $2,000 and a bag of white powder. The police lab would later confirm it was cocaine. It also would confirm that the bundle of money had fingerprints on it. They belonged to Michael Porter.

* * *

Carol Anne sat in her car while the police searched the apartment. She couldn't bear watching them pulling open drawers and cupboards and examining everything, including her underwear, birth control pills, and journal. She felt so exposed, so humiliated. What would they think of her? Would they read her journal?

She clutched a stuffed bear, the one Mikey won at the Kutztown Fair when they first started dating. Cole had inspected it carefully before allowing her to take it to the car. It was just a bear stuffed with polyester fibers and memories. Carol Anne sat hugging the bear. She had nowhere else to go.

She didn't want to reach out to any of her friends, not that she had many. None of them would know what to do or say about Mikey's murder. She wouldn't, either, under the circumstances. And now she certainly didn't want to tell them about the drugs and money that were found or why she knew with absolute certainty that they didn't belong to Mikey.

It was probably a mistake not to work harder at her friendships. But after she met Mikey she was content living in a world of two. Maybe that was because after her parents died her world became too crowded. She was fifteen and went to live with her aunt and uncle. Their white clapboard house had three bedrooms and one bathroom; Aunt Margaret and Uncle Gene had five children. Carol Anne shared a bedroom with her three girl cousins. Their initial sympathy for her being an orphan was soon replaced by resentment that she was given some of their precious space—five hangers and a bureau drawer. After high school graduation, she thanked her aunt and uncle and gave her cousins a gift by moving out.

Carol Anne watched as a German shepherd bounded out of a police SUV. She liked dogs, but she didn't like this one because she knew it would be sticking its nose into her closets and, well, everywhere, searching for drugs. The dog wouldn't find any, though she still couldn't imagine where that bag had come from. She couldn't understand why she never noticed it. She opened the windows all the time. Air conditioning was too expensive.

And all that money. Impossible. They never had more than about twenty dollars in the house. She closed her eyes and prayed this nightmare would go away.

Tap. Tap. Tap.

Carol Anne instinctively hugged the bear tighter and leaned away from the driver's-side window, hoping whoever was tapping would also go away.

"Carol Anne! Carol Anne!" Louise Jenkins was rhythmically tapping her gold pinkie ring on the window. "My dear, you shouldn't be out here all alone."

Carol Anne rolled down the car window as Louise peered in at the stuffed bear. "Well, I see you do have some company. That's comforting."

Carol Anne opened the car door and stumbled out. "They're up there, searching through everything. The police."

Louise looked at the two police cars in the parking lot. "You'd think they'd be more discreet. You're not a criminal."

"Neither is Mikey, but that's how they're treating him. They think he did drugs. He didn't. I promise you, he didn't." She squeezed her eyes shut, trying unsuccessfully to trap her tears.

"Mrs. Jenkins, this is a surprise," said Detective Cole as she stepped outside.

"I'm here to invite Carol Anne to my house. She does not need to witness the raid on her home. It's a disgrace."

"It's a necessity, Mrs. Jenkins, a necessity based on evidence. Miss Jackson gave us permission. We also obtained a search warrant."

"Does she need to stay here?" Louise put her arm around Carol Anne's shoulders.

"No, but we need to be able to reach her."

"Call my house, that's where we'll be."

Louise helped Carol Anne and her bear into the front passenger seat of her Mercedes. She walked around to the driver's side.

22

"Two grand and a bag of coke," said Barnett as he and Cole sat across from Mardi in his office early Tuesday morning. "Nothing else of interest was found in the apartment."

"It's odd," said Cole. "It didn't look like a drug dealer's apartment."

"Other than the bag of coke and two grand." Barnett took a sip of his coffee.

"But it doesn't fit with the apartment," said Cole. "Furniture looks secondhand; the clothes are worn, inexpensive brands. The only other money we found was in a coffee can, $4.98 in change and a crumpled dollar bill. There was nothing in the medicine cabinet except generic ibuprofen, Band-Aids, and toothpaste."

"You never did a drug raid in Trenton where the suspect lived in a rathole with a filthy mattress on the floor?" asked Barnett.

"Yeah, but the dealers were also users. Their profit went up their nose or into a crack pipe. Nothing we found says Porter used drugs, and if he's a dealer, where's his money?"

"In the plastic bag, Detective!" Barnett slammed his coffee cup on the table. "Two thousand dollars. This is not rocket science. Drugs and money were found in Porter's apartment."

"Outside his apartment; taped outside his apartment," corrected Cole.

"Fine! Drugs and money were found *outside* Porter's apartment, though the only way to reach them is from the *inside*, unless you happen to have a twenty-foot ladder with you. And Porter's fingerprints are on the money. Porter was a drug dealer, and that's why he was killed."

"That's a reach," said Cole.

"Let Barnett finish," Mardi snapped.

Barnett grinned. "It's simple. It's a drug deal gone bad. Porter was at Twin Beeches to sell drugs. Guess who the buyer was? James Carter. Maybe Carter decided he didn't want to pay. Maybe Porter was screwing him in the deal. Whatever the reason, Porter's dead, Carter's prints are in the van, and he dies of an overdose. It's full circle."

He walked over to the whiteboard in Mardi's office and drew a circle. "It's like a clock." At twelve o'clock he wrote *Coke*. "It begins with coke." He moved down to three o'clock. "Carter meets Porter at Twin Beeches to buy or steal the coke." Six o'clock. "He kills Porter." Nine o'clock. "He dumps Porter's van in the lake. And then his time ran out." He jabbed the marker at twelve o'clock. "He overdoses on—what else? Coke. Conclusion? We now have two fewer criminals in Bucks County."

Cole leafed through her notes and without looking up said, "It's circumstantial. We don't know that Carter was at the party, and we don't have any concrete evidence that he killed Porter. We only know that he was in Porter's van at some point. If this evidence were presented in court, you wouldn't get a murder conviction."

"I don't give a shit if it holds up in court," Barnett bellowed. "It doesn't need to go to court. They're both dead!"

"Enough!" Mardi grabbed the photo of Carter. "Somebody had to have seen him at the party. Get out there and talk to people."

23

"Good morning, Carol Anne," said Louise as she walked into the kitchen carrying a freshly cut bouquet of flowers. "Did you sleep well?"

"Yes, perfectly," she replied, although she would have been content to remain awake last night, taking in every detail of her bedroom. The crisp white sheets, pale-yellow walls edged in shiny white molding, a chandelier that sent flickers of light dancing across the ceiling. The room even smelled different—clean, fresh. She looked around for a candle or air freshener; she wanted to buy that brand for her apartment. She blushed at her own naiveté. Finally she succumbed to the weight of the day and drifted off quietly, restfully, until the birds sang her awake.

Claudia took the flowers from Louise. "Breakfast is ready."

"Oh, I see we're having a special guest's breakfast, very impressive." An herb and zucchini frittata, maple-smoked bacon, and sautéed mushrooms and tomatoes sat on the granite countertop. Claudia placed the vase of flowers in the center of the kitchen table.

"Carol Anne made the frittata," said Claudia. "She's quite a cook."

"It looks scrumptious." Louise carried her plate to the kitchen table. "Where did you learn to cook?"

"I lived on a farm when I was young; we grew most of our food. Whatever was ripe was what we had for dinner. It's amazing how many ways you can cook zucchini," Carol Anne said with a laugh. "Roasted, stuffed, fried—we even used it in chocolate cake. The zucchini keeps it moist," she added. "I never made anything fancy like this until I got the job at the River's Inn in New Hope.

"I'm a waitress, but two days a week I help prep food for the chef. I watch him and take notes on my breaks. Mikey liked my frittatas, though he called them egg pies." She laughed. "Me and Mikey didn't have much money, so most of the other recipes I learned were too expensive to make, but as Mikey always said, 'We've got our future, Carol Anne, and if you want to make us and the kids fancy food, you can. We'll have the money someday.'"

Carol Anne bit her lip. "Someday was supposed to be our future." The rest of the meal was consumed in silence.

"Carol Anne, let's go sit on the patio with a cup of tea," said Louise. "It's where I spend most mornings. It's very soothing."

Louise and Carol Anne walked through the kitchen and down three steps onto a curving pea gravel path. They followed it around the kitchen garden and on through lush beds of hollyhock, bee balm, dianthus, and wild geranium until they came to a slate patio with a table and chairs.

"Who lives there?" Carol Anne asked. Across a pond stood a small fieldstone structure with oversize windows.

"Plants and my garden library. It was built as an orangery."

"What's an orangery?"

"My great-grandfather built it for his orange trees. They were considered conservatory plants. He grew them in massive clay pots, and before the first frost he would hire workers to lift them onto dollies and roll them into the orangery until spring, when they would roll them out again. My ancestors' lifestyle was one of some extravagance, I must admit. But at least they didn't bring a garden hermit onto the grounds."

"Is that like a garden gnome?"

"Except it was a real person. It once was fashionable to have a hermit living in your garden as part of the landscape design. Originally a hermit was someone who offered spiritual guidance in exchange for living in a small hut on the property, but a couple of centuries later wealthy estate owners liked the concept, but perhaps not the contemplativeness. So a hermit became more or less a garden ornament."

"That's crazy," Carol Anne remarked.

"Yes, it was."

Louise sipped her tea. Their walk had led Carol Anne away from her grief, even if only momentarily.

"You have a perfect life," said Carol Anne as she relaxed back into her chair.

"Oh, my dear, no one has a perfect life."

"Well, some are a lot closer than others. Mine is far, far away," she said simply, "and I don't think I'll ever even get close."

"It will take time. You've experienced a terrible tragedy."

Claudia walked down the path carrying a tray. "I brought you a fresh pot of tea. It's a perfect morning to sit outside."

"See? Even the morning is perfect," said Carol Anne.

"For all of us," Louise replied, patting Carol Anne's hand, "including my new little friends. Look over there."

Goats rounded the orangery and clomped their way along the fence.

"Goats!" squealed Carol Anne. She jumped up from the table and ran to them. "They're LaMancha goats, aren't they?"

"You know goats?"

"My grandfather raised them. LaMancha and Saanens." She scratched behind the ears of the first goat she reached. "I played with them as a child."

"Well, meet my gang. That's Freesia or maybe Hyacinth," said Louise. "I'm still learning who's who."

Carol Anne laughed. "You'll be able to tell them apart in no time. They have their own personalities and usually very nice dispositions."

"As long as they're not so nice that they let my son Elliott land his helicopter in the field."

"He has a helicopter?"

"Yes, but I'm trying to convince him to take the train from New York like everyone else on the weekends. That helicopter is a ridiculous waste of money and not very ecologically friendly. The goats should work. He's a softy at heart, so he won't risk landing with goats in the field."

The goats wandered about, grazing as they went. Louise poured fresh tea. The lemony aroma reminded Carol Anne of her first visit to Twin Beeches, of sitting in the kitchen sipping tea after she had plowed into the shrubs. She had almost lost control of the car, but instead of being screamed at or arrested for trespassing, Carol Anne saw Louise run toward her with open arms to hug her. Hug her! How bizarre. How wonderful.

"I'm going to help you get your life back to normal, Carol Anne," Louise said gently. A baby goat bleated, and Carol Anne watched as its mother made her way through the herd.

"Mrs. Jenkins, you have been so nice to me. I feel stronger than I have since Mikey died. But I know I have to go back to my apartment, to face my life without him."

"Maybe tomorrow, dear. Give yourself one more night to relax. You can tell me more about goats."

Carol Anne really didn't want to leave Twin Beeches. *I should hate this place,* she thought to herself. *It's where Mikey died. But I feel protected here.* She gently set her teacup down.

"Can I ask you something, Mrs. Jenkins?"

"Of course, dear."

"Who are those men on your wall?"

"You mean the portraits in my study?"

Carol Anne nodded. "I hope I'm not being nosy."

"Not at all. They're my family. Let's go inside, and I'll introduce you."

The Samuels watched as Louise brought Carol Anne into the study.

"Misters Jenkins, may I present Miss Carol Anne Jackson. Carol Anne, these are my ancestors."

Louise walked over to the first portrait on the far left. "This is Samuel Jenkins the First, my great-great-great-grandfather. And this is his son, Samuel Junior." As she walked along, Louise gently touched each frame in greeting.

"Here we have Samuel the Third, the orange lover. We were discussing your orangery this morning," she said to the portrait. "And we appreciate your restraint in not bringing a hermit onto the grounds. My grandfather, Samuel the Fourth, and, in fifth place, my father. Hello, Father."

Carol Anne walked slowly past each one, noting their attire, their faces, and their countenance. She paused a bit longer at Samuel the Fourth's portrait and then moved on.

"I thought they belonged to you," she said to Louise. "They seem very watchful and caring. I think they're nice."

Nice. Now that's something the Samuels didn't often hear. Their formal portraits wore a visage that was primarily morally stern with a touch of clever and perhaps gallant, but nice? How refreshing. They were pleased that Carol Anne appreciated them.

"Do you have a portrait?" she asked Louise. "You're the next generation. Or is there one of a brother?"

"Oh, I'm sure the Samuels can't wait to hear my answer."

"Did I say something wrong?" Carol Anne stared down at the floor.

"Oh, not at all, dear." Louise motioned for her to sit in one of the yellow chairs. "In fact, you've just endeared yourself to five generations of my family. This wall of ancestors, the Samuels, as I call them, began with Samuel the First, who built Twin Beeches. The firstborn of the next four generations were sons, duly named Samuel. And then I came along, an only child of Samuel the Fifth and my mother, Lisabeth.

"I didn't want a portrait, much to the chagrin of my father and I'm sure all the others." Louise looked up at them. "They considered it tradition; I thought it pretentious. We're not the royal family; we don't need to document our ancestry with paintings of ourselves. It was just too la-di-da for me."

Carol Anne studied the wall. "I think you would look very nice up there with them. It would make me proud if I was you."

The door to the study suddenly closed.

"Goodness, that was quite a gust of wind," Louise said as she looked at the Samuels reproachfully.

24

"Ask and you shall receive," Barnett gloated as he strode into Mardi's office at the end of the day. He dropped the photo of Carter on his desk. "He was at the party. Smith Phillips recognized him from this photo."

"Smith Phillips?" Mardi flipped through the list of staff and guests at the party.

"He owns the party supplies company that was used that night. I thought that was a good place to start. He recognized him immediately."

"He's listed as a guest," said Mardi. "Why didn't we interview him that night?"

"He said he was only there for about an hour. He wanted to make an appearance to show his support but didn't stay long."

"But long enough to notice Carter? What's their relationship?"

"None, but he's certain he was there, working as a server. He said the guy was either nervous, inexperienced, or on drugs. Phillips watched him carry a tray of glasses to the bar." Barnett chuckled. "He said he heard him before he saw him. Carter was shaking so bad the wineglasses were clanging together. Phillips thought he might drop them. They're his glasses, so he would notice."

"Carter isn't on the staff list."

"I know, but Phillips says he saw him. Why would he lie about that?"

25

"Louise Jenkins said Carol Anne Jackson will be at the house," said Mardi as he and Cole drove to Twin Beeches.

"Of course she'll be here," Louise had said when Mardi called to schedule a meeting. "The poor thing is trying to gather her courage to go back to her apartment to clean up the mess your people left. Shameful, Anthony, just shameful."

Anthony. How is it that hearing his full given name made him feel like a child? He was Tony to friends and acquaintances and Chief Detective Mardi professionally. But *Anthony*? It's what the nuns called him in elementary school, his parents when he was in trouble, and now Louise, shaming him. In a small town you never grow up, at least not in name. He will forever be *Anthony* to Louise Jenkins.

"That's an odd friendship, don't you think?" asked Cole.

"You mean between Louise Jenkins and Carol Anne Jackson?"

"Yeah. A stranger is murdered at your house and the victim's girlfriend becomes a regular visitor there. That's odd."

Mardi shrugged. "Amelia will be there, too. We'll see how she reacts to our report about James Carter. I don't think she or her mother totally trust our investigative work."

"Can't say that I blame them." Cole glanced over at Mardi. He kept his eyes on the road but his jaw clenched.

* * *

"Drug dealing? Here? I simply don't believe it," said Louise, after Mardi provided an update to the investigation that linked James Carter to Michael Porter.

Mardi had expected her reaction and the same from Carol Anne Jackson. Instead Carol Anne slumped her shoulders, dropped her head, and stared at her folded hands.

"This was a historical society benefit," said Amelia, "not one of Frankie Vincent's all-night parties."

Mardi gritted his teeth. Frankie Vincent was a sore point with him.

"Amelia, I'm sure Anthony would rather not revisit that case and its embarrassing outcome," said Louise. "All that work investigating Mr. Vincent and he just goes poof!

"The idea that drugs were at my party is preposterous. I don't think the patrons, many of whom are my friends, are big cocaine users. Maybe drinkers, but drugs? What's your proof?"

"Mrs. Jenkins, investigations are a complicated process. We are not saying that guests at your party engaged in drug use. What we are saying is that *a* guest saw Carter there. We also know that Carter drove Michael's van into the lake and then died of a cocaine overdose.

"I promised you during each of your numerous phone calls that I would provide you with details as appropriate," Mardi said, failing to keep the frustration out of his voice.

"And I appreciate that, but it seems to me that the only thing you know with absolute certainty is that Mr. Porter was murdered here," said Louise. "Of course, that's an easy conclusion. After all, he left his body behind. I'm not at all convinced of this drug connection."

"Did you find Carter's prints on the candlestick?" asked Amelia.

"No. It's not surprising, as the servers all wore gloves," said Cole.

"Mikey didn't do drugs," Carol Anne stammered. "I don't care what you found. They weren't his."

Mardi and Cole stood to leave. "I'm very sorry, Miss Jackson," said Cole as she passed by Carol Anne. "This must be very painful for you to hear."

Carol Anne said nothing.

26

"What cute hors d'oeuvres," Ruth said as she gently picked up a taco the size of a fortune cookie.

"Thank you," said Winnie. "We're having a Mexican fiesta tonight. The recipes are from a restaurant you and Mrs. Jenkins went to in Cabo San Lucas. Dinner is chicken stew. I helped Mrs. Jenkins make it this afternoon; it's been cooking for hours."

"Margarita anyone?" asked Louise as she walked into the study carrying a tray with a pitcher, a plate of sliced limes, and a small bowl of coarse salt.

"Oh, I think I'll stick with a martini," said Ruth. "I had such a terrific headache drinking that margarita the first night of our trip. It must have been too much salt. You know I have to watch my salt intake."

Louise laughed. "Ruthie, it wasn't the salt. You drank three of them before dinner that night."

"Oh, Louise," Ruth scoffed, ignoring the truth about her headache.

"Amelia, would you like one?"

“Sure, thanks, Mom. Let me help.” She took the tray from Louise and set it on the cocktail table. “Is Elliott coming to dinner?”

“He is. Kirby, too. They’ve been out of sorts lately, but hopefully they’ve resolved their squabble. But no Andrew. He’s not back from his trip.”

“I left Elliott a message about Tony’s visit yesterday,” Amelia said, out of earshot of the others. “We need to fill him in.”

“I agree, but not while Winnie is in the room.”

“Hola!” Kirby walked into the study wearing a dazzling fuchsia-and-gold embroidered tunic. Elliott, in a sombrero, was at her side.

“Well, aren’t you two striking,” said Louise as she clapped her hands together.

“Elliott told me you were having a Mexican dinner, so I thought we should dress appropriately.”

“Elliott, you look, you look . . . ,” Amelia stammered.

“I look ridiculous,” he said. “I told Kirby I’d wear it only for the entrance, then the hat comes off. Here, Winnie, a gift for you,” he said as he sailed the hat like a giant Frisbee in her direction.

“Elliott, you’re loosening up!” exclaimed Louise.

“Let’s not get carried away. I’m still very much one of them,” he said as he looked up at the formal portraits of the Samuels.

“Oh, they all had their moments, too, though I suspect my grandfather never thought we would find his croquet mallet.”

The room fell silent, waiting for reason to rise above Louise’s non sequitur.

“He loved the game,” she continued. “Insisted we all wear our whites even though I thought we looked like a bunch of Good Humor men, but he insisted. ‘Rules of the game,’ he said. He liked rules and he liked croquet. So I expect we shouldn’t be surprised that the mallet is there," she said, looking at the portrait of her grandfather.

"Mother, what are you talking about?" Elliott asked.

"The painting, dear. Your great-grandfather hid a mallet in his portrait. I hope he's aware I found it."

"And the fried egg, too?" asked Winnie as she walked over to Samuel the Fourth's portrait.

Louise beamed. "You found the egg? My, but you're observant."

Elliott and Amelia wore identical expressions of confusion. Kirby backed away from the group. Ruth sipped her martini. She was certain Louise was making sense; it would just take Ruth a bit longer to figure it out.

"Yes, it's right there," Winnie continued, pointing to the painting's burled wood table that Samuel the Fourth stood beside. "That's burl," she said of the swirling pattern, "but look closely on the edge of the table. There's a fried egg painted to look like burl. Definitely a fried egg."

Everyone gathered around Samuel the Fourth. He loved the attention.

"Will wonders never cease," exclaimed Ruth. "It is an egg. Why would he put an egg in a painting? I mean, if it were a still life or maybe a breakfast scene, or, oh I don't know, there must be other reasons, but this is a portrait . . ."

Amelia laughed. "It's hilarious. And I always thought these were such serious portraits."

"They are," added Louise, "but with a dash of quirkiness. It's a family trait. Something that I thought was lost on you, Elliott, but I see I was wrong," she said as she eyed the sombrero.

"My father also has a few surprises in his portrait, but dinner is ready. You can search after dinner. The Samuels aren't going anywhere," Louise said as she patted the gold frame of Samuel the Fifth's portrait. "It's time to eat."

* * *

"Louise, the table is splendid," said Kirby as they gathered in the dining room. The table was covered in a deep blue cloth; a multicolored serape table runner ran down the center, displaying clusters of miniature sombreros, maracas, and brightly painted clay pots filled with cacti and succulents.

"I hope the meal is as splendid," said Louise. "Claudia is not here tonight to work her culinary magic. She and Wills are at the Mercer Gallery in Doylestown, overseeing the installation of Wills's paintings. His show opens next Thursday."

"Well, it smells delicious," Amelia said.

"A simple meal, guisado de pollo," said Louise. "Mexican chicken stew."

Louise loved seeing her dining table surrounded by those dearest to her. She felt enormous gratitude that her children made the effort to join her whenever possible. So many of her friends were less engaged with their offspring. Some estranged, others just distanced. Too busy, too far. Perhaps disappointment had pulled too hard on the familial bond, causing it to weaken, or perhaps their children had willingly severed the bond to release the intense pressure they felt trying to live up to expectations.

With her clan the bond was strong, tested at times, but saved by its resiliency, a tensile strength. It could stretch in search of individuality or independence and then spring back when encouragement or validation was needed.

She looked at Ruth and Winnie sitting side by side, one seventy-five, the other eleven. Her friendship with Ruth spanned almost seventy years, throughout which Ruth charged through life to make sure she wasn't left behind. And Winnie, a big brain in such a little body. Thankfully she held on to her wonderment of life. Louise hoped she wouldn't lose it in the crucible of growing up.

As if on cue, Winnie picked up one of the miniature sombreros scattered across the table. "I wonder if Florence would wear one of these? It's the perfect size. Wouldn't that be cute?" She pushed her chair back from the table. "I need to rehearse my lines for my school play. May I be excused but come back when you're serving dessert?"

"Of course, Winnie. I'll let you know when we're ready."

"What play are you in?" asked Amelia.

"*A Midsummer Night's Dream*. I'm Puck."

Elliott waited until Winnie had climbed the stairs. "OK, what did the police tell you?"

"The police were here?" exclaimed Ruth. "Have they solved the murder?"

"They seem to think so," began Louise, "but I'm not so sure. It's all rather distressing and disappointing."

Ruth leaned in, ready to absorb and repeat whatever Louise could tell her about the murder.

"Anthony informed me that Mr. Porter appears to have been involved in selling drugs, cocaine to be exact, and he was killed by a man named James Carter, who subsequently died of a drug overdose, cocaine, after driving Michael's van into Lake Luxembourg."

Elliott held up his hand. "Just so I'm clear, James Carter drove the van into the lake, didn't drown, and then died of an overdose?"

"That's right. He escaped from the van and was found dead

in his apartment nearby. The cocaine he used matched that found in Michael's apartment."

"There was cocaine in Michael's apartment?" Ruth gasped.

"It's all too absurd." Louise sighed. "Carol Anne insists that Michael did not take or sell drugs. I don't know if she was bamboozled by him or if the police have it all wrong."

"Or she was in on it," said Elliott. "Mother, don't get taken in by her."

"Elliott, she's an innocent."

"You don't know that," he snapped.

"I do, dear. I can feel it. She's overwhelmed and exhausted. She stayed here the past two nights and was a wonderful house guest."

"She stayed here? You don't know anything about her!"

"Yes I do, and I trust her."

"Can we stop the debate over Carol Anne for a minute," interrupted Amelia. "There's a bigger issue here."

All eyes turned toward her. "The evidence may point to James Carter killing Michael," said Amelia, "but why? And why here? Neither was on the list of guests or staff. They must have arrived together, otherwise where is James Carter's car? He apparently drove away in Michael's van."

"Maybe they both were dealers and were selling cocaine to guests," said Elliott.

"Oh, Elliott, don't be ridiculous," said Kirby.

Ruth shrugged. "Well, I for one think it's a relief that the murder involved drugs. It means that none of us is in any danger. We don't take drugs."

"May we please change the subject?" said Louise. "I've had enough discussion of Michael's murder for one day."

"Mother, you need to be careful," said Elliott. "Carol Anne . . ."

Louise cut him off. "Elliott, please, I want to enjoy this evening."

As if on cue, footsteps sounded on the stairs.

"Is it time for dessert?" asked Winnie.

"Yes, it is," Louise said with obvious relief. "We'll have it in the study. It's time to play the Jenkins family version of *Where's Waldo*. I'm sure the Samuels are waiting for us to discover their shenanigans."

27

The Samuels were waiting. The last time they had received so much attention was when there was a fire in the study.

"Help me, Wills," Louise had cried. "We have to save the family." She had grabbed her father off the wall.

Wills had quickly pulled down the remaining portraits one by one, dragged them to the living room, and then run for the fire extinguisher. Louise propped the portraits together against the sofa in a group hug. Smoke drifted into the living room, taunting the Samuels with flecks of soot.

And then it was done. The fire was out. The culprit, a brass floor lamp with bad wiring, lay strewn across the lawn like a dead stick figure wearing a wire-frame hat that had once been covered in creamy silk and festooned with a brass pineapple finial. Next to it were the smoldering remains of the damask drapes and two window seat cushions, which Wills had used as oven mitts to protect his hands.

"Well, that was exciting," Louise had exclaimed.

Over the next week a pair of electricians was at the house

every day inspecting lamps, lights, and outlets. And the Samuels were back in the study, where tonight they watched six sets of eyes search their canvases for clues to their personalities.

"I don't think the first three Samuels deviated from the standards of ancestral portraiture," said Louise. "I believe my grandfather was the first to add a little something to his painting."

Winnie strode over to the portrait and looked up at Louise's grandfather. "Hi," she said to him.

Samuel the Fourth was bursting with pride.

Ruth studied the painting. "Once you know the egg is there, it's so obvious. But why a fried egg, I wonder. I do like them myself, but coddled eggs, now that's a different story altogether. They're—"

"Where's the croquet mallet?" asked Elliott, ending Ruth's potential ovoidal filibuster.

"Look at the fireplace," said Louise.

Elliott and Kirby both jumped up for a closer look at the painting. Its fireplace mantel held a pair of brass candlesticks and a Moravian vase. Above it hung a painting by Edward Hicks.

"That's the painting hanging in the living room," exclaimed Elliott. "I never noticed it in this portrait."

"Actually, the one in the living room is a copy," said Louise. "I lent the original to the Philadelphia Museum of Art for its Henri Rousseau exhibit. Hicks's primitive style is said to have influenced Rousseau."

"I see it," said Kirby. "Yes, I found it!" she shouted jubilantly, punching her fist in the air and then quickly turning to the others. "Sorry, I got carried away."

Elliott remained focused on the painting. The search had become a competition.

"Want me to show you?" Kirby teased Elliott.

"OK. I give." Elliott laughed as he put his arm around Kirby. Amelia and Louise exchanged glances.

"Look at the shadow behind the candlestick. It's a mallet slightly tilted, as if it were propped against the wall."

"There's also something fishy about his painting." Winnie giggled as she sat down on the rug next to Louise's chair, resting her head against the upholstered arm. Louise stroked her hair.

"I see it!" Ruth shrieked like a schoolgirl, startling everyone, including the Samuels. "There's a fish. See it? It's in the pipe stand."

"My father and grandfather often went fly-fishing in Montana," said Louise. "There's a nod to that in my father's painting as well."

* * *

All eyes turned to Samuel the Fifth. But he barely noticed. He was busy recalling the day he discovered the trout in his father's painting. It was on the first day he was sitting for his own portrait. He was studying the composition of his father's painting, how it captured his strength and intelligence. And then he spotted the fish—a rainbow trout perched between two of his father's favorite pipes. His serious, sometimes intimidating father had a fish painted into his portrait! Samuel the Fifth decided then to add a fly rod to his own.

That night he told his father he had discovered the trout. It was a cool, crisp evening. They were right here, in the study, where his future generations were now enjoying their own evening together. He and his father sipped a scotch after dinner. "My son," his father whispered to him in an unusually sentimental voice, "those fishing trips were very special to me."

His father died shortly after Samuel the Fifth's portrait was complete. He called the artist back so she could paint two glasses of scotch near the fly rod. A toast. A thank-you. He never wanted to forget that moment, that evening.

Neither of them has.

* * *

"Isn't this fun?" said Winnie.

"It is, my dear," said Louise, "and you are so very observant."

"Mom and Dad have taken me to museums since I was little and we study the art very closely. They show me little details that others might miss. I think I just got used to looking for them. Also, I like to investigate things. Did you know I found a 1937 Buffalo Head Nickel in the pantry? It's worth about a dollar now."

"Well, that's almost a two thousand percent increase in its value," said Elliott.

"Yes, but if the buffalo had only three legs it would have been worth thousands. Do you want to see it? It's in my evidence box."

"Evidence of what?" Ruth was mixing herself another martini.

"The murder," said Winnie.

Ruth dropped her glass.

"I spent two hours in the pantry with my flashlight, magnifying glass, and a butter knife. I kept the doors open and lights on; it was a little scary, thinking about the body that had been there, but exciting, too. I thought I might find a clue that the police missed."

"It's a relief that horror is over," said Ruth, dabbing the rug with a cocktail napkin and searching for her wayward olive. "I still have nightmares about it. There was so much blood—"

"Did you find other things?" interrupted Kirby, sparing

everyone from further graphic details, real or imagined, from Ruth.

"A couple of small things. I checked along the baseboard and in the gaps between the shelves and the back wall. I pried things out with my butter knife."

Winnie quickly looked at Louise. "It wasn't one of your good ones. It's the one I use as a putty knife when I'm making things."

"I used to have a coin collection," said Elliott. "Let's see the nickel."

"I'll bring the whole box," Winnie said as she ran to her room.

She returned a few moments later. "Here it is." Winnie placed the multicolored shoebox on the window seat and opened it. Each item was carefully displayed like a precious artifact on a pillow of Kleenex.

Elliott examined the nickel. "A 1937. This is in very fine shape. It could be worth more."

"That was my first find," said Winnie proudly. "It was wedged in the corner under the baseboard in the far back of the pantry. There's no mint mark on it, which means it was minted in Philadelphia."

"Well, it could have been there since 1937." Louise laughed.

"This looks like a cocktail pick," said Ruth, pulling a thin silver spear from its tissue pillow.

"Oh, I didn't think of that. I figured it was for picking your teeth."

"Ugh." Ruth stabbed it back into its Kleenex pillow. "Germs."

"And here's the last one, a button."

"It looks like a shirt button," said Elliott.

Winnie put the lid back on the shoebox.

"That's a vivid box," said Kirby.

"Thank you. We painted my dresser and I had some paint left over." She paused. "Why, I have a great idea. Would you like to see my dresser? It's really beautiful."

"I'd love to," said Amelia.

"You all can come see my room if you want."

"I think I'll have another martini instead," said Ruth.

"Come along, Ruth." Louise took her arm. "Let's go see Winnie's room," she said as they followed the others up the stairs.

28

"Wow, my room was never this tidy when I was your age," said Amelia. "And the posters on my walls were of my favorite rock bands."

Above Winnie's desk was a poster of the periodic table of elements. "I don't really need the poster anymore. I know all the elements and their atomic mass," she said matter-of-factly, as if it were a poster of the alphabet.

"I keep it because it's so beautiful, so colorful, *and* it's from the Los Alamos National Laboratory, one of the largest institutions for science and technology," Winnie said, gazing up at the poster. "The blue boxes are alkali metals, turquoise are actinides, and the lavender, they're my favorites, are noble gases. Noble gases. What a great name, isn't it? Each emits a truly brilliant color. Neon is a noble gas. So is Krypton."

Winnie picked up a yo-yo from her bookshelf. It was sitting next to Winnie the Pooh and a stuffed Albert Einstein doll. "Do you want to see a trick?" she said as she looped the yo-yo's string over her finger. With a simple flip Winnie sent it spinning out and over her head, and then with a snap reversed its course, and it came hurling backward to her. "It's called a time warp. It's an around-the-world with a reverse. Gravity and momentum," she said simply.

"Winnie, what grade are you in?" asked Elliott.

"I'm a freshman in high school. I skipped a few grades."

"Is it hard being so much younger than the other students?" asked Ruth.

"Not so much anymore. I'm used to it, but I don't really hang out with them after school. I'm a kid and they're teenagers. One girl, Jessica, is a friend. I go to her house sometimes. We study together, and then I hang out with her younger sister, Hannah. We're the same age."

Winnie replaced her yo-yo. "Do any of you like Shakespeare?" She held up the script for *A Midsummer Night's Dream*. "I'm performing in it next Friday. I'm Puck. It's a pretty big role."

Kirby walked over to the dresser. "My, this is gaud . . . grand," she stammered. "A very grandiose use of color." She ran her hand along the carved drawers. "It's a very good reproduction, though the paint is quite nontraditional."

"It's original eighteenth century," said Louise.

"Mom, is that the piece from the upstairs hall?" asked Elliott.

"Yes. Quite a transformation, don't you think?" said Louise.

"You painted an antique?" said Kirby before she could stop herself. "I mean, it's very interesting, but I'm more accustomed to preserving original pieces whenever possible."

"That's understandable," said Louise. "And if Andrew were here he would most definitely agree with you. In fact, he'll probably have a fit when he sees it. But since I don't intend to sell it, it doesn't matter. I think it's quite beautiful now."

"Yes, it is," said Ruth. "And look how nicely it matches the vase from Cabo Pottery."

Kirby picked up the vase. "This is from Cabo Pottery?"

"It is," said Ruth. "I selected this pattern first, and then Louise traded with me."

Kirby inspected it. "I'm sorry to say this, but the quality is terrible. I've bought pottery and tiles from their factory for my clients for years, and I've never seen such poor glazing. This should definitely be replaced."

"That's up to Winnie," said Louise. "It's hers."

"Mrs. Jenkins gave it to me as a gift," Winnie said.

"Well, I can easily replace it for you." Kirby set the vase back on the dresser. "This is far below the factory's standards. The glaze is so thin that it will probably crack in no time." Kirby snapped a photo of the vase with her phone. "I better let the Travel Club know as well. I set that excursion up for them."

"Do you know the club's owner, Robert D'Angelo? He's first-rate and was very attentive to me on our trip." Ruth blushed.

"Yes, he's very good, isn't he? Makes you feel like a queen."

"How old is he?" asked Ruth.

"Ruth is smitten with him," said Louise. "Did you talk to him at the party, Ruth?"

"He was at the party?"

"Yes, I saw him briefly."

"That was just not my night." Ruth sighed.

"I'll get you a replacement, Winnie," Kirby offered. "Sometimes even the best quality inspectors miss something."

"Thank you, Miss Dunbar, that's very nice of you, but I think I'll keep this one."

* * *

"You're very quiet," Elliott said as he and Kirby drove to her house.

"I'm just frustrated. That vase is junk, and I thought my willingness to get it replaced would be appreciated."

"But Winnie likes it as it is. It doesn't matter."

"Yes, it does. This is my area of expertise. I thought your mom would appreciate it."

"I'm sure she did, but if Winnie likes the vase, that's enough for Mom."

"What about the dresser? It was worth a significant amount before she allowed a child's idea of decorating to destroy its value!"

"Probably, but as Mom said, if she's not going to sell it, what does it matter?"

"That's ridiculous."

"No, that's just Mom."

29

It was early Saturday morning when Amelia pulled into the parking lot of Bryson's Bistro. She got out of her car and walked to the rear to get her bike off its rack.

"You're going to love it," said Charlotte Cartwright, one of Bryson's regulars both at the bistro and on the weekly bike treks. "Winding roads, beautiful scenery, and lunch back here."

Elliott walked over and hugged Amelia. "It's a forty-mile ride. Are you sure you're up to it?"

"Sibling rivalry before the first pedal is pushed," said Mitchell Butterfield. "Just ignore him, Amelia. He treats your brother the same way. Where is Andrew? Is he riding today, or did Dean convince him to sleep in?" Mitchell's crush on Andrew was no secret.

"They're out of town on a buying trip," said Amelia.

Steve Bryson gave Amelia a water bottle with his eponymous pub's logo on it. "One of the perks for joining our group."

"How many usually ride?" she asked.

"Eight to ten, it varies." He looked around. "I think you

know everyone, except maybe Richard Powell. He's riding today. Have you met him?"

"Only by name. I know he's married to Leslie Clark."

"Nice guy, though competitive." He looked over at Elliott. "They try to win the race, even though it's not a contest. The rest of us just ride for fun."

"Kirby is on her way," Elliott said, dropping his cell phone into a pocket on the back of his jersey. Amelia's raised eyebrows shot above her sunglasses. Elliott ignored her.

The traffic was light for a Saturday as they rode toward Washington Crossing Historic Park, a favorite location for a picnic in the summer and the site of the Christmas reenactment of George Washington crossing the Delaware River, changing the course of the American Revolutionary War.

Amelia loved the rich history of Bucks County. Philadelphia may have Independence Hall, Betsy Ross's house, and the Liberty Bell, but Bucks County has its battlefields, settlements, and inns, the latter of which purporting that "Washington slept here." Given the significant number of historic inns, Washington was well rested during the Revolution.

Amelia watched as Smith Phillips eased in and out of the group of cyclists. He had joined them just as they were heading from the parking lot at Bryson's. Amelia hoped he would stay for lunch after the ride. She wanted to talk to him about what he saw that night at Twin Beeches.

Her breathing labored with each rotation of her tires as she climbed another hill past woods and farmland. Long bike rides had been her therapy in California; the good weather year-round allowed for very regular sessions. She would ride along the coast, the thrumming of waves creating a natural rhythm, her own salty sweat cooling her body and rinsing her mind of stress. The air felt rinsed as well, as if the ocean had pulled it into its current and then tossed it back out with each wave.

The air in Pennsylvania was entirely different. Humidity wrapped Amelia in a thick, wet embrace. Inescapable. It reminded her of family picnics with her aunt Vita. Vita would open her meaty arms wide to hug Amelia. She was a cauldron of aromas—sweet perfume, suntan oil, and, when she laughed, lime and gin. But Aunt Vita's embraces were loving and protective. Unfortunately, they were also sweaty.

"My dear Amelia, my how you've grown," she would cry while pressing Amelia's face into her pillowy bosom, which carried the additional scent of lilac. Amelia would stand on tiptoe in an attempt to rise above the bosom as it approached her; each year she got closer to reaching fresh air.

As Amelia pedaled through the familiar countryside, the moist air scented with mowed fields, lavender, and the occasional farm animal felt like she was riding into an Aunt Vita hug.

Amelia stayed in the middle of the pack, but as the miles passed she drifted toward the back, joining Mitchell and Charlotte. She watched as Elliott and Richard began to pull away, talking trash each time one passed the other.

"The road straightens just round this bend," gasped Charlotte. "I have to stop for a water break."

"I'm with you," huffed Amelia.

Charlotte steered her bike to the side of the road and swigged the last of her water.

"This is a serious workout, but I'm glad I'm riding again." Amelia leaned on her bike to catch her breath, her back tire still on the edge of the roadway. "I used to ride regularly in LA."

She smiled to herself, realizing she had mentioned LA so casually.

"Ready?" asked Charlotte. "Only three more miles to go."

They paused to allow a car to pass by. Seconds later a black SUV swung around the bend, racing into the straightaway. Amelia dropped her bike and jumped to the side of the road. The SUV swerved to avoid the bike but didn't reduce its speed.

"Slow down, you asshole," Charlotte yelled.

"Car!" Amelia shouted as it gained on the other cyclists. Elliott and Richard were well ahead by a hundred yards, racing side by side to the finish. Behind them, Steve Bryson, who had just pulled out into the lane alongside Kirby, raced to pass her and managed to squeeze in between Kirby and Smith as they furiously pedaled single file at the very edge of the roadway. As the vehicle roared past them, they were forced off the roadway onto the narrow, gravelly shoulder. Suddenly, Steve lost control of his bike and careened down an embankment. He flew over the handlebars and landed in a thicket of loosestrife and vines. His bike continued to roll herky-jerky until it flopped over like a wounded horse. Smith and Kirby managed to stay upright on the shoulder, churning dust and grit into a cloud behind them. They finally rolled to a stop.

"Don't move, Steve." Charlotte raced to him.

Amelia dialed 911. "We need an ambulance."

"No ambulance," yelled Steve. "I'm just scratched up."

"You need to be checked out," implored Charlotte.

"I'm just shook up. I landed on my side; my head's fine," he said as he took off his bike helmet and leaned on Charlotte as he stood up. "Shit." He fell to the ground.

As the sirens wailed in the background, Charlotte took Steve's hand. "I'll come with you to the hospital."

Mitchell grinned. "I knew it. You two . . ."

Amelia elbowed him.

* * *

"The jerk didn't even stop," scowled Mitchell as they crowded around a table at Bryson's after Steve and Charlotte headed to the hospital in an ambulance. "He must have seen Steve lose control of his bike. How dare he not stop?"

"It all happened so fast," said Kirby. "I wish we had gotten the license plate number."

"It was a Pennsylvania plate, but the number was covered in dirt," said Amelia. "And it was an Explorer, I'm positive." She felt less positive that it was simply a reckless driver.

Gus walked over from behind the bar carrying a large pitcher of water and menus. "Charlotte just called. Steve is banged up but OK. Bruised, has a couple of cracked ribs, and a sprained ankle, but they're letting him go home. He also thinks he landed in poison ivy."

They all groaned.

"I'd take a broken rib over that," said Mitchell. "Between poison ivy, oak, and sumac, I don't know how we all survived our childhoods here. It's everywhere."

Gus poured water for everyone while Kirby handed out menus.

"I'm afraid I can't stay for lunch," said Smith as he gulped his water. "I have another engagement."

"What if it wasn't an accident?" asked Amelia.

Elliott shook his head. "You're not trying to link this to the murder, are you?"

"Most of us were there that night."

"Steve wasn't, and he's the one in the hospital," said Elliott.

"It's awfully coincidental."

"Sorry to miss out on the intrigue," said Smith as he set down his empty glass. "I gotta run. Gus, keep me posted on Steve's recovery."

"Smith." Amelia ran after him. "Do you have a minute? I heard you identified James Carter."

"What of it?" he said testily.

"Wow!" Amelia took a step back. "I just wanted to ask you about that night."

"I've already talked to the police. I recognized a man in a photo. That's it." He turned and walked out the door.

"What's wrong?" Elliott asked as Amelia shakily sat back down.

"Smith Phillips. He's offensive."

"Oh, he's hard to read sometimes," said Mitchell. "You never know if he's being condescending or courteous—same behavior, different intention."

"There was nothing courteous about him."

"What did he say?" Kirby refilled her water glass.

"I asked him about James Carter, the man who the police think killed Michael Porter. He's the one who confirmed that Carter was a server at the party. I was just curious how he remembered him if he didn't know him beforehand."

"How do you know Smith hadn't met him previously?" asked Kirby.

"Mardi told me. It struck me as odd that a couple of days after the murder, Smith is shown a photo of James Carter, a man he never met before, and he identifies him as a server at the party."

"That is a bit strange," said Kirby. "But nobody really looks at the servers. They only pay attention to what they're serving."

"My point exactly," said Amelia.

Gus headed in their direction carrying a tray laden with food. He placed a Niçoise salad in front of Kirby.

"Gus," she snapped, "I said dressing on the side. This isn't on the side; the tuna is swimming in it."

Amelia glanced at Elliott while Gus retrieved Kirby's plate.

"Sorry, Kirby," said Gus. The others shared Gus's embarrassment while Kirby picked a French fry off Mitchell's plate. "So unhealthy, but I have to eat something before I faint."

"Kirby, you certainly know Smith better than any of us. What do you think?" Mitchell asked.

Kirby trained her sights on him.

"Oopsie, did I let the proverbial cat out of the bag?"

"Our gossip queen apparently wants you all to be aware that I once dated Smith." Kirby looked across at Elliott. "Briefly. Years ago."

30

"He didn't do it," Carol Anne said.

She had phoned Louise Saturday night asking if she could come over in the morning. She had something to tell her, something very important. She also called Amelia. It was time to be honest.

"Mikey didn't do drugs," Carol Anne said. She sat opposite Amelia and Louise in Louise's study.

Amelia moved to the sofa next to Carol Anne. "I know this is a horrible situation for you. I respect how much you believed in Michael, and it doesn't mean you can't still love him. It's just . . ."

"But Mikey wasn't involved in drugs!" she cried. "Everything the police said is wrong. They're wrong about the drugs, about his fingerprints. They're all wrong." She pounded her fists on her lap. "It's not true. I know it for a fact!"

Carol Anne sobbed as she balled up the clump of soggy Kleenex. It had no more room to hold her tears. She turned her face toward Louise, drew in an unsteady breath, and said, "Mikey was never involved in drugs. I was."

The whispered words slammed Louise back against her chair, mouth agape, eyebrows reaching for her hairline.

"Carol Anne, what are you saying?" Louise gasped.

"I'm so ashamed," she cried. "I should have told you in the beginning. I just never ever thought anyone would believe Mikey was involved in drugs, so that part of the story would go away and I would never have to tell my secret."

"Your secret! The drugs are yours?" demanded Amelia.

"No! I swear to you they aren't mine, and they aren't Mikey's. I don't know where they came from."

"I'm calling Detective Mardi." Amelia reached for her cell phone.

"No, wait! Please wait. I can explain. Then you can call him, but please let me tell you first. I'm so sorry, Mrs. Jenkins. I'm not a bad person."

"Amelia, close the door," demanded Louise. "Carol Anne, compose yourself and tell us everything. Truthfully!"

Amelia picked up a box of tissues from the side table and brought them over to Carol Anne. She then pulled a chair perpendicular to the sofa where Carol Anne sat, blocking her exit.

"A few years ago," Carol Anne began hesitantly, "I was living in a house with four other people and working two jobs, trying to save enough money to move into my own apartment.

"One night, Lynne, one of my roommates, offered me some speed." Carol Anne looked up at Louise. It was like confessing to her mother, if she had had a mother growing up. "That's meth. You snort it; at least that's what Lynne did. I tried it. It gave me so much energy, I felt like I didn't need to eat or sleep. It was great until the day Lynne found me unconscious on the floor in the kitchen. She and two others drove me to a doctor, not to the hospital, just a doctor who they knew wouldn't tell the police. He said if I didn't stop I was going to die. I didn't stop, but I did less. And then I met Mikey. He didn't know about my habit.

"One day we were at the laundromat. Mikey needed some quarters for the dryer and I told him to get them out of my change purse. I forgot I had a little bag of meth in there. He found it.

"He said I had to stop because he didn't want to be involved with a drug addict. He didn't say he was leaving me. He said he wanted me to stop, so he could stay. No one ever cared for me like that. It's been three years. I've never, ever touched it again. Not even now, with Mikey dead. He left me courage.

"So you see, that's why Mikey couldn't possibly be involved in drugs. He worked too hard to help me. We built a new life together, and it was drug-free. Someone put those drugs in the apartment. There is no, no way they belonged to Mikey, and they do *not* belong to me. You can have me tested. I swear to you."

"Why didn't you say something to the police?" asked Louise.

"I was going to admit it to them the day they were here and said the drugs were why he was killed, but then you"—she looked at Amelia—"started asking questions, and I thought maybe they would reinvestigate and I wouldn't have to tell anyone, especially you, Mrs. Jenkins, about my past."

Like a trapped bird desperate to find an open window, Carol Anne's plea darted chaotically about the living room, searching for an escape from Louise's shock and disappointment.

"Carol Anne, you need to tell your tale to the police." Louise left the room.

31

"Can't believe you live here." Mardi looked around Amelia's living room. "I hated this place as a kid. When I walked up your front steps just now, that feeling of dread returned."

"Still the charmer," Amelia said.

"It's not about you," he said with a grin. "It's the library. The only time I ever came here was because I had to." He looked up toward the loft. "The reference section. My eyes would glaze over as soon as I started research for a paper. And remember the librarian? Man, she was scary. She always gave me a look like I was a juvenile delinquent, though Jimmy Boyd and I did carve our initials into one of the tables up there."

"So she was right." Amelia returned the grin.

It was early Monday evening. The light bathed the walls with a warm glow the color of parchment. Everything about the interior of Amelia's home held the imprint of books.

"Would you like something to drink?" Amelia asked. "Coffee, water, a beer?"

"I'll have a beer. I'm off duty." He settled back in a side chair. "I never noticed that fireplace. Was it always here?"

"Yes. Everything is pretty much original. I added a proper kitchen in the back and renovated the attic, which now has two bedrooms and bathrooms. The youth section over there is my library. The loft is a sitting area/media room.

"Glass?" she asked as she set a tray with two bottles of beer and two glasses on the carpenter's chest coffee table.

"Nah, I'm good." He took a swig from the bottle while Amelia carefully poured her beer into a glass and sat down on the sofa.

"You look great, Amelia. It's nice to have you back in town." He studied her as she sipped her beer. She hadn't changed much since he first noticed her in high school when he sat behind her in English class. Her long neck and graceful shoulders. She was taller and thinner than most other girls whose rounded hips and burgeoning breasts created a blossoming softness that guys yearned for. Their bodies, shaped like hourglasses, measured the time when sexual fantasy would become a reality.

But Amelia was elegant. Her slender though shapely legs went on forever. He dreamed of getting tangled up in them. In school, when she was deep in thought, she would scoop up her long brown hair with both hands and twist it into a knot at the back of her head, squeezing out the flowery scent of her shampoo, which Tony breathed in deeply. Then she would secure her mane with a pencil. A neat and tidy bun held by a wooden stick. How she did that he could never figure out.

But he was grateful. It allowed him to gaze at her long neck and shoulders until it became too much of a distraction and he would pull the pencil out, sending her hair cascading down her back. She thought he was teasing her; he was saving himself from an embarrassing shudder.

"I'm intrigued," she said, interrupting his memory. "What is it you wanted to talk to me about?"

Mardi shifted in his chair and leaned in toward Amelia, his hands clasped around the beer bottle, elbows resting on his knees. "Carol Anne Jackson."

"Carol Anne?" She set her glass down on the coffee table.

"She came to see me. She told me about her meth habit. She said she admitted it to you and your mom." Mardi sat back in his chair. "She gave me permission to speak to her therapist, who corroborated her statement about Porter's efforts to keep her straight."

"She's pretty gullible. I wouldn't have let the police talk to my shrink," said Amelia.

"She volunteered, in fact she insisted, and it wasn't just for Porter's sake; it was for your mom's. Carol Anne is devastated over not telling her. And I could hardly take her just on her word. I needed more."

"And you are telling me this because . . ."

"Because I wanted you to know that I looked into her story and while I believe she's sincere, it doesn't change the outcome."

"Why not? If what Carol Anne says is true, then the case doesn't hold together unless Porter was a brilliant manipulator who hid his drug dealing behind the role of a devoted boyfriend who saved his girl from a meth addiction. That's bullshit, Tony. He was a pizza delivery guy whose career aspiration was to be a construction worker, not the head of a cartel."

"Except we have the drugs, the money, and the fingerprints."

"Tony, why did you want to see me? Why are you telling me this?"

"Because of our past. Because I like your family." He took a breath and looked deep into Amelia's eyes. "Because in tomorrow's paper there's a front-pager on it. Chief Sullivan spent a couple of hours with Leslie Clark. Sullivan still hates the media, but he gave Leslie the interview anyway. He said her coverage would showcase the investigative work of our police force.

"I think he just wants vindication from the Frankie Vincent debacle. That case still pisses him off. His nephew Harry Barnett had just joined the force and was working on the Vincent case when Frankie bolted. Harry is the son of Sullivan's sister Martha, who's tight with Richard Powell, Leslie Clark's husband. I expect Leslie was using Martha to push Sullivan. Sullivan gave her a lot of access."

"Were you interviewed?"

"No, word came down that only Sullivan was to be interviewed. Sullivan likes the spotlight; I don't. I'm not happy about this, but it's out of my control. I just wanted you to know."

"Does Leslie know about Carol Anne's past drug problem?"

"I don't know."

"If she talks to her, your case might not look so neat and tidy."

"I don't think Carol Anne is going to bare her soul to a reporter."

"She might if she thinks it can vindicate Michael. She talked to you, didn't she? A recovering meth addict talking to a cop was way riskier."

"Not if she's clean."

"Tony, you found drugs in the apartment. You don't think she considered that before talking to you? Carol Anne would do anything to clear Michael's name."

"Including revealing her drug addiction to the world?"

"Why not? Her world has already crashed in on her. Why not let Leslie dig through the rubble?"

32

"Louise, did you see this?" exclaimed Ruth as she rushed into Louise's kitchen waving the front page of today's *Courier Times* like a distress flag.

"That girl is a drug user! And to think she stayed at your home. Are you sure she didn't steal anything?"

"Oh, Ruth, calm down. Carol Anne says she *was* a drug user, and Michael helped her quit. Her interview explains as much."

"Likely story," snapped Ruth. "They were probably in it together. I'm just lucky I didn't find that boy's body in the pantry any earlier. I could have been caught in the crossfire between him and his killer. He was probably a rival drug lord."

"Ruth, it takes guns to be caught in the crossfire. Michael was killed with a candlestick."

"It's just so upsetting." Ruth plopped down on the living room couch, spent from her self-created melodrama. "Every time I think I've recovered from my night of horror, something like this happens."

She waved the paper in front of Louise again. "What twaddle! The *Courier Times* should have just reported how the police solved the crime, not included that girl's fantasy about her boyfriend being a knight in shining armor. It's probably a ruse so she can now take over his drug empire."

"Ruth, you're being ridiculous."

"Oh, Louise, you always see the best in people. The evidence is there. 'Case closed,' to quote Police Chief Sullivan. Thank goodness for our police department. Weren't those details fascinating? So clever of them to match the murderer's eyeglass prescription with the glasses found in the van; such attention to detail. I'm going to make a nice contribution to the Policeman's Fund this year. They cracked this case in no time."

"Are you too rattled to go to Newtown today?" Louise asked as Ruth fanned herself with the newspaper. "I can wait until tomorrow to pick up the paint for Winnie's room."

"Oh no, let's go. I need to pick up the throw pillows I ordered from Kirby. She was so kind to rush the order. They're custom, you know, for my boudoir. Afterward let's go to La Grenouille. I need a bowl of their French onion soup to calm my nerves and maybe have a nice glass of Chablis."

* * *

"Here they are," Kirby said as she arranged three silk-embroidered pillows on the countertop. "My assistant, Marc, is getting the other two."

"They look absolutely luxurious," exclaimed Ruth, rubbing her hands together like an excited child. "You have such an eye, Kirby." Ruth hugged a blue-and-yellow-striped pillow to her chest as she watched Marc step out of the back room. He was wearing a crisp oxford cloth shirt, khakis, and loafers with no socks. His dazzling grin and piercing blue eyes on top of his choice of clothing made him look like he could have walked off the pages of *GQ* magazine.

"You have a gentle touch for such a muscular young man," Ruth chortled as Marc carefully cocooned each pillow in an elegant Dunbar & Co. drawstring bag and then nestled them into two oversize shopping bags with ribbon handles.

"Are you a designer, too?" she asked, ready to dump Kirby for his services. "I would never have thought to mix stripes and prints, though I guess that is de rigueur for English country estates. And that is the land of my ancestors."

"May I take these to your car?" asked Marc.

Ruth swooned. "You are a charming young man."

"I'll meet you at La Grenouille," said Louise. "I won't be a minute at the hardware store."

"Oh, I'll tag along. Isn't that Marc just adorable? Elliott better watch himself. He may have competition."

* * *

"How's the girl's bedroom coming along?" asked Fred, the owner of Newtown Hardware, as he mixed a can of Sea Foam Green for Louise.

"It's colorful," she replied. "This is for Winnie's floor lamp."

"Is it metal? Make sure you prime it first."

Ruth leaned over the counter and started sniffing Fred.

"Eh, what are you doin', Ruth?" he said as he backed away from her.

"You're wearing Old Spice, aren't you?"

"Yep. Did I overdo it this morning?"

"Oh no, no, but let me ask you, did you know MP?"

"MP?"

"Yes, the man who was murdered at Louise's house."

"Oh, Mike Porter. Yeah, poor kid. Hard to believe what the papers said about him. I guess you never know about somebody, though this one's real surprising."

"Why is that?" asked Louise.

"You can't judge a book by its cover. I see workmen come in here all the time. Some are big and burly, got tattoos. I don't like tattoos. They look like they could start trouble, yet you watch 'em hold the door for a lady or help get something down from a high shelf. They're nice.

"I guess the same's true the other way. Mike seemed like a real decent kid. Who woulda thought he sold drugs. Had a nice girl, too. I met her a couple of times. They'd come in together once in a while for what have you."

He laughed uncomfortably. "So, Ruth, what's this got to do with my aftershave?"

"Well, you see," began Ruth. "By the way, did you know I was the one who found the body? It was just awful; I'll never get over it. Who would ever dream of opening a door and finding a body!"

"Ruth, Fred asked about the Old Spice," said Louise, trying to nudge the narrative along.

"Yes, of course, sorry, whenever I think about that night it gets me going." She took a deep breath. "I recognized the name Michael Porter because of your Old Spice and my husband's military service."

Fred looked to Louise for a translation.

"What I mean is," Ruth continued, "the night he was killed, the police said his name was Michael Porter but he went by MP. I suddenly remembered hearing someone introduce himself by those initials. It was here, and you must have been standing by him, because I remembered smelling Old Spice, which was also my husband's cologne. As you probably know, MP stands for *military police*, and so because of my husband's career in the United States Army and you wearing Old Spice, I made the association that allowed my memory to recall that moment."

"Whew, that's quite a recollection, Ruth," said Fred.

"Do you remember Michael introducing himself to anyone, Fred?" asked Louise.

"Not that I recall. When was it?"

"I think I was last here about a month ago?" replied Ruth.

"Well, Mike was in pretty regular, picking up supplies or checking the board to see if anybody needed help. I keep a bulletin board by the back door so people can post help-wanted notices for fill-in jobs on construction sites, kind of old school, but it still works. We've got a lot of restoration and renovation going on in this town, and they're often shorthanded, though usually they're looking for experienced stonemasons and craftsmen. None of that 'slap up a vinyl-sided box in a week and call it home.'" He chuckled.

"As far as I know, Mike was a good fill-in when a crew was short. He got pretty steady work from Jerry Baker. Maybe he was with him that day. Jerry's a real talker. Could be he introduced Mike to somebody."

"Thank you, Fred. I'm just trying to help the police in any way I can," said Ruth. "It's my duty, particularly given I'm the one who discovered the murder."

"Well, it sounds like the police have figured it out, though I can't say it fits the kid I knew. See that clock?" He pointed to a golden oak wall clock. "Mike and his girl were saving up for that last time I saw them. I said they could open a house account and take it home that day. I trusted them. But Mike said no, they'd save up their money and then buy it. You'd assume if he was a drug dealer he'd have money to spend."

Smith Phillips closed the door behind him and walked down the back steps of Newtown Hardware. He'd heard enough.

33

The morning sun splashed across Amelia's living room as she sipped her coffee and read the *Courier Times*. Even though Tony had alerted her that the story would run today, she was still surprised at the extensive coverage, including a lengthy interview with Chief Sullivan. He was effusive about his leadership and his team's crime-solving abilities. The police department's PR team couldn't have written a more glowing report.

A much smaller article anchored at the bottom of the front page was Leslie Clark's interview with Carol Anne.

Was Murdered Man's Character Assassinated? Now, there was a headline!

As a reporter, Amelia had written so many pieces that were given powerful headlines. She investigated corruption, greed, and malfeasance. In her last article for the *Times*, she was certain she was exposing the CEO of Tripoint, a man who was destroying his company. But her story may have killed him.

Amelia should have been better prepared for the destruction

of her own career. She knew her actions clearly compromised her and the integrity of the paper.

It was all too tantalizing. A plump, juicy revelation, swollen with deception and greed, and Kevin tempting her to slice it open and expose its rotting insides. Her knife was a thumb drive crammed with financial reports, memos, and emails. It was a perfect tool that dug into the bowels of a corporation and exposed Ben Adams as the mastermind behind a complex embezzlement scheme. Amelia carefully excised the evidence, avoiding the occasional traces of doubt that clung to it.

And then she abandoned all pretext of journalistic ethics. She included an interview with Kevin Morgan. You simply don't interview someone you have a personal relationship with and not disclose it. Ever.

Amelia would never know if Ben Adams died out of remorse for what he did or because she had exposed him. Maybe she had assassinated Ben's character.

The evidence against him was convincing, but so was the evidence chronicled in today's paper against Michael Porter, except for Carol Anne's story. She defended Michael's reputation, his innocence. Amelia hoped the powerful headline above Leslie's story would serve as a buoy and attract attention to what lay beneath—facts that raised doubt about the investigation's findings. Leslie Clark revealed another side of Michael Porter's character.

Amelia never afforded Ben the same courtesy.

* * *

"Is Carol Anne Jackson here?" Amelia asked the hostess at the River's Inn.

"Are you a reporter?" she asked testily.

"No, I'm a friend of hers."

"Just a minute."

Amelia watched as the hostess walked to the back of the restaurant. It was lunchtime and the tables were mostly filled with women, nicely dressed, nibbling salads and chatting. Amelia had been to this location years ago when it was called Mother's Restaurant. It was a favorite dinner-and-morning-after spot. A romantic dinner followed the next morning by mimosas and eggs Benedict, a perfect brunch following a passionate Saturday night. Amelia never knew if the name *Mother's* was an intended irony, serving breakfast to more than a few after what was most likely a one-night stand. "Let's go to Mother's" was probably not expected after such an assignation.

Amelia glanced down at the thick, black leather reservation book that sat on the wooden podium. Tucked underneath it was a newspaper, probably shoved there when Amelia walked in the door. She tugged at the paper and out popped Michael Porter's photo alongside Carol Anne's interview.

A man walked toward Amelia, stopping along the way to greet several patrons. "I'm Stanley Wickham. May I help you?" He looked like a maître d' in his crisp white shirt and black slacks. But he carried himself like an owner, confident, cordial, and, toward Amelia, curious.

"I'm a friend of Carol Anne Jackson. I was hoping to speak with her."

Stanley eyed her cautiously. "Your name?"

"Amelia Halliday."

"I prefer that my staff not be interrupted while they are working. What is it you want to see her about?"

"This." She pointed to the news article.

"You're the third person today, and the other two were reporters."

"I'm not. I'm here to see if she's OK."

"I see."

Amelia felt sure he didn't. "I'm not a close friend of Carol Anne's, but I am concerned about her. My mother is Louise Jenkins. It was at her house that Michael Porter was murdered. Twin Beeches. We're worried about Carol Anne. She's been through a lot."

Stanley glanced over his shoulder. Amelia followed his gaze and saw that a group of diners had stopped talking. The woman closest to them was leaning back in her chair, her head turned in profile to Amelia. Her eyes were focused on the potted palm in the far corner, though she would not have reacted if it had suddenly grown legs and walked away. Her hearing was the only sense that was on high alert. She pushed her hair back from her right ear and moved her head ever so slightly, like a satellite in orbit, positioning its antennae to receive optimal reception.

"Let's go back to my office," he said.

Amelia followed him, realizing that they had been caught in the gravitational pull of the diners' curiosity.

"Carol Anne is a nice kid," he said after he closed the door and offered Amelia a seat. "She's worked for me for about two years now. She's primarily a waitress at lunch but a couple of evenings a week she works as a prep cook. She's relatively unsophisticated in her approach to food and doesn't have any basic training, but she's diligent and wants to learn. It's a tedious job chopping vegetables and washing greens, but Carol Anne does it with a smile. And she observes everything. I think she has a talent and I would like to see her get a chance."

"Can I talk to her?" Amelia asked.

"She's not here. She called me this morning and quit. She's humiliated by today's article and is afraid our regular customers will not return if there's a speed freak—her words—in the restaurant. I told her what she did was noble. She defended Mike's reputation at her own expense. I met him a couple of times. He seemed like a nice, hardworking kid. Just like Carol Anne. I told her I wouldn't accept her resignation. Not yet. I asked her to take a few days off to reconsider her decision. She's alone, you know, now that Mike's gone. This job is all she has."

Stanley was quiet for a moment and watched Amelia carefully. "I hope you are who you say you are. Carol Anne is in a fragile state right now. She needs support, not notoriety."

"I understand. She and my mother formed a special bond, odd when you consider the circumstances, but it's there—actually still is, as far as my mother is concerned. Thanks for talking to me." Amelia picked up her purse from the floor next to her chair and stood to leave. "You're a very generous man, Stanley. Carol Anne is lucky to work for you."

"If you see her, tell her the offer is still open and that I wish her well."

Amelia walked through the restaurant. The satellite's orbit shifted, signaling everyone at the table. Amelia walked past them. "Good day, ladies."

She glanced at the newspaper on the podium, at Michael's photo. *Who were you?*

34

Amelia drove to Riverview Apartments and called Carol Anne from the parking lot. Her voice mail was full. She tried the landline. A male voice intoned: *We're not here right now. Leave a message and we'll call you back. Really, we will.* It was followed by a chuckle, an earnest chuckle. It transformed Michael into a person. Not a corpse, not a photograph, but a person who chuckled.

"Carol Anne, this is Amelia Halliday. I'm outside in your parking lot. Please pick up if you're there. I want to help." She paused. Nothing. "And so does my mom," she added, before hanging up.

She'd wait at least a little while. Carol Anne's car was there. She was probably inside sleeping or hiding. She watched the window, hoping to see the drapes part. A Fox News truck pulled into a parking space at the far end of the lot.

"Carol Anne, this is Amelia again. A TV crew has arrived. If you're there, please pick up." Amelia heard a click.

"I'm here," Carol Anne said simply. "I don't want to talk to any more reporters. I can't handle it." She began to cry.

"Let me come up."

Amelia popped her Phillies cap on her head and bounded up the steps to the apartment.

Carol Anne quickly opened the door. She slammed it just as fast once Amelia was inside. "I've made things worse," she said. "I shouldn't have talked to the reporter, but she seemed so nice. She said she wanted to help. It's a horrible story. I made things worse, didn't I?"

"No, you didn't. You did a very brave thing."

"I didn't know she was going to put everything I said in the newspaper. She said she knew that I didn't believe what the police were saying about Mikey. She said she just wanted to understand better before she talked to the police some more. Now the whole world knows. I'm ashamed, and I sound like I'm stupid because I said the police were wrong."

"They've been wrong before," Amelia said as she peered out the window between the drapes. "There's a cameraman and reporter coming up the stairs."

"What do we do?" Fear smothered Carol Anne's humiliation.

"Nothing. We're not going to answer the door. But just so you understand, there will probably be a story on the news tonight with footage of your apartment building." Before Amelia could stop herself, she said, "It's what I would have done."

Carol Anne gasped. "What *you* would have done? Are you a reporter? Is this why you're here?"

"No, Carol Anne, absolutely not. I used to be a reporter, in California. I'm not anymore. I'm here to help you."

There was a knock on the door. Carol Anne looked at Amelia. A second knock, more of a pound, landed. Amelia motioned for Carol Anne to follow her into the kitchen. "Please trust me, Carol Anne. They know we're here," Amelia said in a low voice. "They saw me come up the stairs. We'll just sit this out until they leave."

Amelia stared at the mess. "They really tore this place up."

"I was never the greatest housekeeper, but I never let it get this bad! And now it's too depressing. Every time I try to straighten things up, I see something of Mikey's and start to cry."

"Well, since we can't leave, why don't I help you," said Amelia. "Maybe it will be a little easier." Amelia picked up a pencil that sat next to a to-do list. "May I borrow this?" She twisted her hair into a knot and ran the pencil through it, holding it in place.

Carol Anne stared into the sink. "These dishes are disgusting. It smells like something died here." She sucked in a breath. "I can't believe I just said that!" As she exhaled, a tiny laugh fell out but was quickly slapped away as Carol Anne's hand rushed to her mouth. "That was sick," she said, embarrassed by her inappropriateness.

"It's OK, Carol Anne. It's just a saying."

"I know, but I can't believe *I* said it, you know, considering . . ." And then as Carol Anne stood in the wreckage of her apartment smelling of putrid, rotted food, it happened again. A chuckle this time, like a macabre hiccup, escaped through the space created by a chip in her front tooth. Others tried to follow, clamoring to get out. It was time. Opening her mouth wide, Carol Anne's hysteria raced through the apartment, bouncing off pillows and slamming into walls until it finally collapsed of its own anguish.

Carol Anne sagged into a kitchen chair, wiping her tear-streaked face with her shirtsleeve. Amelia led her to the sofa, where she promptly fell asleep. Amelia covered her with a fleece blanket and began the task of replacing the fetid air with oxygen. She opened the windows and scraped the moldy, congealed food into a plastic bag. Next she filled the sink with hot water and dumped in the plastic dishes. She watched the cups bob like buoys in a bay, the scum from the rotted food floating around them like tiny, toxic spills.

She turned to the refrigerator. Mementos of daily life were held in place by magnets in various shapes. An apple, orange, lemon, and bunch of bananas were clustered together like a flat fruit bowl next to a stethoscope-shaped magnet for an urgent care clinic, and a tow truck with the name "Tom's Towing" on the door. Trapped under each were scraps of paper—receipts for groceries and coupons for soup, shampoo, and hot dogs. Two Dairy Queen magnets in the shape of ice cream cones held a strip of four photos from a photo booth, Carol Anne and Michael grinning at the camera or each other.

On the side of the refrigerator hung a calendar, a diagonal line carefully drawn through each passing day. The last line drawn was the day before Michael died.

Amelia studied the calendar. Initials and work hours neatly filled each square. On the date of Michael's death: *CA 10-6, M 9-3C*. What was the C after Michael's hours? She flipped through the calendar. Michael's times had a *C* or *P* after them. Amelia assumed the *C* meant carpentry or construction and the *P* pizza delivery. Pizza delivery was usually around the dinner hour, though he had numerous afternoon shifts as well. His carpentry dates were clumped together in groups of two to three consecutive days, though most recently full weeks were marked with a *C*.

The inside of the refrigerator was almost empty. A carton of milk, three eggs, a tub of margarine, bulk cheddar, and wilted lettuce. Three Styrofoam cups held individual packets of ketchup, relish, and mustard.

She returned to wiping the counters. A plastic napkin holder held mail, mostly flyers, the Penny Shopper, and a bank statement showing a balance of $172.58. She leafed through the pages—rent, utilities, and an occasional debit of twenty dollars.

The cupboard above held a bounty of space along with tiny packets of salt and pepper, miscellaneous cans of soup, beans, and tomato sauce, and a box of Lucky Charms cereal.

"I know it's expensive, but we like it."

Amelia quickly turned to face Carol Anne. "I was tidying up the kitchen," she stammered.

"I figured you might go through our things. I expect that's why you're here."

Amelia's cheeks flushed. In the past she was never embarrassed over digging into people's lives. She had a story to tell. But this was different; she was not on an assignment. She was prying.

Carol Anne waved her hand. "It's silly." Then noticing Amelia's confusion, added, "The cereal. It's for kids." She laughed. "It's magically delicious."

35

"Is Miss Dunbar here?"

Kirby's assistant, Marc, looked down at Winnie. "I expect she's busy, but I'll check in a minute. Does she know you?"

"Yes. I'm Winnie Miller."

Winnie set her plastic grocery bag on the counter and wandered around Dunbar & Co., looking at the antiques and new furniture, each complemented by accessories to demonstrate Kirby's design capabilities. Winnie picked up a gold-trimmed plate from an antique French country sideboard.

"Young lady!" Marc shrieked.

Kirby rushed in from the back room. "What's wrong?"

"Put that down," Marc commanded Winnie. "It's very, very expensive porcelain."

"Hello, Miss Dunbar," said Winnie. "I was just admiring the china. The botanical on this plate looks like Potentilla fruticosa." Winnie flipped the plate over as Marc gasped.

"See?" She pointed to the inscription on the back. "I'm

studying the Latin names for plants. Butterflies love this one. We have it in the garden."

"Winnie," Kirby stammered. "How nice to see you. Marc, this is Winnie Miller. She and her parents live at Twin Beeches, Louise Jenkins's home." Kirby looked at her watch. "Shouldn't you be in school?"

"We had a half day today. It's kinda nice having an early day in the middle of the week. Did you know that the ancient Romans named the days of the week after the sun, moon and the five planets they could see with the naked eye? Wednesday was named for Mercury. In Latin it's dies Mercurii. The modern romance languages still reflect that. In French it's mercredi, in Italian it's mercoledì.

"However," she raised a finger in the air, "and this is really fascinating, the English names for days of the week were influenced by the Anglo-Saxons and the old German gods. Wednesday is from Woden, king of the gods. So the Saxon name for Wednesday is Wodnesdaeg. I guess that's why we have the silent *d* in our spelling. We certainly don't say it's *Wed nes day*." She laughed. "I just love *The Old Farmer's Almanac.* It's got all sorts of interesting tidbits of information. Mrs. Jenkins gets a new edition every year."

Kirby stared speechless at the eleven year old.

Marc cleared his throat. "Children are not often in our showroom," he sniffed, "and *that* is a thousand-dollar Flora Danica dinner plate."

"Good thing I'm not my usual klutzy self, then." Winnie smiled impishly as she set it back on the display stand. "I know it's valuable. Mrs. Jenkins has a set of these dishes. We used the teacups for a tea party last week; we picked cups and saucers that matched the plants in her garden."

Kirby picked up the grocery bag on the counter and looked at Marc disdainfully. "Is this trash sitting on the counter?"

"Oh no, that's mine," said Winnie. "It's for you, Miss Dunbar. You were right about the vase. It was definitely inferior."

Kirby opened the bag. Inside were the crumbled remains of the gift Louise had given to Winnie. "I'll return it to the factory so they can see for themselves what horrible quality it is." She peeked inside the bag again. "I guess I should say *was*." Her eyes twinkled when she smiled. Winnie hadn't seen her do that before.

Kirby knotted the bag. "I guess you want the replacement after all."

"Thank you. I appreciate it. Well, I better go now. See you later."

Marc followed Winnie to the door. As she passed the china display she tapped a fingernail on the lid of a soup tureen. "Mentha silvestris. Mint. It's a very calming herb. You might enjoy it."

As Winnie walked her bike past Dunbar & Co., she peered in the window to see if Marc was guarding the door to prevent other children from entry. She noticed an antique tea set, crystal goblets, and a silver chest displaying sugar tongs, fancy scissors, and long, skinny forks. Winnie parked her bike and went back inside.

There was no sign of Marc or Kirby. Winnie peeked behind the drapes that separated the showroom from the storage area and saw Kirby slam down the telephone and kick a large cardboard box against the back wall. It burst open, spewing polystyrene packing peanuts everywhere. They skimmed across the counters like tiny hovercraft, danced across a pile of pillows, and attached themselves to everything, including Kirby.

"Excuse me." Winnie stepped from behind the drapes.

Kirby jumped. "Oh my God, Winnie, you startled me! What is it?"

"I'm sorry. I, uh, the little forks in your window reminded me of something I wanted to ask you, but I can help you pick up the peanuts first," she said as she watched them continue their electron-charged dance.

Kirby looked around her workroom and attempted a feeble laugh. "I lost my temper. It's nothing. What is it you want to know?"

"Do you remember the silver pick I found? It was in my evidence box."

Kirby thought for a moment. "Yes, I do remember," she said as she nervously picked up the box off the floor and peered inside. "At least this box was empty." She crunched on the peanuts as she walked toward Winnie. Several clung to her ankles. "What about the pick?"

"I just wanted to know more about them. Do you pick your teeth with them or what?"

Kirby laughed. "I guess you could, but it would be rather crass. They're the nineteenth-century version of today's toothpicks with the frilly tops. You use them to pick up hors d'oeuvres."

"Are they common?"

"They were among a certain class back then. Why are you so curious?"

"Oh, I'm always curious about most everything. But my pick could be a clue to the murder."

"At your age you shouldn't be thinking about such macabre things as murder. I expect the one you found was there for decades, maybe even a century."

Kirby bent down to retrieve a dustpan. Winnie, unable to control herself, giggled.

Kirby looked up. "What are you laughing at?"

"I'm sorry," Winnie said. "It's just that, well, you have peanuts stuck to your legs." She bit her lip in an effort to control another giggle fit. "And on your butt."

"Oh for God's sake," she said as she tried to brush the peanuts off her clothing. They now clung to the backs of her hands. "These things are horrible. They stick to everything."

"It's because they're nonconductive. They pull electrons from other objects and the negative electrical charge stays on it. It doesn't pass through. That's why it's called static electricity. Like a magnet, the negative charges on the peanuts push each other away, but the positive neutrons in your clothes and hair attract them and they stick to you. You know, opposites attract."

Kirby stared at Winnie. "I see," she said as peanuts dotted her hair.

"You know what will help? Moisture. It dissipates the static electricity because moisture is denser than the peanuts, which are almost all air." Winnie spied a bottle of Windex and took the dustpan from Kirby. "Here, this will work great." She sprayed it lightly and scooped up the now complacent peanuts. "See, no static. Isn't that fascinating?"

36

Tony Mardi sat at a table on the patio of the Brick Hotel waiting for Amelia. "The Brick," as the locals called it, was a historic inn in the heart of Newtown, and was yet another place where George Washington purportedly stayed while saving the country from English rule. It's restaurant, Rocco's at The Brick, was a popular after-work meeting spot. Mardi's glass of iced tea was sweating almost as much as he was. He was tempted to take a table inside in the air conditioning, but he would wait. He would let Amelia decide.

He watched her round the corner from the parking lot and walk along the white picket fence surrounding the Brick. She spotted him and smiled happily, or possibly curiously. He would know which if he could see her eyes, but they were hidden behind sunglasses. At least she agreed to meet him. Must be curiosity.

He wasn't sure how much to tell her. Mardi knew she was still digging into the murder. He wasn't surprised. In college, when something piqued her interest, Amelia was like a methodological hoarder. She would collect seemingly endless amounts of information, gather it around her, and then start digging, shoveling away the extraneous or refutable until she found the answer. She was a hoarder with organizational skills.

But could he trust her?

"I was thinking of something a little stronger," she said as she eyed Mardi's iced tea. "Unless that's from Long Island."

Across the street from the Brick, Newtown's First National Bank's clock tower chimed five o'clock, as if signaling happy hour. A server appeared with a menu and a basket of pretzels.

"If it's too hot we could go inside," Mardi said.

"No, I like it here in the garden." She looked up at the server. "I'll have a Chablis."

"A draft beer, thanks," said Mardi. "We may order something more later." He wasn't sure how long their conversation would last.

Amelia moved her chair around the table until she was beside Mardi, instead of opposite him. They both now faced the street.

"I like to people watch," she said as she munched a pretzel.

He wasn't certain if that were true, or if she wanted to avoid eye contact. He grabbed a handful of pretzels. "My lunch. It's nice to see you."

"You, too. How's work? Your boss's interview in the paper was quite a PR bonanza for the police department. Any reaction to it?" Amelia asked.

The server reappeared with their drinks.

Mardi sipped his beer before answering. "Not to the article, but I did receive a complaint related to it."

"About what?"

"You."

Amelia laughed. "You've got to be kidding me!"

"Smith Phillips reported that you're harassing him."

"That's ridiculous! I simply asked him if he could tell me

anything about the party. He was there, and he owns the rental company that provided the linens and glassware."

"You told him you knew he ID'd Carter. I expected you to keep that information to yourself."

"Then you should have said it was confidential!" she snapped.

"Amelia, what are you doing?" Mardi leaned in closer to keep their conversation out of range of the guests at the next table who were now staring at them.

"You know what I'm doing. I'm trying to find the motive behind Michael Porter's murder."

"Helloooo!" Winnie waved to Amelia. She leaned her bike against the picket fence and ran onto the patio. "Hi!"

Amelia and Mardi looked up, unsmiling. "Is everybody in a bad mood today?"

"Sorry, Winnie." Amelia hugged her. "We're not in a bad mood; we were just in a serious conversation."

"Sorry, I didn't mean to interrupt. I'm on my way to my friend Jessica's house."

"Are you running into grumpy grown-ups today?" Mardi asked, holding out the bowl of pretzels to her.

"Oh, way more than grumpy," she said as she took a few pretzels. "I went to Miss Dunbar's store. The vase Mrs. Jenkins gave me broke, and Miss Dunbar said she could get a replacement. First, Miss Dunbar's assistant, Marc, I don't think he likes kids, yelled at me because I picked up a plate in the store. Then Miss Dunbar, who was OK at first, got mad about something. It didn't have anything to do with me," she added hastily, "and she kicked a box filled with packing peanuts. It made a total mess. Actually, that part was kind of funny. You should have seen the peanuts explode from the box. I helped her clean them up."

"It sounds like your behavior was the most grown-up of all of them," Amelia said.

"Thank you, and I did learn a little more about one of the items in my evidence box."

"Your evidence box?" asked Mardi.

"Yes, from the murder." She quickly looked around at the other tables and lowered her voice. "I searched the pantry and found a couple of things."

Mardi looked at Amelia. "There's certainly no lack of investigators on this case." He pulled out a chair for Winnie. "Care to have a seat and tell me what you found?" He was pleased with the diversion. Hopefully it would reset the tone of his conversation with Amelia.

"The most interesting thing to me was a silver toothpick. I'd never seen one before. Miss Dunbar knows a lot about antiques, and she said it's probably from the early 1900s. She thinks it was stuck in a crack in the floorboard for a long, long time. It probably belonged to Mrs. Jenkins's parents or even her grandparents. It's *that* old," she said.

"Doesn't say much about how tidy the Jenkins family kept the pantry over the last hundred years," mused Amelia.

"Doesn't say much about how well we searched the pantry, either," added Mardi.

"Oh, it was stuck in the crack between the brick floor and the wall," said Winnie. "I'm little, so I was able to scoot under the bottom shelf to inspect the area."

"Do you have any other evidence?" asked Mardi.

"I found a Buffalo Head Nickel and a button. Do you know if the murderer was missing a button? Maybe that's a real clue?"

"I'll check our files."

Winnie beamed. "Gee, that would be great. Will you tell me if it's connected to the murder?" She looked around again.

"I will, though I hope you haven't been involved in anything illegal," he teased. "I expect your fingerprints will be on it, and we'll have to run them through our database."

"You won't find my fingerprints. I wore gloves. Well, I better go." She hugged Amelia. "Bye, *Chief* Detective Mardi. I like your title. It sure sounds important."

"Ride carefully," Amelia called after her.

"I will." She waved and then pedaled onto Washington Avenue.

"Why does it matter that I told Smith I knew he ID'd Carter?" Amelia asked, turning her attention back to Mardi. "You closed your investigation."

Mardi sipped his beer. "Here's the thing," he began. "No one else at the party said they saw James Carter. It seems odd that Phillips, who was there for only an hour, remembered him. Said he was a server. It's unusually observant."

"That's what Elliott and I both thought," Amelia offered.

Mardi's frustration returned. "How many people have you discussed this with?"

Amelia looked chagrined. "Members of Bryson's Bike Club. It was the day Steve Bryson was run off the road. Smith was with us. After he snapped at me, I mentioned it to the other riders."

A stretch limo pulled up to the Brick and a group of young women piled out. One was wearing a bride-to-be sash. They made their way to a reserved section on the patio. Their laughter and chatter eased the tension.

"I didn't know it was confidential, Tony. I'm sorry." After a pause she added, "Are you concerned about Smith?"

"I'm more concerned about you. I'd rather you weren't pursuing this."

"You know me, Tony. The murder happened at my mother's house. How can I resist? What would you rather I do?"

"Have dinner with me."

37

Winnie kept checking her mirror. The van was still behind her. She noticed it as soon as she left the Brick Hotel. Now that she was on Sycamore Street, there was plenty of room for him to pass her; she even tried riding along the uneven shoulder, but she was afraid she would fall.

She took a deep breath. She was already almost a mile out of town. She should have turned off at the last intersecting road. There wasn't another one for at least a mile.

The van inched closer to her and then backed off. She had to get away from the van. She saw an oncoming car in the distance. Up ahead was a narrow patch of ground beside the road. Next to it were two large trees. She often pulled off there when she needed a water break. She pedaled faster, trying to reach it before the oncoming car passed her and the van.

Pedal. Pedal.

The van came closer.

Winnie hunkered down over her handlebars, abruptly pulled her bike off the road, and skidded to a stop between the two trees. The van couldn't react in time, and drove past her. Winnie immediately swung her bike around and pedaled back toward town. She knew the van couldn't turn around until the oncoming car passed it.

Winnie pedaled with all her might. Her legs felt like windmills. She could see a driveway just ahead. With a sudden jerk she turned into it. The house was dark. No one was home to rescue her.

She raced past the house into the backyard. *No fence! Please don't let there be a fence.* Liberty Street ran parallel to the road she had just left. It would take time for the van to drive to the next intersection and reach Liberty. It would give her time to hide.

No fence! No fence!

She kept pedaling past bushes and along a garden pathway. *Sorry. Sorry,* she whispered as she mowed down a row of flowers. *Almost there.*

She flew onto Liberty and immediately veered right into an alley behind a row of brick townhouses. On the right were the garages for each home; on the left an ivy-covered brick wall. Winnie knew that a narrow walking path ran along the other side of the wall flanked by a copse of pine trees. No vehicle could get through there.

She raced behind the wall and onto the path. The tree branches reached out to her, shielding her or threatening to knock her off her bike. She stopped midway, dropped her bike onto the ground, and jogged through the trees until she was closer to its exit on Washington Street, just blocks from the Brick Hotel.

"Amelia?" she whispered into her phone. *Please still be at the Brick.* "Amelia?"

"Winnie, what's wrong?"

"Help me. I'm behind the Washington Grove townhouses. A

van is following me. It's gray. Please come get me. I'm in the woods by Washington Street."

"Keep your phone on. I'll be there in a minute with Detective Mardi."

Winnie tucked herself into the boughs of a tree and clutched her phone.

A branch snapped behind her.

She could hear breathing. It was getting closer, but she couldn't move. She squeezed her eyes shut.

A warm, wet nose nuzzled into her and began licking her hand.

Winnie shrieked. The dog jumped back.

"Winnie! Winnie, where are you?" Amelia and Mardi raced through the woods.

"I'm here! Over here." She waved with her phone in her hand. A golden lab stood at her side. They were both panting until Winnie sank to the ground and buried her face in the dog's neck and wept.

"It was gray. A gray van. I think the driver is from Miss Dunbar's shop. I couldn't see him that well in my mirror, but I know it was a man. I think it was him."

"You're a very brave girl, Winnie," consoled Mardi. "Amelia will take you home."

"Can we get my bike? It's just over there."

Amelia walked with Winnie. The golden lab stayed at Winnie's side.

"Charlie!" a woman's voice called. "Charlie!" The dog bounded toward her. "You bad boy! How did you get out of the house?" She spotted Amelia and Winnie, whose face was streaked with tears. "I am so sorry, did Charlie scare you?"

"No, no," Amelia said quickly. "She just had a mishap with her bike. Your dog was actually very sweet."

With a shaky hand, Winnie patted the dog's head. "You're a good boy." Her voice quavered.

* * *

"Good evening, Miss Dunbar." Mardi strode into Dunbar & Co.

"Detective." She paused. "Markson, isn't it?"

"Mardi, Chief Detective Mardi."

"Oh, sorry. Yes, what can I do for you?"

"Do you own a gray van?"

"A van?" She laughed. "Me? You must be kidding. I drive a BMW. Why do you ask?"

"Is your assistant here?"

"Oh, Marc, he drives a van. He just returned from a delivery. What is this about?"

"We have a complaint about an incident. I'd like to talk to him."

"What kind of incident? He works for me, represents my company. What is this about?"

Mardi looked around the showroom. "Where is your assistant, Miss Dunbar?"

"Marc," she called over her shoulder. "Someone is here to see you."

A voice came from the back. "Who is it?"

Kirby turned her back on Mardi and yanked open the drape. "Get out here!"

Marc walked around Kirby. "Yeah?"

"I'm Chief Detective Mardi. You are?"

"What's this about?"

"I'm asking for your name."

"Oh for God's sake, it's Nelson," Kirby blurted out. "Marc Nelson."

Marc glared at Kirby. She returned the look. "If you've done anything to damage my business . . ."

"Miss Dunbar, please," demanded Mardi.

"I haven't done anything," snapped Marc. "What do you want?"

"Were you driving a van on Sycamore Street approximately one hour ago?"

"Yeah, what of it?"

"We have a complaint. A young girl on a bicycle said a van was following her."

"Oh please, *that*?"

"That?" yelled Kirby. "What do you mean *that*?"

"Mr. Nelson. We can go to police headquarters, if you prefer."

"No, I don't prefer. What did the kid tell you?"

"Why don't you tell me what happened."

"Nothing happened. Thankfully!" He turned to Kirby. "It was that girl who was in here earlier. She was riding her bike, weaving back and forth on the road. I kept trying to get past her. Then she suddenly pulls off the road and turns back in this direction."

"You didn't turn and follow her?"

"Why would I? I was trying to get around her!"

38

What had she done? She'd thought she could save Mikey's reputation by talking to the reporter. Now she had ruined both of their reputations. Why would anyone believe Mikey wasn't a drug dealer when she admitted that she did drugs—*used to* do drugs? Who would believe her instead of the police?

Carol Anne hadn't left her apartment since the article ran two days ago. Where would she go? Not to work. Who would want her to wait on them? She knew she'd ruined her life. She'd had one with Mikey. She needed to remember what she once had.

As she sorted through his belongings, Carol Anne felt like she was violating Michael's privacy. He should be the one going through them *with* her, especially this box. He called it his "treasure chest." It was filled with photos, mementos, and a couple of toys from his childhood. Her own memories were stored in a wooden hope chest that had belonged to her mother. Such a different approach to life: he kept treasures; she held on to hope.

Sometimes on a Saturday night after work he would bring a

pizza and a six-pack of beer home and they would play a game they called "My Life." They would randomly retrieve two things from their respective boxes and share their stories. Occasionally Mikey would retrieve an item from his box and study it quizzically, turning it over in search of a recollection, only to discover it was only a memory aspirant.

"It's just easier to throw stuff in a box and decide later if it's important," he would say in defense of his forgetfulness.

She picked up a light-blue braided ribbon. She knew this story. It was one of her favorites. She closed her eyes and listened for the knock on the door of her old apartment.

"Here, I got ya these." Mikey grinned sheepishly as he stood on her doorstep clutching a bunch of daisies wrapped in crinkly cellophane and tied with a light-blue ribbon. She held them tightly against her chest, their soft white petals nuzzling her chin as surprise and joy danced across her face. Mikey looked down shyly and did a slight shuffle on her doormat to brush off his embarrassment.

It was early in their relationship, and the flowers weren't for any special occasion, which made them very special. She arranged the daisies in an empty spaghetti sauce jar. She tied the blue ribbon around it. For the next two weeks, she gently trimmed the stems so they could sip the water that she refreshed daily.

When the flowers were gone and the jar recycled, Carol Anne repurposed the ribbon. She cut it into three pieces and braided it, the way her mother braided her hair when she was a little girl. She sewed a button on one end and knotted a loop at the other. A bracelet. She wore it constantly until last Valentine's Day.

"This one will last longer, Carol Anne," Mikey said to her as he unbuttoned the fraying ribbon from her wrist and replaced it with an enameled bracelet, sky blue and dotted with daisies. "Will you be my valentine?"

Her right hand instinctively, protectively, wrapped itself around the bracelet on her left wrist as Carol Anne stared into his box of memories—old keys, ticket stubs, and matchbooks. She tried to think of it as a junk drawer at a stranger's house; it would hurt less that way. She realized that she didn't know the story behind so many of these things. She wished they had played My Life more often, but then again, there was no rush; they had time.

She closed the box. Only its owner knew all the stories, but he was now just a memory, too. The souvenir of his life sat on Carol Anne's bureau—a small brown box containing his ashes.

It was time to play My Life again. She needed the story behind his ashes, behind why he was killed. She knew who could help her.

39

"What a nice place you have," Carol Anne said, clutching Michael's treasure chest as she stepped over the threshold into Amelia's house the next morning.

"Thanks," said Amelia. "It used to be a library."

"A library?"

"Yes. It was the town's library for almost a hundred years."

Carol Anne set the box on the dining table. "What happened to the books?" She scanned the living and dining rooms rimmed with bookcases that now held Amelia's personality.

"They moved to a new, modern building. This was an antique shop for a while, and then, appropriately enough, a bookstore. And then it sat empty until I bought it.

"My own books are in here." Carol Anne followed her into the adjacent room. "This used to be the library's youth section, and this"—she ran her hand along a shelf—"is the original spot where the library kept Nancy Drew books."

"It looks like they're still here." Carol Anne slipped *The*

Bungalow Mystery from the shelf and ran her hand over the blue cover, its title stamped in orange.

"I collect them. That's a first edition. 1930. I have editions from every decade."

Carol Anne scanned the shelf of Nancy Drew books, each decade reflecting its own design style and color, from periwinkle blue to the blue tweeds and now the more contemporary bright-yellow spines. "I like the pattern of the books grouped this way; it's like wallpaper," Carol Anne said.

They returned to the dining room. "Thanks for letting me come over. I know it would have been easier to show you his things at the apartment, but I needed to get out of there."

Carol Anne lifted the lid of the box. "I thought there might be something in here, maybe about Mikey's past. He called it his 'treasure chest.' I also included some things I found around the house like receipts and lists, just in case they mean something." She held up a plastic bag. "This stuff was in the drawer in his nightstand."

Amelia checked the receipts. "Are any of these unusual?"

"No. They're mostly for gas. His van is a gas hog, but we usually didn't have enough to fill it, so he stopped at gas stations a lot. He always kept an extra ten dollars hidden in the seat cushion as an emergency."

"Here's a receipt for fifty dollars. That didn't fill the tank?"

"That must have come from Jerry Baker. He'd fill the van up once in a while when they were on a job. Jerry was nice like that."

Amelia sipped her coffee as she watched Carol Anne clutch a piece of paper.

"It's hard to look at some of this." She showed Amelia the note. It was just a to-do list. Carol Anne's eyes welled. "Michael! It's Michael's handwriting. I need to call him Michael. My heart can't take hearing me say Mikey." She quietly blotted her eyes. "If I'm going to find out what happened to him, then I have to call him Michael. Michael is formal." She laughed gently. "And that wasn't Mikey."

For two hours Amelia and Carol Anne sorted through the box, searching for signs of a hidden life. If Michael had one, it was secreted far beyond their reach. The box revealed a simple, uneventful life and no hint as to why he was murdered. They replaced the lid.

"Shall we go?" Amelia said. "I can drive."

"I'm a little nervous about having lunch with your mom," Carol Anne said.

"Oh, don't be. She's been worried about you."

"That's music to my ears. I'm so ashamed I didn't tell her about my past."

* * *

Amelia tooted her horn twice as she pulled the car around to the side door at Twin Beeches. "Habit," Amelia said. "We always toot when we arrive."

"Carol Anne, I'm happy to see you." Louise hugged her and then turned to Amelia. "And you, too, darling."

"Glad you noticed me, Mom," Amelia teased.

Carol Anne blushed and stared at the ground.

"We'll have lunch outside."

The sun gleamed through the pergola and left bright, small squares on the flagstone patio, each framed in the shadow created by the geometry of the latticework. A gentle breeze was sprinkled with the twitter of birds tucked into nearby hedges. After lunch the birds would swoop in to nibble at the crumbs left from the crusty baguette that accompanied grilled shrimp over salad greens, the latter picked fresh from the garden that morning.

"I want to apologize to you again, Mrs. Jenkins. I'm sorry and very embarrassed. I'll never be able to repay you for your forgiveness and the comfort you have given me. I really believe the truth about Michael will come out. It just has to."

Louise paused and gently touched Carol Anne's hand. "Michael. It's easier to call him that, isn't it?"

"Yes." Carol Anne looked at her with surprise.

"I understand. After my husband died, I referred to him as Karl when I was making the funeral preparations. His middle name was Fritz. I thought it was more endearing, so he was Fritz or Fritzie to me. It took some time before I could use my nickname for him and not cry."

How does she understand me so well? Carol Anne wondered. "Mr. Jenkins must have been a wonderful man."

"Mr. Jenkins? Oh, you mean my husband? His last name was Keller. Jenkins is my family name. I kept it when I married Fritz."

"Like a celebrity," said Carol Anne.

Louise laughed. "Would you like to see a photo of him?"

"Yes, please."

"There are loads of photos of our family on the shelves to your right," she said as they walked through the patio doors into the study. "The large one in the center is one of my favorites. It's our wedding photo."

"He was very handsome," Carol Anne said, gently touching his face. "You were a beautiful bride, Mrs. Jenkins. And you look like your mom," she said to Amelia. She carefully replaced the photo on the shelf, polishing its silver frame with her shirtsleeve to remove any smudges.

"At least Michael died in a house filled with love. I guess it could have been worse."

"Carol Anne!" squealed Winnie. "I'm happy to see you. Are you doing OK?"

"I'm better and better each day."

"Mrs. Jenkins," said Winnie. "I just came in to tell you that Florence is ringing her bell. Can I let her in and give her a peanut?" She shook the tin.

"Do you know about Florence?" Amelia asked Carol Anne. "She's a squirrel, apparently somewhat trained."

"My little menagerie," said Louise. "I'm also considering getting a couple of herding dogs to round up the goats for me."

"You should get them from the shelter," said Carol Anne. "There are so many poor dogs with no one to care for them." Suddenly aware she may have insulted her host, she stammered, "Of course, I don't know if they have cattle dogs, and I bet they're wonderful. I didn't mean—"

Louise interrupted her. "You're right. That's exactly what we should do. What a kind and thoughtful suggestion."

Carol Anne blushed, but instead of staring at the ground, her default move when uncomfortable, Carol Anne lifted her eyes to meet those of Louise.

Louise smiled. "Let's go meet Florence," she said.

40

"Mrs. Jenkins is amazing," Carol Anne said to Amelia as they drove down the driveway of Twin Beeches. "Imagine, a squirrel named Florence. How funny."

"My mom is a unique individual."

Amelia stopped at the end of the driveway. "I just had a thought. Have you ever been to the Pineville Tavern?"

"No. But Mikey, I mean Michael, went there a couple of times with Jerry and the other guys."

"I want to talk to Jerry again. Do you want to go? Maybe he'll remember something if he sees you."

"Oh, he's never met me. I only heard about him from Michael."

"No problem. I'll run you back to my place for your car."

"No, I want to help, though I hope I don't break down again, you know, in front of other people." She removed two tissues from a box of Kleenex Amelia had in her car and stuffed them in her pocket. "I can do it."

As Amelia pulled into the parking lot of the Pineville Tavern, several smokers who were gathered at the end of the lot glanced up. Jerry was among them.

He ambled over to Amelia as she exited the driver's side. "You tryin' to become a regular here?" He laughed, his eyes twinkling with delight or sarcasm. "I'm heading back in myself. Can I buy you and your friend a drink? I owe it to you. I was a little full of myself last time."

"Jerry, this is Carol Anne Jackson."

Jerry stopped at the door to the Pineville Tavern. "Wait a minute. You MP's girl?"

Carol Anne attempted to smile but her clenched teeth only allowed a grimace to form as she moved her head up and down.

"Oh, man, I'm real sorry for your loss. You hangin' in there? Here, let me get the door."

A flurry of laughter and music slipped out before the door closed with a bang. "Do you want a table? Hey, Barb." He waved to the bartender.

"No, we're fine, Jerry. It looks like there's room at the end of the bar," said Amelia. "We wanted to talk to you about Michael's last couple of weeks."

Amelia glanced over at Carol Anne. Her face was expressionless, but her right hand gripped the strap of her leather shoulder bag with such intensity that her knuckles looked like hard, white marbles. She was hanging on to a lifeline.

"Uh, sure. I couldn't believe it when I heard about him and the drugs. It was on the news. That just about blew me out of my socks."

"He. Didn't. Do. Drugs." Carol Anne spit the words at Jerry.

Jerry raised his hands in surrender. "Whoa, wait, I'm with ya. I think it's a crock of shit. One of my guys used to call him 'church boy' 'cause he was so straight. Sorry"—he looked at Carol Anne—"but I'm telling you like it is. When we had drinks after work, he'd have a beer. One beer, that was it. I tell ya, I just don't believe it." He paused and looked at Amelia. "And I'm sorry I was such a jerk to you last time. Emily, right?"

"Amelia."

"Oh yeah. Amelia. Sorry." He grinned sheepishly. "Barb! He waved at her with one hand and made the motion of drinking a beer with the other. "Let me buy you two a drink."

The bar area was filling up with the smokers returning from their exile. Amelia chose the barstool at the far end; Carol Anne sat next to her. Jerry took the third stool, lifted it with one hand, and set it down opposite Amelia and Carol Anne, forming a triangle. "This will be easier to talk. So what do ya want to know?"

"When did you first meet Michael?"

"Must have been about six months or so ago. He was at Newtown Hardware. I was posting a notice on the jobs board. He told me he delivered a pizza to me once. I didn't remember that. I guess he was better than me at remembering names." He grinned at Amelia.

Barb handed Jerry his beer and set the other two on the counter. "Like I said, he worked for me off and on. He was a good worker, Carol Anne, real good."

"Recently, did he seem different or say anything about another job?" asked Amelia.

"Nah, he seemed like himself. He wanted to join my crew full-time, so he probably wouldn't have said anything about other work."

"He liked working for you," Carol Anne said and then quickly sipped her beer.

"That's nice to hear. Thanks."

"We appreciated those Phillies tickets. Those were good seats." She smiled.

Jerry paused for a moment. "Oh yeah, I forgot about that. I did give him a pair."

"Do you remember anything about his conversations while you were working?" Amelia was anxious to shift from reminiscing to remembering.

"I'm usually running around checking on the work, so I don't talk much with the guys other than about the job they're doing. At lunch it's usually about sports. Eagles. Phillies."

"Was he close to any of the others? Maybe talked to them more?"

"Nah, I don't think so. He kept to himself." He finished his beer and glanced at the clock behind the bar. "Listen, I gotta run in a minute." He handed Amelia and Carol Anne each one of his business cards. "I guess I'm not much help, but I am glad I met you, Carol Anne, and I'm sorry about MP. In my book he was a stand-up guy."

He motioned for Barb. "Put the beers on my tab. I'll be back in an hour. Can you hold the corner table? It's trip-planning night."

"Oh boy. Hope your destination is ready for you," Barb said.

"We wouldn't pick a place that wasn't. That's no fun."

"What kind of trip are you going on?" Carol Anne asked.

"My buddies and me are going to narrow that down tonight. There's five of us. We're all single and we go hunting or fishing, sometimes to Vegas for gambling. This trip we're thinking about is Grand Cayman. Fishing and scuba diving."

Barb laughed. "As well as drinking and carousing."

"Yeah, but we've got Officer Barnett. He's one of the original members, and he's got a badge. They take care of us, professional courtesy."

"I've seen the photos," Barb teased. "There's nothing professional about any of you when you're on vacation."

"Ah, we're harmless." Jerry grinned and winked at Carol Anne. "Don't listen to her."

41

"This reminds me of the old days," Mardi said as he picked an olive from the charcuterie tray.

Amelia had finally agreed to have dinner with Tony. She should have accepted his invitation to dinner at a restaurant instead of suggesting they cook at her place. It seemed like a good idea at the time. But now it felt awkward and too familiar. She also felt frazzled. She and Carol Anne stayed longer at the Pineville Tavern than she had expected. It had left her only forty-five minutes since they returned to her house and Carol Anne had driven off in her Escort. So much for a little downtime before Tony arrived.

When they attended the University of Pennsylvania, they would often cook together on weekends in his apartment when his roommate was away. Simple dishes, usually spaghetti. The day would begin with a trip to the Italian market in South Philly, where they bought fresh tomatoes, parsley, oregano, and maybe an eggplant. The next stop was Di Bruno's on Ninth for a hunk of parmigiano cravero, and then home.

The tiny alley kitchen was soon filled with the aroma of

sizzling garlic, tomatoes, and herbs. The steam from the pasta pot clouded the kitchen window. Amelia would use her finger and write "sauce" on the glass. Tony would draw a line through it and write "gravy." And so it would begin.

"What do you know about Italian cooking?" he would say. "You're Irish, German, and French. I'm pure Italian, and where I come from we call it gravy. Ask anybody in South Philly."

"Look at a menu in any restaurant anywhere and it will say sauce. Gravy is brown or beige, and you put it on turkey and mashed potatoes."

"My ma calls it gravy. My aunt calls it gravy. It's gravy."

Amelia would shake her head. "If you're ever out of town and order gravy with your spaghetti . . ."

"I'll make sure you're with me to translate."

Their relationship ended before she had that opportunity.

Amelia looked out her kitchen window at the pots of herbs on her deck. "Why don't we go outside; I need to pick some basil, thyme, and rosemary." She handed Mardi a glass of prosecco. "Cheers," she said as she nodded her glass in his direction, took a sip, and grabbed a small basket that hung from a hook beside the kitchen door.

Her herb garden was a collection of square terra-cotta pots of varying sizes grouped together in a stairstep fashion. The herbs gracefully drifted down the sides, a waterfall of fragrance.

"This was once the parking lot for the library, wasn't it?" Tony surveyed the deck and the lawn below it, a deep green rug of grass fringed with tiny white alyssum.

"It was once all asphalt," Amelia said as she pinched basil leaves, snipped sprigs of thyme, and dropped them into the basket.

"Quite the transformation." Mardi walked along the deck, down the three plank steps, and followed a flagstone pathway until he reached a corner of the property. Under a stately maple tree, dotted with hanging lanterns on its lower limbs, sat a wooden bench in the midst of a family of hostas.

Amelia walked down the steps to the rosemary plant on the patio. She paused and watched Tony. His familiar gait hadn't changed.

He suddenly turned and smiled at her. She quickly looked away, embarrassed that he had caught her watching him. He sat down on the bench, patting the seat beside him. "Care to join me?"

Flustered, she stumbled on the step. Basil leaves popped out of the basket and scattered at her feet. She hurriedly scooped them up and ran into the kitchen.

"I'll be out in a minute," she called through the open window, needing a few minutes to lose the rosy glow of humiliation. She rinsed the basil and set it aside for the caprese salad, minced rosemary and thyme for the steaks, and took several deep breaths and a sip of wine. Ready.

She heard footsteps on the deck. Mardi peeked in the kitchen door. "Maybe it's better if I come inside and help with dinner. I also need to open the wine I brought. It needs to breathe."

Once again they were side by side preparing a meal. When the prep work was done, Amelia set the table on the deck and returned to the kitchen.

"Shall I do the honors?" Mardi asked as he picked up a tray laden with marinated steaks and vegetables.

"Thanks. The grill should be ready. I'll finish up the salad."

"Cheers," Mardi said as they sat down for dinner.

"It's a perfect night to dine outside," Amelia said as she took a bite of the caprese salad. "I think I missed these the most. Jersey tomatoes. There's nothing like them. California may have wonderful produce, but they don't have Jersey tomatoes."

"They grow fine grapes though," said Mardi as he held up his glass. "This is one of my favorites. Rebel Roan from Carhartt in Los Olivos, near Santa Barbara. It's a Rhone blend."

"Los Olivos? I spent quite a few weekends there when I lived in LA. I always checked out the Carhartt Cabin for a wine tasting. Fun atmosphere, but serious about their wine."

"I order a case periodically. It's for special occasions."

When were you in Los Olivos?"

"Five years ago. May 15."

"May 15? It must have made an impression on you. I don't remember many exact dates, unless they're catastrophic, like 9/11."

"This date didn't start as a catastrophe. I planned a perfect weekend. Booked the Fess Parker Country Inn, rented a convertible, and asked a woman to marry me."

"Oh!" Amelia set down her wineglass. "She said no?"

"Worse, she said yes. We got married and then she dumped me a year later. Decided she didn't want to be married to a cop. Or she decided she wanted to be married to the Phillies first baseman. I don't know which decision came first."

"I'm sorry, Tony."

"I've moved on, and I'm enjoying the region's wine again." He paused. "And your company." He tilted his glass in her direction. "I thought about calling you when I heard you moved back here. You know, for old times' sake. Seemed awkward, though, so I let it pass."

"You were at the party."

"I was. Thought I might bump into you there."

"Were you ever at the house when Frankie Vincent owned it?"

He smiled. "Never legally. One of our officers managed to get himself invited to an occasional party."

"And?"

"And nothing. At least nothing out in the open, but there's no question that drugs were there. We were getting close, and then Frankie walked away."

"Did someone tip him off?"

"Don't know. Once in a while we hear rumors that he's been back to visit, but I doubt it. That would be a boneheaded move."

"Do you think there's any connection to the murder?"

"I've thought about it, but just because drugs are involved doesn't mean there's a connection. Vincent wasn't the only game in town."

Strings of small lights looped through the pergola swayed in the night's breeze. Amelia and Tony sat in silence, digesting their meal and considering where to take the conversation next. Amelia rose and gathered the plates.

"Why don't we have coffee and dessert inside," she said.

"Sounds great. Here, let me take those." He took the plates and followed Amelia into the kitchen.

Amelia sliced two small pieces of apple cake while the coffee brewed. "Ice cream?" she said as she opened the freezer.

"Not for me, thanks." Mardi patted his stomach and laughed. "I shouldn't even have had the cake. Hold on, is that Limoncello?" he asked, peering over her shoulder into the freezer.

"Yes, I thought we'd have a small one after the cake."

"A little *digestivo*. My family would be proud."

After dessert and coffee at the kitchen island, they carried glasses of Limoncello into the living room.

Mardi walked over to Amelia's collection of antique boxes. He noticed a square chestnut box, its corners inlaid with mother-of-pearl. "Didn't I give you that box?"

"Yes, you did." Amelia smiled, surprised that he would remember.

"I always thought it was odd that you wanted a box for a gift. Usually that's what the gift comes in."

Mardi joined Amelia on the sofa. "This is a nice evening, Amelia." He stretched out his legs and left them hovering over the coffee table. "May I?"

"Of course. It's indestructible." Amelia patted the carpenter's chest, its surface nicked and marred by missed hammer swings. "Its imperfections give it character. I like that about it."

They sat together in silence, sipping their drinks. Amelia was surprised by the ease; perhaps it was because of the intimacy they'd once shared.

"I have something to tell you," she said.

Tony turned to face her, hopefulness in his smile.

"I followed you to Core Creek Park."

His shoulders slumped. "I know."

"You know?"

"You're on tape."

"I am?" Her incredulity quickly turned to alarm.

"We sometimes record particular operations. It's good for training or documenting our actions. There's also a chance that someone in the crowd may appear overly interested. That's more the case with arsonists. They want to see their work, like moths to a flame. That day was both training and documenting. We fully expected to find a body in the van.

"So, Amelia . . ." Mardi smiled broadly. "We've got you on tape. Darting between trees like a ninja was particularly entertaining."

Amelia buried her head in her hands. "How humiliating!"

"I kind of admired your determination."

"A ninja? I looked like a ninja?" She laughed, trying to hide her embarrassment.

Mardi jumped to his feet and started jerking his body left and right as if navigating an obstacle course.

Amelia howled with laughter. "OK, OK, I get the picture." Still consumed with laughter, she retrieved her laptop. "Here, have a look. I'm not the only one in a video."

Mardi watched as Amelia's video scanned the parking lot then slowly moved down toward the dock. Mardi was standing on it, motioning to the divers. Slowly the van rose from the water. Mardi and the others walked around the van repeatedly. Someone removed an object from the back. The sounds were unintelligible, but the person dropped the item to the ground and walked away. Mardi returned to the van, stooped, and picked it up. He carried it to the water's edge.

"What's that in your hand?" Amelia asked.

Mardi remembered the fish drowning in air. "A fish. It was still alive, so I released it into the lake."

"Tampering with evidence?" Amelia grinned, though inwardly she was touched by his action.

"No, I didn't see the point of letting it die," he said tersely.

"I'm sorry," Amelia said. "I was just being a smart-ass. It was a very humane thing to do." She propped her feet on the coffee table, leaned them against Mardi's, and then quickly moved them away.

"Tony, do you still believe Michael Porter was a drug dealer?"

"The evidence says he was. I know you don't agree."

"Nope. You may be right about who murdered whom, but there's more to it. It just feels off, and I believe Carol Anne."

"I believe facts." He looked over at Amelia, knowing he had

just ruined the evening. “If any new evidence turns up, I’ll follow it.” Mardi finished his Limoncello and stood up. “I should go.”

Amelia followed him to the door. “It was a nice night.”

“Can we do it again?”

She gave him a quick hug and then backed away, not wanting her feelings to linger. “Yes, I’ll gather new evidence.”

“And if you don’t find any?”

“Oh, I will, but . . . it’s yes, even if I don’t.”

42

Stanley Wickham had refused to accept her resignation. He had given her time to collect herself after her interview appeared in the newspaper. That alone was a reason to return to work—he cared about her. But Carol Anne also needed the money. She had $2.12 in her bank account. Ready or not, she had walked back into the River's Inn.

It was a rough start. Saturdays were always busy. She mixed up the orders. She spilled water on a customer when refilling his glass, an amateur's mistake of not shaking down the ice in the pitcher before pouring. The couple that shared two appetizers received a bill for two lobster rolls, a Caesar salad, and a bottle of wine. She said "I'm sorry for my mistake" more often than "May I take your order?" But toward the end of her shift she was back in her groove, with only an occasional misstep. One couple even welcomed her back, saying they had missed her.

It was a good day until she returned to her apartment. Grief met her at the door as usual. It blocked her view from the kitchen window of the bright afternoon sky, blue with puffs of white clouds gently floating past. It pushed and shoved her in her bed as she attempted to take a nap. It had become an abusive roommate since Mikey died. Now it was stealing their things.

It already owned everything that once belonged to Mikey—his baseball glove, the posters that hung on the walls, even the sofa and lamps. When Carol Anne slipped her hand into his glove, searching for the imprint of his fingers, grief would give her a few moments of comfort and then rip it away. It was the same with all of Mikey's things. And now it was attacking her belongings. Carol Anne could barely look at the photos of her and Mikey or the gifts he gave her without grief pawing at her. She had to move. Her bank account told her she had to stay with this cruel companion. She knew that was impossible, as impossible as being able to move.

* * *

When she arrived at work the next day, her boss called her into his office. Carol Anne's default reaction was to assume he was going to fire her. Maybe too many customers complained. Instead, he asked how she was coping. She confided in him that she was managing but needed to move out of her apartment.

"Well then," Mr. Wickham said, "this is fortuitous timing, because the apartment in my carriage house next door is vacant." Carol Anne was sure the rent was beyond what she could afford, but he insisted on showing it to her.

A wooden staircase along the side of the carriage house led to a second-floor apartment, a charming space with open beams, stucco walls, and wooden floors. It had one bedroom and bathroom, a small living room, and a very spacious kitchen, which was anchored by a large oak farmer's table. It reminded Carol Anne of the table in her grandmother's house. As a child she would climb onto one of the ladder-back chairs and watch her grandmother knead bread and make jam.

"The ground floor is for storage for the restaurant," he said, "so there's no garage for your car, and you'll have to put up with delivery trucks unloading pallets of supplies, but it's nice up here. The furnishings are relatively new. My wife and I lived here while our house was being built."

It was just too good to be true. So it couldn't be. "I know I can't afford it, but thank you for showing it to me. Maybe someday," she said.

"I know what you earn," he said with a gentle smile. "If you like it, I want you to move in. You can pay a reduced rent for now. You deserve a chance to rebuild your life. I've seen you taking notes as the chef prepares dishes, while the other servers take a coffee break. You have a solid work ethic, Carol Anne. Let me help you. You can move in as soon as you want."

Carol Anne stared into the kind face of Stanley Wickham. She was afraid to blink; he might disappear.

43

Armed with a roll of packing tape and a Sharpie, Carol Anne scrambled from box to box, sealing them before she could change her mind. She was moving into the carriage house, of that she was certain. It was her decisions on what to take and what to donate that kept changing.

For two days, she filled boxes and then picked through them, moving items from the donate boxes to those she was taking with her. Mikey's things moved the most. She couldn't bear parting with them. She felt like she was giving him away.

What if the wooden bookends, carved in the shape of bears, had some special meaning? Or the guitar pick? He didn't play guitar, so why did he have it? Did someone famous use it?

His clothes were the most difficult. She nuzzled them, searching for his scent, afraid his memory had faded after she had laundered them. She slipped a few of his T-shirts in her "take with" boxes. She would sleep in them; sleep with him.

But the rest, she knew she had to let go. Each screech from the packing tape as she rolled it across the boxes began to sound less like a cry of pain.

The Salvation Army would arrive in the next two hours. She had to be ready. The old sofa, kitchenette set, and nightstands were clustered together near the door, waiting for the truck to take them to a new home.

"Your donations will go to people who have so little," Louise had reassured her on the first day, the most difficult day, of packing.

Carol Anne stacked the donation boxes on the dinette table. Most everything she and Mikey had was secondhand. She never considered that it might be worth anything to someone else. She felt generous.

She heard a knock at the door. "Here we go," she said to the boxes.

"Carol Anne?" Louise's lilting voice floated through the open window. "I've brought lunch."

"And me," Amelia chimed in.

Carol Anne hurriedly let them in and moved the boxes off the table.

"We have hoagies, iced tea, and"—Amelia held up two white waxed bags, each holding a dill pickle the size of a fist—"pickles!"

They gathered around the table. White deli paper rustled as they dug into lunch.

Louise surveyed the apartment, which now resembled a small warehouse of boxes. "It looks like you're about done."

"I am. All the Salvation Army boxes are ready. I just have a few more things to pack to take to the apartment," she said as she gobbled the last bite of her cheese hoagie, anxious to finish packing.

She reached for Mikey's baseball glove, hugged it, and slipped it over her hand. It felt warm, like holding his hand. She was reclaiming the things grief had tried to steal.

"When is your friend bringing his truck?" Louise asked.

"Who? Oh yes, around four." Carol Anne didn't know what to consider him. A friend? He was Mikey's boss.

The packing tape screeched as she sealed the final box.

"Thank you, ma'am, and God bless you," the Salvation Army volunteer said as he handed Carol Anne the pink donation slip. "With your help, we are doing the most good."

Carol Anne blushed. How different it felt to be on the giving end. She felt an abundance of pride for her meager contributions. She looked around the apartment's bare walls and at the small tower of boxes, far fewer than were riding in the back of the Salvation Army truck. She patted the top of Michael's treasure chest, assuring it that she was not abandoning Michael by giving so many of his things away.

"One guy and a truck, at your service." Jerry Baker bounded through the open door and then skidded to a halt at the sight of Amelia.

"Emily, no, Amelia! Damn, I'm bad with names. How's it going?"

"Hi, Jerry," Amelia said as she turned toward the bedroom. "Just checking to see if everything is packed."

"Jerry, this is Mrs. Jenkins," said Carol Anne awkwardly.

"Hello, ma'am. It's nice to meet you."

"It's nice to meet you, too, Jerry."

After an awkward moment Jerry turned to Carol Anne. "Is this everything?"

Carol Anne nodded toward the boxes.

"No problem. It'll only take one trip."

* * *

What's he up to? Amelia wondered. Carol Anne told her Jerry'd had lunch at the River's Inn a few times. Now he was helping her move? Amelia thought back to Tim Watson telling her about Jerry's unease, maybe even alarm, that Amelia was asking questions about Michael.

Amelia had learned a lot about the lives of Carol Anne and Michael as she helped fill cardboard boxes and sort through worn-out garments. The paucity of their belongings was evident as the tableau of the one-bedroom apartment was disassembled. Taken together, the furnishings, the books and knickknacks, the closets and cupboards gave weight and substance. But as closets were emptied and their belongings spread out on the floor, they revealed an inventory of scarcity. Mismatched cutlery and jelly jar drinking glasses, clothing with shiny patches on the elbows and knees from repeated washing and pressing, a frayed coverlet draped across a sofa cushion to hide a deep tear.

The apartment didn't reflect the life of a drug dealer, not even one just starting out in such an ignoble career. If the drugs and money the police found really belonged to Porter, surely he would have slipped a twenty from the wad of money now and again to splurge on a saucepan to replace the scratched and dented one with its broken handle of jagged plastic, or bought Carol Anne a new pair of slippers so she wouldn't have to wrap duct tape around the right foot to keep the sole from flapping open like a weary yawn. Amelia remembered when Carol Anne caught her staring at her slippers. "We're big fans of duct tape," she had said, blushing, "but always blue or neon pink. The gray tape is depressing."

Amelia never saw a flash of doubt pass Carol Anne's face in an unguarded moment as she pulled a box or bag from beneath the bed or from a closet shelf. Carol Anne was certain she wouldn't find anything to implicate Michael. He wasn't guilty. He couldn't be, except for the evidence saying he was.

"I think we're ready," Carol Anne said nervously to Amelia and Louise. Jerry was already at the truck, checking the straps that held her belongings in place for the ride to the new apartment.

"Call if you need anything." Louise hugged her.

"Are you OK to drive?" Amelia asked as she saw Carol Anne tremble when she closed the front door.

"This is hard," she whispered. She tugged on the door to make sure it was locked. Maybe the grief would remain inside. She smiled weakly. "I'll be OK."

Amelia and Louise watched as Carol Anne pulled her car in front of Jerry's truck and, with a brief wave, turned onto River Road.

44

Amelia had twenty minutes to get from Carol Anne's apartment to Tim Watson's house. She grabbed a Clif Bar out of her purse. Dinner would have to wait. His reaction when she called him surprised her; he invited her over, even after she told him she wanted to discuss Jerry Baker.

Amelia pulled up to a beautifully restored fieldstone farmhouse. She rechecked the address she had written down. *Maybe he still lives with his parents,* she thought.

"Thanks for inviting me over," she said as Tim led her through the foyer into the living room. The midcentury modern furnishings and cool gray and blue hues complemented the high ceilings, exposed beams, and wide-plank oak floors. And he had art.

A large vibrant yellow and cobalt blue abstract painting hung above the fireplace. On the opposite wall, a tall window framed a stone garden sculpture reminiscent of Henry Moore. The open floor plan stretched from the living room through the dining room and into the kitchen.

"You have a very nice place."

"Thanks." He motioned for her to take a seat on the sofa. "I bought it a year ago. My plan was to flip it, though I've gotten pretty comfortable here. Can I get you something to drink?"

"No thanks. I won't stay long. I only have a couple of questions."

"Shoot." He sat down at the opposite end of the sofa.

"Would you tell me again the conversation you overheard between Jerry Baker and Michael Porter?"

"Yeah, but I don't think I left anything out. I heard Jerry offer MP some extra work. Like I said, I remembered because I was surprised he didn't ask me first; he usually does. Then MP is killed, and Jerry gets bent out of shape when you talked to him about it."

Amelia looked around his living room. "You still take on odd jobs? It would seem those days are over."

Tim let out a guffaw. "Looks can deceive. I've done all the renovations here, bit by bit. If an odd job turns up, I'm not too proud to take it. I may be able to do the renovations myself, but I still need to pay for the supplies."

"I'm impressed. This is fabulous."

Tim casually draped his arm over the back of the sofa. "Jerry hasn't said anything about MP or the murder since then. But we've been busy. We're in the final stages of one job and shifting some of our time to the next project." He laughed. "I haven't been to the Pineville Tavern after work lately so I don't have any fresh gossip. Been too busy working on that." He pointed to the kitchen island. "I finished installing it yesterday."

From a rectangular skylight centered above, sunlight bounced off the mica embedded in the deep blue granite island. It sparkled like a night sky.

"It was a mother to install, but I'm real pleased with how it came out."

"You should be, it's beautiful." Amelia walked over to examine the island while trying to decide how to frame her next question. She couldn't come up with anything, so she went for the direct approach. "Do you know if Jerry socialized with Michael Porter?"

"Socialized? If beers at the Pineville count, then yeah." He snorted. "Jerry doesn't fraternize with us workers. He hangs with his own crowd. He invites the crew to join him for a drink at the Pineville. He's generous that way, but I think he does it so he can show off. He's a regular there. Why are you asking?"

"Jerry has visited Michael's fiancée, Carol Anne, at work, and helped her move into her apartment."

"You think they're hooking up?" Tim couldn't resist chuckling. "He dates a lot of girls, brags about it. Moving Carol Anne's stuff is way too—I don't know—sensitive? It seems out of character." He paused and then added, "What do you think is going on with Jerry and MP's girl?"

"I don't know. I just think it's interesting. Have you reconsidered telling the police about the conversation between Jerry and Michael?"

"Nope. I don't know for certain the job was for that night, only that he asked him that day. I don't want to jeopardize my job. I've got a mortgage to pay, you know." His smile was carefree but his eyes had grown dark, like the granite without the sparkle.

Amelia didn't know if he was uneasy or afraid.

45

"Amelia, welcome to New York." Elliott hugged his sister.

"I wasn't as convinced this morning when I boarded the seven fifteen train. Wow. What a view." Walking into his living room, Amelia felt like she was floating above the city. The open floor plan stretched fifty feet until it reached the windows. Two-story-tall panes of glass were filled with sky and buildings.

The furnishings were sleek with clean, minimalist lines. On the far right a solid wall painted slate gray held three original Ansel Adams black-and-white photographs of chiseled rock and falling water. Monuments of nature looking outside at the industrial landscape of buildings.

"These photos are exquisite," said Amelia.

"I once read that Adams preferred black and white because color could be distracting, diverting an artist's attention when taking a photograph," said Elliott. "And you know how I hate distractions. So how was your meeting?" he asked as they settled onto the leather sofa.

"Worth the trip. It was great to get together with Kathy Hacker, plus I finally get to see your apartment.

"Do you remember Kathy? We worked together at *The Bulletin*." Amelia glanced up as a helicopter flew in the distance. "I'm editing her book of essays. Initially it felt like she was doing charity work by offering me the opportunity. And maybe she is, but I am a good editor. It's the reporter part of me that imploded. How was your day?"

Better this afternoon. I wasn't thrilled over my call with Mom this morning. She said you two helped Carol Anne move to a new place yesterday. Why are you involved with her?"

Amelia bristled. "Because she doesn't seem to have anyone else to turn to, and Mom and I don't believe she or her fiancé were drug dealers."

Elliott shook his head.

"Elliott, I came here to see you. Let's change the subject. You said your afternoon was better. Tell me about it."

After an awkward silence, Amelia watched Elliott switch into business mode.

"I closed on the Whitmore Building in Midtown, another mixed-use project. Condos on top, retail below. I also might get involved in a residential project outside Newtown. I want to invest more in Bucks County properties. Richard Powell would be my partner."

Amelia arched her eyebrows. "Leslie Clark's husband?"

"Yeah, we're keeping it quiet for now. He's trying to close the deal before it's formally listed. It's a big parcel."

Amelia grinned. "So is your apartment. Did Kirby help you furnish it?"

"No. I used a New York firm, though she did find a few choice pieces for me—like that game table."

Amelia walked over to a square glass table surrounded by

four black suede chairs. A rectangular black suede box sat on the table. She lifted the lid. Inside, Monopoly playing pieces were tucked into a suede compartment—gold playing pieces. Amelia picked up the tiny top hat; its underside was protected with suede. "Well, this is a major upgrade from the game we played when we were kids."

She lifted the tray of playing pieces. "A silver Monopoly board?"

"Yep." Elliott laughed. "Kirby gave it to me for my birthday. You know I love the game; it's real estate."

"But sterling silver and gold? Don't tell me you play with real money!"

Elliott laughed. "Only in real life."

"What time do we need to go?" Amelia asked as she looked at her watch.

"About ten minutes. The helipad is only seven blocks away."

"Since Mom put goats in the field, where do you land Skip? By the way, I can't believe you gave your helicopter such a goofy name."

"You complain I'm too serious. Yet another example of you being wrong." He nudged her and laughed. "Ken Riess lets me land it on his property. Let me give you a quick tour of the apartment before we head out."

"I'd love it. The last time I was in New York you were still in a two-bedroom condo waiting for this to be completed."

"This is two bedrooms as well, but I also have a gym, terrace, and study."

"Elliott, this is beautifully done," Amelia said as they wandered through each room. "The kitchen is incredible. I didn't know you cooked." She laughed.

"I don't. At least not often. I cater. This kitchen is perfect for that. I host a fair number of client events and fundraisers. "You should come to one of my parties."

"I guarantee it, now that I'm on the East Coast."

As they walked back to the living room, Elliott paused. "Hang on, I forgot Kirby's suitcases." He walked out of the bedroom and set two suitcases by the front door.

"Is Kirby coming with us?" asked Amelia.

"No, she's staying in the city tonight. I'm bringing these back so she doesn't have to schlep them on the train tomorrow. She brought a load of fabric samples for a client."

"If your deal with Richard Powell goes through, will you spend more time in Bucks?" Amelia asked as they were driven to the heliport.

"Deal or no deal, I'm already spending about half my time there. Kirby's in Bucks most of the time, not to mention I like my place there, or I will if it's ever completed so I can move in."

Elliott's 1882 barn in New Hope, Pennsylvania, was structurally similar to his New York apartment in that it had big open spaces inside and out, but the views were significantly different. Instead of a steel-and-glass landscape, the barn's windows offered views of an apple orchard, rolling hills striped with grapevines, and a gently flowing stream. Ansel Adams probably would have preferred his photos hung in the barn.

46

"Ten grand? Why would Frankie leave it behind?" asked Smith Phillips as Robert D'Angelo removed a stack of money from his desk at the Travel Club.

Robert shrugged. "Who knows?"

"Where'd you find it?"

"In a hidden compartment in the pantry at Twin Beeches. It's nifty. Frankie got the idea for the compartment from a friend who owned a bodega in the city. Behind his counter he had shelves, and two of them were shallower but you wouldn't notice just glancing at them. He built a fake wall behind them. Stick a toothpick through a pinhole in the wall and it presses a button that releases a magnet. The wall comes loose and you've got a hidden storage space."

"What did the guy keep in it? Drugs?" asked Smith.

"Nope. Cigarettes. Buy them in Delaware; sell them in Philly. No taxes. He made a bundle until a cop noticed the discrepancy in the shelves. I think he was tipped off; who notices shelf sizes?

"The Twin Beeches version is better. Frankie told me his

nephew made it. I figured while we were at the party we might as well see what was in it."

"Do you know where Frankie went?"

Robert looked incredulous. "You're kidding me, right? You think he's gonna send me a postcard?"

"Just curious."

"We got what we wanted at the house." Robert waved the stack of bills in front of Smith. "This was a bonus. Talk about killing two birds with one stone."

"Poor choice of words."

Robert snorted. "Never was it so apt."

"That's cold."

Robert shrugged. "Hey, shit happens. What should we have done? Porter saw the money. He freaked. Left me no choice. There's nothing that connects us to him."

"Except that we were there that night."

"Yeah, but I was invisible. I'm not on the guest list, and I didn't talk to a soul."

Smith eyed him warily.

"Hang tight. It's foolproof. You saying Carter was at the party was a stroke of genius."

"As if I had a choice."

"Yeah, well, it worked. You said he was at the house, so he was at the house."

"Even though he wasn't. It's just another complication."

"It led the cops to the conclusion we wanted." Robert raised his index finger. "One, you said Carter was at the house. Two"—he raised the next finger—"the van was found in the lake with his fingerprints in it. That's real proof." He smirked. "Three, Carter OD'd on coke. Conclusion?" He wiggled his three fingers. "Carter killed Porter, drove the van into the lake, and then OD'd while celebrating. End of story."

Smith mirrored Robert's fingers, then lowered his index and ring fingers. "Or we're all screwed. Why bring Carter in after Porter was killed?"

"Sometimes you just need to improvise. Anyway, it's been more than a week since you said Carter was there and no one's questioning your statement. You made our problem disappear."

"Just call me Houdini."

"Here, Houdini, a reward." He handed Smith half the money. "And to sweeten the deal, I've got an unopened bottle of single malt scotch at the house. Let's go sit on my patio and have a drink."

47

Robert steered Smith's BMW into his driveway. "C'mon buddy, you're home. Get out here and I'll park your car in the garage." He removed the house key from Smith's key ring and handed it to him.

"Thanks, man." Smith clutched his key as he stumbled out of the passenger side, leaned against the car for balance, and then pushed off toward the front door.

It had been a long night of drinking—for Smith. After one scotch Robert switched to vodka. Smith stayed with scotch; Robert knew he would. What Smith didn't know was the vodka bottle was filled with water.

Robert drove the car twenty feet farther and parked it in the garage. With gloved hands he pushed the ignition switch to turn off the car and grabbed the key ring from the console and a duffel bag he had thrown onto the back seat. He hit the automatic garage door button and dashed under the closing door, almost losing one of his shoe covers.

Robert remained by the garage, watching Smith's failed attempts to unlock his front door.

"Wheresh the lights?" he heard him say as Smith swayed against the railing, barely catching himself from toppling over. Turning and bracing his back against the front door, he tried to steady himself.

"You're schhpossed to be on," Smith mumbled to the lamp-post. He pushed off against the door, hovered briefly, and fell back again. "Son of a—" He grabbed the railing, swerved to and fro as if slow dancing, swooned, and fell face-first down the steps.

Robert still didn't move. The closest house was a hundred yards away, so it was unlikely that anyone heard them, and there was no need to rush. He could wait.

No lights, no movement. It was time to finish the job.

He walked over to Smith and nudged him with his foot. Nothing. He removed a tarp from the duffel, spread it out on the walkway next to Smith, and rolled him onto it. He found the house key on the walkway, reattached it to the key ring, and dropped the keys onto the tarp. He dragged the tarp along the paved walkway to the back of the house.

He crossed the patio and continued along a path that led to a wooden dock with two Adirondack chairs and a small table in between.

The Delaware River swirled around the dock's posts, creating neat, concentric circles. Robert dragged the tarp onto the edge of the dock. On the arm of one of the chairs he put Smith's keys and wallet. The five grand he had given him was now back in Robert's possession. *No point in wasting good money,* he thought. He lifted one of the life jackets off a hook on the side of a wooden shed and slipped it over Smith's left shoulder. Then he removed an almost empty fifth of scotch from his duffel bag, the same bottle from which Smith had poured shots all night. He unscrewed the top and dropped it and the bottle into the canoe, which was on the river's bank. Robert removed one of the paddles before sliding the boat into the river's current. It floated away into the darkness.

He wrapped Smith's right hand around the remaining paddle handle and then placed that paddle next to the tarp. He tilted the tarp until Smith slid facedown into the water. Robert used the paddle to push Smith into the current. Smith's left arm, held afloat by the life vest, appeared to be waving goodbye. Robert dropped the paddle into the water and waved back.

He folded the tarp, returned it to the duffel, and retraced his steps. As he passed each of the three backyard light sensors, he stood behind them and screwed the LED light tightly into its socket. When he reached the front path, he did the same to the bulb in the lamppost.

He waited another ten minutes. Not a sound. He raised his cell phone aloft and turned on the flashlight app for three seconds. He heard a truck approach; it was invisible in the darkness.

Robert tossed the duffel bag in the back and climbed into the passenger's seat. Even the interior light didn't go on. Robert had been very clear with his instructions.

"Thanks," he said. "You can turn on your headlights when you pull onto River Road."

Robert remembered Smith saying, *"Just call me Houdini."* Robert almost laughed when he said it. Smith's comment would have been prescient if it hadn't been a myth that Houdini died by drowning. He stared out the passenger window. They were driving parallel to the Delaware River. He wondered if Smith's body had passed them yet.

"We need to stop at the dump before you take me to my car."

The driver clenched the steering wheel.

After disposing of the duffel bag there, they arrived at Saint Mary's Hospital. "Go around back to the dumpsters."

Robert tossed the gloves and booties into one of them, thinking how ironic it was that the same protection he used while killing Smith kept others safe from contamination and disease. He reached for the bottle of Purell that was in the console of the truck. "Do you mind?" He held up the bottle.

"Help yourself."

"Thanks. Hospitals give me the creeps. All those germs. My car's in Lot C. I believe our work here is done."

"This got way too complicated."

"We had to improvise."

"Improvise? It was a trainwreck."

"We got what we wanted. Too bad for Smith. If he'd kept his cool about lying to the cops about Carter, he'd be sharing in the riches. Some of us can improvise, others can't. Those who can't become collateral damage."

"Man, you've got balls."

"Hey, trust me, this will all go away."

"How do you know?"

"If I told you, I'd have to kill you."

"That's not funny."

"True."

"What's true?"

"That it's not funny. Stay copacetic. I got your back."

"You better."

Robert grabbed his arm. "Smith panicked. I handled things. If Smith admitted to the cops that he lied about seeing Carter, then their obvious follow-up would be, *Why*? Which would lead to *who*, and the *who* is what would have gotten us into trouble. I tried to get him to chill."

"Your drive-by warning during the bike club ride was not something that said 'chill.'"

"That, my friend, wasn't about Smith. Hey, man, you need to chill."

"You need to stop killing people. That was never in the plan."

Robert eased out of the truck, casually jangling his car keys. "No worries, bro. No blood got on my clothes this time." He laughed and strolled to his car.

* * *

The truck pulled onto Langhorne Yardley Road toward Newtown. A couple of blocks later, the driver realized that the car following him was a police cruiser. He glanced over at the passenger side of his truck. Anything incriminating? *Nah, buddy, you already dropped off the murderer.* He checked the speedometer; he was doing thirty in a forty-five mph zone. *That's gonna get you pulled over faster than if you were speeding.* He accelerated and entered Newtown. *Slow down, it's twenty-five here!*

And then it happened.

The cruiser's lights came on, washing the truck in blue and red, mostly red, bloodred. He felt like his truck was filling with blood. His hands clenched the steering wheel as he jerkily pulled over. The streetlights were pixelating, there was a whooshing sound in his ears, and his chest heaved as he gasped for air. He was going down. He punched his chest. *Breathe. If you pass out, the next scene will be you in Saint Mary's with cops firing questions at you.*

He slowed the truck to a stop.

The cruiser raced past him, its siren wailing.

He opened his door and threw up in the street. This was the last time improvisation was going to play the lead role. It was time to take control.

48

The door opened into an oasis of calm.

"I'm so happy to see you," Carol Anne gushed as she invited Louise and Amelia into her new apartment.

Carol Anne wore a simple T-shirt and blue jeans, her blonde hair pulled back in a loose ponytail. Amelia remembered their first meeting—Carol Anne's slumped shoulders, jeans barely able to hang on to her slender hips. Today her clothes were still simple, her jeans still loose, but she displayed confidence. It was a new look for Carol Anne. And a new role. She had invited them to lunch despite the fact that she had moved only two days ago.

The foyer opened to the living room. Its honey-colored oak floors, stucco walls the color of buttercream frosting, and furnishings perfectly proportioned to the small living space were dressed in shades of wheat, milk, and gosling feathers.

"Would you like to see the apartment first? You won't believe how beautiful it is. I mean, it's a little messy because I still have some boxes to unpack, but, well, since I didn't have that much stuff, it's not taking too long."

Louise squeezed her hand. "It was very generous of you to invite us. Lead the way."

"OK, so this is the living room. Of course, that's obvious," she added awkwardly. Between the white slipcovered sofa and a pair of upholstered chairs was a coffee table, a former piano bench painted the color of cappuccino foam. On it was a plastic cafeteria tray, which held a bouquet of daisies in a Mason jar. It had been Michael's TV tray until Carol Anne moved in with him and insisted they eat dinner together at the dinette table.

The living room was light and airy despite its small size. Two windows fronted Main Street and a third on the adjacent wall, surrounded by built-in bookshelves and a window seat, offered a pleasant view of a magnolia tree.

* * *

Amelia noticed that Carol Anne had stacked Michael Porter's treasure chest and her hope chest against the wall between the two front windows. On top were Michael's baseball glove and a candle. It reminded Amelia of a church altar. She wondered if that was intentional.

Louise walked over to the window seat. "This would be my favorite spot. It's a perfect place to read." She smoothed the fronds of a large fern hanging from an exposed beam nearby. "A nice Davallia fejeensis."

Carol Anne and Amelia looked at her blankly.

"The rabbit's foot fern?" Carol Anne asked.

"Davallia fejeensis is its botanic name. I always liked its furry feet. They're called rhizomes; basically they're the plant's roots. They like a lot of humidity, so make sure you spritz it regularly."

"I will. I just got it yesterday. It was a housewarming present from Michael's boss."

"Jerry Baker?" asked Amelia.

"Yes. He has been so nice to me. He came to the restaurant for lunch and brought me the plant. He said he got it because rabbit's feet are supposed to bring good luck, and since that's what these, um, rhizo"—she paused—"these roots look like, he thought that would make a good gift."

"That was very nice of him," said Amelia, trying to hide her unease.

Carol Anne led them through the short hallway to the bedroom. Amelia recognized other items from the old apartment. The poster of sunflowers mounted on foam board was propped against the wall. The worn navy-blue-and-white quilt that had faded into shades of evening covered the bed. At the foot lay a carefully folded down comforter.

Carol Anne gently patted its puffy surface. "This came with the apartment. It's beautiful, but I want to sleep under the quilt we had."

Louise leaned over the bed and picked up the stuffed bear, hugged it, and then carefully tucked it back between the two bed pillows.

"Through that door is the bathroom, and guess what's in the hall closet?" Carol Anne flung open the double doors. "A washer and dryer! No more Laundromat for me. It's incredible. And now on to my favorite room, the kitchen."

She opened every cupboard and drawer. "This kitchen has everything. A microwave, gas stove, a blender, toaster oven, and lots of dishes and glasses and even napkins. And they all match." A wooden block on the granite counter held a set of knives; next to it an earthenware jug sprouted a bouquet of wooden spoons.

"Even when I make scrambled eggs I feel like I'm on the set of Martha Stewart's cooking show," she exclaimed. Her face flushed, but it wasn't embarrassment; Carol Anne was beaming.

Her once sullen cheeks were plumped like ripe cherries balancing on the ends of her smile.

"Are you ready for lunch?"

"Carol Anne, your table looks beautiful!" exclaimed Louise. The table was set with pale-blue placements and crisp white linen napkins.

"Please sit down. I'll bring the food. It's a lemon chicken with pine nuts and seasoned with lavender salt. Can you believe it? Lavender is in the salt. And there's potato salad with fresh herbs in it, not the dried stuff in jars. It's all from the restaurant. Mr. Wickham wanted me to treat you."

Amelia took a seat across from Louise. Carol Anne set a plate on each placemat and then took her seat at the head of the table.

A cluster of small clay flowerpots formed the table's centerpiece. Each one sprouted daisies, begonias, or violets. A ladybug sat on one of the begonia's leaves.

"They're cakes!" Carol Anne beamed. "Buttermilk cake topped with crumbled dark chocolate, so it looks like dirt. The flowers are made of icing called fondant. The ladybug was my idea. We're making them for a special party a garden club is having at the restaurant. Jacqueline, the restaurant's pastry chef, is letting me help. She said you could sample them if you gave her feedback. There is a special guest coming all the way from England, so we want them to be perfect."

"Well, isn't this exciting. These are such dear little things," mused Louise. "I almost don't want to eat them."

Carol Anne picked up a daisy pot. "This one is to take home. It's for Winnie. I buried a gummy worm in the cake batter."

"Cheers to you, Carol Anne." Louise held up her iced tea.

"Thanks." She dug into her food.

"It sounds like you're working a lot," said Amelia.

"I am. It's good because I don't feel so alone. Sometimes after my shift I go for a walk and think about Mikey. I tell him not to worry about me, and also that I know the police are wrong about him."

"It's good to tell him that. I'm sure it's a relief for him to know you're doing OK," said Louise.

"You don't think it's crazy? I mean, I don't talk out loud, but I do feel sure that he's with me."

"Of course he is. Some people are just afraid of it, or maybe they can't tune in to those moments. If they did, they would have lovely conversations."

They ate in silence, Amelia wondering how she was going to broach the subject of Jerry Baker.

"You know what the hardest thing is?" Carol Anne said as she finished her last bite of chicken. "I feel guilty that my life seems to be better since Mikey died." She bit her lip. "It's hard for me to even say that, but it's kinda true. I mean about the material things." She rubbed the daisy bangle bracelet on her arm. "I would trade it all right now if it would bring him back."

Louise reached for Carol Anne's hand. "Let people help you. You were an innocent victim in a terrible tragedy."

"Mikey was, too. I'm sorry, I know I should be thankful for what everyone has done, especially you and Amelia. And I am forever grateful. It's just that I miss him so. It hurts and I'm afraid I'll forget him if I don't keep the hurt, the missing him.

"I'm also kind of angry. Not just at the guy who killed him but at the police. They don't believe me about Mikey. But Jerry tells me that I would know better than anybody if Mikey was involved in drugs. He believes me."

"He's been a good friend to you, hasn't he?" Amelia said.

"He has. I never met him when Mikey worked for him, and I assumed he was a lot older, you know, having his own company and all. But he's not much older than me, though he's smarter about things. I guess that's why he's so successful. When he comes in for lunch, some of the other waitresses flirt with him," she said.

"Is that awkward?" Amelia asked.

"Awkward? You mean them flirting with him? Of course not." Carol Anne looked at Amelia wide-eyed. "Oh, he's not a boyfriend or anything like that. I couldn't do that; it would be cheating on Mikey," she stammered.

"I'm sorry, I didn't mean to embarrass you."

"I don't want you to get the wrong impression. He was Mikey's boss, and he said he wants to help me. He told me he had challenges, too, so he knows how important it is to have people around who look out for you. He asked me if that was OK, and I said yeah."

"Perhaps we're being overly protective of you," said Louise.

"It's good to feel like someone is looking out for you," Carol Anne said. "It's kinda strange to say, but it's like your family, you know, the Samuels. When I'm at your house, I get the feeling they're watching over everybody in a protective way. You and Amelia and, I think, maybe Jerry are doing that for me in real life. It's nice."

49

Winnie sat on the window seat in Louise's study, her legs dangling outside. Amelia and Louise were rearranging plants on the patio directly below her.

"Did you have a nice lunch today? Is her apartment nice?" Winnie asked.

"It's lovely," said Louise. "I think Carol Anne will be very happy there."

"Her flowerpot cake is delicious. A perfect after-school snack," she said, leaning out over the windowsill. "Don't worry, I won't get any crumbs on the cushions. Do you think Carol Anne's boyfriend was a drug dealer?"

Amelia and Louise both abruptly turned toward Winnie.

She popped a fondant daisy into her mouth. "It's impossible to think of Carol Anne and not think about the murder. The evidence says he was, but do you believe it?"

"No, I don't," admitted Amelia, "though my opinion is compromised."

"Because you like Carol Anne?"

"Because I believe Carol Anne's account that Michael helped

her overcome a drug addiction. And if I believe that, then it's difficult to imagine he was a drug dealer. One behavior doesn't support the other."

"Then why was he murdered?"

"I don't know. I don't even know why he was here."

"I need to get my journal." Winnie climbed back into the study.

She reappeared on the patio minutes later. Louise and Amelia were relaxing on chaise lounges. Winnie sat down on the edge of Amelia's and paged through a vivid pink Moleskine notebook. "There are so many gaps, I must know more. I was at the party the whole time."

Amelia smiled at her. "We all were."

"But how could someone commit a murder and nobody notice? There were people everywhere."

"That's part of the problem. With so many people it's easy to blend in, either as a guest or as someone working at the party. And he committed the murder behind closed doors."

"It's like a play," Winnie said. "Everyone had a part, everyone wore the right costume. There was music playing, people talking, and lots of distractions. The murderer strikes and then walks out of the house and drives away. Kind of a perfect crime."

Winnie paged through her journal. "I wrote down everything I could think of about that night. It's for my writing class assignment. I wrote the first draft, but it's not complete yet." Her smile hinted at embarrassment. "I thought maybe I could solve the murder before it was due."

"That's certainly a unique topic for a class assignment," said Louise.

"We were told we could write about anything. Mine is mostly about how grown-ups don't really pay attention to kids at parties.

Hmmm, that's what I just said about murderers, too. That's pretty weird. Anyway, my story is called 'A Kid at a Cocktail Party.' The murder is my surprise ending. Do you want me to read what I have so far? It's not that long."

"We're all ears," said Amelia.

Winnie stood up to face both of them, cleared her throat, and began:

"I have attended several big parties at my house."

Winnie paused and looked at Louise. "I know it's not my house, but I wanted my prose to be simple."

"It's your house, too. You live here."

Winnie smiled and continued.

"A good party is a feast for the senses: the food, the outfits, perfume that either smells delicious or gives me asthma. But the conversations that adults have are the most fun.

"As a kid, nobody notices you. Mainly because you're shorter, and they're too busy looking around the room to see who it is they want to talk to instead of the person next to them. They never look down in search of a conversationalist. Basically, kids at parties are ignored and it's great. We can move through the crowds without much notice and listen in on all sorts of conversations. Even though some parties can be kind of snooty, it's important not to be intimidated."

Winnie looked up. "I hope you don't mind that I said that. It wasn't really all that snooty, but if someone my age was experiencing this for the first time, I'm sure they would feel that way. I'm appealing to my reader."

"Lots of shiny fabric and sparkles, probably diamonds but you never know. Cubic zirconia is hard to tell from the real thing."

"These are just notes. And I have a few photos that I can refer to when I write this part."

"The food is always great. Lots and lots of hors d'oeuvres. They're my favorite. I wish every meal could be hors d'oeuvres, except for breakfast. I love

waffles. But hors d'oeuvres are the highlight for a kid at a party. You can eat whatever you want and no one notices. Waiters walk around all evening carrying trays of deliciousness. Shrimp cocktail, crab claws, puff pastry filled with tasty stuff, and my most favorite of all—dessert! There are always plates and plates of chocolates, tarts, tiny cakes, and petit fours. The best part is adults rarely eat them because they're always watching their weight.

"I never wait until the end to have dessert. I eat it in between the shrimp and chicken satay, though sometimes I have to be patient because they don't put the desserts on the table until later in the evening. In fact, at my last party, I almost got caught taking some petit fours before they were supposed to be served. I thought no one else was in the room until I heard footsteps behind me. I quickly ducked under a table.

"It was two men. Even though the men were guests at the party (I could tell because they wore dark suits and shiny black shoes) and should have been having a good time, they were in bad moods. One of them couldn't find his wife or girlfriend (if they came together, how did he lose her?) and the other just stood at the table I was under, drinking something. I could tell because he kept clunking the glass on the table. I heard him say he wanted to leave soon. Hard to imagine why they even showed up.

"Advice to adults: if you're going to go to a party, think like a kid. Have fun and eat the food or stay home."

Amelia couldn't stop laughing. "Winnie, you should write a Miss Manners column."

Winnie smiled. "Thank you. I'm almost at the end of part one."

"There are also fancy cocktails and wine, too. Usually the more guests drink the funnier they become, even when they don't mean to be. When that happens someone always says, 'Oh, don't listen to her; it's the alcohol talking.' Alcohol never had a chance to say anything at this party. There wasn't enough time. Why?

"Because someone was murdered AT THE PARTY! Yes, a real-life murder! It was so exciting to be a kid at the scene of a crime.

"End of part one."

Winnie looked at Amelia and Louise. "This is a kid's point of view. I hope it's not offensive."

"Of course not. Where does your story go next?" asked Louise.

"Well, I have my notes about the police questioning me, and that could be interesting, though I don't like that the police investigation ended with Michael being a bad person. I guess I would have accepted that if I hadn't gotten to know Carol Anne, but now Michael seems more real, and it sounds like he was nice. I was hoping that maybe he would turn out to be a hero of some sort."

50

It was early evening when Amelia returned home. She sat cross-legged on the sofa in her loft, her laptop balanced on her lap. To her right was her favorite architectural detail, the semicircular window that rose from the floor about a third of the way to the ceiling. Its six panes of glass formed a fanlight over the front door, a Romanesque feature that reminded her of the sun rising. From her perch in the loft she had a bird's-eye view of Maple Avenue.

She thought back through the years when her home was still a library, and she sat up here doing homework at a long library table. The window served as a lookout for friends, their heads bobbing as they climbed the steps to the front door. She and her classmate Susan often studied there together. Amelia usually got there first. Susan would climb the steps and look up at the window. Amelia would let her know she was there by slipping off her shoes and wiggling her toes in the window. Feet in a window seemed so funny then.

This loft space was still a reference room of sorts. But instead of shelves laden with encyclopedias and maps of the world, it held a sofa and two upholstered chairs. A large television hung above a set of lateral file cabinets. There was little in them. Her laptop and two external hard drives held most everything she needed, including her notes on Michael Porter's death.

She looked down through the window again and then back at her watch. Mardi was late, only by twenty minutes, but he should have called.

The front gate clanged shut. Mardi ambled up the walkway carrying a large bag.

"Sorry I'm late. I stopped for snacks," he said as Amelia opened the door to him.

"And wine." He smiled.

Amelia did not return the smile.

"What? What's wrong?" he asked.

"Nothing." Except that her heart was racing.

"Are you all right?"

"I'm fine. I thought you were just dropping by."

"I am." He paused and looked at her quizzically. "With food. No ulterior motive, just snacks. You asked me over. Remember?"

"Of course I remember," she fumed.

Mardi followed her to the kitchen. Amelia opened the refrigerator, pulled out a bottle of water, and sat down at the island.

"Amelia." Mardi looked down at her hands gripping the water bottle. "You're going to crush it. What's wrong?"

She knew what was wrong. Kevin Morgan. The bastard. He also showed up at her door with bags—dinner and the Tripoint files. Amelia thought it was all real, Kevin's feelings for her, his gift of an explosive article for the *Times*. He used her. She never saw it coming.

She released her stranglehold on the bottle and pushed the bag of groceries toward Mardi. "I'll be right back. Help yourself to whatever you brought." She walked out of the kitchen adding, over her shoulder, "I'm fine."

* * *

The house was silent, except for the ticking of the tall case clock. Mardi had barely noticed it in his previous visit, which had been filled with conversation and laughter. The ticking was just a rhythmic addition; its marking of the time could be easily overlooked. But now its sound filled the air, punctuating the tension. Tick, tick, tick. He opened the kitchen window, hoping birdsong or even a lawnmower could distract him from the metronomic pulse.

Amelia had called him earlier in the day. She wanted to talk to him about Jerry Baker. Mardi stopped for food and wine on the way, a ploy to stay longer.

He heard footsteps. Amelia walked down the hall toward the kitchen. She set copies of the *LA Times* on the counter, the top featuring the suicide of the CEO of Tripoint. "I caused this, and your bag of groceries brought the whole ugly incident back into my life."

"Amelia, I . . ."

"No, listen to me! I was investigating the embezzlement of funds from *this company.*" She jabbed her finger at the word "Tripoint" in the headline. "My source was Kevin Morgan. I was in a relationship with him and didn't tell my editor. A minor faux pas," Amelia said sardonically. "Someone else should have taken over the story, but I couldn't let it go. I believed everything Kevin told me. I even quoted him in my articles, the most egregious violation of my myriad conflicts of interest.

"So the CEO dies and I lose my job. Your bag of groceries, well, it was a surprise. I mean, not a surprise that you brought groceries, though I didn't expect it." She stumbled along. "It was a surprise that they were such a trigger point for me." Amelia inhaled deeply. "When I was working on the Tripoint story, Kevin would come to my apartment. He would show up at my door with two bags—in one was dinner, the other confidential files from the company."

Mardi sat down opposite the newspapers. Amelia picked up the bottle of water. This time she opened it and drank. They sat in silence as Mardi read the first article. The suicide. He noted Amelia's byline was not there; she had already been fired. But he knew this. He knew all about what had happened in LA, except her relationship with Kevin Morgan.

"Well, there's a lot more in my bag of groceries than I intended," he said hesitantly, not wanting to make light of the situation, but also needing to restart the conversation, in part because the ticking of the clock was becoming unbearable.

"I'm sorry. This is my issue," Amelia said.

The clock began to chime; Mardi jumped.

Amelia laughed. "I love that clock. It knows how to move on."

"I don't know how you stand it."

"I don't even hear it anymore." As if on cue the chimes stopped, and the clock gonged seven times. "I do notice that," she said, laughing. "I turn it off at night. I'm enough of an insomniac as it is. I don't need my clock to count out the hours for me."

She reached for the brown bag. "Let's move past my PTSD episode. What did you bring? And please tell me there's no sushi in the bag. That was Kevin's go-to meal."

"Italian, of course. Give me a platter and I'll have an antipasto spread ready before you can say *gravy*."

* * *

"Never going to happen. It's sauce." Amelia was back on familiar ground. "So tell me about Jerry Baker." She opened jars of olives and pepperoncini. "Did you know he has a drug conviction?"

"Of course. Why are you looking into his past?"

"Because of his interest in Carol Anne Jackson. He's visiting her at work, and he helped her move into her new apartment."

"Maybe there's an attraction."

"She's not his type."

"According to you?"

"According to people I've talked to, but that's beside the point."

"Actually it's not beside the point, Amelia. It *is* the point. What's your endgame?"

"My endgame? Prove Michael Porter wasn't a drug dealer."

"You're investigating with a foregone conclusion. That's a dangerous approach."

"OK, I overstated my motive. I want to find out if Michael really *was* a drug dealer. And right now I think Jerry Baker's behavior is suspicious. He was busted for coke. Maybe there's a link."

"We interviewed him after the murder; there's no apparent link, other than Porter worked for him. He was cooperative."

"The first time I talked to him he was far from cooperative."

"There's a difference between a police officer talking to him and you asking questions."

Amelia ignored him. "Jerry agreed to meet me at the Pineville Tavern, and then he was pissed off when I showed up. He humiliated me, so I flipped him off when I left."

Mardi broke into a broad grin. "I would have loved to have seen that."

Amelia filled her plate with Italian meats and cheeses. "More wine?" She held out the bottle.

"Thanks."

"Also, Jerry Baker warned his crew not to talk to me."

"How do you know?"

She swallowed and took too large a sip of wine. "Someone mentioned it to me. He said Jerry was worried that any publicity could hurt his business."

"That's a legitimate concern."

"Yeah, but it doesn't feel right. There's something else going on. I just don't know what it is."

"Amelia, I know you're not going to give up on this pursuit of yours."

She shot him a look.

"Wait, don't get defensive, just hear me out. People don't like being questioned, even unofficially, about a murder. Just be careful."

"So you think there's more to this?"

"I think you're on a quest to prove Michael Porter's innocence, and I don't think you're going to find it."

"We'll see."

The clock chimed.

"I think that's last call," Mardi said.

Amelia gave him a small splash of wine and took the rest.

51

Jerry Baker hadn't responded to her phone messages, so Amelia decided to find him. She knew her best chance was at the Pineville Tavern after work, but that was his clubhouse. She wanted a private conversation with him. She was on her way to his latest work site when she decided to make a slight departure from the route and swing past the River's Inn. It was noon. Maybe Jerry was there for lunch.

His truck was in the lot. She parked next to it. Thirty minutes passed. Amelia periodically started her car to run the air conditioner. The day was oppressively muggy. She wondered if Carol Anne had called him after Amelia and Louise had lunch with her. Perhaps she was questioning Jerry's intentions. Perhaps she was questioning Amelia's.

The door to the River's Inn opened and Jerry stepped out into the blinding sunlight. He pulled his sunglasses from his shirt pocket and strode toward his truck. He passed in front of Amelia's car as he hit the unlock button on his key fob. His truck beeped as he reached for his door handle. Amelia lowered her passenger-side window.

Jerry stooped down and peered in. "Well, well."

"You didn't return my calls."

"I was busy."

"Jerry, give me a break. I'm just looking out for Carol Anne."

"So am I," he snapped.

"You warned your crew not to talk to me about Michael Porter, and now you're spending time with Carol Anne. I don't get it."

Jerry opened her car door and got inside. "OK. Let's hear it, what don't you get? But first, turn on the air. It's frickin' hot."

Amelia moved her seat back to give herself room to face him.

"Don't get too comfortable. I've only got a few minutes."

"Jerry, for God's sake, this is what I don't get. One minute you're a nice guy, the next you're a jerk."

"I was Nice Guy in there; you get Jerk."

Amelia rolled her eyes.

"I never warned my crew about talking to you. And I'm not hitting on Carol Anne, if that's what you're getting at. As far as Carol Anne is concerned, I'm just trying to help her."

"Why?"

"Why not? We all go through tough times. I've been there. So have you."

Amelia unintentionally crossed her arms over her chest.

"Google." He smirked. "You know better than most how easy it is to find information on people. You were a reporter. I guess that explains it."

"No, it doesn't."

"Well, you must like asking questions. It's what you do for a living."

"Did. What I did for a living."

"I know that. Look, I'm not judging you, but don't judge me for wanting to look out for Carol Anne."

"So again, why are you? Whether Porter was a drug dealer or not, cocaine is involved. You were convicted of possession five years ago." *Right back at you!*

Jerry's face flushed red and he clenched his fists. Amelia moved her hand over to the car door handle, ready to bolt if he got any closer.

"You know what the connection is?" he yelled. "I'm worried about her. I know how good it feels to get high. So does she. I'm just trying to give her some support so she doesn't go back there. She said MP saved her. Who's she got now?"

Jerry yanked open the door. "And here's another thing. There was coke at their apartment. Either someone planted it or MP was a dealer. Did you ever consider that either way someone might think Carol Anne knows something? Did you ever think she could be in danger?"

Jerry climbed into his truck, and she watched him slam his palm into the steering wheel before he sped out of the parking lot.

Amelia slumped in her seat. *What just happened? How could I be so wrong? Or am I?*

Her phone vibrated. A text.

Are you still coming to my play tonight?

Absolutely, Amelia replied to Winnie. She needed a diversion. Desperately.

52

"Come, young Puck, your fans await," Claudia said as they arrived at Rocco's at the Brick. They followed the hostess to the corner table at the end of a long, glassed-in porch that provided a charming view of the Brick's gardens and the street beyond.

Winnie let out a squeal as Louise, Ruth, Amelia, and Winnie's father, Wills, all stood and clapped. Winnie danced a little jig and then, realizing that other patrons were watching, quickly took her seat.

Claudia hugged her daughter. "Puck, our own sweet imp."

"What a night I'm having," Winnie said, beaming. It was her first performance at George School.

"You received a standing ovation," said Wills. "I am so proud of you, my girl."

"Wonderful performance, Winnie, just wonderful," gushed Ruth. "I was never a big fan of Shakespeare. His English is too difficult to follow, but you were wonderful. So realistic as an elf."

"Thank you, Mrs. Richards. I loved being onstage."

"How did you remember all your lines?"

"Oh, that part was easy. It was remembering my cues that I had trouble with. I would get so caught up listening to the other actors that sometimes I almost missed the signal for me to go onstage."

"You had great stage presence," said Amelia, "and it looked like you were having fun."

"Thou speak'st aright; I am that merry wanderer of the night!" Winnie stood and bowed. "And now I must wander to the bathroom."

"I'll walk with you," said Amelia. "I left my phone in the car, and I want to take a few photos of your celebration."

* * *

"Amelia?" Winnie and Amelia turned toward the voice. Tim Watson was standing at the bar.

"Tim," said Amelia. "What brings you to the Brick?"

He laughed. "I do go to other bars besides the Pineville Tavern. I'm waiting for a friend."

He looked down at Winnie dressed in a tunic festooned with flowers, leaves, and sequins. A trail of ivy was cinched around her waist and held in place by a clasp of acorns. "That's quite a fashion statement!"

Winnie smoothed her green wig to reveal pointed ears. "I'm Puck from *A Midsummer Night's Dream*."

Tim extended his hand. "I'm very pleased to meet you, Puck."

"My real name's Winnie." As she shook his hand she noticed his gold ring. "That's a cool ring."

"Thank you. It's my family's crest."

Winnie studied it closely. "It's nice. Is your family royalty?"

"Oh, hardly." He laughed. "Is this your daughter?" he asked Amelia.

"No, but she has become part of the family. Her parents are artists and have studios at my mother's. They also look after the property. Winnie is like a granddaughter to my mom. She's the smartest kid I've ever met. She's eleven, going on PhD."

Winnie laughed out loud. "I'm still in high school."

"Can I offer you a drink, Amelia? Maybe a soda for you, Puck?"

"Thanks," said Amelia, "but we're having a celebration on the porch for Winnie."

"And I have to go." Winnie giggled at her own words and ran off to the bathroom.

* * *

"Yummy, calamari," said Winnie as the server set down a platter of hors d'oeuvres. "Look, Amelia, your friend's leaving." Winnie pointed to Tim Watson, who was crossing State Street. "Maybe his friend couldn't make it. We could have invited him to our table."

"That's nice of you, Winnie," said Amelia, "but I don't know him that well."

"Who?" asked Ruth.

Winnie pointed out the window. "That man standing at the corner. He was in the bar. He said hi to Amelia."

"He's a nice-looking young man," said Ruth, raising her eyebrows expectantly.

"Look, Ruthie, there's your boyfriend, Robert D'Angelo," Louise teased.

"You have a boyfriend?" asked Winnie incredulously.

"Where?" said Ruth.

"At the corner. He's driving that black SUV," said Louise.

The SUV stopped at the intersection where Tim was standing. The driver's forearm rested languidly along the open window, his chiseled profile glowing as the interior light came on.

Ruth clasped her hands together and gushed, "Isn't he handsome?"

Winnie stared at Ruth.

As Robert turned left onto Washington Avenue, Winnie and the rest of the table turned their heads in unison, following the SUV as it passed in front of the Brick. People at nearby tables briefly followed their gaze, then returned to their meals, unsure why the vehicle was so captivating.

"He's not really my boyfriend." Ruth chuckled. "But a girl can dream, can't she?"

Winnie scooped a forkful of calamari into her mouth. She needed to distract herself from Mrs. Richards's boy crush. It was too weird. She's a very nice lady, but she's too old to have a crush on somebody.

Winnie thought of her friend Sarah, whose neck broke out in hives whenever Jason Drummond walked past her locker at school. Of course, Sarah was only fourteen, but still, how could you be so goofy over a boy that it could make your skin itch?

Winnie liked Walter Zappulla, but not like that. She liked him because he knew a lot about the Large Hadron Collider in Switzerland. She could talk to him for hours about smashing protons. And he never gave her hives.

53

Amelia was having a productive morning editing an essay when her doorbell rang. She debated answering. It was probably someone with a petition to fight air pollution or a lawn service interested in fighting her dandelions.

Another ring and then a third. She looked down through the half-circle window in the loft. Tony Mardi was at her door, his cell phone up to his ear.

Her phone rang.

She ran down and flung the door open. "What's wrong?"

Mardi stepped across the threshold and shut the door.

"What is it?" Amelia's heart was racing. "Tony, you're scaring me."

"Smith Phillips is dead. Kids tubing down the Delaware found his body snagged by tree roots. His canoe was a couple of miles downriver."

He followed Amelia into her living room. She plopped onto the sofa.

"He drowned?" she asked. Before he could answer, she said, "He was murdered, wasn't he?"

"His blood alcohol level was 0.25. Preliminary results say he drowned, but we have to consider everything, given the circumstances."

"Now there's a good idea."

"Amelia," Mardi snapped, "enough with the sarcasm. I'm not in the mood. I've got bodies piling up."

Amelia swallowed her sarcasm. "Sorry. When? When did it happen?"

"Still undetermined, but judging by the condition of the body, at least a couple of days ago. His clothing was odd for canoeing, especially his choice of shoes. He was wearing loafers."

"What else was he wearing?"

"Street clothes: khakis, golf shirt, leather belt. His PFD was unzipped and hanging off one shoulder."

"PFD?"

"Personal flotation device, his life jacket. An empty bottle of scotch was in the canoe, along with one of the paddles."

"Where's the other paddle?"

"We're still searching the river for it."

The case clock chimed three times. "Listen, I gotta get back to the station."

Amelia grabbed his arm. "Why were you so anxious to tell me?"

"You've been talking to a lot of people, asking a lot of questions."

"But none of the answers have helped me figure out why Michael Porter was killed."

"But they don't know that. I'll let you know if I learn anything else." He paused at the front door. "Amelia, be careful. Watch your back."

Amelia didn't even know what to watch for in front of her. None of it made sense, except that Porter was bludgeoned to death, Carter OD'd, and now Smith drowned. A gunshot to the head seemed to be all that was missing—that, and maybe a stabbing.

She returned to her loft, opened her laptop, and scrolled down to the essay she had been editing before Mardi arrived. She clicked it closed. She needed to think.

54

Amelia sat on her deck, watching birds dart back and forth between the maple tree and the bird feeder, while others took turns splashing in the birdbath. Watching birds was a form of meditation to her. Their clicking, chirping, and chattering created a transforming chant. She desperately needed it right now.

She smiled as she thought of the first birds she had become enamored with—the bluebirds that helped Cinderella dress for the ball. They were so sweet and wore funny brown shoes. She asked for bluebird boxes for a birthday when she was seven, maybe eight. She knew at that age that the birds didn't really wear brown shoes, but that they needed a safe place to build their nests. Her father helped her hang them on the fence posts. Years later, he gave her an Audubon print of a bluebird; it now hung in her powder room. He said bluebirds were full of innocent vivacity.

Vivacity, that's what she needed now. She was exhausted from dredging up people's secrets in search of answers to

Michael Porter's death. She felt like she was ransacking people's emotions. Now someone else was dead.

Amelia's phone vibrated and lit up with Winnie's smiling face. "Hello, Winnie."

"Amelia, I'm glad I reached you. I remember where I saw the ring."

"The ring?"

"You know, the one that your friend was wearing when we saw him at the Brick Hotel?"

"Tim Watson?"

"Yes. I was working on my essay about being a kid at a party and something jarred my memory. It's the part about the men with bad moods. Didn't you get my texts?"

Amelia looked at her screen and saw she had three new text messages. "I'm sorry, I didn't notice them."

"That's OK. One of the men at the party was wearing a ring like your friend. It's all in my notes."

"You have my full attention."

"Just a minute, I'll get my book." Amelia heard her running across her room and then turning the pages of a book. "It was when I was hiding under the table. OK, here we go:

"First man: 'Where is she?' And next to it I wrote '*cranky voice.*'

"Second man: 'I don't know. There must be two hundred people here. You find her.'

"First man: 'Here, I got you a drink.'

"Second man: 'Thanks. We need to be out of here soon.'

"Next to that part I wrote '*arm hanging down, gold ring with duck beak, lemon.*' That's my own shorthand. I now know what the duck beak is. It's a family crest. When I saw Mr. Watson's ring, he said it was his family's crest. It's shaped like a shield. That's what I thought was a duck beak. Was Mr. Watson at the party?"

"I don't think so." Amelia felt on edge. "What's *lemon* mean?"

"Oh, that was what was in the man's drink. I came out from under the table after he left. I saw his glass. It had a piece of lemon peel in it. I was trying to remember details so my writing would be more colorful."

"Very good, Winnie."

"Also, I know what time it was. The reason I know is that I looked at my watch before I took the petit fours. It was only seven thirty. I knew they wouldn't uncover the desserts for a while, so I'd have to sneak them."

"Did you see either of these men later?"

"I don't know. I never saw their faces, only that they wore dark suits and shiny black shoes, just like most of the other men that night. After I took some dessert, I hurried to the breakfast room to eat it. I didn't want to get caught."

"Thanks, Winnie. I'll ask my friend if he was there," she said, failing in her attempt to sound nonchalant.

"If he was at the party, don't tell him that I said he was in a bad mood, OK? He seems like a nice person."

Amelia was no longer so sure, but there was one way to find out.

* * *

"Tim, it's Amelia. I'm sorry to bother you, but I've got a quick question. Did you attend the party at Twin Beeches?" Amelia hurried through her question over the phone, no preface and no lead-in.

Tim paused ever so briefly. "You mean when MP was killed?"

"Yes." *What other party would there be?*

"No. Why are you asking?"

"Because I hadn't already done so. I don't like making assumptions." She knew it was a lame excuse, but she didn't want to involve Winnie.

Silence.

"Tim?"

"Yeah. I don't like making assumptions, either, so what are you getting at?"

"You told me you had plans that night. I'm just asking if it was the party."

"Of course it wasn't. Check your guest list."

"Where did you go?"

"That's none of your business. In fact, this is insulting. I contacted you, remember? I wanted to help." He ended the call.

Tim said he wanted to help. Jerry Baker told her the same. Yet she felt more confused than aided. Each time she met with one of them, her view of their intentions changed. Tim was sincere, until now. Of course, she had just treated him like a suspect.

Jerry was the opposite. He was arrogant, or maybe just showboating, during her first encounter with him; then he was helpful, though possibly still showboating, when Carol Anne was present. But in the parking lot of the River's Inn he was angry, actually furious. *"Did you ever think she could be in danger?"* he had asked. She was convinced that he was trying to protect Carol Anne, but from what or whom?

Jerry and Tim were like the angel and the devil on her shoulders. The good one perched on the right, whispering in her ear, while the devil on the left distracted her from the truth. But they kept trading places.

She remembered Tim waiting at the bar at Bryson's to speak to her after her interview with Leslie. He said Gus told him that she would be there. What seemed like a logical explanation then seemed illogical now. Gus was a great bartender and might know a lot of people, but how would he have known she'd be there that night?

It was time for a drink at Bryson's.

55

"Tim Watson? Yeah, I know him," Gus said as he poured Amelia a glass of Viognier at the bar. "He doesn't seem to be your type, though." He winked. "How do you know Tim?"

"Gus, I don't know him. I only met him when he came in here to see me. Remember? You told him I was here."

"Me? No, Amelia, it wasn't me." He rubbed his hands on the bar towel hanging from his side. "No reason Tim would ask me, and even if he did I wouldn't have told him. Client confidentiality." He laughed. "I'm a bartender; I pour drinks and listen." He took his cell phone out of his pocket. "We've all got 'em, so if you're not answering your own phone, then that means you don't want to talk to whoever's trying to reach you. I'm not getting in the middle of that."

In the reflection of the mirror above the bar, Amelia saw a guy three stools away trying to get Gus's attention. "I think someone's thirsty." She nodded to her left.

"Ralph! It's been a dog's age." Gus shook the hand of a

short, stocky guy perched on the edge of a barstool, his feet barely touching the footrest. "Your usual?"

Amelia studied him in the mirror. Dog's age, how apt. He looked like a bulldog with his protruding lower jaw, close-cropped hair, and thick neck.

"How's the appliance biz going?" Amelia heard Gus ask him as he handed him his drink.

A Maytag man, she thought, *except in place of the white jumpsuit he wore a work shirt and chinos. Must be in sales.*

"Busy." He tipped his Manhattan toward Gus. "Cheers, buddy. Good to see you. Haven't been out much. I've been working like a dog."

Amelia smiled to herself.

"But payday is coming, baby," he continued. "If all goes well, next month I'll be drinking champagne. I'm working on another acquisition."

Gus gave him a high five. "How big?" he asked.

"Big, buddy, big. Bricks and mortar in seven states; but online, now that's the sweet spot. Ginny wants me to buy her a winter place in Palm Beach. She may just get it." He laughed and took a swig of his Manhattan. "Nah, forget the champagne. I'm sticking with these. You make a fine drink, buddy."

Amelia sipped her wine. Never make assumptions about people. That's probably rule number one in the bartender's guide to success. She wasn't even close with the bulldog.

She watched Gus mix drinks and trade barbs with his regulars. She wasn't a regular yet, more of a frequenter, which made it all the more curious that Tim knew or assumed that she would be here the night they met. And he was at the Brick the night of Winnie's play. Was that just a coincidence? She scanned the bar, suddenly feeling paranoid.

Amelia motioned to Gus for the check.

He walked over and leaned in slightly. His countenance had changed from affable to concerned. "Amelia, I don't want to be nosy about you and Tim."

"Gus, it's not what you think." She patted his hand. "But I appreciate you looking out for me."

"Oh, no worries, it's just strange, given your families."

Amelia looked at him quizzically, her hand still resting atop his.

Gus's furrowed brow looked more like a frown. "You know about Tim's uncle and the drugs, right?"

"Gus, I barely know Tim."

"Ah, so this is one of those six degrees of separation things between you and him. Tim's uncle owned your mom's house." Gus mistook Amelia's shock for incomprehension, so he continued. "Frankie Vincent bought your mother's . . ."

It wasn't incomprehension; it was a freeze-frame moment. Gus's words hung there in front of Amelia. She recognized them all: *Tim, mom, house, drugs, Frankie.* But they didn't belong together; they were separate topics, until Amelia's brain shrieked *WHAT?* Though she managed to tamp down the decibels before it became audible to Gus, she couldn't control her iron grip on his hand.

"Yeah, none other than big Frankie," he said, rubbing his hand after Amelia finally released it.

"Sorry," Amelia said, embarrassed to see the imprint of her fingers on his flesh.

"I'm not saying there's any connection between Tim and his uncle other than, you know, they're related, but if you include facts like your mom's house, the murder, and now you asking me about Tim, it becomes more weird than coincidence."

"Did you know that Tim worked with Michael Porter, the man who was murdered?"

"There ya go."

"Hey, Gus, can I get a refill?" the bulldog called as he popped a maraschino cherry in his mouth.

Amelia laid a few bills on the counter. "Keep the change, Gus."

"Keep your eyes open, Amelia."

56

The next day was warm and sunny. Amelia drove to Twin Beeches to pick up a table Louise had offered her. She considered staying home to try to figure out what Smith's death and Gus's revelation about Tim might have to do with Michael's murder, but she needed to let the information percolate on its own first. Sometimes distractions bring clarity to a situation. She also decided she would keep her mouth shut, at least for now. No need to worry her mom or feed Ruth's appetite for gossip.

* * *

The air carried the fragrance of flowers from the cutting garden and the baa-ing of goats through the open windows at Twin Beeches. Louise sat at the kitchen table reviewing the guest list for the garden club's upcoming luncheon. A round marble and iron bistro table sat on the floor nearby.

"What do you think?" she asked Amelia. "I bought it years

ago in France at a truffle market. It needs a good home instead of being stuck up in my attic."

"Sold," said Amelia. "Thanks, Mom." Amelia sat down next to Louise and noticed the list of names. "Planning another party?"

Louise let out a loud laugh. "Not here. This is the guest list for thc garden club luncheon where Carol Anne's flowerpot cakes will be served."

"Hello?" Kirby called from the open side door.

"Kirby, come in," said Louise. "How nice to see you."

"I hope I'm not interrupting anything. I'm on my way to a client's house nearby so I can't stay long, but I have a gift for Winnie." She set a box on the table and removed a brilliantly colored vase. "And an apology from Cabo Pottery. One of the clerks was new and had taken the vase for your order from the irregulars shelf."

"It's beautiful. It was very kind of you to get Winnie a replacement," said Louise.

"Thank you. I've done business with them for such a long time. It's the least they could do. I'm sure they fired the clerk."

"That would be rather harsh. I'm sure it was an honest mistake."

"Well, I don't think carelessness or incompetence should ever be tolerated," she said.

Louise was incredulous over how quickly Kirby's mood could shift. She seemed to carry kindness and intolerance in the same hand, ever ready to hold out a benevolent gift or lob a ball of anger with equal ease. "Let me get her. She's in the barn working on an art project."

"I'll go," volunteered Amelia.

Louise watched Kirby look around the kitchen and spy the bistro table by the back door.

"That's a remarkable piece," said Kirby. "Are you getting rid of it?"

"No. It's for Amelia."

"I could get a good price if she wants to sell it."

"I just gave it to her."

"Oh, of course, sorry. I get a bit overly enthusiastic when I see quality antiques," Kirby said.

Louise returned to her guest list.

"Hello, Miss Dunbar," Winnie said as she and Amelia entered the kitchen. Winnie rubbed her hands on her beige smock that was smeared with dried clay.

Kirby handed Winnie the vase.

"It's beautiful! Oh, thank you so much." She set the vase on the table and moved to hug Kirby, who backed away ever so slightly before bending down and giving Winnie a quick squeeze, making sure no part of her clothing touched the smock.

"The colors are luminescent." Winnie turned back to the vase. "It's great! Much more vivid than the original one."

"Are you throwing pots, Winnie?" asked Kirby, noting her smock.

"No, Mom is. I'm trying to make a mosaic frame. Mom has a bin full of broken pottery. She's a perfectionist." Winnie laughed. "If it's not perfect, whack! And into the bin it goes. I'm using the pieces in my mosaic."

"Artistic recycling," said Kirby.

"It is! I like that," exclaimed Winnie.

"How is it coming along?" Kirby asked.

Louise smiled. She could tell Kirby was enjoying a connection with Winnie—for once.

"Actually, not so well, Miss Dunbar. You don't know how you've lightened my spirit bringing me that beautiful vase. My project is crumbling. No, it's disintegrating."

"What's wrong?" Amelia asked.

"The pieces from Mom's Morning in Spring series worked great. But I couldn't use the two pieces I saved from my old vase. They were flowers. I wanted to put them in the top corners of the frame I'm making. It's going to have a mirror in it and hang above my dresser. It would have looked so cool."

"What went wrong?" Louise asked.

"The first piece dissolved when I washed it."

"They were from your first vase?" Kirby asked.

"Yes. I had hoped to salvage something from it."

"Is the remaining shard still in the studio?" Amelia asked.

"Mom may have already thrown it away."

They followed Winnie to the barn.

Amelia examined the piece of pottery. And then she called Tony Mardi.

* * *

"It's not clay and definitely not porcelain. It's some kind of a compressed substance," Claudia told Mardi and Cole. "It definitely wasn't fired in a kiln."

Cole scraped a small piece off the shard and placed it in a pouch from her narcotics test kit. She crushed an ampoule into it and agitated the pouch. Her knowing nod when the liquid turned blue confirmed what Amelia had suspected.

"Would you all mind going into the house?" Mardi said crisply.

"Of course," said Louise. She turned and ushered the others toward the door.

"Miss Miller, would you please stay for a few more minutes. And you, too, Mrs. Miller."

It took Winnie a minute to realize she was the Miss Miller he was referring to. "Me? Really?" She beamed. "Yes, of course!"

"Thank you."

The others returned to the kitchen.

"What do you think they found?" Louise asked.

"I think they found cocaine," Amelia said.

"Oh my God!" exclaimed Kirby. "In the vase?"

"I'll make some ginger tea," Louise said. "It's very calming."

Fifteen minutes later, Winnie strode into the kitchen, head up, shoulders back, eyes dancing. "This is so fun. Detective Mardi said someone else will be here in a minute. He's some sort of specialist. Look, there he is walking to the studio. Isn't it exciting?"

Winnie paced around the kitchen. "I do hope they hurry up and let us know what they found."

"Well, my dear," said Louise. "It's possible they won't be able to divulge anything until their investigation is complete."

Winnie stopped pacing. "Investigation? You mean the murder? Whoa! I need to get my evidence box and show them what I've discovered."

Winnie returned and sat at the kitchen table, her leg jiggling a Morse code of excitement.

"Finally," Winnie exclaimed when her mom, Mardi and his team entered the kitchen. "Here's the evidence box I told you about." Winnie said to Mardi. "The button I found in the pantry may be a clue. I think it's from a shirt."

"An evidence box?" asked Cole.

"Winnie is extremely observant," said Mardi. "Winnie, why don't you let Detective Cole examine it. She's an expert in collecting evidence."

Winnie gleefully opened the box.

"And after you show Detective Cole what you found, we'll head upstairs," said Winnie's mom.

Mardi turned to Louise. "I understand there are dishes that match the vase."

"Yes, they're in the pantry."

* * *

Mardi and the forensics analyst followed Louise.

"Ruth Richards actually bought these," said Louise said as she watched them examine the pottery. I purchased another pattern, but Ruthie's rather fickle and decided she liked mine better, so we swapped. Both are very nice patterns."

"Did you exchange the dishes before or after Michael Porter's murder?" asked Mardi, while the agent unpacked equipment from his case.

Louise laughed. "Oh, well before. We had barely landed at the airport here when Ruthie wanted to trade. The luggage was lined up outside the hangar. Our driver loaded my luggage and boxes into the car. Ruth's weren't out yet, so we went to the hangar to retrieve hers."

"In the hangar? Was this private?"

"It was with the Travel Club. They have their own plane, actually a couple. Staff travels with you and handles everything."

Satisfied that the pottery did not contain cocaine, they returned to the kitchen.

"Miss Dunbar," said Mardi. "I understand you brought Winnie a new vase today."

"I did. It's there on the table. Please tell me that there are no drugs in it. I've worked with Cabo Pottery for years. I'm confident they know nothing about this."

The agent examined it closely. He turned it over and tapped it against the table. "It's solid. Completely different composition. It's your basic pottery."

"Well, it's more than basic," Kirby snapped. "It's *Cabo Pottery*! Oh, I'm sorry. That was unnecessary. I'm just relieved. I don't want any association with drugs. It could ruin my business." Kirby looked at her watch. "Oh good Lord, I'm late for a meeting with a client." She turned to Mardi. "I must leave." She handed him her card. "Call me if you need contact information for Cabo Pottery."

* * *

"Tell me, why did you suspect drugs?" Louise asked Amelia after the police left.

"It reminded me of a drug bust I covered a few years ago in LA. The DEA showed me a giant Buddha whose belly was filled with fifteen kilos of coke, and that was just one of about fifty statues. There were also tiles and platters made from compressed cocaine. They looked like bisque, white, no gloss. Smugglers have certainly improved their products since then. The colors in Winnie's original vase looked pretty vibrant. Maybe they painted the pattern on the vase."

"But why give it to me?" said Louise.

"Was it in the same box as the dishes?" Amelia asked.

"Yes, there were two boxes," Louise said. "The vase was in the one with the bowls, cups, and saucers. I opened it first so I could give Winnie her present."

"Did you notice any difference in color from the rest of the dishes?"

Louise thought for a moment. "They were individually

wrapped. I don't think I unwrapped any of the others until later." Louise excitedly grabbed Amelia's arm. "Amelia, we didn't unpack the dishes until after the party. Claudia and I had too much to do to get ready for the house tour. We left them in their boxes on the floor of the pantry."

57

Ruth barely slept last night after Louise had called with the news about finding cocaine in the vase. She rushed through breakfast and tried on three different dresses before settling on the blue one. It was slimming and somewhat youthful, she thought as she modeled it in front of her full-length mirror. She added a long pearl necklace, pearl earrings, and a heavy spritz of tuberose perfume. She was ready.

"I'd like to see Mr. Robert D'Angelo, please."

The woman behind the front desk at the Travel Club looked up at Ruth. "Is there something I may assist you with?" she asked.

"Oh no, this is personal. Well, not exactly personal," Ruth said, blushing, "but something I would like to discuss with Robert, with Mr. D'Angelo, privately. Just tell him Ruth Richards is here. He'll know who I am."

Ruth watched as Vanessa Van Born, according to her name-plate, adjusted her headset and tapped a button with a long, emerald-green-polished nail. *Vanessa Van Born,* Ruth thought. *That's a stripper's name, or maybe a socialite.*

"A Mrs. Richards is here to see you." Vanessa looked up at Ruth and smiled. "She says you know her." Vanessa arched an eyebrow.

"Tell him I'm *Ruth* Richards. He has escorted me on a number of Travel Club trips. I'm profiled in your magazine this month," she huffed.

"Mrs. Richards!" Robert bounded out of his office. "What can I do for you?"

"Well, first of all"—she looked at him sternly and then broke into a smile—"it's Ruth to you, dear. No sense in such formality after all our trips together," she tittered, before turning back to Vanessa with a knowing glance. "I would like a private word, Robert, if I may."

Ruth almost swooned as he held out his arm to her. "Allow me," and after a brief pause, he added emphatically, "Ruth."

"I just love how handsome your office is," said Ruth as Robert showed her to a plush armchair opposite his desk. "It's very spacious," she added as she looked past the desk into a sitting area complete with a black leather sofa and armchairs and a coffee table. Along one wall was a large flat-screen TV wrapped in shelves filled with globes of various sizes. Next to it was a tall, inlaid wood cabinet, its top doors opened to reveal a bar.

Robert followed her gaze. "Would you like a cocktail?"

"Oh, goodness no! Although I'm sure somewhere in the world it's five o'clock. But I'm afraid if I had a martini now I'd end up napping on your divan." *Napping on his divan! Ruth, calm down.*

"May I offer you a nonalcoholic refreshment? Sparkling water, coffee, soda?" He sat on the edge of his desk.

"Sparkling water would be very nice. I am a bit parched."

Robert reached across his desk and called Vanessa. "Two

sparkling waters," and then turning to Ruth, "lime and ice?" She nodded happily. "Served the way I like it." He clicked off and, to Ruth's delight, sat down on the chair next to her. "So to what do I owe this pleasure?"

"Well, Robert, I just wanted to make sure you're OK." Ruth abruptly stopped talking when she heard the tap at the door.

Vanessa walked into the office carrying a silver tray.

"What service! You must have been a waitress," said Ruth, watching her as she balanced the tray on one hand while placing two coasters on the desk, followed by glasses of water, a platter of cookies, and two small plates.

Vanessa closed the door just a little too hard as she left.

"I didn't want to say anything while she was here," Ruth said, tilting her head toward the door.

"Would you like a biscuit?" Robert asked.

"Oh, thank you." She reached for a chocolate-covered cookie. "You say it just like the English, 'biscuits' instead of 'cookies.' I've traveled there frequently, particularly to the hamlets outside London. Very charming. Some of the estates reminded me of Bryn Mawr. You should arrange a Travel Club trip to the United Kingdom. I'd happily sign up. I just love your trips. In fact, I have oodles of scrapbooks from all my travels with the club. They're filled with programs, ticket stubs"—she blushed demurely—"and, of course, lots of photos that include you."

Ruth took a bite of cookie. "Robert, I just had a thought! My photographs would be useful for your brochures." Her mind raced toward the possibility of working with Robert. "I take photos in the moment, not posed. They're very natural. I'd gladly offer them to you to enhance your marketing materials, though I recommend we leave out the pottery store photos from our last trip, even though there are some quite good ones of the interior and, of course, you." She smiled, imagining sitting in her own office reviewing photos. "Certainly not after what happened."

"Ruth, whatever are you talking about?"

"Oh goodness, I do tend to run off on tangents, don't I?" She giggled. "That's why I'm here. I want to make sure you're not in any kind of trouble." Ruth pursed her lips, soured by the word she was about to say. "Drugs, Robert." She lowered her voice to almost a whisper, forcing Robert to lean in. "I have been informed that cocaine was smuggled into the country in the vase I acquired in Cabo. So, of course, I came right over to see you, in case you need me to vouch for your character. I wouldn't want your reputation or that of the Travel Club to be besmirched by Mexican drug lords preying on innocent tourists."

Robert sipped his water, slowly set down the glass, and looked into Ruth's eyes. "Ruth, you are a remarkable woman," he said while gently stroking her hand, "and so very thoughtful. How did you come by this information?"

"Well." Ruth drew a deep breath. "You see, Louise Jenkins, my friend who came on the trip, traded dishes with me. I hope you're not upset with me after all the time you took to personally help me at the store, but Louise liked the pattern, too. You have such good taste, Robert, and Louise is my dear friend, so what could I say. I traded with her and then, lo and behold, cocaine was found in Louise's vase—well, my vase, actually. I only found out last night. It was too late to call you, so I rushed here this morning."

"But why would you think such a thing could come back to me?"

"Well," said Ruth, overwhelmed by the warmth of Robert's hand on hers. "Well." She pulled her hand away and shoved a cookie into her mouth, chewing furiously. "You see . . ." Crumbs shot out from between her lips. "I'm sorry," she said, covering her mouth with her hand and then swallowing.

"It's OK, Ruth, take your time." Robert handed her her glass of water.

"You picked out the pattern for me. It could look suspicious, don't you think?"

Robert looked pensively at Ruth. "I see your logic, though it's preposterous that I would engage in such a thing."

"I know that. I just wanted to assure you that I'm here to help in any way I can. You know rumors can destroy a person's reputation. Just read the gossip columns. They're filled with examples."

"That's very kind of you. As one of our special VIP travelers, it's gratifying that you're watching out for our reputation." He took her hand again and gave it a squeeze.

"Goodness, I'm a VIP? Well, isn't that thrilling."

"I hope your other purchases are OK. I recall you bought quite a lot. You're such a savvy shopper."

"Yes, I do like a good deal when I see one," Ruth admitted with a giggle. "Everything else is fine. The police checked. But someone at that shop is up to no good, and I was the unlucky one to get the contraband. Me, of all people!"

"I'm sure the police will turn to the Mexican authorities to get to the bottom of this. I'm just thankful the smugglers didn't try to track you down. I shudder to think what they might have done to get their drugs back."

Ruth clutched her throat. "Oh my, I never thought of that."

Robert glanced at his watch and stood up. "Ruth, I'm sorry to rush you, but I have a full schedule today. Of course, I was more than happy to delay my next meeting when I heard you were here. I appreciate your concern about me."

"It's my pleasure. As I told the police, the Travel Club is a high-class operation, and you would be more than happy to help them."

"Of course. Thank you, Ruth. You're a wealth of information."

"Well, I try to stay on top of the goings-on in our town." She reached for another cookie. "Do you mind?"

"Please, help yourself."

Ruth selected a cookie and wrapped it in a napkin. She also grabbed a Travel Club coaster and shoved them both in her purse.

Robert took her arm again and escorted her to the front door. Ruth smiled at Vanessa as she passed. "Goodbye, dear, thank you for the excellent service." She turned to Robert. "I hope you pay her well. It's hard to find good help these days."

A file drawer slammed shut, causing Ruth to jump. Robert moved Ruth along to the door and held it for her.

"You are such a gentleman. I'll let you know if I hear any more about what we discussed," she said conspiratorially. "Doesn't it make you wonder if it's connected?"

"Connected to what?"

"Why, the murder at my friend Louise's home. Surely you read about it."

58

"Good morning!" Amelia walked into the study at Twin Beeches.

"Amelia!" Louise exclaimed. "Two days in a row. What a treat. Any news about the cocaine in the vase?"

"No, but I do want to ask Wills about something that happened the night of the party."

"He'll be back any minute," said Claudia. "He drove to Doylestown to pick up goat feed."

"The goats only eat organic," added Louise. She picked a book from a shelf in her study and immediately returned it to its spot. "I'm making a donation to the book drive, but these books are like friends. How can I give them away?"

She turned to Claudia, who was filling a box with books. "Keep Shakespeare. Melville, too, and Hawthorne. Did you know they were lovers, possibly unrequited, but lovers nonetheless? I always keep them on the same shelf. They should be together."

Amelia picked up a book on Louise's desk. "Is this a romance?"

"In a manner of speaking. *Merry Hall* is filled with passion and unexpected pleasure."

Amelia felt her cheeks tinge with embarrassment at Louise's broad grin.

"It's about gardening," Louise said. "Well, much more than that, but the gardens are luscious. It's a wonderful story of how Beverley Nichols restored thc gardens of his Georgian home in the country. I just adored him and his books. I met him at a house party when I lived in England. He was irreverent, witty, and quite the bon vivant, the perfect dinner-party guest. He was an Oscar Wilde but with a happy ending. I don't think the towns-people knew quite what to make of him. Gossiping about him was a full-time avocation; he didn't disappoint."

"Are you giving it away?" Amelia said, noting four other books by Nichols on Louise's desk.

"Oh, heavens no. They're treasures. I'm moving it and his other children to the orangery among the gardening books. But I do need to thin this literary herd in here. I have far too many books. Either I give some away or relocate the Samuels and build more bookshelves."

The room fell quiet, uncomfortably so. "Oh, don't worry, dears." Louise grabbed a feather duster and fluttered it under Samuel the First's nose. "You're old classics, too. I'm just kidding about moving you."

The gravel crunched on the driveway. "I'm sure that's Wills," said Claudia, taping closed a full box of books. "I'll tell him to come see you, Amelia, after he unloads the truck."

"Would you like some iced tea, Amelia?" Louise asked as she poured herself a glass from a pitcher on a trolley, which also held a plate of sandwiches. "It's herbal, with a dash of honey. Speaking of which, we're going to start an apiary."

"An aviary?" asked Amelia.

Louise laughed. "We don't need cages for birds. They have the full run of my property. An apiary, a bee yard. Wills has done all the research and will set it up. Imagine, our own honey. Here, have a sandwich."

"I'm OK. I'll have something later." Amelia watched her mom as she took a gingerly bite of a tea sandwich. Even when chewing she had a faint smile on her face, happy with her world. She lived in the same world as everyone else. She just moved around in it differently, guided by fascination and curiosity, and solving dilemmas with an abstract sense of logic. She put goats in the field to fend off Elliott's helicopter, sold and then repurchased Twin Beeches to get a fresh take on it, and seemed to maintain a friendly rapport with the Samuels. The oddest element was that it made sense to Amelia. It was part of her own genetic makeup, though she had inherited a weaker strain that needed nurturing. She had left it to starve for years. Facts, logic, and practical solutions had ruled her world. And look where that got her.

"I think I will have a sandwich. They look delicious," Amelia said. She glanced up at the Samuels, confident they understood.

The study door opened and Wills walked in.

Louise handed him her glass of iced tea. "I just poured this. You look thirsty."

"Thanks." He gulped half the glass and smiled appreciatively. "Claudia's herbal blend, isn't it?"

"Imagine how delicious it will be when we use our own honey," added Louise.

"This afternoon I'll plot out where we should put the hives," said Wills. He turned to Amelia. "Now what can I do for you?"

"It has to do with the murder."

"The murder?" Wills and Louise said in unison.

"Well, this is—" said Louise.

"What is it you want—" Wills interrupted.

"—exciting!"

"—to know?"

"It's pretty mundane," Amelia said. "It's about boxes."

"Boxes?" Again Louise and Wills answered in unison.

"Mom, please!"

"Sorry, dear," she said. "But boxes? What on earth?" She caught Amelia's look. "Go ahead."

"Wills, you said that the night of the party you had some boxes removed from the pantry."

"That's right."

"Do you know what was in them?"

"Supplies for the party, I assume. They were blocking the door to the dining room."

"Could one of them have been dishes from Mexico? Mom said she didn't have time to unpack them before the party, so she left the box in the pantry."

"It was two boxes, dear," Louise interjected.

"Wills, is it possible they were the boxes you had moved?" asked Amelia.

"They couldn't be," said Louise. "They were still there. Claudia and I unpacked them a couple of days after Mr. Porter was killed."

"Maybe they were replaced," said Amelia.

Wills set his glass on the side table. "I'm not following."

"Do you remember their size?"

"About that size," he said, motioning to the book boxes. "I didn't pay much attention to them other than they needed to be moved so we could open the pantry door that leads to the dining room."

"Mom, what did you do with your boxes after you unpacked the dishes?" Amelia asked as Claudia walked into the room carrying a fresh roll of packing tape.

"They're right there," Claudia said, motioning to the two boxes that held books. "I knew we'd need them for the book drive, so I stashed them in my studio."

Amelia examined the plain brown boxes. "Mom, didn't you say others in your group bought pottery?"

"Yes, including Ruth. These are her boxes."

"So if they were unmarked, how did you know whose was whose when they unloaded your luggage?"

Louise closed her eyes. "Give me a minute. I need to visualize that day."

Amelia looked up at the Samuels. They seemed equally interested in what Louise might see.

"All the boxes were marked and lined up next to our luggage! I'm sure of it," she exclaimed. "They had a 'Cabo Pottery' label on one side and our last names written in black marker on the other. Oh, but Ruth's boxes and luggage weren't there yet, so we walked into the hangar to retrieve them. They were labeled the same way—a Cabo label and her last name."

"That's right," said Claudia. "When we put the boxes in the pantry, we turned them so Ruth's name was on the side facing the wall; the label faced out. They were positioned so when the door leading to the dining room was open, the boxes were behind it on the lower shelf. No one would see them during the tour." Claudia examined the boxes. "But these are definitely the boxes we unpacked, and they have no label on them."

"The boxes must have been switched." Amelia looked at Wills, suddenly fearful that he might be involved.

"That's what I'm thinking," he said, with no trace of nervousness.

"Heavens! Cocaine may have been in all the pottery," exclaimed Louise.

"And I was right there," said Wills. "Man, that's wild!"

"Wills, what do you remember?" asked Amelia.

"I was finishing up a walk-through of the house, making sure everything was in place. The dining room was my last stop. The rope and stanchions in front of the pantry door were set, but the door was closed. When I tried to open it, something was blocking it, so I walked around through the kitchen to enter the pantry from there. A waiter was in the pantry with a box. I saw a second box against the door leading to the dining room. I told the waiter that the room was off-limits and to remove them." Wills paused for a moment. "Another waiter was nearby and said he'd help. That was it."

"One of them must have been Michael Porter," said Louise, clutching her hands together. "Oh my, that means he was involved in drugs after all."

"Maybe he was hired to pick up the boxes and didn't know what was in them," said Wills.

"Why hire some random guy to move drugs?" Amelia asked.

"I had hoped Michael was innocent, for Carol Anne's sake," said Louise sadly.

"Have the police interviewed Ruth about the dishes?"

"I don't know, though she said she would call me after they talked to her."

"Mom, Tony asked you not to say anything."

"I know, but just imagine Ruth's reaction if the police showed up at her door and told her cocaine was smuggled into the country in her dishes. She'd have a meltdown. Hysteria is her default reaction. How could a little advance warning hurt?"

59

"Oh, Robert, this is so thrilling," Ruth gushed as she followed him up the steps of the Gulfstream. "I thought the Travel Club only had two big planes. This is so, so intimate!" She blushed as she surveyed the interior: six large leather seats, a divan, a credenza, and a galley in the back with wood so highly polished it looked like topaz.

"We reserve it for our most special guests," he said while easing the cork off a bottle of champagne. "Your visit yesterday and the concern you expressed over my reputation and that of my company were exemplary, Ruth. This is my way of thanking you. I know it's spur of the moment, but isn't that what makes life worth living?"

Pop!

Ruth jumped. "Oh my!" She watched him fill two crystal flutes. "I hope you're not flying the plane," she tittered.

"We'll let the pilots handle that. This trip is to thank you for your loyalty to the Travel Club. But I have to warn you, I have an ulterior motive."

"You do?" Ruth tried to take a sip of her champagne. It

spilled down the front of her. "Oh my goodness!" She grabbed a tissue from her pocket and frantically blotted her bosom.

"Yes, I do." He arched his eyebrow and winked at her.

Ruth steadied herself against the credenza. *What big eyes you have!* Ruth pulled her red shawl across her chest.

Robert patted the suede divan. "Have a seat, Ruth." He reached for a linen napkin and handed it to her. "On this trip I want to really get to know you," he said, smiling broadly.

What big teeth you have! Ruth clenched the napkin.

"Many of our clients take one or two excursions with us. But you, Ruth, have logged more time on our planes than some of our pilots. I want you to share your fantasies with me."

"My fantasies?" she squeaked.

"Yes, your travel fantasies. What makes our trips so alluring, so desirable to you? That is what I want to learn on this trip together. How is Ruth's wanderlust fulfilled by the Travel Club?"

"Oh, I see." Ruth's bosom heaved. "Well, I'll do my best to satisfy you." She nonchalantly put her champagne flute to her lips. It was empty.

Robert refilled her glass. "Sit back and relax, Ruth." He glanced at his gold Rolex Daytona. "We'll be wheels up as soon as Vanessa arrives."

"Your secretary is coming with us?" Jealousy and relief scrambled Ruth's features.

"I have caviar!" Vanessa announced as she slipped into the cabin and blew a kiss to the two pilots. "Hello, Mrs. Richards." Vanessa leaned over and gave Robert a peck on the cheek. "And you, bad boy, I had to go to three gourmet shops before I could find the caviar you like."

She carried a picnic basket back to the galley. "Let me get these things stored so we can lift off. Have you ever flown on a G5 before, Mrs. Richards?"

"This is my first time." Ruth watched as Vanessa emptied the contents of the basket into refrigerated drawers.

"Time for me to have a quick glass of bubbly before we take off." Vanessa clicked open the glass door of a cabinet where the crystal stemware sparkled under recessed halogen lights.

"Ruth, let's you and I take the two seats up front," said Robert. "It's thrilling to watch our takeoff. Once we're airborne we can return to the divan for a tête-a-tête."

Ruth settled into the wide leather chair. "This is lovely. All these buttons." She pushed a button on the outside arm. "Wooo!" Ruth exclaimed as she grabbed the armrests. Her chair slid partially into the aisle and swiveled. "Goodness, that startled me."

Robert laughed. "We'll keep it locked for takeoff, but once airborne your seat can turn almost 180 degrees, and, of course, it reclines."

"My dear departed husband would have wanted one of these in our TV room. It's the Cadillac of recliners. Goodness, what will they think of next?"

Robert locked her seat back in place and settled in across the aisle from her.

One of the pilots left the cockpit and doffed his cap toward Ruth. "Welcome aboard, Mrs. Richards. I'm Captain Schmidt. Our flight time to Martha's Vineyard will be forty-seven minutes. Joining me in the cockpit is Captain Moore. Before we take off, I'd like to familiarize you with the safety equipment on board."

Ruth sat in rapt attention.

"And now, please sit back and enjoy the flight."

* * *

"Louise, guess where I am," Ruth whispered into her cell phone as she stood in the bathroom of the G5, sampling the perfume and lotion in the basket beside the sink. "I'm on a private jet with Robert! He whisked me away this morning for a special VIP mystery trip. I'll be back home tonight."

"Are you OK, Ruth?" Robert asked as he knocked on the door.

"I have to go," she whispered into her cell phone. "I'll call when I get home tonight. I hope you get this message." She quickly put her phone in her purse. "I'm just fine, Robert, just powdering my nose." She flushed the toilet and ran the water.

"I thought I heard you talking." He eyed her purse as she stepped out of the bathroom.

"Talking? No, you must have heard me singing." She smiled coquettishly. "How embarrassing. I do that when I'm happy. The facilities certainly match the grandiose decor of this plane. There's Hermès hand lotion in the lavatory." She stuck her hand under Robert's nose. "Doesn't it smell wonderful? French, you know."

Vanessa had pulled the tabletop from its compartment between the double set of seats and set it with china and linen. In the center of the table on an oval silver tray was the jar of caviar nestled in a bowl of ice and surrounded by small crystal bowls of chopped onion, egg yolk, egg whites, and crème fraîche. Toast points were layered in a herringbone pattern around the edge of the tray. On the credenza were glasses and a frosted bottle of vodka. "We have wine, if you prefer," she said to Ruth.

"Oh, I'm a martini girl, the dirtier the better," she scoffed.

"Not a problem." Vanessa went to the galley.

Ruth picked up the mother-of-pearl spoon and scooped a generous amount of caviar onto a toast point. She topped it off with a dollop of crème fraîche and popped it into her mouth. "Mmm, I just love caviar."

Vanessa gave Ruth her martini.

"Thank you, dear, I better drink it slow. I have a bit of a buzz from the champagne." She smiled broadly.

Vanessa put her fingernail up to her front tooth. Ruth looked at her quizzically. "Caviar, Ruth. You have caviar between your teeth."

Ruth took a sip of her martini, swished it around in her mouth, and swallowed. "Did I get it all?"

"No more martinis for Ruth," Robert whispered. "I want her tipsy, not plastered."

* * *

"I hope you like seafood," Robert said as a Range Rover pulled up alongside the plane. "We'll have lunch and take a stroll around town."

They settled into the back seat.

"This is so exciting! Oh, how I wish I had brought my camera. We might see some celebrities while we're here."

Robert leaned over and stroked Ruth's hair. "Sometimes our memories are so much better when they remain private."

"Oh my," Ruth gasped.

Robert lowered the window as Vanessa walked up to the car.

"I'll see you at the restaurant," she said.

"Vanessa has a few things to handle for our return flight," Robert said to Ruth.

"All work and no play . . ." Ruth wriggled a finger at Vanessa.

"Don't worry, Vanessa has plenty of time to play, don't you?"

"You know I do. I'll see you at the restaurant."

The restaurant was bustling as Ruth and Robert were shown to a table overlooking the marina. Pelicans swooped around the boats, which bobbed in a pointless attempt to avoid their droppings.

"Drink?" asked Robert.

"I better stick with water. I've had quite a bit already." She giggled.

"They make the best Bloody Mary on the island."

"Well, if you insist. Shall we order one for Vanessa?"

"No, she can decide what she wants when she gets here. I don't think she'll be long."

"I just love it here, Robert. I've always dreamed of going to Martha's Vineyard. It's so quaint and popular. I just hope there's enough time to do a little shopping."

Robert sipped his drink and studied the yachts anchored offshore. That would be his next purchase. A tender craft from one of them motored toward the dock.

He realized Ruth was chattering away. "Delicious. I'm so glad you recommended this cocktail. Goodness, it has quite a kick to it. What a day."

"I'm sorry, Ruth, I was just thinking what a great day this is."

"Oh, me, too."

"Shall we order?"

"What do you recommend?"

"Lobster rolls are always good, or soft-shell crab."

"I'll have whatever you're having. I need to visit the little girl's room." The waiter directed her to the "Buoys" and "Gulls" signs at the far end of the dining room.

* * *

"Louise? I'm so glad I reached you," Ruth gushed as she locked herself in one of the stalls. "I'm having the most splendiferous time!"

"Ruth, where are you?" asked Louise.

"Martha's Vineyard. Can you believe it? We flew here this morning. Robert said it's a surprise trip because I'm one of their top travelers. Did you know they have a small VIP jet? It's a B5 or a G5. I'm not sure, but is it fancy! I'll be home tonight, so you don't have to worry about any hanky-panky going on." She chuckled. "What a trip!"

"Ruth, listen to me. It's possible that your dishes had cocaine in them, not just the vase."

"That's impossible. You told me the police checked them and they were fine."

"The dishes in my pantry are, but they may have been switched with an identical set, quite possibly the night of the murder. You could be in danger."

"What?" Ruth yelled and then quickly cupped her hand over the phone and whispered, "Why would I be in danger?"

"Because Robert may be involved. Think about it."

"Robert? Oh, that's impossible. Robert would never be involved in something like that. It would ruin his stellar reputation and that of the Travel Club."

"Hold on, Ruth, I have you on speaker and Amelia wants to say something."

"Hi, Ruth. Mom and I just want you to be very careful. If anything seems off, you need to protect yourself. Do you know the tail number of the plane?"

"No, Amelia, I don't, but I'm perfectly safe. This is a trip in my honor. Robert is interviewing me to find out how he can enhance other expeditions. Did you know I have more air miles than some of the pilots? Isn't that remarkable? Thankfully, I haven't been asked to fly the plane." She chuckled. "I must go now, we're having lunch. You're worrying for no reason."

"Where are you right now?" Amelia asked.

"Why, I'm in the bathroom," Ruth tittered. "I'll call you when I get home. Ta-ta!" She dropped the phone into her pocket. As she tugged her purse off the door hook, the front pouch snapped open and her travel sanitizer fell out. Ruth bent down to retrieve it and noticed a pair of blue-and-yellow sandals in the stall next to hers. They looked like the pair Vanessa was wearing.

Ruth returned to the table and saw the third place setting had been removed. "Vanessa isn't having lunch with us?"

"No, she called and said she'll meet us at the plane."

* * *

"Ruth, you're looking pensive," said Robert as the plane taxied down the runway for the flight home. "Is everything OK?"

She glanced back at Vanessa, who was reading a magazine in the last row. "I called my friend Louise from the restaurant and she said it's possible that cocaine was in all the pottery, not just the vase. She's worried about me."

"Worried?" asked Robert, his eyes matching the word.

"Yes, because I'm here with you." Ruth's breasts heaved. "I just don't know what to make of it."

"Ruth, you said the dishes were fine."

"They are. It's fantastical thinking on her part. She thinks the dishes were switched. Now, how could she know that? And, of course, you're not involved, though you should check the backgrounds of your employees, especially . . ." Ruth tilted her head toward Vanessa. "I think she was spying on me when I went to the ladies' room," Ruth whispered.

"She was here at the hangar, Ruth. There's no reason she would spy on you, though I wouldn't be surprised if she was jealous of you." Robert squeezed Ruth's hand. "Your friend Louise needs to keep her wild allegations to herself. I won't hesitate to defend my company and myself against slander."

"I'll take care of things, Robert. She's barking up the wrong tree." Ruth peered out the window at the sunset. *She's just jealous.* Ruth smiled at the thought and picked a piece of dried caviar off her left breast.

60

"Ruth? Where are you?"

"In a limousine!" She laughed. "Are you still up? I thought I'd have the driver drop me off at your house. I can't wait to tell you about my stupendous day!"

"Of course I am, Ruth. It's only eight o'clock," said Louise. "Amelia and I were just finishing dinner. We've been worried about you."

Ruth giggled. "Worried? There was no need to worry. I've had the time of my life. I can't believe I did so much in just a few hours."

* * *

A car horn beeped repeatedly. Louise and Amelia watched from the front door as a black stretch limo drove up the driveway. From the open sunroof Ruth's head appeared. "Yoo-hoo!" With one hand she hung on to the lip of the sunroof, and with the other she gave the Queen's wave, more of a turn of the wrist than a hand flapping.

"Ruth, you be careful," shouted Louise.

As the car rolled to a stop, Ruth popped back inside.

"Thank you, Gino, wonderful driving," she exclaimed as the driver held the door for her.

"What a day!" Ruth beamed, her hair tucked into a pink Black Dog baseball cap. A pink sweater embroidered with tiny green anchors completed her Edgartown attire. "I went on such a shopping spree." She laughed as Gino removed her shopping bags from the trunk. Ruth draped the cord and ribbon handles over her arms like bracelets.

"Have you had dinner?" Louise asked.

"We had a late lunch and some snacks on the plane on the way home. I wouldn't mind a cocktail, though. I have so much to tell you. Maybe a little cheese and crackers."

Louise and Amelia sat patiently while Ruth gushed about the flights, the shopping, and the lunch. When she finally took a breath, Louise jumped in. "Your day sounds like a wonderful adventure. But how did this trip come about?"

"Oh, it was quite a surprise. Robert called me last night. I almost didn't answer because I didn't recognize the number. Am I glad I did! That's when he invited me to lunch today." She took a gulp of her martini. "Little did I know that lunch was going to be on Martha's Vineyard! Ooh, what a thrill. I almost forgot . . ." She set her drink on the end table. "I bought you a little something, Louise." Ruth rummaged through her pile of shopping bags. "Here it is!" She handed Louise a Vineyard Vines shopping bag.

"Oh, Ruth, how thoughtful," Louise said as she held up a bathroom floor mat that was white with a large pink whale outlined in navy blue under which read, "Every day should feel this good."

"I bought one for myself, too. It just spoke to me. My day

certainly did feel good. In fact, it was great. I thought the mat would look darling in your blue-and-white guest bathroom."

Amelia smiled. "It's very Martha's Vineyard-y."

Ruth took a deep breath and settled into the sofa, her drink back in her hand. "What a day! But I must say, I do not understand why you were so worried. I'm a grown woman, you know." She brushed her hair back and realized she was still wearing the pink baseball cap with a large black dog on it. She pulled it off and gave the dog a pat before placing it on the sofa next to her. "Did you know this dog was real? He belonged to a Captain Douglas on Martha's Vineyard; he was his faithful companion. The captain named him after Black Dog in *Treasure Island.* I just love learning new things." She paused ever so briefly. "So what were your worries about me? You can see I've had a stupendous time."

"It's quite possible," began Amelia, "that not only did the vase you bought have cocaine in it but the rest of your dishes did, too."

Ruth waved her hand in the air. "Oh, that. Louise told me about that when I called her today."

Louise interrupted. "Ruth, when we returned from our trip, all the luggage and boxes were lined up curbside outside the Travel Club's hangar. All except for yours!"

"Well, somebody had to be last; they just hadn't brought mine out yet."

"But when we went into the hangar to get your things, the luggage handler stopped us."

"I'm sure he just didn't want someone else claiming my things."

"Or they hadn't had a chance to switch your dishes. It's possible that there were two sets in your pattern—one with the drugs, one without."

"That doesn't make sense." Ruth took another gulp of her martini. "Why give me the druggy dishes if there was another set on the plane?"

"Because that set was already at the airport before we arrived home."

"But what if I picked a different set?"

Louise paused. "Ruth, that's where Robert comes in. He picked the pattern for you, didn't he?"

"Well, he made a recommendation, but I was looking at others, too. I think you're barking up the wrong tree. Anyway, we traded, remember," Ruth said with a bristle in her voice, "so they're not actually mine."

"Ruthie, that's beside the point."

"This may tie into the murder," said Amelia. "The dishes were still in their boxes in the pantry—the boxes that had your name on them. It's possible that the night of the party, someone, maybe Michael Porter, switched them."

"Ruthie," Louise jumped in, "the boxes that Claudia and I unpacked a few days later were plain, no name, no Cabo label. They weren't the same boxes we brought home from the airport. That's why we've been so worried. Robert could be involved. And out of the clear blue he whisks you off in a private plane. I was afraid something would happen to you."

"Well." Ruth looked at the floor mat. "Every day should feel this good, at least up until your best friend tells you the man you had this good day with used you as a drug donkey, or whatever it's called."

"Oh, Ruth, we're not saying he's a smuggler. We're saying there's a chance he's involved."

"Well, just so you know, I told Robert your suspicions on the flight home, and he was shocked. He's a very successful businessman, and you should be careful about what you say about him. You could ruin his reputation."

"I understand, Ruth," Louise said gently. "It's also possible that it's someone in Robert's company who is behind this, and that would certainly damage his reputation."

Ruth looked up hopefully. "You know who it could be? Vanessa. She's the receptionist at the Travel Club and was the stewardess on the plane today. Yes, now that I think about it, it could be her. I think she was spying on me when Robert and I were at lunch."

Ruth picked an olive out of her empty martini glass. "Louise! Vanessa was also on our Cabo trip. She must be involved. Poor, dear Robert."

"Let's not jump to conclusions, Ruthie."

Ruth looked at her watch. On the same wrist was a new bracelet, a pink-and-navy sailor knot with a gold whale clasp. Martha's Vineyard retailers also had a good day.

"Goodness, it's only nine thirty, but I'm bushed." Ruth yawned.

"Can I give you a ride home?" asked Amelia. "I need to get going as well, although my car isn't as luxurious as your stretch limo."

"Just one more of Robert's extravagances." She chuckled. "He hired the car just for me."

Amelia helped Ruth gather her shopping bags.

"You know, my dear departed husband always told me, 'If you can't go first class, stay home.' Well, he never flew private. I'm spoiled now!"

Ruth popped her baseball cap back on her head. "Come along, Black Dog, time to go home."

* * *

Amelia drove cautiously along the back roads to Ruth's house, watching for the glint from the eyes of deer. Bucks County was aptly named.

"I'm sorry if we upset you, Ruth," said Amelia. "You know how dear you are to Mom. You have a long history together."

"We certainly do." Ruth chuckled. "My father called us 'Frick' and 'Frack.' As young girls we were always up to something. Usually your mother was the instigator, and I happily went along. But you both needn't worry about me. You don't know Robert the way I do."

The rest of the drive was in silence other than an occasional snore from Ruth. Her head rested against the side window, giving Black Dog a view of cornfields and woods that edged the roadside.

Amelia followed Ruth up the brick stairs of her Colonial house. To the right of the entrance was a Shaker bench with a twig broom resting against it. Ruth set her purse on the bench while she rummaged for her keys.

"Ah, here we are," she said. "Would you mind coming in while I turn on some lights? I didn't expect to arrive home so late."

The decor belonged on the pages of *Country Living* magazine, though some decluttering would be required. The center hallway featured a pierced tin chandelier and an oval braided rug. A blanket chest, which was flanked by two wing chairs, displayed a collection of milk glass vases, bowls, hens, and cake plates.

Amelia followed Ruth into the kitchen, where a menagerie of ceramic roosters marched across the top of the kitchen cabinets. The one at the farthest end seemed to be peering down at the antique butter churn standing to the side of the back door.

"This is strange," said Amelia. A four-inch length of thin

fishing line was dangling from a piece of tape on the doorframe, and another piece of tape clung to the door itself.

"I tape it across the door opening when I go out," Ruth explained. "Someone's opened the door!"

"Maybe the tape wasn't secure enough and it just fell," said Amelia, hoping it was true. She opened the door and studied the exterior lock. It had scratch marks around the keyhole, hardly unusual given the age of the door and the lock. "I'll check the house," she said. "It's probably nothing." Amelia pulled out her cell phone, ready to hit "Emergency SOS" just in case.

Ten minutes later, Ruth's house glowed brightly in the darkness outside. Every interior light was on, as well as the backyard floodlights, which startled a raccoon family that was wandering across Ruth's lawn furniture. A weather satellite could have mistaken the site for a fire.

"Nothing seems to be missing," called Ruth. "I checked my jewels; they're all in my jewelry box. And the silver's here." She closed the drawer of the sideboard and plopped down in a dining room chair.

Amelia joined her in the dining room. "Nothing seems to be disturbed in the cellar," Amelia said, though she couldn't be sure, since it was crammed with boxes, trunks, and furniture. In one corner stood several artificial Christmas trees. The pegboard wall adjacent to it held accessories to celebrate most every holiday. There were plastic pumpkins, a large witch, a skeleton, Easter baskets, straw bunnies, an oversize leprechaun, and a large, plastic American flag that appeared to be covered in red, white, and blue Christmas lights. Martha Stewart meets the Dollar Store.

"Does my arrangement look off-center?" Ruth asked as she studied her vase of sunflowers on the dining room table.

Amelia slid it to the left until it was centered under the chandelier. "I recommend you put a dead bolt on your back door."

"When I was young, we didn't even lock our doors, but times have changed."

"Will you be OK here alone?"

"Of course, dear. My Paul's been gone fifteen years now. I'm used to it. You know, I got the fishing line idea from an Audrey Hepburn movie, *Chartreuse*—no that's not right—but it was called something like that. Cary Grant was in it. He used it across a hotel door to see if anyone entered when he was out, though I think he used a hair. I remember now." She snapped her fingers. "*Charade*, the movie was called *Charade*. I should remember that. My Paul and I used to play that game when we had parties."

Ruth's eyes twinkled. "Your mother was especially good at it. Well, I best be off to bed."

"Good night, Ruth." Amelia stood outside Ruth's front door until she heard the click of the lock and the chain slide into its track. Ruth's lights were out before Amelia was down the driveway.

61

Tim Watson admired his handiwork. It had taken him three months to complete his kitchen island. The granite top, five drawers, and two double-door cabinets would serve their intended purpose. It was the custom work that he was most proud of. Work that very few knew about, and those who did paid handsomely for it.

He had Uncle Frankie to thank. As a teenager, Tim helped his uncle make wooden boxes with secret compartments. They were simple ones with a false bottom. Frankie gave them to his nieces and nephews at Christmas. He hid a $100 bill in the compartment. Later, Tim added a level of complexity in accessing the bottom chamber. Even Uncle Frankie was impressed.

Tim expanded his skill well beyond boxes. Creating a place for people's secrets was a lucrative business. Most of it was paid for under the table. Funny, given that some of his compartments were literally under a table. Others were inside carved wooden sculptures or behind a wall. He built two for Uncle Frankie; one was behind the wall in the pantry at Twin Beeches.

Tim slid open his kitchen island's second drawer about two inches until he heard an almost imperceptible click. Then he opened the cabinet on the far right and reached inside until he felt a block of wood. He pulled it toward him. Another click, this time louder. He grinned as he made a selection from the onyx-and-marble cube that sat in the middle of the island. It was pierced with sixteen long, silver toothpicks, each topped with a tiny silver playing card—a king, queen, jack, and ace for each of the four suits.

The ace of spades was designed for the task at hand. He inserted it into the keyhole of the middle drawer on the island. Tim glided the pick along the bottom of the keyhole until it reached the sweet spot. He pushed. The panel in between the two cabinets swung out, revealing a large compartment. It was his most complicated and precise design to date. Only the exact order, the exact pressure, and the ace of spades could open it.

He sifted through the contents. On top was a list of who owned his custom creations. He liked to speculate what the owners kept in their secret places. He was certain some of them kept family jewels there—belonging to other families. There was also a pile of Cayman money from his last trip, plus a gun—never used—and his travel wallet. The latter held his passport. Uncle Frankie always told him to keep his passport current and have extra cash on hand.

Tucked underneath Tim's wallet was Frankie's passport. He flipped through its pages. Turks and Caicos, Switzerland, France, Italy, Luxembourg, Mexico. The guy knew how to live. Tim wondered if he was still alive. Why leave his passport? It violated Frankie's first rule for a quick escape. Grab your passport and cash and go.

Not even Frankie had the balls to stay when Tim showed Frankie the bug that was in the chandelier in Frankie's dining room at Twin Beeches. He handed it to Frankie, said goodbye, and never set foot in that house again. Until the night of the party at Twin Beeches.

What a fiasco!

It was supposed to be so simple: swap the boxes of dishes, open the compartment in the pantry, and get the hell out of there.

He told Robert he would help with the box swap because it would get him into the pantry. Get him access to the compartment that only he and Frankie knew how to open. Tim hoped Frankie had left a clue in there about where he was.

Tim felt partly responsible for Michael Porter's murder. Who was he kidding; it *was* his fault. He hired Porter for the job. Two boxes meant two guys, and to Porter it meant a few hundred bucks.

They arrived in Porter's van, parking along the service drive at the back of the house. Tim told him to wait in the van while he checked in at the house. Tim entered the kitchen through the back door, carrying his suit jacket. As expected, the place was crawling with servers, and the kitchen was the usual chaos at the beginning of any big party. No one was going to notice two more guys wearing black pants and white shirts.

He slipped his jacket on once he reached the breakfast room—from server to guest. He found Robert in the dining room, just outside the pantry door. A small table with a large flower arrangement partially blocked the view of the pantry from the living room. Robert handed him a drink. They watched the flow of cocktail-party traffic. People stayed where the drinks were. Robert and Tim were alone in the dining room.

Robert walked over to the pantry, reached beyond the rope-and-post stanchions, and, using a napkin, closed the door.

Tim strolled through the kitchen and out the back door. He

left his suit jacket in the van. He and Porter walked into the kitchen, boxes in hand.

Tim set his box of coke-free dishes in the pantry against the door to the dining room, so it couldn't be opened from the outside. He then casually stood in the kitchen as Porter carried the second box into the pantry.

Suddenly a man appeared, telling Porter to get the boxes out of there and close the pantry's door to the kitchen. Tim almost laughed out loud. It was precisely what he planned on doing. He graciously volunteered to help.

They switched boxes, tucking the "clean" ones back under the shelf where the others had been. Porter took his box to the van. He was supposed to stay there and wait for Tim. Instead, he came back and saw him removing the contents from the hidden compartment. Porter, thinking Tim was stealing, yanked open the door to the dining room to alert someone. He ran to Robert thinking he was a guest. Damn, he'd still be alive today if he hadn't done that.

Robert pushed him back into the pantry. Tim grabbed the box and bag from the compartment and walked out, closing the door to the kitchen behind him. Tim soon realized how bad things had turned. Robert's suit was spattered with blood.

What a disaster! He thought he had been so clever slipping into the party in a suit and slipping out as a server. Take away the jacket and you're pretty much dressed like a server, except with better shoes. No one would remember him at the party. He had been confident of that—until last Saturday when Amelia called him. Why had she asked him if he was there? Why would she even think that?

Tim put Frankie's passport back into the island safe. Robert didn't know he had it. Tim had taken it out of the bag. He left the money for Robert. He didn't want it. It was tainted by

Michael Porter's blood. Tim knew he was complicit in what happened, but he sure as hell wasn't a murderer. He'd never killed anyone; he didn't have the stomach for it. Frankie didn't, either; they were alike in that way. Robert, on the other hand, seemed to have no qualms about it.

Tim snapped his safe shut. The island was back to normal. Tim's life, not so much.

62

Robert sat alone in his office. The silence was a relief. Ruth's incessant calls to him the past two days thanking him for the "adventure of my life" were almost worse than spending the day with her.

Everyone had gone home, even Vanessa. It had been a while since they last had drinks together in his office after work. It always led to sex on the sofa. Amazing sex. She was always willing. And today she was dressed for undressing. Her black leather skirt barely hid the straps of her garter belt. Her white silk blouse was unbuttoned just enough so when she leaned over his desk to give him a file, and a hard-on, he could glimpse her nipples hiding behind black lace. She was the perfect accessory for his office. He hated to disappoint her and deprive himself, but he needed to think.

He opened the cocktail cabinet, triggering the halogen lights inside, and poured himself two fingers of scotch. The interior reminded him of the galley in the G5, one of the many extravagances he enjoyed. He liked his Travel Club fleet, although the two "tourist" planes seemed like buses compared to his G5. But those buses were useful; they always held at least one unsuspecting candidate for his import business.

Business had been good. He could barely spend or move the money fast enough, and it was strictly business-to-business. He and his partners could have made a lot more money if they sold smaller quantities, but that would mean selling to consumers, and those who consumed cocaine became less careful and less discreet as they became more dependent. That's how you get busted. Some desperate son of a bitch showing up at your door at all hours looking for a gram or two, or a regular customer introducing you to his new best friend who just happens to want larger and larger quantities, until the day he arrives with a badge instead of cash. Nope, they were strictly B2B.

His job was easy. Seduce the old ladies into buying dishes, statues—whatever vessel was needed to bring coke into the country. They were his mules. Dependable Ruth Richards was the leader of the pack. Four successful trips; sixty kilos of coke.

And she had been clueless. There was always plenty of time to switch her purchases once they landed. She was the last one to leave the airport lounge, insisting on having one more glass of wine *for the road* and following him around, jabbering about their next trip *together*.

He should have realized it would get complicated when she brought her friend on this last trip. Louise Jenkins wanted nothing to do with his schmoozing, so Robert had to divide and conquer. Ruth bought the dishes. Another success, until Ruth walked into the hangar with Louise and a driver, and the coke left with them.

He'd have to put her out to pasture now. But there would be others.

His phone vibrated. He looked at the text message.

I'm in the parking lot.

Robert unlocked the back door.

63

Amelia watched as Tim Watson pulled into the parking lot of the State Street shops and found a spot near the Travel Club. She had been following him off and on since she found out he was Frankie Vincent's nephew. His destinations were not unusual—work, home, grocery store, bar. However, this was unexpected. First the FedEx office and now here. *Was he planning a trip?* She thought of Ruth's trip two days ago with Robert D'Angelo. *Is there a connection?*

Tim walked to the club's back door.

She found a parking spot in the middle row and backed in, facing away from the row of stores, which included a yarn shop, Bangle & Butterfield Boutique, a florist, Dunbar & Co., and the Travel Club. Tim's truck was a dozen spaces to her right in the first row. There would be no reason for him to walk in the direction of her car. She raised her headrest as far as it would go, slouched down in her seat, and adjusted the rearview mirror. She had a perfect view.

Half an hour later the lot began to empty as employees and customers headed home. Amelia hoped Kirby Dunbar was working late. She would be her excuse if Tim spotted her—just waiting for a friend.

She glanced at her text messages.

Mardi: Call me.

Louise: Dinner? It was Thursday. Dinner with the family.

Mardi: A drink?

Winnie: Are you coming to dinner? Any news on our case? She added a spyglass emoji.

She saw a flash of a light in her side-view mirror. It was a motion sensor light at the back door of Dunbar & Co. Kirby was leaving, probably going to dinner with Elliott at the house. So much for an excuse if Tim saw her. She turned back to her messages and replied.

Louise: Don't hold dinner. I'm running late. Sorry.

Mardi: Will call in a bit. May be up for a drink if it's not too late.

Winnie: Detective, I look forward to providing a full report, Amelia wrote, thinking about how gleeful Winnie would be when she found out that Amelia had been on a stakeout when they texted. She hit send and checked her rearview mirror.

* * *

"Hey, man, how goes it?" Robert asked as he opened the back door of the Travel Club.

"Good, I'm good," said Tim, giving a quick glance around the office to make sure they were alone.

Robert poured a finger of scotch. "Neat or rocks?"

"Neat. Thanks."

Robert picked up a remote. Pavarotti loudly joined them in the room. "I sweep the place for bugs, but you can never be too careful," he said.

Tim sipped his drink as he wandered around the office. Why

did he recognize the song? Opera was not his thing. *The Simpsons*, that was it. Sideshow Bob sang it. He strolled over to the collection of globes.

"So tell me what's on your mind." Robert casually sat on the sofa.

"It's about Frankie." Tim's voice was strong; his nerves were jangled.

"Yeah?" Robert laughed as if Tim had made a joke. "He's your uncle. You probably know more about him than I do."

"But not where he is. Do you know?"

Robert studied Tim carefully. "You know who else asked me that? You wanna guess?"

Tim looked at him quizzically.

"Smith Phillips asked me the same thing."

Tim flushed down the bile in his throat with a swig of scotch. "Why would Smith ask about him?"

"I don't know, and as you are well aware, it's too late for me to find out. Why are you interested?"

"I'm curious. Sometimes I wonder if he's still in the area."

"Frankie's probably livin' the life with Phyllis, drinking margaritas in the Caribbean."

Pavarotti boomed.

Ridi, Pagliaccio,

sul tuo amore infranto!

Ridi del duol, che t'avvelena il cor!

"The Master," Robert said, motioning upward. Tim knew he meant Pavarotti. Robert could not be close to God.

"*Pagliacci* was my grandfather's favorite opera, and he would replay 'Vesti la giubba' over and over again. It's the end of the first act."

"What's it about?"

"Betrayal." Robert took a slow sip of his drink.

64

Amelia sat in her car, wondering just how much longer Tim would be in the Travel Club. She would need a bathroom break soon.

A car drove past the Travel Club and stopped at the door to the yarn shop. *Beep! Beep!* A woman emerged and climbed into the passenger seat. As the car pulled away, Tim emerged from the Travel Club.

He backed his truck out of his space and drove toward the exit, but instead of turning onto the road, he slowly drove along the row of parking spaces where Amelia was parked.

Amelia ducked down. The truck stopped in front of her car, blocking her.

Tim climbed out of his truck, tucked a scrap of paper under her windshield wiper, and, giving her a nervous glance, walked back to his truck. Amelia waited until he was gone to retrieve the note.

Meet me in the parking lot of the Brick.

Amelia found the last free parking space at the Brick at the far end of the lot, near the firehouse. She backed in and watched as three cars circled in search of an open space. She slid her can of Mace out of her purse and tucked it beside her; her phone was in the center console. She removed her silk scarf and dropped it over the phone. She hoped it didn't muffle their conversation, if Tim actually showed up.

And then she saw him, crouched beside her car just behind the driver's door.

"Amelia," he whispered, "let me in."

She felt for her Mace and unlocked the car. Tim slipped into the back seat.

"What are you doing?"

"I'm hiding. What do you think I'm doing?"

Amelia unexpectedly started laughing. "This is ridiculous. You've got ten seconds to tell me what's going on, or I'm out of the car and calling the police."

"Here, look at this." He reached between the front seats and handed her Frankie's passport. "You should know that Frankie Vincent is my uncle."

Amelia flipped through it and set it back on the console. "Tell me something I don't know, and you have two seconds left."

"I don't think Uncle Frankie ran. He didn't take his passport. I think Robert killed him."

"Or Frankie didn't need his passport."

"Why wouldn't he take it? And there was a lot of cash with the passport. No reason to leave that behind."

"How did you get his passport?"

Tim hesitated.

Amelia waited.

"I took it," he said finally. "I took it from your mother's house the night Porter was killed. It was in a hidden compartment I built for Uncle Frankie in the pantry."

Amelia gasped.

"Wait! Hear me out, Amelia."

Thirty minutes later, he was still in her back seat.

"OK"—she threw up her hands—"my brain is about to explode."

"Don't make a scene."

"A scene? You're hiding in the back seat of my car telling me about two murders, drugs, and a secret stash in my mother's pantry? And you don't want to go to the police? Are you out of your mind?"

"No, scared. I only agreed to move the boxes that night so that I could get into the pantry compartment to see if Uncle Frankie left a clue for me about where he went. We were close. When I saw his passport, I freaked. He's dead, Amelia, I'm sure of it.

"Robert killed Porter and Smith, why not Uncle Frankie? I don't have enough proof for any of it, and if I don't get some, I'm screwed." He palmed the passport. "Amelia, I'm trusting you. Give me a pen and paper.

"The reason I was at FedEx today was to send you a package," Tim said as he drew on the paper. "It will arrive in two days. I mailed it to you just in case my meeting with Robert ended badly. In it is a key to my house and instructions on how to open a compartment I built into my kitchen island. You're the only one who knows it's there. Inside is a letter with the details of everything I've just told you. If you haven't heard from me by the time the package arrives, follow the instructions and go to the police."

The reason I was at FedEx today. "Wait, did you know I was following you?"

"That's what gave me the balls to talk to Robert. I figured if he was going to send me to Glory Land, he wouldn't do it in his office, and you'd follow us when we left. You've been tailing me for a couple of days, right?"

"Well, off and on," said Amelia, her surveillance confidence shattered.

"When I spotted you again this morning, I decided to make my move before you gave up."

He handed Amelia the paper and pen. "Here's a diagram of how to get into the compartment at Twin Beeches."

Amelia studied the drawing as Tim opened the door. "I'm telling you the truth. It's too insane not to be. I'll call you."

He paused briefly. "You'll need a toothpick."

He slipped out of the car and into the shadows.

65

Amelia followed the laughter into the dining room. Louise, Elliott, and Kirby were gathered around the table.

"Amelia, you made it. Sit down, dear, I'll get you a plate."

"I'm fine, Mom. I've been running all day. I'll just pour myself a glass of wine for now."

Amelia slipped into the pantry. With the shelves filled with dishes and glassware, it was difficult to notice the discrepancy—a two-foot-long section of shelves was at least three inches shallower than the others. Amelia peered under the lowest of the three shelves. It looked like tiny woodpeckers had attacked the wall, leaving pinhole-size scars.

Amelia tapped a toothpick into the tiny holes. On the fifth try she found the spot. Carefully she lifted the front row of shelves as if she were opening the trunk of a car. The compartment was empty, but it satisfied Amelia that Tim was telling the truth, at least about this.

"Amelia, you're here!" Winnie stood at the door to the pantry, staring at the raised shelves.

Startled, Amelia let go of the shelves, which dropped down forcefully, causing the vases and glasses to knock into each other. Two large vases tipped and shattered on the brick floor.

"What's the commotion?" Louise ran to the pantry. Elliott and Kirby were close behind.

"It's a secret hiding place!" Winnie exclaimed, bouncing up and down.

"Where?" Louise stared at the shards of glass glinting off the floor.

"Sorry, Mom." Amelia inserted the pick back into the hole and lifted the shelves.

"It's empty." Winnie frowned.

"Your ancestors certainly loved secrets," said Kirby. "Hidden things in their portraits, and now this. What do you think was kept in here?"

"It wasn't the Samuels," said Amelia. "Frankie Vincent had it built." Amelia showed them the sketch.

"Where did you get that?" Elliott asked.

"I can't say."

"Is this connected to the murder?"

"Yes."

"Woah," Winnie said quietly. "I did find evidence after all." Winnie ran from the pantry. She returned clutching her evidence box.

"The silver toothpick. Remember? I found it in the pantry!"

66

Ruth strode past Vanessa's empty desk toward Robert's office. She would settle this once and for all. She couldn't bear going into the weekend not knowing the truth. Tuesday, Robert wined and dined her in Martha's Vineyard. Wednesday, she called to invite him to dinner. He declined and not even graciously. Thursday, he didn't even have the decency to return her calls.

"I don't care what you think! You do what I tell you to do," Robert yelled.

Ruth froze outside his door.

"In your dreams!"

Ruth recognized Vanessa's voice, though she had never heard it so shrill. "You're despicable, conning old ladies. And our relationship is over!"

Robert laughed. "You set a pretty low bar for a relationship if sex in my office qualifies."

"You're a pig! I'd watch what you say to me."

Robert's voice turned menacing. "Threatening me is a very bad idea."

"You don't scare me!" Vanessa whipped open the door. "Mrs. Richards!"

Ruth stepped around Vanessa and marched into Robert's office. "That's no way to talk to a lady, not even your secretary."

"I'm not his secretary!"

"Well, whatever they call it today." She turned to Robert. "I need to have a word with you."

"Ruth, I'm busy. We had a nice trip and I appreciate your calls, but I have work to do. And as you no doubt heard, I'm not in a very good mood."

"Then I'll get to the point. Did you take my photo album?"

"What are you talking about?"

"My album with the photos from Mexico is missing. I wanted to put my mementos from our trip to Martha's Vineyard in it. I don't have any photos, but I do have postcards, a menu, and a coaster from the plane." She looked at him hesitantly. "I hope it was all right to take the coaster."

"Ruth, I have no need for your album, and I couldn't care less if you took a coaster. I'm actually surprised you didn't stash a champagne flute in your purse."

Ruth was taken aback. "That's hardly the tone to take with one of your VIP clients, particularly after we talked about my possibly working with you."

"Ruth, I'm busy."

Ruth clutched the strap of her shoulder bag like the strap of a rifle. She was ready to do battle.

"I showed you the album when you came to my house to interview me about our trip to Cabo. You certainly seemed to enjoy looking at it then. If you had used anything from it—photos, passages from my journaling, ticket stubs—it would have made for a much more interesting article in the club's magazine.

You should know that I was very disappointed when it came out."

Robert, seated behind his desk, stared at Ruth incredulously. "Ruth, I don't have time to listen to you babble about your album. You probably forgot where you put it."

"Robert, you're hurting my feelings."

Ruth knew she shouldn't have started out accusing him of taking her album, but she was angry. That appeared to be the prevailing mood in the office. She took a deep breath and exhaled, hoping to blow away Robert's insults. She knew what she wanted to say. Maybe he didn't realize how she felt about him.

"Those photos from Cabo are very personal to me," Ruth began. "You're in them. They capture the start of our special relationship. There, I've said it. We have a special relationship, don't we?"

"Ruth, dear Ruth, the Travel Club is my business. My job is to make people like you feel special."

Ruth's voice quavered. "People like me?" She grabbed the edge of Robert's desk to steady herself. Tears filled her eyes. "People like me? Oh, I'm such an old fool."

Vanessa stormed back into the office. "No, you're not. He's despicable!" Vanessa shoved a large envelope into Ruth's hand. "Here's your album. Your trip to Martha's Vineyard was to get you out of the house so someone could steal it." She glared at Robert.

"Robbie didn't like the photos of Cabo Pottery, particularly those that showed him in the storeroom. He told me to shred them." Vanessa paused and then sneered, "Oops, Robbie, I forgot!"

Robert leaped from behind his desk, shoved Ruth out of the way, and lunged at Vanessa, knocking her to the floor.

"Let go of her!" Ruth screamed.

Robert was on top of Vanessa, his knee on her chest and his hands around her neck. Ruth grabbed at his shoulder, trying to pull him off Vanessa. Robert grabbed Ruth's leg, and with a quick jerk sent her sprawling to the floor on her back.

Ruth rolled away from Robert and tried to get to her knees before collapsing again, this time face-first onto the floor. She heard Vanessa gasping, "I can't breathe. Get off me."

Ruth lifted her head and saw her purse under the armchair. She dragged herself over to it and reached into the front flap. *You can do this, Ruth.* It was more of a plea than an affirmation. She used the chair to brace herself as she slowly rose to her feet.

Vanessa was clawing at Robert's hands. Her face was the color of rage. And fear.

"You bastard," shrieked Ruth. "Close your eyes, Vanessa!"

Robert twisted his head toward Ruth's voice. The Mace hit him directly in the face. He and Vanessa cried out as the Mace enveloped them, forcing their eyes closed. Robert's hands flew to his face. Vanessa blindly shoved him off and crawled away.

"Ruth," she gasped, "get help."

Ruth ran toward the back door that led to the parking lot. As she passed the cocktail cabinet, she suddenly stopped and turned back. Robert was kneeling, one hand on his desk trying to pull himself up, the other frantically rubbing his burning eyes.

Ruth raised a bottle of scotch in both hands and swung it like a bat, slamming it into Robert's head. He crumbled to the floor. She kicked him twice.

"How dare you, you heathen." Ruth's voice was unrecognizable even to her—menacing and empowered.

Ruth dragged Vanessa through the back door and propped her into a sitting position against the wall. "Breathe in the fresh air."

A couple emerged from the florist next door. They stopped, staring at the two disheveled women.

"Don't just stand there," Ruth barked. "Call the police."

She slumped down next to Vanessa and clutched her hand. "We women have to stick together."

67

"They should give him life!" demanded Ruth. "How dare he take advantage of me!"

"But you showed him, didn't you, Ruthie," Louise said from a chair next to Ruth's hospital bed in the ER. "You're a hero."

"Well, you know, self-defense means self-preservation. I carry my Mace wherever I go." Ruth whipped a small can from under her pillow. "See?"

Louise instinctively drew back.

"Don't worry, it has a safety lock on it."

"All the same, Ruthie," said Louise, "why don't you put it away."

"It saved my life and Vanessa's, too. That evil man was choking the life out of her before I came to her rescue, at great risk to my own life, I might add."

"Thankfully, the doctor said you're going to be fine and can go home. I would like you to stay with me. You shouldn't be alone. Amelia said she'll come by and can run to your house to pick up anything you might need."

Detective Mardi knocked on the door to Ruth's room. "May I come in?"

"Oh, please do," said Ruth. "Did you catch him?"

"Not yet, but there is an all-points bulletin out for Robert D'Angelo's arrest."

"Anthony, is Ruth safe?" Louise asked.

"Mr. D'Angelo is on the run. I don't expect he'll attempt anything, but you should remain cautious until we apprehend him. If you see anything suspicious, call 911 or this number." He gave each of them a card.

"I can't believe he got away," fumed Ruth. "I thought I knocked him out cold."

"We'll find him," Mardi said.

"I hope you throw the book at him. I'm very embarrassed. I was such a fool."

"Hardly a fool, Mrs. Richards. You weren't the only one who fell for his charms. Vanessa Van Born is being very cooperative."

"And she's so much younger than me! I guess I still have it."

68

She didn't expect it to be a crime scene; though, considering the circumstances, she should have realized that it was a possibility.

She should have been more careful. Should have tried not to disturb any potential evidence. What had she touched? The back door and the kitchen island were a given, especially the island. Her fingerprints were everywhere. But once she saw the blood, she stopped touching things and called Tony Mardi.

* * *

Amelia had looked forward to a quiet morning after last night's visit with Ruth at Twin Beeches. Robert's attack on Ruth and Vanessa was more violent with each retelling, Ruth's response more heroic.

When the FedEx driver handed Amelia the package from Tim Watson, she feared that a deadly assault may also have occurred, just as Tim forewarned. The note inside was simple:

Amelia, if you haven't heard from me, then Robert succeeded. Use the information I left you to get him! Tim.

Folded in the note was a key with a tag marked "back door" and a diagram for accessing the hidden compartment in his kitchen. It reminded her of instructions for building IKEA furniture, except instead of an Allen wrench, she would use Tim's preferred tool, a toothpick.

She parked two streets away, next to a small park with tennis courts, and walked to Tim's house. She slipped in through the back door while calling his name. Silence mingled with the smell of bleach.

Even with instructions it took Amelia thirty minutes to open the hidden compartment in the kitchen island. It required smooth, precise movements. Amelia's furtive glances at the windows and sweating palms stymied the first dozen attempts. And then she heard the click. Inside the compartment was a thick envelope with Amelia's name on it. She quickly scanned the letter inside, signed by Tim. It read like a confession, though the most damning sins had Robert D'Angelo's name attached to them.

She'd read it carefully later. She needed to get out of the house. It was giving her the heebie-jeebies. But so was the smell of bleach. She needed to find where it was coming from. She returned the island to its original state and began her search.

It wasn't the kitchen. The cleaning products there, including those under the sink, were natural—Mrs. Meyer's, Seventh Generation, white vinegar, and baking soda. She checked the bathroom. No bleach. She crept down the hallway and found it. In the bedroom.

She also found blood. At least she was pretty sure it was blood. It was a large, dark stain on the bed, more on the floor.

Bleach had partially whitened the carpet, but the stains were still there.

* * *

Amelia hid behind the bushes in Tim's backyard until the police arrived. Barnett was first on the scene, quickly followed by Mardi and Cole. She gave them Tim's note, house key, and instructions for opening the safe. Then she handed over the letter. In it Tim had said that he wanted her to "get" Robert. She'd let the police do that.

She spent the next three hours with Detective Cole at the police station, elaborating on what Tim had confided in her: that he had admitted he was at Twin Beeches the night of the murder, that he had built the hidden compartment in the pantry at Twin Beeches, that he believed Robert D'Angelo killed Michael Porter and Smith Phillips, that he suspected Frankie Vincent was dead, and that he thought he was next on D'Angelo's hit list.

Cole's left eyebrow twitched each time Amelia said anything significant. It was doing a crazy dance by the time Amelia was done.

Toward the end of the interview, Cole briefly stepped out of the room. When she returned, she said Tim's body had not been found at the house. An empty bottle of bleach was discovered under his bed.

69

Traffic was bumper-to-bumper on State Street in Newtown as Amelia headed home from the police station. She decided to avoid the congestion by cutting through the parking lot behind the State Street shops. A police car and several black SUVs with government plates were parked at the back of the Travel Club, blocking the lane between the businesses and the parking lot. Amelia steered her car along the first row of parking spaces.

A woman rolling two suitcases was walking in the middle of it, forcing Amelia to stop. Amelia rolled down her window. "Can I get by?" Amelia called.

The woman stopped, let go of the suitcase in her left hand, and pointed her middle finger toward the sky. "You'll just have to wait," she yelled as she turned to face the car.

"Amelia?" Kirby exclaimed. "God, I'm sorry. The police blocked the lane so I can't pull my car up to the door. I had to park way the hell over there," she said, pointing to the back of the lot.

"I'll drive you to your car."

"Thanks. I'm sorry I was so rude. I'm totally stressed out. I've got to get to a meeting in New York, and the parking lot looks like a crime scene."

It is, Amelia thought to herself as she and Kirby lifted the two suitcases into the trunk of her Audi. "These weigh a ton."

"I know. Who would think fabric samples and sketches could be so heavy. Were you coming to see me?"

"No, I'm on the way to my mother's and cut through the parking lot because State Street is moving at a crawl." Amelia looked back at the Travel Club. "I assume you know about Robert D'Angelo."

"Everybody's talking about it. Did he really attack Ruth Richards and a woman who works at the Travel Club?"

"Yes. And he may be involved in smuggling drugs."

"What?" Kirby's eyes darted to the police cars and back to Amelia. "Is this about the vase?" Suddenly she grabbed Amelia's arm. "I could be dragged into this because of that damn vase? That just can't happen."

Amelia didn't dare mention the possibility that Robert might be a murderer, too. "Did you ever see him at any social events?" She wanted to move the conversation along to avoid Kirby's self-induced hysteria about her own reputation.

"Never. No, that's not right. I once attended a hangar party when he unveiled his second plane, but that was just a professional courtesy."

"Did you see him at Twin Beeches the night of the murder?"

"Oh my God! He was there?"

Amelia stopped her car by Kirby's and hit the trunk release. The popping sound made Kirby jump.

"This is all unbelievable!" Kirby continued. "Have they arrested him?"

"I don't know. I think they're still looking for him."

"I'm glad I'm going to New York. If I saw him I'd run him down with my car. The creep! We don't need people like him endangering our community. Drugs! That's despicable." Kirby drew a deep breath and got out of the car. She and Amelia loaded the suitcases into her BMW. "They better catch him. I'll be back tomorrow or the next day."

Amelia hoped Robert would be caught before Kirby returned and laid eyes—or tires—on him.

Kirby walked around to the driver's side of her car, then stopped and turned back to Amelia. "Again, I'm sorry about the, you know . . ." She held up her middle finger and laughed.

Amelia was in awe of Kirby's amplitude of emotions.

70

Monday morning Amelia reread the letter Tim had left her, glad that she had used her phone to photograph it before turning it over to the police.

Why didn't he mention the dump?

She set the letter aside and clicked on her iPhone's voice memo. The recording was surprisingly clear, given that the phone had been in her center console underneath a scarf the night Tim slipped into the back seat.

"I drove Robert to the dump. He threw away a duffel bag, and then I drove him to Saint Mary's, where his car . . ."

She played the entire recording one more time. It was time to share. She sent a text to Mardi: I've got to talk to you about Tim.

The swoosh as her text made its way to him sounded like an ill wind, or perhaps a sigh of relief. She would know which very soon.

Her phone pinged. Amelia glanced down, expecting it to be Mardi.

It's me. Hurt, but alive. I've got to see you.

Amelia didn't recognize the phone number, but it had to be Tim Watson. She replied: Where are you?

Drive to Core Creek Park. Leave car unlocked in the parking lot off Tollhouse Road. Walk around for 10 min. If no one followed you, I'll get in the back seat of your car.

When?

Now.

This time she'd tell him she was recording.

* * *

A walk in the woods would have been enjoyable if an injured man running away from a murderer hadn't ordered it.

Amelia jumped each time a jogger overtook her at Core Creek Park as she wandered along the path that threaded through a dense grove of trees. The joggers were unintentionally stealthy, except for a dad pushing his daughter in a baby jogger stroller. Amelia heard them coming, the child giggling and yelling, "Faster, Daddy." She waved as she rolled past Amelia. The other joggers were so quiet they seemed to suddenly overtake her, causing her nerves to send a jolt of energy through her body, as if she was slowly being electrocuted.

She kept walking. Seven minutes. Eight minutes. Finally, it was time for Amelia to turn around and retrace her steps. The dad was heading back in her direction. She'd jog behind him. Safety in numbers, even if one was a toddler.

The dad nodded as he passed her. She gave him a ten-foot lead, then turned and began her own rhythmic jog back to the car. The child's cooing sounded like a refrain from a hymn, calming her. She breathed in the pine air, relaxed her shoulders, and increased her stride. The father and child turned off onto a path on the left. No matter, her car was just around the next bend. The sun warmed her shoulders as it cast her shadow in front of her. Another shadow appeared on her left, growing in size as it approached. Amelia moved farther to the right to share the path. The shadow disappeared behind her. Until she saw an arm extend.

He was holding something. *A baton? Is he holding a baton? Is he running a relay?*

Before the absurdity of that notion sunk in, she felt an exploding pain on the left side of her head. Her body lurched to the right even as her feet tried to propel her forward. Long green arms seemed to wave her away, but still she fell into them. They clawed at her face while she tumbled onto a blanket of pine needles, dirt, and nothingness.

* * *

"Turn them off, please, they're too bright." Amelia tried to shield her eyes but her arms were pinned at her sides.

"It's OK, Miss Halliday. You're safe. You're in an ambulance."

She tried to look at the man who was talking, but there were four of him, four of everything.

"I'm going to throw up," she mumbled before losing consciousness.

A swarm of bees was rushing toward her. She could hear their approach. Louder. Louder. She raised her arms to shoo them away and felt a piercing sting on the inside of her right arm.

"Bees," Amelia cried. "Help me! Bees!"

"Amelia, honey, it's Mom. Can you hear me? She's awake! Nurse, she's awake!"

"They're stinging me. It hurts!" Amelia cried.

A nurse rushed to Amelia's bedside. "It's OK, honey, it's OK," she said as she straightened Amelia's arm, examined the IV, and secured it with more tape.

Amelia opened her eyes, tried to move her head, and grimaced. "Ohhh."

Louise took Amelia's hand. "Everything's going to be OK. You're in the hospital."

"What happened?"

"You were attacked at the park yesterday."

"Who attacked me?"

"We don't know yet, but the police are searching for him. You need to rest."

Amelia closed her eyes again. "Who found me?"

"Someone called 911."

Tim Watson. She was supposed to meet him. Did he do this? No, no that doesn't make sense. It hurt even to think. She smelled pine.

"A tree tried to catch me," she mumbled as she floated away into sleep. "It wasn't strong enough. I hope it's OK."

Louise stroked Amelia's hand. "Rest, my sweet."

* * *

"You look so glamorous," gushed Carol Anne as she walked into Amelia's hospital room.

Amelia was sitting in a reclining chair by the window. She wore a pink chenille robe. And sunglasses.

"I'm still sensitive to the light, but thanks for the compliment."

It had been two days since the attack. The first night in the ICU was a blur. Literally. Even with her eyes closed, images swam laps around her head. At least now she could walk, slowly, and turn her head, very slowly. She still needed to master looking down without the urge to throw up before she could be discharged.

"Did they catch the guy?" Carol Anne asked.

"Not yet."

"It's about the murder, isn't it?"

Amelia shrugged and then grabbed the arm of the chair to stop Carol Anne from spinning in front of her. "Ooh, can't make that move, either," said Amelia as she sat perfectly still and took a deep breath. "I don't know what else it could be. Hard to imagine some random guy going for a run carrying a blunt force object."

Carol Anne handed her a white box. "I made you these. I hope you're allowed to eat cookies."

"Absolutely." Amelia smiled. "Thank you. You're very thoughtful. How are you doing?"

"I'm good. Working a lot. I'm on my break. There's something I need to tell you. It's about Jerry, or maybe it isn't. I hope it isn't."

"What about Jerry?"

"I remembered something that Mikey told me when he called me about that job. Usually when he got extra work he would say so-and-so called him and offered him a job. But that day, the day he died, he said a guy *at* work wanted him to help him out. Him and Mikey were gonna do the job together. After Mikey was killed I was in shock, I guess, so I blocked it in my memory. It was the last time Mikey spoke to me." She bit her lip. "I couldn't play it back in my head. He sounded so happy. And when I finally did think about it, I was afraid to say something because maybe it was Jerry. I should have said something sooner. Maybe then you wouldn't have been hurt. I'm so sorry." Carol Anne sat on the edge of Amelia's bed and began to cry. "I really messed up. It's my fault you got hurt. I'm sorry. I really am."

"Carol Anne, I don't think anything would have changed if you had told me sooner. So this is not your fault." Amelia slowly rose from her chair. "I have to get back in bed."

The door to Amelia's room opened slightly.

"Knock, knock." Amelia's doctor peered in the room. He saw Carol Anne quickly press a wad of tissues against her eyes. "I'll come back in a minute," he said.

Carol Anne's face was mottled with red blotches. She blew her nose loudly. "I'll go so the doctor can take care of you."

Amelia wearily climbed into bed. *Who attacked her?* Amelia was afraid of the answer, just as Carol Anne had been about who hired Michael.

71

Amelia carefully sat up and leaned against the bed pillows. After three days in the hospital she was home—almost. The condition for her discharge was she could not be alone. She was back in her bedroom at Twin Beeches. She ate her breakfast off the same white wicker breakfast tray from her childhood. She was ten years old again, eating oatmeal and blueberries.

Amelia's cell phone pinged.

Her head still hurt when she read, but surely she could read a text.

You OK?

And then she realized who it was from. Am I OK? she texted Tim Watson. Did you attack me?

No! I was hiding near your car waiting for you to return. I saw you take the path.

Before Amelia could respond another text appeared.

I left a photo in the mailbox at your mother's house. It's the guy who attacked you.

More text.

He ran from the trees by the path. Sorry. Had to leave. Too dangerous.

You took a picture instead of helping me! I could have been killed!

No response. Not even the bubbles showing he was writing something. Nothing.

Hey, how do you know I'm at my mother's house? "Bastard!" Amelia flung her legs over the side of the bed. "Ooh," she groaned and grabbed her head. She gingerly took the stairs to the kitchen.

Claudia ran to her. "Let me help you."

"I'm OK, really. I just need to walk slow, really, really slow."

Claudia held out a chair at the kitchen table. "What can I make you?"

"Actually, could you do something for me? I think there's a photo in the mailbox."

Claudia looked at her quizzically.

Amelia lowered herself into a chair and propped her chin on her folded hands. "My head weighs a ton, but I'm not imagining things. I got a text that there's a photo in the mailbox of the person who attacked me."

"Good Lord," Claudia said as she hurried out the kitchen door.

* * *

Amelia studied the blurry photo of a medium-built figure in gray sweats, a black baseball cap, and sunglasses.

"Amelia!" Winnie squealed and raced into the kitchen, dropping her backpack with a thud on the floor. She skidded to a stop when she saw Amelia grimace.

"I'm sorry," she whispered. "I'm just so happy you're OK.

Well, not totally OK, but you know, you're not dead." Winnie clamped her hands over her mouth.

Amelia patted the seat next to her. "I'm happy to see you, too. In fact, I need your help."

Winnie beamed. *"Anything!"* She quickly covered her mouth and whispered, "Sorry, anything. I don't have much homework, so I have plenty of time to help."

Amelia handed Winnie her phone. "My eyes are still too jiggly to focus. I need you to forward these messages to Detective Mardi."

Winnie scrolled down the messages. "All of them?"

"Yes, and then take a picture of this on my phone." She handed Winnie the photo. "And send it to him as well."

Amelia heard a soft "Wow!"

"I know. He may be my attacker. Please add a message that these are from Tim Watson, and that I think he's using burner phones."

"What's that?" Winnie asked.

"It's a prepaid phone. People buy them to hide their identities. You use the phone and then toss it."

"Whoa" was all Winnie could say as her little fingers sent the messages. She leaned over to Amelia and gently hugged her arm.

Amelia waited for Mardi to call.

72

"Amelia!" Kirby roared. "Detective Mardi just called me. Is it true?"

Amelia jerked the phone away from her ear. "Kirby, please, I have a hellacious headache.

I just found out myself."

Mardi's call earlier this morning had stunned Amelia. A suspect had already been identified—Marc Nelson, Kirby's assistant. Mardi said he saw the resemblance after the photo she sent him was enhanced. It was his chin. He had noticed how square Marc's chin was the night he questioned him about following Winnie. It jutted out like a boxer's, and that night Mardi wanted to hit it. Instead he took down his license number and address.

"I can't believe it." Kirby's incredulity reduced the decibels only slightly. "Why would Marc attack you? He's fired, I promise you! I told the police to tell him so. Has he been arrested?"

"Kirby, I don't know. Are you back?"

"No, I'm still in New York. I left Marc in charge. That

bastard!" she yelled. "How dare he close when I'm gone? *My* clerk locks up *my* store and goes for a jog?"

"Kirby, please, my head is pounding."

"Sorry, I'm just in shock, in disbelief. What did you do to provoke him?"

"Provoke him! Are you crazy?"

"Wait, wait, I'm sorry. I didn't mean to say you caused it. I'm just overwhelmed by this news. It's all so horrifying. Why would he attack you?"

"Kirby, I don't know. I don't even know if it was him. Detective Mardi told me he's a suspect."

"This is a nightmare. My reputation, Amelia, this could ruin my reputation."

"When are you coming back?"

"Well, as soon as I can. But I have so much to do here. I don't know. Do I need to?" A nervous twinge punctuated her question.

"I just assumed the police might want to check"—she wasn't about to say *search*—"your store for any evidence against Marc."

Silence. "Kirby? Are you still there?" Amelia detected what sounded like a sob.

"I just can't get involved in this. Whatever it is. My reputation is at stake. If my clients sense any hint of something illegal related to my business, I'm toast. This is my moment! If Marc screws this up for me, I'll kill him!"

"Kirby, he's not going to screw things up for you."

"But I hired him. If Marc is arrested and Dunbar & Co. is mentioned, my reputation's shot."

"Kirby, I have to go." Amelia felt like an earthquake was rumbling between her ears, ready to split her head open.

"I understand. I just had to talk to someone. Elliott is in a board meeting all day."

That's it? Kirby needed to talk to someone?

"Call me if you hear anything more," Kirby said. "Oh, and take care. You need your rest."

If she had been on a landline, Amelia would have slammed down the phone. There should be an app for that. It would be a nice complement to the old phone ringtone.

73

Welcome home. Amelia heard the case clock chime as she opened her front door. The late-afternoon sun offered her a game of checkers across the oak floor as its rays marked off squares of light through the small square Queen Anne-style windowpanes. She climbed the stairs, enjoying their familiar creaks, a conversation of sorts, and dropped her bag next to the bed.

The room was cozy, calming. The pale-blue walls and soft-yellow drapes were the colors of serenity. On her bed floated a puffy white cloud. Amelia was tempted to climb in for a nap. How easy it would be to sink into it and sleep.

But the past week had consisted of almost nothing but sleep. During the few hours she was awake, her brain revolted against her every move. It pounded and throbbed when she peered into the daylight, spun the room when she tried to walk, and roiled her stomach at every meal. *Sleep,* it demanded.

Amelia acquiesced.

Now it was time to make sense of things. Tim Watson's texts

had stopped. She wondered if it was intentional. Perhaps he was dead for real this time.

Murder. There were so many of them, each apparently with the same motive—to silence. Michael Porter. Smith Phillips. She wondered about James Carter. His overdose seemed too convenient. Are there more bodies to be found? Frankie Vincent's? Tim Watson's? Could one man really have killed them all?

Perhaps after the first it's easy.

Amelia left her bedroom and walked down the stairs, allowing each step to have its say. She needed to set the table. Elliott and Kirby were coming to dinner. Fortunately they offered to bring takeout.

"What an ordeal," Elliott said as he hugged Amelia.

"It certainly was," said an exasperated Kirby as she unpacked containers from La Grenouille. "You'd think no one ever ordered French takeout before."

"I meant Amelia's assault."

"Of course," stammered Kirby, "but you must admit it was like twisting Jerome's arm to let us order carry out."

"Takeaway? Non, mademoiselle," said Elliott, mimicking Chef Jerome. "Takeaway is for pizza, not *gastronomie Française*."

"Well, he does have a point," Amelia said as she carefully unwrapped three porcelain dishes, each holding six escargots. "These are rather expensive takeout containers."

Kirby laughed. "I promised Jerome I would return them. I'm a regular. I thought French would be a celebratory meal for you, Amelia, after your *ordeal*." She turned toward Elliott as she emphasized the last word.

"Cin, cin," Elliott said, raising his glass. "So are you really OK?" he asked as he stroked Amelia's arm.

Amelia smiled. "I'm fine. It's a relief to be home. I'm not a very good patient."

"Why were you in the park?" Kirby asked.

"Because Tim Watson asked me to meet him there. It was all very stealth. Park my car, go for a walk, return to my car. Next thing I know, I'm in the hospital."

"And Marc attacked you? My Marc?" Kirby was still incredulous.

"That's who the police suspect. I don't know. I didn't see who it was."

"I always thought that jogging path was too isolated," Kirby said. "I never run on it. The trail around the lake is so much better. But you're safe now, thank goodness."

"Any fallout with your clients because of Marc?" Amelia asked.

Kirby waved her hand dismissively. "I didn't even mention Marc, and I'm sorry I freaked out over the phone. I was so shocked when the police called me. I should have realized that my standing with my clients wasn't going to be jeopardized by a clerk who worked for me." She lifted her wineglass as if toasting herself. "I already called in a temporary replacement, someone who interned with me last year. I'll look for a permanent employee when I have more time."

After pieces of crunchy baguette sopped up the last bit of snail butter, Amelia cleared the ceramic dishes and escargot forks, replacing them with bowls of beef bourguignon.

"These are a very nice design," said Kirby, admiring the pottery.

"Thanks. I bought them in Portugal last year." The pottery triggered a thought. "Kirby, did Marc handle replacing Winnie's vase?"

Kirby looked startled. "No. Why do you ask?"

"Maybe he's involved in the cocaine shipment from Cabo."

"Amelia, I finally calmed myself down over hiring such a

loser; don't get me apoplectic over the idea that he was a drug dealer," Kirby said. "My rep in Mexico sent the new vase. He did it as a favor to me."

"Your rep?"

"Yes, I have a relationship with a design firm in Mexico. It's a professional courtesy. I told him the pattern, and he shipped the vase."

"Did you send him the broken one?" Amelia asked.

"No. There was nothing left of it but a bag full of rubble. I threw it away."

Elliott laughed. "You probably pitched a thousand dollars' worth of coke."

"Elliott, that's not funny!" Kirby shivered. "Cocaine in my store. Disgusting."

"Would you like coffee and dessert?" asked Amelia. "I don't have much. A little sorbet and maybe a couple of peanut butter cups stashed in the freezer."

"Thanks, but we really should get going," Elliott said. "You need your rest. Kirby and I will clean up."

"Leave the dishes," Amelia said. "I can do it, and I'll take the escargot dishes back to La Grenouille tomorrow. It'll feel good to get back to some kind of normal."

"At least let us help clear the table," Elliott said.

"Damn it," Kirby snapped. "I splashed sauce on my silk scarf. It's Hermès."

"Give it to me," said Amelia. "I can get it out."

"No, I'll deal with it later."

"I insist. I'm a wizard at removing stains. The secret is dish detergent. I'll treat it and drop it off at your shop tomorrow when I return the dishes."

Amelia walked them to the door.

Elliott searched his pockets for his keys.

Kirby dangled them in front of him. "They were on the kitchen counter."

Amelia looked puzzled.

"You OK?" Elliott asked.

"Yep, I'm fine. Drive safely."

Amelia returned to the kitchen and checked the key bowl by her back door. Only one set of car keys was there. The keys she used to drive herself home this morning. Where was the other one?

She loaded the dishwasher, wiped the counters, and checked on Kirby's scarf. The stain appeared to be gone, though she would check in the morning once it was dry. She carefully blotted the scarf with a flour-sack dish towel.

What was it about her car keys that confused her? And then she remembered. Tony—or was it her mother?—asked her in the hospital where her keys were.

In the car. They were in the car.

She called her mother.

"Amelia, you're up rather late. Is everything all right?" Louise asked.

"I'm fine, but I'm a little hazy about my car keys. When I was in the hospital, did you ask me where I kept the spare set?"

"Yes. I wanted to move your car, but it was locked and the keys weren't with you."

"But I left it unlocked. My keys were under the driver's-side floor mat."

"No, dear, your car was locked, though your keys were just where you said they were. We used your spare key to get into the car. I forgot to give them to you before you left. They're here. Why are you wondering about that at this late hour?"

"I'm just trying to piece things together."

"You should get some sleep, dear. I'll bring your keys over tomorrow."

"That's OK. I'll pick them up next time I'm there."

"Whoopsie!" Louise exclaimed.

Amelia heard glass breaking. "Mom?"

"I have to go, dear. I just dropped a gigantic bowl of potpourri that I made with flowers and herbs from the garden. The kitchen may smell strongly of lemon verbena next time you come over."

Amelia made her way upstairs. Her headache was back, but it wasn't from the attack.

It was *about* the attack.

74

Normal. Amelia awoke feeling normal. The remnants of her concussion had finally washed away. No more mind-bending headaches or bouts of vertigo. Her energy was good. Not perfect, but good.

Grabbing a granola bar, Amelia added *grocery shopping* to her mental list of errands. She would have to stop for a coffee along the way. The milk in her fridge looked like cottage cheese. She tucked Kirby's scarf, now stain-free, into her purse, packed the restaurant's dishes in a small box, and grabbed her keys. Even the good night's sleep hadn't sorted out her confusion over why her car was locked the day she was attacked. What did it matter? She just wanted to run errands, to enjoy the mundane.

As she loaded the box onto the back seat of her car, she noticed an envelope wedged between the front seat and the console. Inside was a photo of an armoire and a note: *Don't know where it is. Thought D'Angelo had it, but it's not at the Travel Club. Maybe at the club's hangar? Check the trunk. Bye.*

On the back of the photo were the instructions for opening its hidden compartment. She looked in her trunk. It held an unfamiliar black plastic garbage bag. She cautiously opened it and saw a duffel bag.

So much for mundane activities.

* * *

"I'm here to see Chief Detective Mardi," Amelia said to the officer at the front desk. He leaned back in his swivel chair, his belly straining against the buttons of his uniform. Amelia guessed he was in his sixties, though his thinning hair and fleshy jowls may have added unearned extra years to his appearance. He reminded Amelia of a bulldog. Or a walrus.

"What's it in reference to?" he barked.

"Amelia Halliday!" A door on the right opened and a familiar voice rose above the wave of blue uniforms that streamed out. "How are you feeling?" Cole asked.

"Recovered."

"Are you looking for Mardi?" she asked, smiling.

"Yes, I am," Amelia stammered, not sure if Cole's smile was friendly or curious.

"I don't think he's back yet." She turned to the desk clerk. "Has Chief Detective Mardi returned?"

"No, Rita, he hasn't."

Cole's gaze remained on the clerk.

"No, Detective Cole, he hasn't."

"Thank you," she said tersely. She turned to Amelia, who was holding the trash bag she had found in her trunk. "Can I help you?"

Cole and Amelia walked to the conference room that had just been vacated. "The last of the old school," Cole said, tilting her head in the direction of the clerk.

Amelia set the trash bag on the chair next to her. "You know about what happened to me, right?" Amelia asked once Cole closed the door.

"I was at the hospital when you were brought in. We didn't know the extent of your attack."

Amelia looked confused.

"Your clothes were disheveled. Sweatpants partially pulled down."

Amelia turned ashen. "Oh my God!"

"It wasn't a sexual assault, Amelia. Everything points to the perpetrator searching your clothes, looking for something." Cole took a bottle of water from the mini fridge in the conference room and handed it to her.

"Thanks. It's horrifying not to know what happened." Amelia shivered and then reached into her purse, looking to change the subject. "This is why I'm here." She pulled an envelope from her purse and handed it to Cole.

"I found this in my car today. Tim Watson said he built two things for his uncle: the fake wall in the pantry at Twin Beeches and an armoire. This must be the armoire. The back of the photo has directions on how to access the compartment."

Amelia picked up the trash bag and put it on the table. "This was in my trunk. I think Tim retrieved it from the dump. There's a duffel bag containing what looks like a tarp in it. I didn't touch anything but the zipper on the bag. I unzipped it and then closed it when I saw what was in there. I think it's from the night Smith Phillips was killed."

Amelia spied a Keurig coffee maker across the room. "Do you mind?"

"Help yourself," said Cole.

Amelia added milk and a packet of sugar to her coffee and took a sip. "Ahh. I usually don't leave home without it."

Amelia held up her hand. "Wait, something just clicked. I

think he was looking for my keys. Not Tim; the guy who attacked me. Maybe he saw Tim put the bag and note in my car. Tim probably assumed I had my keys with me, so he hit the door lock before he closed the car door. That's why my spare keys were needed to move my car. The man who attacked me must have searched my clothes for my keys."

"Have you heard anything more from Tim Watson?"

"Not since I forwarded his last texts and the photo of the man who may be my attacker."

"Why do you think Tim Watson has divulged all this to you? Why doesn't he go to the police himself?"

"He's complicit, isn't he?"

"It appears so."

Amelia shrugged. "Well, that's a good reason."

"Have you considered that perhaps you're a pawn in whatever game he's playing?" Cole asked.

Amelia bristled. "I'd hardly call it a game. I think he's acting out of self-preservation. He knows Robert D'Angelo killed Michael Porter, probably Smith Phillips, and maybe Frankie Vincent. He could be next."

Cole pulled the trash bag toward her. "We'll have everything analyzed." She slipped the photo and note from Tim Watson into a folder. "I'm sorry you're in the middle of this. We'll solve it, I promise you."

"I'd like a copy of the note and photo."

Cole raised her eyebrows.

"Tim left them for me. I'd like a copy."

Cole made copies and held them out to Amelia. "If you hear from Tim Watson again, you'll contact us." It wasn't a question. Cole released her grip.

"And when you find the armoire, you'll let me know."

75

Amelia found a parking space on State Street just down from La Grenouille. As she carried the box of escargot dishes to the restaurant, she saw one of the sidewalk bistro tables was available. The day was warm and sunny. It was time to let the police handle the investigation and for her to enjoy life a little. She took a seat, handed over the dishes, and ordered a cappuccino and a *pain au chocolat*.

Instead of scanning her phone for messages, Amelia sipped her cappuccino and watched the world go by, the part of the world that traveled through downtown Newtown. Brick and field-stone buildings over a hundred years old lined both sides of State Street. A bank, hardware store, florist, clothing and antique shops, even a five-and-dime.

She watched as a woman wearing a green gardening apron stepped out of Bergen's Florist. She pulled a pair of pruners from her apron pocket and trimmed ivy that was trailing down the large urns on either side of the entrance. She dropped the wayward tendrils into a basket that was draped over her arm like a large bracelet. Next she pinched back the geraniums.

Along the sidewalk, wooden benches were positioned every half block. From their armrests hung small, rectangular baskets filled with flowers, reminding shoppers to stop and smell the roses or whatever seasonal flower was tucked within the sphagnum moss. Amelia needed to do more of that. She finished her coffee, paid the bill, and walked over to the florist to buy a bunch of Gerbera daisies.

Dunbar & Co. was her next stop. She crossed the street and passed the Travel Club. Etched in its front window was the club's logo, a plane soaring through the sky. A large gray shade hung behind it, blocking any sunlight or eyes. The plane hovered; it had nowhere to go.

Amelia opened the door to Kirby's shop. A young woman with a broad smile emerged dramatically from behind a pair of peacock-blue drapes at the back of the shop and strode toward her.

The scene reminded Amelia of a beauty pageant.

"May I be of assistance?" she asked.

"I'm Amelia Halliday."

"Hello, Miss Halliday, I'm Tracey Rutledge." She shook Amelia's hand. "Miss Dunbar told me you might stop by to drop off her scarf."

Tracey could have stepped off the pages of a Talbots catalog: a black pencil skirt, crisp white blouse, and a fitted blazer. Her glossy blonde hair was firmly held in place by a thin rose-hued headband. "I'm afraid Miss Dunbar is at a client meeting." She glanced at her watch. "She should be back in less than an hour."

Through the parted curtains Amelia could see boxes piled everywhere. Tracey caught her look.

"Oh dear, I shouldn't have left the curtains open." She quickly tugged the drapes closed. "Never let the public see where the work really happens." She smiled nervously. "I hope you won't mention to Miss Dunbar that I left the curtains open," Tracey said as she nervously rearranged a candle and an enameled box that sat on a silver tray.

"No worries," Amelia said and handed Tracey the scarf. "Stain's out!"

"Miss Dunbar will be thrilled. She told me she was afraid she had ruined it. Ooh, it's an Hermès, no wonder she was upset."

"I won't keep you," Amelia said. "I can see you're busy. Tell Kirby hello for me."

"I certainly will," she said.

Tracey was a shoo-in for Miss Congeniality.

76

"Oh, Amelia, how sweet of you." Louise hugged her with one arm while holding the Gerbera daisies with the other.

"A small thanks for taking care of me. I'm back to my old self."

"Your memory is all right? No confusion?" Louise asked. "Your call last night about keys was a bit concerning." Louise walked over to the counter and retrieved Amelia's keys. "Here they are."

"It turns out the keys were important." Amelia relayed the events of the morning and showed her the photo of the armoire and the note.

"Curiouser and curiouser, as Alice would say," Louise mused. She opened the refrigerator. "Would you like a snack? It's time for my afternoon pick-me-up."

"No thanks. I can only stay a minute. I have errands to run."

Louise sat down to a plate of cheese and crackers and picked up the photo of the armoire.

"Where do you think it is?"

"Tim's guess is it's at the airport in the Travel Club's hangar."

"That's plausible," said Louise. "Fly in pottery, do whatever one does to extract the cocaine, store it in this cabinet, and deliver it wherever."

"What's being delivered?" A voice came from outside the kitchen door.

"Amelia and I are just hypothesizing something," Louise said as Winnie walked in. "How was school?"

"Boring. May I have an apple?"

"Of course." Louise held up her plate. "Would you like some cheese?"

"No thanks." She looked down at the photo on the counter.

"That's nice. Did you buy it?"

"No, but it may be related to the smuggled drugs."

"Really?" Winnie studied the photo, then flipped it over and studied the diagram. "Another hidden compartment? Cool! Can we go see it and open it up?"

"We're not sure where it is," said Amelia.

Winnie looked puzzled. "It's at Miss Dunbar's store." When she saw the startled look on Louise's and Amelia's faces, she added, "At least I'm pretty sure it is."

"When did you see it there?"

Winnie chewed on her lower lip and crinkled her eyes. "I saw it when I brought her the broken vase." Her eyes popped open. "To be precise, it was when I helped her clean up the packing peanuts in the back room. What a mess. It looked like they were attacking her. They were in her hair, on her legs, and her butt." Winnie giggled. "Boy, was she upset."

"The armoire was in her back room?" Amelia asked.

"Yep. It had these same doodads on it. They reminded me of

checkers." A row of round carved discs ran across the front of the armoire.

"And it had a red 'Sold' tag hanging from the door handle," Winnie continued. "Looking at this picture, the checkers look more like cookies." Winnie reached over and took a cracker off Louise's plate.

"Winnie, you are the most observant kid I know," said Amelia. "I take that back. You're the most observant *person* I know." Amelia hugged her. "Kirby should be back by now, and let's hope the armoire is still there. If not, at least we can find out who bought it."

"Can I come?" Winnie pleaded.

"It's better if I go alone. Kirby is pretty sensitive about her reputation. Selling a piece of furniture that was probably used to smuggle drugs is not going to be well received."

"And she doesn't like kids, either." Winnie crossed her arms.

77

A police car was parked on State Street near Dunbar & Co. when Amelia arrived. She found an open spot a few cars behind it. Selfishly she was disappointed. She wanted to be the first to open the armoire. If it was still there.

Or maybe the presence of a police car had nothing to do with the armoire. Maybe it was a coffee break or a little shopping on taxpayer time. Just as Amelia was trying to decide if she should go in to see Kirby, Tracey stepped out of the shop and walked toward the Temperance House. Amelia got out of her car and called to her.

"Hello, miss, um, I'm sorry, Halloway?" Tracey blushed.

"Halliday, but call me Amelia."

"I'm so sorry. I'm usually very good with names."

"How are you?" Amelia asked, noting that Tracey appeared emotionally disheveled.

"Miss Dunbar said I should go home for the day." She leaned in closer and whispered, "A police officer is in there. I don't know what it's about. Oh, don't misunderstand, I'm sure she didn't do anything wrong. The officer is very professional, even friendly.

Miss Dunbar walked me to the door and told me she would see me tomorrow."

"She may be helping with an investigation," Amelia whispered. "But keep that to yourself."

Tracey put her hand to her heart. "Such a relief. I'll sleep much better tonight. Thank you for trusting me enough to tell me. I won't say anything. You know reputation is everything in this business."

Kirby had found her ideal assistant.

Amelia was certain that Tony Mardi would not be amused if she tried to butt in, so she returned to her car and waited.

After twenty minutes, the front door opened, but Officer Barnett, not Tony, stepped onto the sidewalk. He walked past his patrol car, crossed the street, and entered the Starbucks on the corner.

Time to visit Kirby. Amelia walked into the shop to the shrill sound of a drill.

"Hello, Kirby?" she called, not wanting to startle her by suddenly appearing in the back room. "Kirby?" she called again as she walked toward the back of the shop.

The drilling stopped.

As Amelia approached the curtains, she heard a man's muffled voice.

"Will it all fit?"

"Barely. You're lucky I moved a lot of this already," she heard Kirby say testily.

Amelia stopped at the curtains.

"This got totally out of control," Kirby continued.

"There were complications, Kirby. I handled it."

Amelia froze when she recognized the voice. It was Tim Watson. She ducked out of sight behind an upholstered chair.

The front door opened. It was Barnett. *What a relief,* thought Amelia.

She was ready to run to him when she noticed he was holding three coffees in a cardboard tray. Amelia dropped back down to her hands and knees. If Barnett turned even slightly to the right, he would see her.

Instead he stepped inside and turned his back to Amelia. She heard the click of the front door locking. And then the lights went out.

Barnett passed within two feet of her and walked straight to the back room.

"What took you so long?" Kirby demanded.

"There was a line. You're ridiculous, sending me out for a latte. You need to get out of here."

"Did you lock up?" Kirby asked, ignoring Barnett's complaint.

"Yeah, you're closed for business. Permanently." He laughed.

Amelia crawled closer to the curtains.

"You never should have trusted Robert," Kirby said.

"Hey, you set this deal up. Don't blame me," argued Tim.

"You should have controlled him better," Kirby snapped.

"Consider him now under control."

"If you hadn't screwed things up at the party, we wouldn't be leaving."

"You knew at some point this could happen," said Tim. "If you hadn't fallen for your boyfriend, you'd have no trouble leaving."

"How dare you! You shut your mouth."

"Would the two of you shut up and finish packing the cash!" Barnett snarled.

"Stay cool," said Tim. "I know what I'm doing. And don't you complain. Payday's here."

"Damn straight," said Barnett.

"Stop squabbling! Tim, back the truck up to the door," demanded Kirby.

"You can't use Tim's truck," said Barnett. "There's an APB out on him."

"Oh gosh, why didn't we think of that?" Kirby said sardonically.

Tim laughed. "Robert lent me his. His final act. Plates switched with the unlucky owner of another black SUV that was parked at the Amtrak station."

Amelia heard the sound of wheels rolling across the floor.

And then silence.

She crawled toward the edge of the curtains and peeked into the back room. There was no sign of Kirby, Tim, or Barnett. But the armoire was in plain sight, standing along the wall to the right. Its double doors were ajar.

Amelia crept up to it, keeping her eyes on the back door. She reached for the armoire door nearest her and tried to open it farther. Its creak sent her scrambling behind a stack of boxes.

The murmur of voices outside continued.

She slowly moved back to the armoire, this time trying the left door. It silently swung open. The armoire was empty, but two hinged panels pressed against its ceiling were all Amelia needed to see. They matched the diagram exactly. When locked in place vertically, the panels created a deep compartment between them and the sides of the armoire. Fresh screws permanently held the panels in place above. The interior space of the armoire now matched the exterior. Whatever had been hidden inside was gone. Amelia took several pictures with her phone and then hurried to the front of the store, flipped the dead-bolt lock, and raced to her car.

She pulled onto East Centre Street and saw the SUV backed

up to Dunbar & Co. Tim Watson was loading two suitcases into it.

She drove past and stopped at the corner. "Tony, call me. It's urgent. Barnett is working for Kirby and Tim Watson. The armoire is at her store. They're loading a black SUV with suitcases. I'm going to follow them. It's Barnett, Tony. He's involved."

The car behind her laid on its horn. Startled, she dropped her phone on the floor. She made a hasty right turn, pulled up to the curb, and reached down to retrieve her phone. When she sat back up, she was startled to see Barnett's squad car passing her.

Amelia held her breath, waiting. If he saw her, his brake lights would go on. The patrol car continued down the road.

By the time she looped back around to the parking lot, the SUV was gone. She frantically raced through the parking lot and shot onto Washington Street in time to see it heading west and onto Sycamore Street. She followed at a distance, grateful there were several cars separating them. She hit Mardi's number again. Voice mail. "Tony, call me. I'm following them. I think they're heading to the Bucks County airport."

Several miles later, the SUV turned right into the entrance to the airport. Amelia drove past, watching in her sideview mirror. She saw another car also make the turn. She looped back, thankful for the cover. She drove past several office buildings, the A1 Flying School, and to her surprise, a sign with the Travel Club logo and an arrow pointing straight ahead.

The SUV drove another half mile, turned into the next drive, and pulled up to a gate. Beyond it Amelia could see a fenced-in parking lot of trucks and cargo vans. The sign said "Maintenance Depot." Amelia sped up, looking for a place to make a U-turn. As she closed in on the car ahead of her, she realized it was a black BMW. Amelia had assumed Kirby was in the SUV with Tim. She was wrong.

Who to follow? Kirby's brake lights suddenly came on. Amelia watched her pull into a parking lot for Executive Aviation Services. Amelia drove past and found a drive marked "Deliveries Only." She pulled in and tried Tony again.

"Tony! I need you to call me. Kirby is at the airport, Executive Aviation Services. Tim's nearby. I don't know what he's doing, but she's obviously flying somewhere."

78

"Good evening, Mrs. Flanders."

"Good evening." Kirby left her suitcase just inside the door and walked over to the reception desk. She looked at the woman's photo ID. "Deirdre, are you short on staff this evening?" Kirby tilted her head toward her suitcase.

"I'm so sorry." The young woman rushed from behind the desk. "I just asked Jeffrey to check on catering for your flight."

"I see. My husband will be here momentarily," she called over her shoulder as Deirdre rolled Kirby's suitcase up to the desk.

"Would you like to wait for him in the lounge?"

"Thank you, but I'd rather get settled on the plane. Are we on schedule?"

Deirdre hurried behind the desk and glanced at her computer screen. "We may have a brief delay. Two flights were diverted from Allentown."

Kirby frowned. "That's certainly not what I wanted to hear."

"It shouldn't affect your arrival time in Miami."

"It better not."

Deirdre flinched.

"Make sure someone is watching for my husband. I want his luggage loaded on the plane with us, not in the cargo hold. Do you understand?"

"Perfectly," Deirdre said icily.

Kirby arched an eyebrow, and Deirdre quickly looked down at her screen.

Kirby turned her back to Deirdre and pulled her phone from her purse. "All clear, come on in, Mr. Flanders," she texted and walked toward a uniformed guard standing at the door to the staging area for private planes.

"Welcome, Mrs. Flanders."

"Thank you." Kirby stopped and looked back. "Deirdre, my bag?"

"I've got it, Mrs. Flanders," a young man called as he hurried toward the suitcase.

"Good." She turned and walked to the plane, escorted by the guard.

In the galley of the Gulfstream, Kirby opened a bottle of wine and poured herself a glass. Only a few more minutes and she would transform herself once again. A rich woman. No, a richer woman. She regretted leaving Elliott. He was what she always wanted. She could have maintained her lifestyle with him without smuggling. Of course, she never would have met him if she hadn't traveled in the right social circles, which her green-card ex-husband financed with the fifty grand he paid her to go away. She exceeded even her own expectations. She thought she would be satisfied with her interior design shop servicing wealthy clients, but it became boring. There was nothing boring about drug smuggling. Or Tim. Though maybe it was time to be done with him, too.

She and Tim would have to lay low for a while, but then they'd start their new lives. Maybe together. Maybe not. The south of France appealed to her. She would decide in due time. Now she just wanted to feel the vibration of the plane rolling down the runway.

"There's my sweetheart!"

Kirby rolled her eyes as Tim walked back to the galley after directing the attendant where to place the two suitcases. "Are we all set?"

"Ready to go. No more complications," said Tim.

"We might be delayed."

Tim looked troubled. "Why?"

"A couple of planes were diverted here."

A plane touched down in the distance.

"That's one." Tim smiled and poured a scotch. "Relax, we're fine."

"There was a car behind me when I pulled onto Airport Road, a silver Audi. Amelia has a silver Audi. Why did you leave her that friggin' photo of the armoire?"

"It was a diversion. I knew she'd take it to the police, along with the trash bag with the tarp in it. Robert's prints are all over it." He laughed. "The police are probably swarming his house and headed to the Travel Club's hangar. No one knows we're involved, and who but us would have the balls to book a private plane at the same airport where the cops are searching a nearby hangar? It's brilliant."

"Then why was Amelia following us?" Kirby asked.

"Don't get paranoid. She was probably on her way to the Travel Club's hangar. Do a little investigating herself." He laughed again. "The focus is on Robert, and maybe searching for my body." He took a slug of his scotch. "Which, as you may get to experience firsthand tonight, is alive and well."

Kirby laughed. “Let’s not get carried away with the Mr. and Mrs. Flanders bit.” She held up their passports. “These will be replaced in Miami.” She poured herself another glass of wine.

The pilot stepped out from the cockpit. “A few more minutes and we’ll be wheels up. Weather’s clear all the way to Miami. Do you need anything before we lift off?”

“We’re fine,” Kirby replied, smiling radiantly. “And we can help ourselves. We’ll be just fine back here alone.”

“If you know what I mean,” Tim added with a smirk.

The pilot doffed his cap. “Well, fasten your seat belts for takeoff.”

“You’re impossible!” Kirby smacked Tim’s arm.

As the plane lifted off, Kirby saw the flashing lights of police cars. She reached over and grabbed Tim’s arm.

“Relax, they’re at the Travel Club hangar. What’d I tell you?”

79

Amelia had watched helplessly as Tim had pulled into Executive Aviation Services and minutes later a jet lifted off. She slammed her palm into the steering wheel, took a deep breath, and pulled next to Tim's SUV. She walked into the lounge.

"Hi." She quickly looked at Deirdre Hamilton's name tag. "Miss Hamilton, I'm Amelia Halliday." She looked around the empty lounge. "I think I just missed my friends. I was supposed to see them off but got caught in traffic. Can you tell me who just took off?"

"I'm very sorry. We can't divulge any information."

"I understand." Amelia smiled. "Thanks anyway." She walked toward the door, then changed her mind. "May I ask you something? *If* it was a couple who just took off, would you say that the woman was an uppity bitch?"

Deirdre let out a howl of laughter before quickly covering her mouth.

"Thanks." Amelia gave her a thumbs-up and strolled out the door.

Amelia grabbed her phone on the first ring. "Detective Mardi, so nice of you to get back to me. But they're gone."

"Amelia, where the hell are you?"

"Same place as my last message to you. Executive Aviation Services."

"I'll be right there."

Amelia stared in disbelief as a patrol car screeched to a stop beside her. "You weren't kidding."

"I was at the Travel Club hangar, along with a cavalry of feds."

"The armoire's not there."

"I know it's not there. I do listen to your messages. Another team is at Dunbar & Co."

"But you missed Kirby and Tim." She pointed to the sky.

"I needed to bring Barnett in first."

"Did you?"

"Yeah, after a shouting match with Chief Sullivan. I hope to God you're sure about his nephew's involvement."

"I have a recording." Amelia held up her phone. "It may be difficult to hear, but hopefully you can enhance it." She navigated to the recording and turned up the volume.

"If you hadn't screwed things up at the party, we wouldn't be leaving." "That's Kirby speaking," Amelia said.

"You knew at some point this could happen. If you hadn't fallen for your boyfriend, you'd have no trouble leaving." "And that's Tim."

"How dare you! You shut your mouth." "Kirby."

"Would the two of you shut up and finish packing the cash!" "And that's Barnett."

"Stay cool. I know what I'm doing. And don't you complain. Payday's here." "Tim again."

"Damn straight." "Barnett. And that should put an end to your concern." Amelia laughed.

80

The copilot carefully peered into the back of the plane. "Sorry to interrupt. There's nothing to be alarmed about, but a door sensor indicator is lit. It's probably just a malfunctioning light, but we can't take a chance. We're returning to the airport. It shouldn't take long. I'm sorry for the inconvenience."

"Shit!" Kirby yelled.

The copilot stepped forward. "We're perfectly safe, ma'am. It's just a precaution."

Tim squeezed Kirby's arm. "Relax. It's OK."

They stared out the windows as the plane made its approach.

"Look, there's a maintenance truck. We're going to be fine."

The plane taxied to a stop. The copilot opened the door and released the stairs.

Kirby watched the truck stop beside the cargo area. Two men in blue jumpsuits climbed out of the truck.

"We'll just wait here," Tim said.

"I'm sorry, but we prefer you deplane while they come onboard to check the door."

Kirby and Tim followed the first pilot down the stairs. He moved aside as the maintenance men stepped next to Kirby and Tim. Before they could react, their arms were pulled behind them and they were handcuffed and Mirandized.

Kirby let out a shriek and turned to headbutt Mardi.

He grabbed her shoulder and pushed her down onto the tarmac. "It's over," he said simply.

As Tim and Kirby were led into the lounge, they passed a woman reading a magazine. The magazine slowly lowered. Amelia smiled at Kirby.

Kirby glared at her in anger and contempt.

Amelia took a sip from a flute of champagne. "Cheers." She tilted her glass toward her.

Deirdre hurried over to Amelia. "Please, let me refill your glass, Miss Halliday." She then turned to Kirby. "No worries about your luggage. I'm sure these gentlemen will be happy to carry them for you."

81

One month later

Amelia and Carol Anne walked into the study at Twin Beeches. Tony Mardi followed behind them.

"Carol Anne, I'm glad to see you." Louise rose from her seat to hug her. "And congratulations! I hear you're now working in the kitchen at the River's Inn."

"I am. Mr. Wickham has been great. He even helped me apply for a special scholarship at Arbor College to take culinary classes. I don't know who gave the money; it was anonymous. But I'm sending a thank-you note to the school. I just can't believe it."

Louise's eyes twinkled. "Isn't that nice."

Amelia, sitting at the window seat with Winnie, glanced over at her mother. Another Yoda moment.

"But the most important thing," Carol Anne continued, "is that it's been proved that Mikey didn't do anything wrong. I mean, I always knew he was innocent, but now everyone will know." She took a seat next to Louise, who squeezed her hand. "And did you know that Officer Barnett planted the drugs and money in our apartment?"

"Oh my! But how did Michael's fingerprints get on the money?" Louise asked.

"Tim Watson hired him," interjected Mardi. "May I?" He gestured to the chair next to Ruth. "He apparently paid him before they switched the dishes. Michael Porter left the cash in his van. His fingerprints were on it. That allowed Barnett to use the money to frame him."

"And Kirby was the brains behind the drugs?" Ruth asked.

"We don't know just yet," said Mardi. "We do know that Kirby Dunbar laundered the money through her interior design business. Robert D'Angelo handled the import side of the business with the help of several employees at Cabo Pottery. Tim Watson was sales, and Barnett was the police insider.

"Initially, the coke was sold here at Twin Beeches. Frankie Vincent may have hosted the parties, but we think it was his nephew, Tim Watson, who moved the coke. Tim didn't just stumble on the bug in the chandelier. Barnett told him it was there. Barnett was integral to their operation. He kept them informed of any investigations. He was probably the protector during arranged rendezvous with buyers, and according to Amelia, he also bought Kirby and Tim lattes." He chuckled. "We think they, or at least Tim, convinced Frankie Vincent to run. They wanted him to look guilty."

"But why run if he wasn't guilty?" asked Ruth.

"He wasn't exactly innocent," said Mardi. "They were his parties. The coke was at his house. After he ran, Kirby used her business to make the deliveries. It all broke down because Robert, as it turns out, was very comfortable killing people if there was a screwup."

"Robert almost added a double homicide to his killing spree," said Ruth.

The room went silent.

"Vanessa and me. Robert would have killed Vanessa and me if I hadn't saved us."

"Yes, Ruthie, that was quick thinking," said Louise. "So Robert killed Michael Porter and Smith Phillips?"

"And possibly James Carter," Amelia said.

"The man who was here with Michael?" Winnie asked.

"Except he wasn't," Mardi said. "We believe Robert pressured Smith Phillips, the party supplies owner, to lie about seeing Carter here. And then Robert killed him so he couldn't change his story."

"But James Carter had to have been here. He drove away in Michael's van," said Louise.

"Actually, Tim drove Michael's van, and then he or Robert hired Carter to dump it in Lake Luxembourg."

"Why on earth would he agree to that?" exclaimed Ruth. "He could have drowned."

"He was a scuba diver with rescue diver status," said Mardi. "He knew how to get out of a submerged vehicle. We think he did it for money. He deposited three thousand dollars in cash the day after the party and then took a trip to Nassau. He returned and twenty-four hours later was found dead of a cocaine overdose, either accidentally or with Robert's help. The night Carter died, his neighbor, Claire Green, saw what we believe was Robert's SUV in the parking lot. She noticed it because it was parked in her usual parking space in front of her apartment.

"It's not a proud moment for my team, but we were convinced, and, I might add, impressed, when Officer Barnett made the connection between James Carter and Michael Porter's van. Of course, Barnett already knew the van was in the lake. He quickly steered the evidence to support the theory that Carter killed Michael."

"Robert was the most horrible, evil man of all of them," said Ruth. "To think I was cavorting with him. What a fool I was."

"I feel like a fool, too, Ruth," said Amelia. "Tim used me to keep the police looking everywhere but at him and Kirby. And his final insulting diversion was to attack me in the park."

"Tim Watson attacked you?" Ruth gasped. "I thought it was Marc. Well, that's at least some good news. I mean about Marc, not the attack. Marc seems like a very nice young man. Handsome, too. Perhaps he'll take over Kirby's business. I do have a bit of decorating I need done." She paused. "But there's a photo of Marc at the park?"

"Tim took the photo of Marc with his phone, which we now have," said Mardi. "It's time-stamped 12:47 p.m. When Amelia was attacked, at 6:32 p.m., Marc Nelson was having a drink with his girlfriend at a restaurant in Lambertville. We have witnesses. Kirby Dunbar knew that Marc jogged on that same path every day at lunchtime, so it was easy for Tim to take the photo."

"Marc has a girlfriend?" Ruth frowned.

Amelia snapped her fingers. "I should have realized Kirby was somehow involved. After my attack she said that jogging path was too isolated. How did she know where I was? But why would Tim attack me and put the plastic bag and photo in my car?"

"To buy more time. Tim was diverting attention. As long as he was considered a victim, he thought he was safe, and he and Kirby had to finish moving the money out of her shop."

"But he could have killed you!" cried Winnie.

"Maybe he knew that I've got a really hard head." She smiled and hugged Winnie.

"So Kirby, Tim, and Robert were in cahoots with Frankie Vincent?" asked Louise.

"Possibly," said Mardi. "There's still no lead on Vincent's whereabouts or Robert D'Angelo's."

"Tim told me he thought Robert had killed Frankie," said Amelia. "Maybe Tim ordered it?"

The Samuels's stoic expressions belied their revulsion over the thought of a man ordering the killing of his own relative. They didn't believe Frankie, or as they liked to refer to him, Franklin, was a drug dealer. It was that horrible nephew of his. While the Samuels didn't approve of Frankie's parties or even his terrible taste in decorating, he was a scotch drinker, just like them. And he was jocular. They shared a quiet moment in his honor.

Sitting next to Amelia on the window seat in the study, Winnie was furiously writing in her murder journal. "This is an amazing story! I'm sure to get an A."

"How's poor Elliott?" Ruth asked. "To think he fell for that evil woman."

"Throwing himself into his work," said Louise.

"And helping with the investigation," added Mardi. "The suitcases that Kirby carried back and forth to New York were for moving coke and money, not for her interior design work. Elliott led the DEA to her office in New York."

"They found a large safe." Amelia broke into a grin. "The safe was stuffed with cash and a laptop. More to come on that."

Louise stood. "Well, here's to justice for Michael Porter."

The Samuels quietly exhaled a collective sigh of relief. It sounded like an evening breeze.

Louise turned to Mardi. "And here's to a successful drug bust. Well done, Anthony."

Amelia walked Tony to the front door. “I’m glad it’s all over.”

“All of it?” he asked, his eyes twinkling.

“Well, you know, the crime. The crimes. The whole mess.”

“Good night, Amelia.” Tony smiled and walked to his car.

82

Frankie Vincent and Robert D'Angelo were still missing. Then a couple canoeing in the Pine Barrens in New Jersey found a body—Robert D'Angelo with a bullet in his head. Tim Watson had apparently overcome his aversion to killing. It was his gun. Perhaps he wanted to test Robert's theory that killing could tie up loose ends. It didn't work.

Amelia wondered how Kirby Dunbar was going to survive in a prison cell. Her interior design expertise didn't offer much for metal beds and windows sans curtains. She didn't even want to think about how Kirby would relate to her new neighbors.

Amelia's doorbell rang. A UPS guy handed her a package the size of a toaster oven. It was postmarked Key West. Inside was a box made of teak with an intricately carved mother-of-pearl medallion in the center.

Amelia lifted the lid and found another box, red leather, from Cartier. She slipped the golden nail bracelet, which was nestled inside, onto her wrist and opened the note card.

Phyllis said Cartier is a good brand, and I trust her. The bracelet's got a fancy French name, Juste un Clou, *but I like it 'cause it's just a nail.*

Seems like a good gift because you must be tough as nails (that's not an insult). Wear it in good health and use it as a key. The box was made for it. Frankie Vincent

Amelia stared at the note, then the bracelet, and then the note again.

He knows where I live! He lives in Key West?

She removed the bracelet from her wrist. *The box was made for it. Of course the Cartier box is made for it,* Amelia thought. Does he mean the wooden box? Did Tim make it? While the point of the nail could be used like a toothpick as in Tim's creations, the bracelet was round, which meant the end of the nail could only be inserted into a hole on the very edge of the box.

Amelia turned the box every which way, looking for a hole. Nothing. On the underside of the box was a carving of an olive branch wreath. It was beautifully carved. It seemed like such a waste, given that no one would see it unless the box was turned upside down. She flipped it back and studied the medallion in the center. It had several small holes, but she couldn't maneuver the bracelet's nail end into them without bending the bangle. Amelia broke into a smile and flipped the box upside down again.

She set the bracelet on top of the wreath; it sank into the engraving. She pushed and the left side of the box popped open, revealing a gap between the outer and inner walls. It held a photo and a letter.

So this is Frankie. A smiling, overly tanned man wearing khaki shorts, a Hawaiian shirt, and a thick gold chain beamed at her. On his head was a captain's cap. Next to him stood a blonde wearing large sunglasses and a pink first-mate's cap. She stood several inches taller than Frankie. They were in a marina.

Dear Amelia,

I hope you used the bracelet and not a hammer to open the box. My friend tells me you tidied things up back there. Good job. A murder at Twin Beeches is some bad juju.

Just so you know, I'm no drug dealer. I don't even do the stuff. I'm a scotch man. The only coke I ever sold went with my burgers and fries at Steer Here. But I admit there was some of the illegal kind at my parties. You know, buy a case of wine, some scotch, some coke, and it's a party. I could of shit when I realized my nephew was selling coke out of my house, not just bringing a little over for a party. He was selling kilos!

Tim knew I kept my passport and cash in the pantry. So I got a new passport by reporting the one I had as lost. The one in the pantry is the old one. It's no good, but I hoped it might confuse Tim and make him think I was still in the area.

I knew it was time to leave when Tim showed up at my house to rewire the chandelier in my dining room. I never asked him to, and as far as I know, it was just fine. He must've known the bug was there. I figured some cop was involved. I guessed it was Detective Mardi. That Barnett guy was too much of a buffoon. Just goes to show you there's a brain even in dummies.

I think Tim wanted me to run so it would look like I was guilty, but I ran to get away from him. He's dangerous. I wanted nothing to do with him anymore. It breaks my heart, but there you go.

I bought a nice boat for Phyllis and me to stay on. Phyllis says it's a yacht. I say as long as it floats I'm happy. I've got a couple of other houses elsewhere, but we've stayed away from them in case Tim found us. Tell your mom her house was extra special.

I'm no saint, but my nephew must be the devil. I bought a Mass card for him just in case there's a chance for redemption, but I doubt it.

Just so you know, I taught Tim how to make the boxes. I made them for him and his cousins every Christmas and hid a C note in them.

Tim was creative and clever. He took it to a whole new level. He helped me make the compartment in the pantry. That's where I kept my expensive booze and Phyllis's jewelry.

So, Amelia, I wanted you to know the truth. I'm not a bad person. I worked hard and made a lot of dough. On behalf of the Vincent family, I extend my apologies for my nephew's bad behavior. He's getting what he deserves. Family or not, you don't go around offing people to clean up your mess. At least not this family.

Phyllis says I need to stop writing and get this in the mail while we're still in port, so I'll sign off. Maybe we'll meet someday.

Frankie

P.S. You probably figured out who my friend is. I mean, it's not like I only got one, but without Jerry Baker I wouldn't have been so successful. When everybody else thought I was some goombah from South Philly who was gonna fall flat on his face, Jerry got behind my burger joints. He built the first three at cost and the promise of a percent of the business when I turned a profit. He took the risk and it paid off. I kept my word (I always do). He should have been my nephew. Him I like. He kept an eye on that girl until the cops (or you) figured out why her boyfriend was killed. OK, I gotta go. Phyllis is looking real impatient.

83

It was dusk, and Amelia had just finished the final edit to Kathy Hacker's book of essays. She was happy with the results.

She looked around her house. It felt like the walls were purring. And then it hit her. While editing the essays, she often read them out loud to better appreciate their cadence. She was reading to her library once again. And it was happy.

Her doorbell rang. She knew it was Tony. He had asked if he could come by.

She opened the door to find him standing there holding the handle of a wheeled cooler. It looked like a leashed dog at his side.

"I brought snacks. And wine. But no grocery bag. Are we good?"

Amelia opened the door wider and let him in.

The End (for now)

A BRIEF HISTORY OF THE LANGHORNE LIBRARY

Photograph courtesy of the Historic Langhorne Association

The town in *Murder at Twin Beeches* is called Four Lanes End, Langhorne's original name, and an apt name for a mystery series.

- 1691—Langhorne's first lending library is established by the Religious Society of Friends (Quakers). It circulated 23 books among its members.

- 1718—The collection grows to 300 books, kept in private homes.
- 1802—Pennsylvania Governor Thomas McKean issues a charter to establish a library. The books are moved to a small building in town.
- 1888—Thanks to a bequest made in the 1886 will of Anna Mary Williamson, the Langhorne Library is built to provide a permanent, more spacious home for the books.
- 1961—Author Maria Leonhauser begins her dream of someday living in the library.
- 1977—A new library is built. The Historic Langhorne Association moves into the original building where it continues to operate a research library and museum.
- 1986—The original library building is added to the National Register of Historic Places.
- 2023—Amelia Halliday, a character in *Murder at Twin Beeches*, moves in.

Acknowledgments

Writing a book is a solitary endeavor until your characters believe in you. Louise, Amelia, Winnie, Tony, and the rest of the gang, you were more than patient with me. I left you in limbo for months—dare I say years—as you sat midchapter or waited in the wings for your entrance. Thank you for taking charge.

As a child I was a proud, card-carrying member of the Langhorne Library, which was a fount of knowledge, inspiration, and more books than I could ever read. It is now home to the Historic Langhorne Association. Thank you to its dedicated team, especially Larry Langhans, who opened the archives to me. And a special thanks for allowing Amelia Halliday to make her home there.

Thank you to my Beta Book Club members: Mary Ackerman, Valerie Atkin, Janet Belcoure, Jane DeLorenzo, Anita Gevinson, Mary Ivers, Debra Kraus, and Marilynn Paine. This book is better because of you. Please don't leave the club, I need you for the next book.

Thank you, Linda Mahlmeister of MOMUS, Inc. for your interior design expertise for Kirby Dunbar's business.

To my beloved daughter, Ariel L. Gold (1985-2020). Anyone who knew her will recognize that Winnie Miller embraces her optimism, inquisitiveness, and fascination with tiny objects found in unexpected places. Ariel's colors were her sentences, paint brushes her pens, and her canvases visual stories filled with love, energy, and wonder.

My most heartfelt thanks goes to my husband, Peter Brown, whose love, patience, editing brilliance, and reminders to eat lunch, sustained me through this adventure.